THE
MINOR
APOCALYPSE
OF
MEENA KREJCI

A NOVEL

BY

SUSAN TAYLOR CHEHAK

FOREVERLAND PRESS
Silverthorne, Colorado
www.foreverlandpress.com

ISBN: 978-0-9960408-8-4

Cover Design by www.ebooklaunch.com

And all shall be well and
All manner of thing shall be well
When the tongues of flame are in-folded
Into the crowned knot of fire
And the fire and the rose are one.

—T.S. Eliot, "Little Gidding"

However I choose to understand what brought
you to the fence, I bring my own hand
up to the latch. There are no cardinal rules
in the treatment of one human by another. In the teeming
air
of our narrow escapes, we freely observe our species
advance, capable and composed, toward
extinction, increasingly eager

for what must appear,
as it approaches, more beautiful
and superior
with every step.

—Jean Monahan, "Letter to Robin Silverman"

Sweet thought that I may yet live and grow green,
That leaves may yet spring from the withered root,
And buds and flowers and berries half unseen;
Then if you haply muse upon the past,
Say this: Poor child, she hath her wish at last;
Barren through life, but in death bearing fruit.

—Christina Rossetti, "Looking Forward"

The moon is full here every night,
And I can bathe here in his light.
The leaves will bury every year,
And no one knows I'm gone.

—Tom Waits, "No One Knows I'm Gone"

As one rose dies another blooms
It's always been that way
I remember the showers
But no one puts flowers
On a flower's grave

—Tom Waits, "Flower's Grave"

It begins...

...like a storm—with that pensive heavy stillness of dead air pressing in, with a soft rustle of the wind just barely stirring in the trees, a bruising over of the summer sky, a somber gray and yellow horizon glittery with lightning, bloated full of thunder, swept by sheets of rain—it begins when old man Krejci bumps his head.

And then—like that same storm spent, blown past to leave the ground and the air around feeling new and fresh and washed crisp clean—the next morning when Meena peeks into her father's sun-spilled bedroom to find that he has not moved, but is still lying on the bed with his head flat back on the pillow, in just exactly the same way she left him there eight hours before, everything will be changed...

July 2006

It begins on a Friday evening in July, when Josef and Meena Krejci go over to Larks Cafe to eat supper and then off to see a movie at the new theater complex out in the Westside Mall. Just the two of them: Joe an old man in his late nineties and Meena his daughter, in her middle middle-age. Nothing fancy: he in his yellow golf shirt and blue trousers and she in a light green cotton shift that she's tried to dress up a little with a flowered pink and turquoise chiffon scarf. If you were to see them out together like this you might think she's his nurse or his caretaker, a paid companion who's been hired to look after the old man.

She is solicitous of him, but he is clearly still in charge. He does the driving. She slows her pace to match his and leans forward to listen to him, raises her voice to be sure he can hear whatever she might have to say to him in reply.

Or if you were to look closer you might think you see a family resemblance and then maybe you would guess that the father is a widower, the mother is dead and Meena is a devoted daughter, maybe never married, maybe divorced, alone and childless, maybe even widowed herself, although this is not in fact the case.

At Larks they sit at their usual table, in a corner near a window that looks out over the parking lot, newly paved and painted, shimmery with the lingering midsummer heat. Joe's back is to the wall because, he says, he likes to see what's coming, but Meena knows that if there's anything coming it's probably not worth waiting for. The place is almost empty at this early hour, and the Krejcis have the young waitress to themselves. The plastic nametag on her lapel says her name is Prairie, and Joe finds this amusing. His blue eyes twinkle as he flirts with her—"What kind of name is that?" he wants to know. The girl shrugs. "My parents were hippies," she answers, matter-of-factly. This must be something that she's been asked to explain many times. "Would you care for any water, sir?" Her face is blank; she's just doing her job. Maybe she knows already, just by looking at him, that this guy is not going to leave her much of a tip. The old ones never do.

But Prairie's chilly demeanor annoys Meena—Why can't she at least smile? How hard is it to be pleasant to a harmless old man who doesn't get out much anymore and is only doing his best to be friendly? Joe Krejci could teach this girl a thing or two about customer relations. With an attitude like that, she wouldn't have lasted ten minutes working for him.

Used to be you had to stand in line to get a table in this place, but not anymore, and no wonder. When Meena was little, coming here for dinner with her father was a special treat, reserved for special occasions, but lately it's become a weekly event. Back then the waitresses bent over backwards to be nice—they had seemed like motherly old ladies to her at the time, but in fact they were probably younger than she is now.

Joe would tell you he loves Larks because the food's pretty good and for only $6.95 you can get all you can eat at the early-bird buffet, seconds and thirds and even fourths if that's what it takes to fill you up, plus unlimited helpings of pie. He's always had a healthy appetite; even now, even at this advanced age, when other men are withering down to skin and bone,

Joe Krejci is still plump. He still has a pinkish glow of health in his cheeks. His laugh is still hearty. He looks years younger than he is and always has: that's what everybody says.

He catches Meena watching him and frowns, "What is it?"

She shakes her head. "Nothing."

Meena has the meat loaf and mashed potatoes, with a little green and pink Jell-O salad and a slice of sponge cake for dessert, and Josef has the fried fish and coleslaw with boiled spinach and stewed tomatoes and a scoop of macaroni and cheese on the side. Plus the pie—one piece of Boston cream, one of rhubarb, and a slice of pecan, which he tries to get Meena to finish for him but she doesn't want it.

It's the yellowy color of the mayonnaise that will lead them both to wonder later whether maybe the tartar sauce was bad, was that it? Was that why he was in the bathroom being sick after they got home, and not because of how he'd bumped his head, not just once but twice that night? At his age he was lucky not to have broken any bones, and they will both of them be thankful for that.

They leave Larks to drive through downtown and across Bohemie Bridge, on over to the new developments on the far west side of Linwood, all the way along to where Hill Parkway widens into four lanes near the Interstate, with Joe at the wheel because even if he is an old man and maybe age has slowed his reaction time some, still after last year's cataract surgeries his eyes are pretty good and he is competent enough to pass a driving test on his birthday every year. Besides, he's Meena's father and he's not anywhere near ready to turn over his independence to her, not now and as far as he's concerned, not ever.

The handicapped parking spaces are all taken, so he has to squeeze into a regular spot on the end instead, a little ways away, and this angers him. Then, when he's climbing out of the car, Joe loses his footing and careens backward, thrashing for balance and chocking his head against the cinder block wall behind him.

Angered further, he kicks at the bumper of the car. He buffs at the knot on the back of his head with his knuckles, rubbing his fist hard across the shiny mottled surface of his scalp. He shrugs Meena off when she comes around and tries to help him. He lurches away from her, staggers and stumbles forward bear-like, into the pool of light that falls across the asphalt from the street lamp overhead.

"I'm all right," he growls when Meena tries to draw his fist away and get a look at the goose egg that's started to swell there on the back of his head. He's angrier than he should be, snapping at her even though she knows he doesn't really mean it.

"Dammit, I said I was all right."

And after all the years that she's been living with him, she surely should know better than to argue with her father. He has never in her lifetime had much of a mind for anything that she might have to tell him, and she learned long ago how to give up and let go of what she can. Joe Krejci is, by his own description, a stubborn old bohunk, and he's just as likely to do a thing twice knowing how it maybe bothers somebody else when he does. Better all around if only you can find a way instead to bite your tongue and bide your time, wait awhile until his anger has cooled off and blown on by and been forgotten.

She tries to take his arm, but he brushes her off and continues on. There is a Boy Scout standing under the theater marquee, holding a flat box of yellow ribbons. On the sandwich board beside him is a blurred blow-up of a man's face.

"Would you like a ribbon, sir?" The Scout thrusts the box of ribbons toward Joe.

But the old man just growls and keeps on walking, while Meena has slowed for a closer look at the sandwich board. The caption reads: "$25,000 Reward For Any Information That Directly Leads To The Return Of RALPH WENDELL. 54 yrs of age, white male, 5'10", 180 lbs, blue eyes, gray/brown hair.

"Ma'am?"

The Scout is offering the ribbons to her. She takes one and starts to pin it to her dress.

"It costs a dollar."

Meena apologizes and puts it back, then joins her father in the ticket line, behind two teenage girls, scantily clad in the usual mallrat slut-wear. He is working to get his wallet out of his back pocket. The girls turn to him, then look at each other and giggle.

"Go fuck yourself," Joe barks.

"Dad!" Meena apologizes to the girls, but they aren't having it.

They edge away from him. "Asshole."

He wobbles and she puts a hand on his arm to steady him. Another early warning sign of Alzheimer's: inappropriate anger. "Are you okay?"

"Stop asking me that, will ya"? Joe has his wallet out and is opening it. His hands are shaking. Before he can stop her, Meena has fished out her five-dollar bill, and she's gone back to the Scout.

He grins. "Change your mind?"

"I'll take two." She hands him the money and helps herself to the ribbons. He starts to give her change, but she stops him. "No, it's okay," she says. "You keep it. It's for a good cause." She puts the ribbons in her purse and goes back to the line.

She tries again to see the bump on her father's head, but again he pushes her away.

"I'm telling you, Meena. Leave it."

So is there anyone who will say it was all her fault? Didn't she try to help him? Didn't she do just as much as she could do? And didn't he push her away and tell her to leave him alone? But Meena will blame herself, anyway. She won't be able to help it.

Because what happens next is that one minute the two of them are standing together, shoulder to shoulder, waiting to buy their movie tickets outside the theater, and then the next minute Joe is going down. She hears his squeak, so shrill and so unlike him that right away Meena knows there must be something wrong, and she turns to look, to see why in the world he might have made such an improbable sound. And what she sees is her father collapsing away from her, like a crumpled paper bag. The two girls are standing right there in front of them in the ticket line, and they sense the awkward movement of the old man's body as his legs give out and he starts toppling over toward them, so they turn around just in time to see him coming. But instead of doing the decent thing by reaching out to try and catch him, these girls jump back. His shoulder hits the ground first, and he turns his head. The girls screech at the hollow hard thunking sound that his face makes when it smacks against the pavement at their feet, bounces, smacks the pavement again.

A shock wave moves through the line and Meena is on her knees. The cement of the sidewalk is snagging holes in her pantyhose, but she doesn't mind that, not a bit. She's bending her own body over her father's, as if she thinks she can shield him from something, maybe just the eager view of all these Friday night movie-goers who are standing around in a tight circle already, drawn to the real-life drama of Joe Krejci's real-life fall. She can feel the warmth of their bodies in the air and she can sense their restless, craning movements as they begin to press in closer to see better whatever there is for them to see. She can hear, too, the rough shuffle of their shoes against the sidewalk and the coarse incomprehensible rumble of their voices murmuring in the air over her head, and it scares her. She sees her own hands as if maybe they belong to someone else; she watches as they flutter uselessly above her father's body, hovering around his hips and then his head, lighting in his hair, landing on his arm, brushing up against his neck, his shoulder blades, his back.

One of his arms has been pinned beneath him; the other is outstretched above his head, turned at the wrist so his hand is twisted, its empty palm held up and out as if in some kind of supplication. Meena is shocked by how unlikely this seems, how wrong it is, how indecent really, for her father, of all people, to be lying here like this, in public, unconscious and exposed. She cups both hands around the curve of his far shoulder and, sobbing with the effort of it, she pulls against his dead weight. He is still a large man. She has rolled him over onto his back.

The front of his yellow shirt is spattered with a fine lacy pattern of sprayed blood, and one whole side of his face—from the flat edge of his temple, across the swell of his cheekbone, down to the rise of his jaw and over onto the point of his chin—has been scraped raw.

Meena isn't sure what she's supposed to do next. She sits back on her haunches, with her hands folded helplessly in her lap, and she can only stare at Joe as if he might be a stranger that she's never laid eyes on before in her life.

Later Meena will think it was because she was weak that she got up and turned away. But she just couldn't bear to look. He was Josef Krejci, he was her father, and she had given most of her life to his, so it was just too much for her to have to see him lying there that way, defenseless and brought down. She didn't mean to turn her back on him, and she wasn't intending to go off and leave him there alone either, but just then someone else stepped aside and a space opened up for her. Meena simply stepped into it, and then it seemed as if the circle around him sucked itself shut again behind her, so that for a moment she lost sight of Joe. At that moment, Meena might have been anybody, just another onlooker, but then there he was again, he had come to and he was lurching up to his feet. He charged toward her, lumbering heavily, with one hand splayed across his injured face, shouldering everybody else out of his way.

He was bellowing her name: "Meena!"

She was embarrassed and she didn't want to have anything to do with him.

A woman had stepped forward and was speaking to him, offering help most likely, but Joe wouldn't have it. He swiped out with a backward swing of his opened hand, just missing her, and the woman reared back.

He had seen Meena and he barreled toward her. He grabbed hold of her arm, curling his thick fingers around it, getting some blood on the sleeve of her green dress—ruining it—and then half pulling on her and half leaning on her for support, he led the way over to the end of the parking lot, where they'd left the car.

Meena untied the scarf from around her neck and gave it to her father. He wadded it in his fist and pressed the soft porous fabric to the raw side of his face. She wanted him to stop and hold still for long enough at least so she could take a look at him to see just how badly he was hurt.

"Maybe we ought to call an ambulance. Maybe you should sit down here on the bumper for a minute to collect yourself. Take a second and wait."

But Joe had opened the car door, and he was standing there with one hand enmeshed in the floral pattern of Meena's scarf and the other hand on the handle of the door, holding it open for her.

"Get in," he said, and obediently she did, smoothing the skirt of her dress with one hand and fingering the holes that had been torn in the knees of her stockings with the other. She perched there on the wide front seat clutching her purse in her lap beneath her folded hands, looking through the grimy windshield into the pitch black of an empty field on the far side of the lot, waiting for Joe to let her know what he wanted her to do next.

"Slide over," he said, his voice low, tight.

He got into the car, ducking under the roof, bumping up against Meena's ankle and her calf with the clumsy weight of his hard, heavy shoes, and she startled away from him, struggling across the wide front seat, her feet tangling up with his, her purse caught under her hip. She was fumbling clumsily with the keys, rolling them through her fingers because she couldn't tell which was which, and when she finally did find what she thought might be the right one, then she couldn't get it to fit into the ignition, but she knew she had to do it so she kept poking it and poking, scraping her knuckles and bruising her palm.

Later she will realize she must have been screaming, too. There seemed to be a lot of noise.

Finally Joe reached over and wrested the keys from her, jabbed the right one into the ignition, turning it so at last the engine came to life, with a disturbing roar because she was already pressing her foot down hard on the gas.

Joe sat beside her, deflated, with his head back and his eyes closed, one hand holding the scarf to his face and the other hanging uselessly, loose between his knees. And at that moment the truth flashed through Meena like a cold hard light: this man was her father, her invincible dad, the indestructible Josef Krejci, and now just look at him. He was hurt and he was helpless, and that put him at her mercy, didn't it?

And with that thought there was a coldness that came over her, a serenity that replaced the whirling panic and settled down upon her like a numbing blanket of snow. Or was it a kind of a stillness that rose up from someplace deep within until she was frozen over from the inside out, hardened her into something as smooth and solid-seeming as ice?

Meena turned around farther, aware even then that he wasn't going to go and see a doctor, certain that he wouldn't allow her to take him to the hospital and that he was unlikely to ask for or accept any other kind of outside help, either. He was ninety-eight years old. He couldn't live forever, could he?

She followed the parkway into downtown—deserted at that hour on an early Friday evening—and then crossed back over Bohemie Bridge into a shanty neighborhood that called itself Nowhere, an eyesore at western edge of Wellington Heights. The trees beyond the windows on either side of the car were dark forms that flipped past, bunched together like a mob that might be swarming toward her, reaching out to tap the windows, craning for a glimpse inside. She turned left onto Old River Road, with its deep ditches that dropped off toward the rabble of the trees on one side and toward the river on the other, and then she turned again, onto Otis Road where she lived with her father in the house where she'd grown up, and the headlights swept the serene blank face of the modest stone structure as she pulled the car up into the drive and rocked to a hard stop around back near the kitchen door.

And just as Meena had known it, Joe was not going to have anything to do with anything remotely medical. He wouldn't let her take him to the hospital, and when she begged him to let her call the doctor he refused and told her she was overreacting. Insisted that it was nothing serious—he'd just lost his footing that was all. No big deal. And then he went into the bathroom and was sick.

Soon Meena will be blaming herself for what happened. She will think she should have known it wasn't the mayonnaise in the tartar sauce at Larks that was bad, as her father kept insisting. He is such an old man and his face has paled, his skin is so cold to her touch and now his eyes seem to be losing focus. She helps him to his bed. He sits there at the edge of the mattress for a moment to collect himself, with his hands out flat on either side of him for balance. His breathing is shallow, labored even. She sees him wince and wonders whether he might be in pain, but she's afraid to ask. She knows that is not something he would want his daughter to know about. He refuses both her sympathy and her concern; he rejects her love as if he doesn't need it. Never did. He takes a deep breath and toes off his loafers, one by one.

"I'm okay," he says, not because he wants to reassure either his daughter or himself, but because he wants her to go away and leave him alone. Still, she bends over him, patting gently at the raw scraped skin of his cheek with a cold washcloth, but he flinches at her touch and snarls and turns his head away so now there really is nothing left for her to do but respect his wishes and step back.

He brings his legs around and lies down, fully clothed, on the bed. He licks his lips. His blue eyes gleam and stare and then seem to gather some of their focus again, and Meena understands that he has something he wants to say to her, so she leans in close again.

She watches as he struggles to speak. She leans closer still, cooperating. She holds her breath. She listens hard.

"Be at peace, Meena," he says.

She starts to respond, but he raises a hand to stop her.

"Remember." He closes his eyes.

"What? Remember what?"

"Remember…" He pauses. "Who…"

She doesn't know what he means. What is he trying to say? Who is it he wants her to remember?"

He swallows. He raises a hand and points a finger at her.

"You."

She shakes her head.

"Are."

Is that it? Are these to be his last words to her? It seems important that she get it right. She really does want so much to understand. She really does want to still believe that this man, her father, knows infinitely more than she does or ever will, about the world, about himself, and about her. He is so old. And she's always been a good girl. She's always respected him, even when he didn't deserve respect. She is his only daughter. She is a motherless child. She wants to behave herself and do as she's told because she still believes that her obedience to him will be rewarded, that it will redeem her, someday.

But he does not elaborate, he doesn't wait for her to answer, and now it seems that Josef Krejci has nothing more to say. He waves her away. He licks his lips, then sinks back into the pillows again, and settles down into the privacy of his own unknowable inwardness, miles away from here, worlds away from his daughter. His eyes are closed. His hands are folded on his chest. His breathing slows, and his body is still: he is asleep.

Meena is left reeling with confusion. What did he mean? Is she supposed to know?

This isn't the first time she's heard this: "Remember who you are." It's one of the things that her grandmother, Matka, said often when Meena was a girl growing up. Sometimes it seemed to mean one thing, and other times another. Maybe she was in danger of forgetting herself? Or, of overstepping her place? Maybe she hadn't been giving herself enough credit, maybe that was it.

And then the old woman was likely to go on to ask, as if it were a test—sitting back, her arms folded against her breasts: "Well, Meena, who is it that you are then?"

Her answer, whispered, choked: "I am myself?"

The old woman's hand waving, dismissing this: "Yes, yes, of course you are. But," louder then, "WHO ARE YOU?"

What could she say? Blushing furiously, her pulse pounding in her ears, with confusion, embarrassment, shame. "I am Meena Krejci?"

And with this would come the sunrise of Matka's warm smile, creeping up into her face as her cheeks filled out and pinkened and her dark eyes went bright with light. She leaned toward Meena, smelling of

13

ferment and vegetables, and touched her thumb to the little girl's cheek. She nodded her big head, sat back again, sipped her tea, looked off as if lost in thought. Then, she turned to Meena again, and her look was slyer now, conspiratorial, as if they shared a secret of some kind between them. "*Ano,*" Matka said. "Yes."

She leaves her father sleeping. She turns off the lamp and slips out of the room, pulling the door quietly closed. She creeps down the darkened hallway to her own bedroom at its other end and sits for a while in the chair by the window, watching the summer twilight dwindle into night. When finally it's fully dark, she rouses herself, gets up and crosses the hall to her own bathroom, where the pieces of her lingerie, sheer flesh-colored stockings and lacy bras, a rubbery girdle and bright white underpants, waft ghostly on the clothes hooks and towel bars.

Meena slips out of her shoes. She pulls off the torn pantyhose and steps out of the blood-stained green dress. She leaves the light off. She stands naked at the sink, her body soft and white and shapeless, and brushes her teeth, washes her face, runs a comb through her wild hair without once looking up to eye the hint of her own reflection in the mirror. A cotton nightgown hangs from a hook on the back of the door and this she lifts and slips on over her head. Pads barefoot to her bed and pulls the blanket back and gets in. The springs creak with her shifting weight until she has settled and lies still.

The window at the far side of the room is open and beyond the screen she can see the tangle of trees that she knows to be the woods that climb the hill behind the house, toward the park. The night is full of familiar sounds that Meena hears without hearing them:

crickets, an owl, a dog, a car trolling slowly up the street, pausing at the top before shifting gears and moving on.

She might have been cut loose from any mooring, she might have been floating, she might have been a speck of dust spinning in a world of infinite inky empty space. As if the rest of the world had dissipated and disappeared, until, with dawn it would be recreated and take on its shape, its pieces coming back together to form the whole, then settling hardened and firm and solid again, each into its proper place.

Sunrise cracks through the curtains with one thin beam of hot white light that falls across Meena's face and ought to awaken her, but it doesn't, not right away. She is dreaming—something about water, something about floating, something about a sound that seems to be coming to her from somewhere else. A ball bouncing on the sidewalk, maybe, or a body rolling down a staircase. Shoes tumbling in a dryer. The thump and thud of her father going about the daily business of opening up his grocery store. She seems to hear him coughing, his morning hack and spit. Maybe he is moving boxes from one side of the room to another, but what for? Maybe he is stacking cans upon a shelf: soup, meat, vegetables, juice, and what else? Meena thinks she can see him clearly, in his apron, his white shirt shining, his heavy shoes, his wide bright tie. His sleeves rolled up and a bracelet of rubber bands pinching at the skin of his wrist. A smell of pipe smoke clinging to him, his skin, his hair, his clothes. He will be opening up the safe behind the counter; he will be putting the drawer into the register; he will be counting out the cash inside and, licking his pencil, making careful note of how much of this money he has to call his own.

He seems to guess that she's been watching him, and he looks up so sharply that her first instinct is to duck away and hide, but instead she wakes and the dream is quickly gone. Forgotten and replaced by thoughts of how much she has to do today. Household chores that Meena tackles every Saturday—grocery shopping, laundry, housecleaning, and maybe in the afternoon there will be time for some work in the garden, which needs attention, weeding and picking. The zucchinis will soon be too big to be any good anymore, and the tomatoes are in danger of over-ripening: maybe she will make a spaghetti sauce for supper tonight, use the lettuce and cucumbers for a salad…

And now Meena remembers.

Dinner at Larks. How Josef stumbled getting out of the car, how he fell outside the theater, how he was sick when they got home.

She sits up, holds her breath, listens hard, hears nothing.

And after she has put on her bathrobe, after she's used the toilet and brushed her teeth and splashed water on her face, then, she will go down the hall and check on him, then, she will see that he is still there on the bed, then, she will understand that he hasn't moved since she closed the door on him last night, that he has not been sleeping, that he is dead.

Meena Krejci stands here in her father's bedroom, holding herself just as still as she can, hardly daring to breathe, as she listens with some reassurance to the pounding steady strength of her own blood surging in her veins. Her legs seem to her to be as sturdy and thick as two posts rising up side by side out of the deep dark grain of the hardwood floor. Her bare feet look heavy and square planted there, firmly rooted in the bright splash of early morning sunlight that comes tumbling in through the opened window and onto the elaborate geography of her father's bed. That cold stillness that settled over her in the car outside the movie theater last night hasn't yet thawed but lingers still, and it keeps her solid and steady and numb.

She can't take her eyes off him: he doesn't look real, he doesn't look like himself. His skin seems to sag—as if he might be made of wax and has softened slightly—and it's lost its pinkish glow. The scrape on his cheek gleams. His eyes are as blue as ever, though: they gaze up at the ceiling, wide with belief.

When a sob begins to hitch in Meena's throat, she swallows it back, shakes her head, knows that if she were to cry right now it would be less for the loss of her father than for what she has come to clearly see has been the steady slow trickle of her own smaller self—what she used to want, what she thought she had, the girl she can remember that she had been at one time, a long time ago—and of her own life bleeding away from her, unstaunched.

There are so many things that Meena needs to do now, and she has no idea where to start, who should she call first? An ambulance? A doctor? The police? It seems too late for that, but too soon to be contacting the mortuary and making funeral arrangements either. There has long been a place reserved for Josef Krejci out at the Bohemie Cemetery, Meena knows, between his parents and his wife.

Just now the morning seems very still—if there is traffic outside, if there are animal sounds or the squeals of children playing or adult voices calling out, she doesn't hear them—and alone here in the house she's feeling a kind of peace, although she supposes it isn't likely to last long.

First, she takes a shower. She washes her hair and shaves her legs. When she feels the sting of soap on her skinned knees, her heart tumbles in her chest, and for that moment she can't breathe. But she leans into the water and wills herself to be calm. She will get dressed, she will eat some breakfast to fortify herself, and then she will decide what she's supposed to do next.

Meena knows that just as soon as word of what's happened gets out this house is going to start to fill as people come around, buzzing at the front door or rattling at the back. They'll bring food, they'll track in dirt, they'll want to offer their condolences, their sympathy, their prayers and support, and they'll want her to be appropriately grateful for it, too. They'll be searching her face to try to read her reaction to her loss, the sudden change in her situation that she'll have to learn to live with, maybe even be grateful for, and then, they'll go off to discuss it among themselves, later.

Meena isn't quite sure what it is she's feeling just now. Sorrow or relief, anger, guilt, or fear. It might be all of these. Or maybe it isn't anything at all.

Someone to Look After You

1951-1957

Once upon a time you were a little girl, and your name was Meena Krejci. You were born a grocer's daughter, on the coldest day of a cold winter, in January, 1951, when your father was already almost fifty and your mother was forty-two. This was too late in life for a woman to be having her first child, your grandmother told you, many times. According to Matka, Agnes Krejci should have been happy with things the way they were, she ought to have been grateful for all that she already had and not tried to add to it anything more. It was a long time before you came to understand just what the old woman meant by this, and when you asked, "But what about me?" Matka only shook her big powdery head. "Well Meena," she replied, "you were the price that was paid."

"You're just lucky you aren't a moron," Libbie Grandon would say later, touching her hair and smiling at the joke.

Your father was a large man, with big wrists and thick thumbs. His shoes were heavy on the stairs when he came up to bed at night. Matka was his mother, and she lived in the apartment rooms above the grocery store.

Krejci's was on the corner of 4th Avenue and 16th Street on the southeast side of Linwood, Iowa, in the heart of Wellington Heights. This was before there was such a thing as a supermarket. The store was small, a family business, and because there were a lot of Czechs in Linwood, the name was a common and familiar one, pronounced *cray-chee*, with the emphasis on the first syllable.

Krejci's was a popular neighborhood store, within walking distance for a lot of its customers, who came with their own carts or called in their orders to be delivered to their homes. later. The building itself wasn't much to look at—just a thick square box with green trim and white slat sides that your father paid to have repainted every year, a lit sign above the door, a long display window in the front, and a gravel parking lot out back.

Josef Krejci worked behind the counter, ringing up orders, taking cash, and making change. He had a wide smile that he saved for the ladies who came into Krejci's to shop. He was a man of dignity, and under his apron he wore a white shirt and a colorful tie. Dark pants with broad cuffs, heavy black shoes. A feather duster in his back pocket, rubber bands collected around one thick wrist, a gold watch strapped on the other. His hair was cropped so close to his skull that when his pink scalp caught the light from overhead, it shone. In his pocket he carried a thick roll of cash, bound by a rubber band, and he'd lick his thumb and uncurl a bill, then snap it with a flourish as he pulled it free.

Your mother was smaller but not in a delicate way. In the silver-framed photograph, Agnes stood next to Josef, and the top of her head was at his shoulder. She was wearing a dress with short sleeves that exposed her thickish arms. She held her hands folded in a pose under her chin; her hair was wavy and dark, her eyes deep set, her smile prim. Her hips were full and her legs were sturdy, feet planted solidly in low-heeled leather shoes.

It was Agnes's job to keep the books and look after the accounts, and she did this with precision at a desk under the stairs that led up to the apartment where Matka lived. When it was quiet in the store one could hear the old woman moving around up there; the floorboards creaked across the ceiling as she walked from room to room.

That winter after you were born your father insisted that his wife stay home with the baby until the weather warmed with the spring and when it did, then she brought you with her in to work. You were quiet and good, content to lie on your blanket in the buggy and listen to the clatter of the keys on the adding machine while your mother punched in the numbers, tallying up the accounts and keeping track of the invoices, sending out statements and paying off bills.

They say that real memory only just begins at four years old, that anything before that is no more than a concoction, a fantastic muddled dream, and maybe this is so. Nevertheless, you would have a picture of your mother in your mind, and whether it was something you remembered or whether it was something your father told you or whether it was something you'd made up is impossible to know. What you saw was your mother perched on the edge of her chair with her back straight and her feet crossed at the ankle. She was wearing a plain brown skirt that hit her legs at mid-calf and a cream-colored silk blouse with a collar that tied into a bow at her throat, held in place there by a gold and garnet brooch. Agnes's eyes swam big behind the thick lenses of her glasses, and her lips pursed thoughtfully as she wrote a careful row of numbers down a column at the edge of a customer's bill. This she folded and tucked into an envelope, moistened the flap with a flick of her tongue, then sealed it and set it on a pile, to be mailed later in the box on the corner that you'd pass on the walk back home.

The bell above the door chimed, and Josef's voice boomed as he greeted a customer who'd come in at the front of the store. The phone rang, and Agnes answered it, listened intently, then pulled out a piece of paper and a pencil and licked the lead before she carefully wrote down, in neat round letters, the order that she would pass on to her husband to fill. Overhead, the ceiling groaned, and then the door at the top of the stairs opened and Matka in her black dress was descending like a shadow, a slow-moving shape on swollen feet that hobbled up the aisle to settle on her stool behind the counter, as torpid as a toad.

Then you were older, and you were loose in your father's store, toddling up and down the narrow aisles between the towering shelves, caroming past stacked boxes of cereal and crackers, cans of vegetables and soup, racks of bread and buns. You careened, squealing, around the corner by the meat case, where heavy slabs of pink beef lay on beds of crushed ice, fresh parsley curled around the brown knots of the pork knuckles, the dimpled pale skin of the chicken breasts seemed to shiver in the cold, and you were a mere shimmer in the glassy ogle of a fish's eye. The pop machine in the corner hummed around its hoarded treasure—jewel-like bottles of ginger ale and root beer, cream soda, orangeade, grapeade, and Coke. The freezer case let out an icy sigh; the produce bins—piled high with ragged heads of lettuce, papery-skinned onions, dusty potatoes, bearded corn—shuddered at the pounding of your father's footsteps behind you. You squealed again at the hard grab of his hands—to your own ears it was a scream, part terror, part delight—as he snatched you off your feet and swung you up high over his head, swooped you around and then plopped you down on the top of the highest shelf. Where you sat, head spinning, legs dangling above the grown-ups' heads, including your father's—his pink scalp shone, Agnes's hairpins glinted, Matka lifted her chin and her big face was like a powdery moon rising over the blue-black sky of her dress. You were drawn downward by your fear, and you leaned into it, wailing. Hands outstretched, you fell into your father's open arms.

"That'll teach you, Meena," he said, as your mother whisked you away.

Or, from a place on a step halfway down the basement stairs, you were watching the play of your father's shadow as it moved, hugely, over the rugged limestone walls below. You were sitting on your hands because if he caught you sucking your thumb then he was going to thump you on the forehead with a quick hard flick of his finger that would blind you for a moment. Josef carried boxes from one side of the basement to the other. He pried open a crate of oranges with the claw of a hammer, and the nails screamed in the wood. He whistled through his teeth as he worked. He stopped and dusted his hands on his pants. He fished his pipe out of his apron pocket and packed a pinch of tobacco down with the flat of his thumb. A match flared, the fragrant smoke wafted up and swallowed him.

Or, you nuzzled next to him in the frozen dawn. The wool of his coat scratched your cheek and the cold leather of the truck's front seat was warmed by the bare backs of your legs under your skirt. Hot air blew out of the vents into your face; it lifted your hair. Icicles whiskered the trees; branches bent and broke under the dead weight of the piled snow. Yours was the only vehicle moving on the street, and all around you the city of Linwood looked abandoned, asleep. Josef gripped the wheel with both gloved hands. He cursed as he turned a corner and the car skidded, corrected, then crawled on, over the leaden river, past the frozen stares of the frowning statues of the saints on Bohemie Bridge.

Or, you were sitting on the kitchen floor in a buttery pool of warm sunlight. The breeze from a fan stirred your mother's hair, which was strewn across the yellow linoleum, where Agnes Krejci lay on her back with her hands out-flung, palms up, fingers softly curled. One leg was straight; the other was bent. Her skirt was hiked up to reveal the lacy hem of her slip against a varicose tangle of blue veins on the low inside of her thigh. Her eyes behind her glasses were open, unblinking, and her plain features now seemed delicate and fragile, beautiful even. You were tracing the outline of your mother's face with a fingertip—from temple to jaw, chin to lips, nose to brow—skin as cold and flawless as the polished porcelain at the bottom of the bathtub, as smooth and pale as the softened wax of the Christmas candles in church.

An angry wasp buzzed in a raised window, trapped somewhere, between glass and screen.

It was 1955, and you were four years old. You had been cranky all morning and unusually willful, and your mother had been complaining—she had a headache, she was sleepy, it was so hot and muggy she felt strangled, she couldn't concentrate, the light from the lamp on the desk, dim as it was, hurt her eyes. Annoyed, Josef sent his wife home to put you down for a nap.

He closed the store at seven o'clock that night, as always—took the cash out of the drawer and put it in the safe behind the counter, swept the floor and turned off the lights, and as Matka plodded up the stairs to her apartment overhead, he locked the doors, front and back, then drove home to the house on Otis Road. He brought the evening paper in off the porch. This was his favorite time of day. He was expecting the smell of his dinner cooking, the sound of polka music playing on the radio, the sight of his little girl toddling toward him, the feel of his wife's lips nipping a quick kiss at his chin. But not tonight. Silence, stillness, shadows instead. Puzzled, he slapped the paper against his leg and called out as he passed through the front room—"Agnes?"—then the dining room—"Meena?"—then the swinging door—"Hello?"—and finally into the kitchen, where Agnes was sprawled on the floor and you lay curled against her.

It was an aneurysm, a subarachnoid hemorrhage that burst within her skull; it flooded her brain with blood, she fell, and in that instant Agnes Krejci was dead. By the time Josef came home that evening, she had been dead for hours, probably all afternoon, the doctor said.

You were only four years old. Why weren't you crying when your father found you? What did you think had happened?

Had you seen your mother fall? Or maybe you'd only heard the sound—the gasp of sudden pain, a hand scrabbling for support against the tiled countertop as vision dimmed—and then you turned to see your mother's knees buckle and her body fold toward the floor.

What look on Agnes's face, of astonishment, of puzzlement, of fear? Did she know? Did she call out to her baby? "Meena!" Her thick glasses, one lens shattered. A sheen of spittle at the corner of her mouth. Such a terrible stillness; the world in long, silent pause.

And then did you call out to her? "Mama!" Crab crawl on all fours to her side? "Mama?" No answer. Agnes didn't blink or breathe or stir.

How long then, before you would begin to understand that your mother was gone for good?

When you asked Matka where your mother was, the old woman answered, "Your mother is an angel. Your mother is a star. She's everywhere and nowhere." Then pointing a finger straight at you: "She is right here." You could peer at Agnes Krejci's face in that old photograph on your father's dresser and then find it again, a shadow in hiding there behind the clear features of your own girl's face in the mirror.

And then you were all alone in your bed in your room in your father's house, and you were supposed to be asleep but there was only darkness all around you and so you were awake, and you were alone. No movement and no sound. The door was closed and the room was dark, and you understood that there wasn't any way for you to know for sure whether the world was still out there somewhere on the other side beyond it, unchanged. It might have been worse to dare to look and see. Because, what if you were right and there was nothing? No sound, no movement, and no light. You leaned against the window sill to peer out at the deep shadows of the woods that climbed the hill toward the park behind the house, and you could just make out the tangle of the branches at the tops of the trees, against the lightening sky. The glass was cold against your cheek. You would wait for morning that way, hunched over upon yourself as if you might be aboard a boat set loose to float upon a sea of nothing.

After your mother's death, Josef brought you with him into the store every morning and all day Matka looked after you in the apartment upstairs: two bedrooms, a bathroom, a living room, and a kitchen. The ceilings all were slant.

You started school, at Arthur Elementary, in the fall when you were five years old, and it was there in Miss Temple's morning kindergarten that you first became aware of Libbie Grandon, whose family had sometime that summer moved into the house next door on Otis Road. You lived in houses set side by side, with yards and driveways in between, but such can be the closed world of early childhood that it wasn't until school started in September that you knew that Libbie was there.

Miss Temple was a beatnik. She had wavy brown hair and a mole on her chin, and she wore long dark skirts and loose silky blouses and black tights and soft leather flats. Hers was a kindergarten just like any other one. The children sat in a circle on a braided rag rug and listened to their teacher read a story or call out the alphabet or play her guitar and sing, tapping her foot upon the floor. You in a red and green plaid dress with a full skirt and puffed sleeves, smocking on the front, white socks, buckled shoes. Libbie close by, wearing brown corduroy trousers and a forest green sweater and yellow rubber boots. Or dungarees with red plaid flannel lining. A black velvet jumper with pink silk roses embroidered on the straps. Her fine blond hair was tied back with a ribbon or woven into a pair of narrow braids.

Every day just before lunchtime Miss Temple led the children in single file out to the courtyard at the front of the school, where the mothers would be sitting in their cars, parked at the curb. On days when it was raining, Matka stood on the sidewalk, planted there in her black rubber galoshes as firmly as if she were a tree that had sprouted from the pavement that morning while you were away inside the school. In one hand she held an umbrella. Her head was wrapped in a gray scarf that she'd tied into a knot under her chin. She took your hand and walked you back to Krejci's, where you would spend the rest of the day together, until it was time for the store to close up and then Josef could take you home.

Each night as you followed your father up the limestone steps up to your own dark and silent house, next door at the Grandons' it was another world altogether, a bewildering muddle of sound and sight—Mr. Grandon hammering at something in the garage; John banging a basketball against the concrete; Libbie riding a bicycle in circles around him, training wheels squeaking; Mrs. Grandon framed by a square of light at the back door, calling to the dog; Rags frantic in the side yard, barking at you and your father before you went inside.

The small stone house in Wellington Heights was in a good part of town, with long lawns and spacious homes on broad tree-lined streets that led up the hill to Ellis Park, with its woods and creek and small zoo. There was an aviary there that kept an eagle and an owl and a family of peafowl. A chicken-wired monkey house. Small animal cages, with badgers and skunks and a bobcat and a wolf behind wrought iron bars. And off to the side, apart from the rest, in a more modern concrete-walled compound of their own, a pair of black bears.

Wellington Heights formed a trapezoid, framed by Otis Road on one side, the park on another, the river on the third, and Vernon Boulevard on the fourth. Across Vernon Boulevard was an area known as Nowhere, and on the other side of the river was the Czech village that was called Bohemietown.

There was a stillness inside that solemn stone house on Otis Road. There was a darkness in the woods that climbed the hill out back and sprawled away farther, toward the park. There was you, a lonely little girl lying sleepless in her bed, listening for your father's heavy footsteps on the stairs and hearing instead the cries of the peacocks, monkey chatter, wolf howl, sometimes the bobcat's other-worldly scream. And there was Libbie Grandon, whose full name was Elizabeth Mellencamp Grandon, whose father sold houses and drove a blue convertible, whose mother played bridge and ordered groceries from your father's store, who had an older brother named John and a cocker spaniel named Rags and a tabby cat that she called Smith. Who had moved into the big green house with the flower boxes and sunny yellow trim next door at the end of the summer, when you were five.

Josef Krejci was proud of where he lived and of his house. He'd come a long way, he said, from the cramped clapboard bungalow where he'd grown up with his widowed mother in Bohemietown across the river to there, Wellington Heights. Both his parents were first generation Czechs. But, your mother was a princess and your father was a king—that's what Matka promised.

And when you asked, "What about me?"
"You are a miracle," she said.

The park behind the house and the woods that surrounded it loomed in the dreams of your childhood as deep and dark and dangerous as the Bohemian forests that figured in the tales and legends that your grandmother conjured up on those long afternoons spent upstairs in the apartment, where you waited for and at the same time dreaded the end of the day when your father would come to collect you and take you home. Matka's warnings sang in your ears. Beware of wolves and witches, trolls and dwarves, the old woman cautioned, and said that when the long cold winters closed down over Bohemia, then the fathers there might turn to the sweet meat of their own children for survival. Loving dads would be transformed into bloodthirsty monsters, men who thrilled to the taste of babies that even after the snow had melted and the ice had thawed, when the gardens were full and the geese were fat again, still they craved that soft fresh flesh, and when they came upon a child alone...

Mrs. Grandon's worries for Libbie were far more modern and worldly and common than that. She feared drunk drivers in speeding cars, radioactive light waves from the television screen, a lightning strike that could ride the phone line into your ear and short out the circuits of your brain. Polio. Communism. The atom bomb. All of which seemed as unlikely to you as Matka's malevolent monsters did to Libbie.

Your father's stone house was halfway up the hill—the back yard rose up wild and overgrown toward the park, where you could mount the stile at the corner of the wire fence and then follow the path that twined through the trees until it opened up into a grassy clearing that was maintained by city workers at the back side of the zoo.

Or you could follow the pavement of Otis Road itself into the park, climb the cobbles to the pavilion at its top, where there was a store that sold candy and pop and snacks and ice. Behind the pavilion the land dipped down toward the crease of Ellis Creek, then rose abruptly up again to the deeper woods of Hollow Hill. From there you could see past Old River Road, across the bunched buildings of downtown Linwood and beyond, the streetlights stretching out through the neighborhoods toward the fields far away where, abruptly, they stopped—as if the city might have been a mere island of life in an otherwise empty ocean, adrift, there seemed to be nothing but utter darkness on beyond.

The neighborhood kids are all out playing in the yards on Otis Road at dusk, and Libbie Grandon and her brother John are among them. Bike tires churn in the gravel driveways, balls are tossed from hand to hand, a back screen door slams shut, the street lamps snap on, porch lights are swarmed by a flutter of pale moths. You are standing at your window on the second floor of your father's house, and from that height you can see almost all of what goes on below you. You are above and apart and alone because your father will not allow you to join in. The world is a dangerous place, he says. And at five years old, you are still too young for it. You don't have a mother, and that means there is no one who can be counted on to look after you out there—you would be on your own.

Until there came a chilly Sunday morning in the late spring, when Libbie's mother was out working in her garden, getting it ready for summer by putting in tomato stakes, unbundling the roses, and raking away winter's debris and dead leaves. You were watching from your window, as usual. You let the glass catch your breath in a circle of fog, wiped it away with a fingertip, and peered down at Mrs. Grandon, who looked as exotic as a jungle bird out there—her body a bright splash of color against the drab background of browned grass and turned earth.

"Your mother is a princess," Matka said, and you were only five years old, but already you understood that this was just a story. It was a game you played, it was a tale you told each other, as pretend as the hand puppets that Miss Temple had at school—alive with gesture and bearing and voice at the cuffs of her sleeves when she held them out before her, but otherwise as limp and dead as a pair of old socks at the bottom of the box in the cupboard where they were kept when they weren't being used.

But Libbie's mother, she was something else. Faye Grandon was the real thing, flesh and blood, living and breathing, a woman as real and as beautiful as one of her own flowers, even on a Sunday morning when the roses were still just tight green buds and she'd changed out of her church dress and was outside working in the yard just like anybody else. Dirt was smudged on her cheek and she wore big gloves, faded yellow pedal pushers, heavy wool socks that sagged over the tops of her torn canvas Keds, and an old pink sweater that had begun to pill across the front and along the backsides of the sleeves. Her head was covered by the cloud of a chiffon scarf and her black hair had been bobby-pinned into a row of tight flat spit curls across her forehead.

Libbie was sitting on the back step eating an orange. She'd dropped the shreds of rind in the dirt near her feet, and they littered the ground around her. She licked the juice off her fingers. She pushed back the thin strands of hair that cobwebbed her eyes, then looked up to where your face was framed by the window, watching. Libbie smiled, and when you didn't respond she raised one hand and waved. You were not expecting to be noticed, and the gesture startled you. You jerked back and heard your heartbeat pounding in her ears. Then you crept forward again and you waved back.

Josef closed the store on Sundays in those days. He never took vacations otherwise. Sunday was his one day of the week to stay home and take it easy, he said, and he did not like to be bothered on his afternoon of rest. He didn't go to church. He slept late, then took his coffee into his study to read the newspaper there, smoke his pipe, and listen to an opera on the hi-fi. In time he'd have to extend his hours, when the Hawkeye Supermarket moved in and began to cut into his business, but back then he still had the luxury of that one day to call his own.

And so when the doorbell rang that morning, he didn't answer it. He might not have heard it; the music in his study was that loud. Or he might have been asleep. It rang again, but he still didn't respond. The third time, you went down and opened the door yourself.

There was Mrs. Grandon on the stoop, smiling expectantly. She'd wiped the dirt from her cheek and dabbed her lips with fresh color, the same pale pink of the roses that would bloom for her that summer. She leaned down so her face, framed by the gauze of her scarf, was close enough to yours that you could see the soft powder that shimmered on the surface of her skin.

"Hi there," Mrs. Grandon said. "Is your father at

home?"

Her breath smelled like cloves, and later you would learn that she chewed clove gum because she believed it made her teeth white. Before you could answer that yes he was home, but no he didn't want to be disturbed, you felt a movement at your back and you turned to see your father, looming in the doorway behind you. He held a folded section of the newspaper, and he slapped it against his leg. Mrs. Grandon pulled off a glove and put her hand out to him. He looked at it, not knowing, it seemed, what it was that she expected him to do.

"I'm Faye Grandon?" she said, as if she wasn't really sure whether that was in fact true.

Josef, silent, slapped the paper against his leg again and waited for her to go on.

"From next door?" Mrs. Grandon added, still asking him, it seemed.

He cleared his throat. "If it's about your bill...," he began, prepared to inform her that this was his only day off, he worked six days a week and deserved a little peace on Sunday, didn't he? But before he could go on, her laugh, abrupt as a hiccup, stopped him.

"Oh gosh, no," she said, "it's nothing like that. It's just that, well, my daughter..." She turned and waved a glove at Libbie, who was standing at the bottom of the steps. Libbie ducked her head, then looked up, grinning.

"Hi there, Mr. Krejci," she said, pronouncing the name just right. He squinted at her, frowning.

Mrs. Grandon went on, still asking him: "They're in the same class at school? Your daughter and mine?"

You felt his big hand on your head, as if he were claiming you, or holding you in place. He asked a question of his own. "Just what exactly is it that you want?"

Mrs. Grandon's smile widened; his frown deepened. "Well," she said, "they're friends?" As if that were a question that, for the asking, should explain everything. She waited, the smile frozen on her face, and that moment of silent impasse seemed to stretch out forever, until finally Libbie stepped up and broke it.

"Mr. Krejci," she said. "Please, can Meena come out and play?"

An aria howled from the hi-fi in the study. Josef didn't seem to know what to say. You didn't dare look at him. You held your breath and waited, and then Mrs. Grandon added the magic words that you would remember later as having changed your life: "I'll look after her," she said.

Four words, a promise, a connection, and that was it: you had been released. No more going to the store after school with Matka, no more standing at the upstairs window alone, watching the world go by as if you were a single passenger on a passing ship. After that you went home with Libbie and you spent most of your days together—at Libbie's house, in Libbie's room or in the den watching television or in the basement at John's train table or in the yard or in the driveway or on the sidewalk or even, sometimes, in the woods.

July 2006

"Sometimes it will be just when you think you are lost that you have in fact been found." This was more smoke that Matka blew into the ear of her granddaughter during the times when the child was in her care. And then she might bend her huge head in the direction of her own son Josef Krejci who walked and walked, who roamed the streets of Linwood and wore down the heels of his shoes while he tried to lose himself there but couldn't do it. Linwood wasn't a big enough place for a man of his great size to get lost in, was it?

"Your father, he is a real Pilgrim of Prague, "Matka said and nodded knowingly.

What might at first seem to be time off, away from the comings and goings of the everyday, turns out to be time on, a logical progression from then to now, from here to there. This wasn't how Matka put it. What she said was, "Keep your eye on the bread crumbs, *dcera.* "

Already it's almost noon and Meena still hasn't figured out what she's going to do about what's happened. Instead of making any phone calls, she's spent the morning going about her business as usual, doing her chores as if nothing's changed. The silence from upstairs looms over her, but she has managed, so far, to ignore it. She did pick up the telephone once, with what intention she couldn't say. Held the receiver to her ear, listened to the dial tone for a moment, and then, her heart pounding, she hung up.

She fixes herself a sandwich for lunch—tuna fish on rye with a slice of tomato from the garden—and sits at the kitchen table eating it, gazing out through the picture window at the woods, trying not to think much beyond the sound of her own chewing in her ears.

She goes on from there to finish sorting laundry and taking out trash, dusting bookshelves, vacuuming carpets, scouring sinks and toilets, mopping linoleum and scrubbing tile. By mid-afternoon, though, it's clear that Meena is going to have to do more than this, and soon.

She thinks she should at least go to the Hawkeye Market first, before the house starts to fill up with mourners and well-wishers. They'll be hungry and thirsty, and this being Saturday, the day that she would do her grocery shopping under normal circumstances, there isn't much left in the cupboards or in the refrigerator either. Meena has become the kind of woman who plans her menus ahead and then goes out and shops for the ingredients she'll need for them. Hamburger meat and pork chops, lasagna noodles, fresh mushrooms, mozzarella, parmesan, dill pickles and baking potatoes and bread. None of this will be necessary now, of course she knows that, but still she thinks she should go to the grocery store anyway, to at least stock up on coffee, brandy, and beer. She's begun to make a list of what it seems she'll need, as if she might be planning for a party. Paper plates. Plastic cups. Napkins.

On the straw mat outside the back door there lies the bloodied body of a dead sparrow, an offering from the neighbor's cat, all feather and gristle and bone. The woods feel especially deep to Meena just now: thick with humidity, wild growth, insects, shadows, heat. Poised on a pole in the back yard is the marten house that Josef spent the winter building, although no martens ever came, and for some time now it has been inhabited by bats. Meena thinks of Leo Spivak: a boy in a striped T-shirt, baggy shorts, sagging socks, black high-tops. Crewcut. Freckles. How he stood out there in the middle of Otis Road where everyone could see him aiming his pellet gun upward. Squinted, fired, and whooped in triumph when a bat fell from the sky to land at his feet with a moist thump. It wasn't until many years later that Meena found out the truth: it's no great feat to bring down a bat. Blind, they fly right into the shot, thinking it's a swarm of winged bugs, some providential meal.

She wraps the bird in tissue, throws it in the trash.

Her father's car, a black Jetta, is still parked where she left it last night, close by the back door. The Hawkeye Market is down on 19th Street, but Meena takes take a left and heads uphill to go the long way around, through Ellis Park. This is the route she always takes, but by now it's no longer the disappointment that it was when Meena still harbored the secret hope that by some miracle it would revert back to the park that it once was, when she was a little girl tripping up the paths with Libbie Grandon. But of course that never happened, and it never would, and she has accepted this fact, so she has no expectations anymore. Just an old habit of turning left at the bottom of the driveway instead of right.

For one thing, the candy pavilion isn't there anymore. And for another, there is a wide grassy meadow dotted with picnic tables and barbecue grills where the zoo used to be. In its last days, it wasn't much of an attraction anyway—the bobcat had died some time ago, there was only one bear left, the wolf cage was empty, and the alligator pond had dried up. But the monkeys had endured and the birds were still plentiful—including the peacocks and the peahens, an old horned owl, a chicken hawk, and a splashy flock of finches.

Now it's gone altogether, and this is at least partly thanks to a series of incidents that started innocently enough, with some high school senior pranksters breaking into the cages to let the monkeys out, free to roam the surrounding neighborhoods, screaming in the trees. Before the animals could be rounded up, one had attacked a child and another was torn to pieces by a dog. Not long after that someone tossed a pipe bomb into the bear compound, and when it exploded in the curious animal's face, she was so maimed that the responding police officers had no choice but to put her out of her howling misery by shooting her in the head. The last straw was a fire in a trash can that spread to the aviary and suffocated the trapped birds that hadn't already been burned alive in the flames.

After that the little wrought iron park zoo was altogether razed, what animals remained were sold off to other cities elsewhere, and Linwood was left zoo-less. Now no longer are there any peacock cries to tear a wakeful hole into the still fabric of the night.

Meena drives through the park and on around onto Beaver Avenue, then turns right to head west toward downtown. There have been changes here, too. What used to be the prim edges of Wellington Heights is now corrupted by the messier sprawl of Nowhere. It's crept across Vernon Blvd, and like a fungus, mold, mushrooms, moss, the squalor has spread and grown.

Grass grows wild and unmown in the lawns. Chain link fences rust along the sidewalks, caging in dogs with bristled backs and bared teeth. These big old houses have been broken up into apartments now, and they're bursting at the seams with people whose bodies and belongings spill out onto the porches, the yards, the sidewalks and the streets. And everywhere, there's sound. Music and voices from kitchen radios, bedroom stereos, boom boxes, television sets, cars.

One thing hasn't changed, though, and that's the stench from the cereal factories: a burnt baked scent of roasted wheat and oats and corn, with an unpleasant syrupy under-smell that coats the throat and makes Meena want a cigarette.

In front of her, an elderly woman in a battered Cadillac creeps along. Poor old thing, scared out of her wits to find herself driving alone through this part of town, even if it is the middle of the day. She expects the people here to attack her. Leap down into the street from their porches, guns in hand, and force her from her car, drag her into an alley, beat her and rape her and rob her and leave her there for dead.

Wellington Heights has become a part of Nowhere, which is just what Joe Krejci has all along so adamantly resisted, dreaded, fought against, and feared. Where once house after house was an implacable façade set back a safe distance from the street across a stretch of perfectly manicured lawn and not a citizen in sight, now there are folks sitting outside on their porches and lounging in their yards. They drink coffee, smoke cigarettes, gaze upward at the sky. Kids on bikes wheel down the long driveways, skid around the corners, huddle at an intersection. Up to no good, Joe would say, smirking. A woman is hanging sheets out on a line. A man hoses the bugs off the grille of his car. It's just another day in just another neighborhood in just one more small Midwestern city, and the air is warm and the sky is blue, life is fine and the world is safe and there are no enemies, everyone is a friend. Everyone is alive and well, it seems.

Meena takes a left on 19th Street, and there on the alley is the Hawkeye Market which used to be the big new supermarket but now seems small and local compared to the huge sprawl of the Food King out on Edgewood Road—and that's why she shops here. She parks in a handicapped space and only feels the slightest pang of guilt, but in this heat she's grateful for that blue plate on her father's car. She gathers up her purse, gets out, gives a hard look around that's meant to dare anybody to challenge her right to be here, but no one does, no one notices, no one cares.

Just before the door swings open for her, there it is again, that face on a flyer: *MISSING!* The color photo is a blurred close-up of a man who has been posed against the background of what looks to be his own front door. He winces, seems to be flinching back from the flashbulb, and the smile on his face looks more like a grimace and a gritting of his teeth—forbearance in the face of scrutiny.

"$25,000 Reward For Any Information That Directly Leads To The Return Of Ralph Wendell. 54 yrs of age, white male, 5'10", 180 lbs, blue eyes, gray/brown hair. Last seen Friday August 3 at Coral Lake with plans to return to his SE Linwood home that evening. Wearing a blue T-shirt, beige shorts, and tennis shoes. He was driving a 1967 blue 4-door Ford Galaxie Sunliner convertible with Cedar County plates #934CRX. Call 1-800-LWCRIME or Linwood Police 420-397-6502."

There's even a snapshot of the car, parked at the curb. Who takes a picture of their car?

Meena figures that the reward money has been raised by the man's family and friends. They must want very much to find him, she thinks, and have him back safe and sound among them again. He is obviously a valued person: grandfather, father, husband, tennis partner, business colleague, friend.

She pauses here for a moment, with the door half open before her, to take in again Ralph Wendell's look of... what is it? Desperation? And then, she makes her way into the cool interior of the store, grateful for the cool clean light, the soothing music that's piped in through speakers overhead, and the industrious aproned workers, busy shelving or pricing cans and boxes and jars of every kind of food that anybody could ever want or need to eat. Meena Krejci has been known to spend whole afternoons here, rolling her cart up and down the aisles, selecting this and that, consulting her list, reading labels, then remembering something else that she needs from someplace over on the far other side of the store and taking the time to go back and get it. She stops now to help an older man find the can of soup that he wants—Campbell's bean with bacon, on sale, half price, with a double coupon.

But other than just that, Meena will not allow herself to linger this afternoon. She knows what she needs and she knows where to find it, and so it doesn't take her more than fifteen minutes to fill her cart and wheel it into the checkout line at the front.

As she is placing her things on the conveyer belt, she hears that the woman in front of her is in a conversation with the cashier about the missing man, Ralph Wendell, whose flyer has also been taped to the backside of the register.

"If you ask me," the cashier says, "I'll bet he's dead."

"Trapped!" That's what Josef Krejci said when he saw that same photo on the front page of the newspaper. Looked like a man gnawing at his own paw, didn't he? Josef scoffed at the idea that Mr. Wendell might have been the victim of some kind of foul play—a bungled burglary, kidnapping, murder even, and said it was clear to anybody who had the eyes to see it that this man had made for himself an escape, from his harpy wife, probably, and their bunch of nattering kids. Probably had planned it for a long time, got himself another name and another Social Security number, bank account and credit cards, and disappeared. Why else would it be that the authorities had been unable to find the car? Even after they searched the woods and the creeks and even the ditches alongside the highway on horseback. Family and friends, Scouts and cops and volunteers have all combed the countryside for two weekends in a row, but so far, they've found nothing at all. Not a trace.

"That's because he's not himself anymore!" Josef exclaimed, standing in the doorway, slapping the newspaper against his leg. He grinned: "Abracadabra!" Then, he blew out through his lips: "Whoosh! That man's long gone!"

Watching him do this Meena wondered: what made her father think he knew anything about it? Was there something in his own heart, had there been times in his own life when all he wanted was to get away, become someone other than himself? Was that why he was always walking? Such a thought came as a revelation to her, his only daughter, and remembering it now, at this moment, is a shock all over again. Here she is, Meena Krejci, who has all these years been pining for an escape of her own, without either the mind or the means to plan for it with any seriousness, realizing now that she has never once in her lifetime thought to consider that her father, too, might have had dreams and expectations that he sacrificed first to necessity and, after that, to time.

She plucks a copy of "The Whole Truth" from the magazine rack. It's a newsprint tabloid that's famous for wallowing shamelessly in rumor and hearsay about everything from celebrity gossip and health fads to unnatural phenomena and far-fetched true crime, and Meena has long been captivated by it, regardless of her father's frequent snorting scorn. "Hogwash! Claptrap! Lies!" She also adds a couple of packs of cigarettes to her order. Marlboro Lights. She likes the gold color on the outside of the pack. She told her father on his birthday in May that she was going to quit smoking, to please him, and mostly she's been successful in this, but it's been a such a hard struggle and she's thinking, why bother with that anymore? Might just as well please herself, now.

The woman ahead of her is a housewife, dressed in tennis togs. She turns to look back at Meena. "Yeah, well, I wouldn't mind collecting that $25,000," she says.

Meena finds herself smiling a smile that feels as if it's been glued onto her face.

The cashier smiles back. "So what do you think, hon?" she asks. "Where is he?"

Meana shrugs and shakes her head. "I have no idea."

But the fact is, Meena does happen to know the Wendells, if only vaguely. They used to shop at Krejci's, years ago when everybody else did too, and they live not far away, just around the corner in fact, on the good side of Vernon Boulevard.

"His wife took out an ad in the paper the week before her husband vanished," the housewife says. "You know. One of those self-congratulatory bits on the 'Milestones' page? To mark their first wedding anniversary, I think it was." She raises her eyebrows, as if this is supposed to mean something, but what?

She's leaning toward Meena; she's nudging at her with an elbow, winking and clucking. "Want to know what I think?" she asks. The cashier hands her the credit card receipt to sign. When Meena doesn't reply, the housewife moves closer. "He's dead," she says. "And she killed him," she adds.

"What? Who?"

"The wife, that's who," the housewife replies, and then she pulls her chin in, smug, knowing.

"Unless he killed himself," the cashier says.

"That guy?" The housewife points to the flyer. "Nah. Hell," she says, "just take a look at him. Poor fella. No balls. Trust me."

Meena peers at the flyer. "Maybe he ran away."

The housewife stops, turns back to face Meena. "What?"

She wishes she'd said nothing. "I don't know, I... Well, maybe he just took off, you know? I mean, maybe he's starting all over again someplace else."

"You mean like he's hiding somewhere?" the cashier asks.

Meena nods. "Yeah. I guess. Yeah. Something like that."

"Why would he do that?"

"I don't know. Maybe he didn't like his life. Maybe he didn't like himself. Maybe he wanted something else."

"So he takes on another identity?"

Meena shrugs. "Maybe."

The cashier shakes her head, dismissing this. "Nah. That's not real. That only happens in movies."

"I'm telling you," the housewife says, "the guy's dead. And he didn't kill himself either; he was murdered. By his wife. She had enough, and so she did him in, and that was the end of that."

And now this woman has turned and pushed her cart away, while the cashier goes on to scan Meena's groceries and the missing man in the flyer looks on with all that troublesome blurred worry in his face.

Meena takes the other way back home again on purpose just so she can pass by the Wendells' house. She's trying to remember what else she knows about the family. They owned the car dealership on 2nd Avenue, Wendell Ford—so maybe that explains the photo of the car. And wasn't there an older brother that everybody said got more than his fair share when the business was sold? Maybe Mr. Wendell was depressed.

Now there is a mini-van parked in the driveway out front, and on its side, that same flyer again, now blown up into poster size. Underneath, in big letters: "Have You Seen Ralph?"

Otherwise, the house looks just fine. Quiet. Peaceful. A wreath of dried wildflowers on the front door, plants blooming on the porch. It just looks empty that's all. Abandoned and nobody home. If you didn't know any better, you might not think that there was anything gone wrong here at all.

The same could be said of the Krejci house at 2338 Otis Road, and Meena realizes this as she pulls into the driveway and feels a pang of, what? Guilt? Shame? Embarrassment?

She thinks of the dreams she still has sometimes, even at this age: where she's supposed to be in school, at a class, history or mathematics, but for one reason or another she hasn't ever gone to it, every day she's missed it and now the year is almost over and she's in big trouble, how will she ever explain? That's how it feels to approach the house right now. She's dizzied for a second by a flutter of panic that flies through her and then is gone.

She knows she's going to have to make a phone call now, of course. She has to tell somebody, she can't be putting it off anymore. But who to call? And what to say? What is everybody going to think later, when they find out how long she's waited? She takes a look at the street, expecting to see an ambulance or a police car pull up, but it isn't going to be that easy. That's just laziness. It's wishful thinking, is all. Because in that case then someone else would be in charge and that would simplify everything, wouldn't it, by taking all the burden and responsibility from her hands? But no, the street's quiet, and the houses are all closed up, here in the thick summer heat of the middle of the day.

She carries her bags of groceries into the house, then puts the things away, carefully and neatly, using the work of it to calm herself again. By the time she's finished, she is damp with sweat. She thinks she'll cool off for just a minute, fixes a glass of lemonade, takes it into the living room, plants herself in the chair in front of the fan. This house is not air-conditioned, because Josef wouldn't have it. Too expensive, he said, and besides he didn't like that cold air blowing on him all the time. Felt unnatural, like breathing chemicals. But now, Meena is thinking, now she can do anything she wants and he's not here to stop her.

She lights a cigarette and watches the smoke roil lazily upward and away from her. No need to hide the pack now. She leafs through the tabloid—a boy who looks like a bat, an alien burial on the moon, a pair of Siamese twin calves, turtles with two heads, and her horoscope: "An unusual opportunity might arise to make some extra money by selling a body part."

She supposes that the proper thing for her to do now would be to call up Dr. Montgomery. He's been caring for her father for as far back as Meena can remember, and he'll know what to do. She'll have to concoct some explanation for why she's waited this long to call him, though, because can't they tell when somebody's been dead for a while? She'll say she got up early and went out for a walk, because she does that sometimes. She'll say she thought her father was asleep in his bed down the hall and she didn't want to wake him. And then she went about the business of cleaning the house and time got away from her so the next thing she knew it was afternoon and he was still up there and that wasn't like him, so she finally decided she'd better go check.

She will do that now. Meena will go upstairs as if she doesn't yet know what she's going to find there, as if she isn't aware of anything wrong, as if she's only just now begun to worry and to wonder, Why is he still asleep? She'll go to into his room, she'll go to his side, she'll look at him and see that he's not moving. She'll become alarmed. She'll think to feel for a pulse, to lean over close to listen for his breathing. She'll call out to him, then maybe she'll even give him a little shake, would that be too much? Then and only then will she fully understand. Then she'll realize the truth, and this will cause her to scream and rush from the room, down the hall to the telephone, to call Dr. Montgomery. All of this will leave her breathless and that will sound just right, and what she tells him then won't be a lie either, not exactly. It will be almost the truth. Close enough anyway.

Meena swings her feet back down to the floor and gets up and goes into the kitchen. She drops her cigarette into the sink, grinds it in the disposal, then rinses out her glass and sets it on the counter to dry. All right then. She takes a deep breath, squares her shoulders, grits her teeth. All right. She's ready. She will do it now.

But even as she climbs the stairs, even as she stands there in the hallway outside his door Meena is still thinking: maybe it's all a mistake. Maybe he isn't dead, after all, maybe he really is just sleeping. Or could be he's unconscious, in a coma that he'll come out of later. Maybe she didn't check carefully enough earlier. Maybe he is waking up right now. Maybe she'll go in, and there he'll be sitting up in bed, looking at her, annoyed that she didn't have the courtesy to knock.

With her hand on the knob, Meena almost turns away. She almost goes right back downstairs, to smoke another cigarette, to wait a while longer, to think. But she manages to shake this impulse off. Scolds herself, just as she knows he would: "No!"

She opens the door, quickly. Almost falls into the room.

Bare wood floor, braided rag rug that Matka made out of old socks and wool pants and sweaters. Single bed, narrow. When had he got rid of the bed he'd slept in with his wife? Meena doesn't know, she can't remember. Has he always slept this way? Blanket, pillow, green bedspread. Table lamp. No ornaments. On the table his medication. Closet, dresser. The old photograph of Agnes, in her thick glasses and solid shoes.

And there he is, same as before. Nothing's changed. Josef hasn't moved. She crosses over to the bed. She stands near him and looks closer. This isn't as hard to do as she thought it was going to be. He stares but doesn't see, and that makes him seem unreal. She is thinking: Do I see some movement? His chest rising, ever so slightly, a flutter of his eyelids, a pulse in his temple? Maybe he's still breathing? No, he's not.

Meena stands back and studies him for a moment.

He looks pretty bad. In fact, he looks just awful. His face is gray, his lips are blue, the scrape on his cheek is a livid bloom. He looks battered. He looks like he's been beat up. She notices the blood on his yellow shirt, dried brown. There seems to be some blood on the pillow, too. And a ghastly-looking bruise on his forearm—maybe it's broken?

Meena knows that in his pocket there will be the cash that he has always carried with him, that thick roll of bills wrapped in a rubber band, and she's thinking that she'd better take it from him now, before anybody else gets here. He would want her to have it, wouldn't he? But to get it, she will have to get closer, lean over him, reach across… She'll have to touch him.

She does this quickly, but even so he is disturbed and there is a smell, a fevered stench that rises up from his body and gags her.

Meena forgets about calling out to him. She doesn't shake him. She even forgets to scream, as she had planned to do. She is backing out of the room with one hand holding the roll of bills and the other hand over her face. She pulls the door hard shut and heads down the hallway to the telephone.

Not until she's started to dial the doctor's number will Meena realize what people are going to think when they see Josef Krejci lying dead in his bed and battered as he is. The blood. The scrape on his face. His arm, broken. His head, bruised. And then what they'll say when they figure out just how long it's taken his daughter to tell.

"Daddy?"

Meena's face is wet with tears. She leans toward him.

"I'm sorry."

She takes a deep breath, then bends closer to un-button his shirt. She only has to grope under his collar for a moment before she finds the silver chain. She tugs on it, and his body rocks, but the chain is strong and it holds. She pulls it again, and his arm shakes free and drops to the side, where it hangs awkwardly, fingertips brushing the floor.

"Please…"

Meena yanks one more time, harder, and his body flails as the chain breaks at last and the key comes away in her hand.

Meena Krejci is sitting at her father's desk. She has opened the bottom drawer and pulled out the fireproof box. She unlocks it with the key, lifts the lid, then reaches in and removes the small pile of documents from inside. She rifles through these. A wedding li-cense: Josef Krejci and Agnes Skvor. A deed to the house: 2338 Otis Road. Her Social Security card: Meena Ludmilla Krejci. A pink slip: 2004 black Volkswagen Jetta. And last: a thick leather packet full of cash.

King of the Wood

1961

On a Saturday afternoon Mr. Grandon might hand out quarters for buying candy at the snack stand in the pavilion, and then Mrs. Grandon would be scolding you and Libbie as you headed off toward the park: "Stay out of the street, steer clear of stray dogs even if they seem friendly, don't drink the water at the fountain, and if a stranger approaches you, you scream and run the other way." She didn't tell John these things—she didn't consider the world to be as dangerous for him as it was for you. Because he was older and because he was a boy.

Libbie was four years younger than her brother John. She was fair like their father, and she was jokey like him, too, with a ready smile and quick laugh, but John had his mother's serene beauty—dark hair, green eyes, and pale skin. John was a tall, thin, studious kid. He was known to hang around with Leo Spivak, who lived across the street and had earned a reputation for wildness that he seemed to feel he had a duty to live up to. There always seemed to be something wrong with Leo—he was a mess of old chicken pox scabs and scars, bee stings and mosquito bites that he scratched and picked at until they bled and bled again. Bruises bloomed on his shins, his knees and elbows were plated with scabs, his nose dripped green and gold snot all winter, he had his tonsils taken out, his appendix burst, he lost a front tooth to the tetherball pole at school. He slammed his sled into a tree at the bottom of the toboggan chute on Hollow Hill and was unconscious for two days afterward. He fell—or jumped?—off the limestone wall at Dead Man's Drop down at Ellis Creek and broke his leg in two places. The rumor that went around afterward was that he'd done it on a dare.

But John was just the opposite: thoughtful, cautious, contained, precise. He was always neatly dressed, in a collared white short-sleeved shirt, a navy blue V-neck sweater vest, crisply creased khaki pants, and clean black high-tops. Around his neck he wore a St. Christopher medal on a silver chain. It lay in the hollow of his chest as if it were a part of him; when he went swimming he'd hold it in his mouth like a lozenge so that if the chain broke, at least the medal wouldn't be lost.

Bohemie Bridge was Linwood's version of the Charles Bridge in Prague, and like its source of inspiration, its promenade was lined with statues of the saints. One winter afternoon when you and Libbie strayed that way on your walk home from school, John pointed out St. Christopher to you. The figure was of a large man, bearded and robed, holding a child perched on one shoulder like a bird. "Christ-over," John explained. His words came out a cloud, suspended in the cold air, as if in awe. Leo had been clowning around, puffing on a stick he'd found and blowing out his breath, pretending it was smoke. The baby was Jesus, John said, and the man was carrying him across a flooded river to the safety of the other side, which act of pure goodness would ensure his blessedness before God forever. The medal that John wore was his protection, he went on, and that made Leo spurt with laughter. As if John needed any protection. "Protection from what?" asked Leo, as the ice above the roller dam cracked with a bang as loud and deep as thunder underground.

The roller dam was a low flat concrete structure that crossed the river just downstream from the pillars of Bohemie Bridge. It had powered the cereal mill at one time, but that eventually went over to Cooke Electric and then the roller dam didn't serve any real purpose anymore. It didn't have a high spill and so its draw was deep and unexpected: the lake that it formed upstream might have seemed placid and peaceful to a boater or a swimmer who didn't know any better or who chose not to heed the bright yellow warning signs that were posted—"Danger! Deep Turbulent Water!"—at regular intervals along both banks. Water crossed over the top fast and strong, drawn down hard and foaming toward the place below the limestone palisades, where the river took a sharp turn, creating the whirlpool that was known as the deep eddy, a swirl of water so slow and lazy as to be almost imperceptible if you didn't know what you were looking for there in the middle of the river's seemingly placid flow.

"The deep eddy is deep," John explained. It was a huge hole that gaped like a drain at the bottom of the river and swirled down and down and down from there, for miles and miles and miles, all the way, he claimed, to the very center of the earth.

He went on: If you could ride a rocket down into the deep eddy, it would be the same as sending a rocket out into space—you could go in and in and in or out and out and out, but no matter where you started, you would always end up right back at the beginning again—there on the bridge in Linwood, standing in the cold shadow of a saint. That was infinity—a snake eating its own tail in one long continuous, twisting loop.

You and Libbie were ten then, and Leo and John were fourteen. A soft faint caterpillar of fine dark hair had settled on John's upper lip, and his Adam's apple had grown to become a knot of awkwardness in his throat that seemed to strangle him and cause his voice to squeak and crack.

This was 1961: Freedom Riders, Alan Shepard, Malcolm X., Bay of Pigs. Mr. Grandon was building a bomb shelter in his back yard. John was going to be an astronaut, he said. He had a telescope in his window that he kept trained on the sky. One day he would go there, he said as solemnly as if it were a promise he was making, carried up into the heavens on a rocket that he would name The Christopher, borne off into the simple purity of space—cold, empty, dark, and flawless, spattered with perfect and pitiless stars.

You and Libbie were a familiar sight, a pair of fearless girls skipping up the sidewalk in denim shorts and canvas sneakers. Mrs. Grandon's opinion was that safety was to be had in numbers, and so you were instructed to stay together and never ever let the other go off anywhere alone. You could walk up to the candy pavilion in the park, if you went by way of the street, but you were not to take the shortcut through the woods, even though that was the better route because it circled the edge of the zoo, passing by the aviary and the monkey cages and the bear compound before veering up the hill into the trees along a path that would bring you eventually into your own back yards. To come through the woods was forbidden, and you both knew it, so when Libbie insisted on taking that path anyway it made you skittish and in a hurry to get it over with and be home.

Libbie was taking her time, dawdling in the warm sun-dapple of the afternoon and the church-like hush of the woods, but you had run ahead, urging her to keep up, and that was why you didn't see the man when he emerged from the trees and stepped out toward the path. Libbie didn't see him either, at first. Until he moved, he might have been a tree himself. His big wool coat was dark and rough, like bark, and his hair hung long and wild around his head, tangled with sticks and leaves, and his beard was so full and hairy that it hid much of his face. Only his eyes were clearly visible, red-rimmed and yellowy, their irises the pale green of new moss. He smiled and swayed back and forth, then leaned toward Libbie to sing, in a slow deep voice that sounded as if it were clogged with mud, on breath that smelled like leafy decay:

"Catch a falling star and put it in your pocket, never let it fade away…"

He opened his coat. His body was filthy, his skin blackened by grime, his chest, belly, and groin furred with wiry dark hair, his penis purplish with blood. His eyes gleamed. He leaned closer, and Libbie, entranced by the sight of him, and in thrall to the rough murmur of his song, might have stayed put, she might have allowed him to reach for her and to touch her with his knotty fingers, if you hadn't taken hold of her arm and yanked at her, pushed her off ahead and urged her to run away.

Later, you named the man Deep Eddie. You called him the King of the Wood.

Jack Grandon liked to sit down with a cocktail when he came home from work—at the end of a long day selling houses or whatever it was he did down there at his office: morning meetings, lunch, open houses, driving around in his convertible with young house-wives, giving them a glimpse of all their dreams come true—and he deserved it, a little bit of peace and quiet, with the newspaper and the radio. He liked the old standards. A man crooning something sweet. He hummed along, snapped the paper, licked his thumb and turned the page.

You and Libbie were on the floor, playing cards. The game was Spit and it was fast. You played in si-lence, so the only sound was the swish of the cards, the slap of your hands. Every so often one of you squeaked, you couldn't help it, but otherwise all you used to communicate with each other were hand signals and facial expressions. Wide eyes, mean frown, grimace of concentrated effort.

Mrs. Grandon stood in the doorway. She looked like something from a magazine, all dressed up, an apron on. The smell of meat cooking, and vegetables, followed her as she entered the room. A pot roast may-be. Your stomach growled.

Mrs. Grandon glided over to the couch. She lit a cigarette. Her silk stockings glistened at eye level. She teetered to the song that was playing, blew smoke, tapped ash, then crossed over to the television to turn it on, muting the volume so it was just the picture playing. The music didn't fit the film, which was in black and white, a western. Dust and heat. A man with a hat and a bandana. Horses rearing.

Libbie slapped the pile. She'd won the game, again, because you weren't paying attention. The song changed to something else. Mr. Grandon snapped his newspaper. Libbie smirked at you, signed an obscenity, then scooped up the cards, shuffled, dealt again. The western was interrupted by a commercial. *Veddy good,* the boy mouthed. And you could smell that pot roast, and you were hoping you'd be invited to stay for dinner. Mrs. Grandon swirled the ice in her drink.

There was thunder in the distance, presaging another storm. It had been raining and storming for days already. One after the other, rolling in over the whole state. Not too far to the south, in Keokuk County, hail had killed a pig, dented cars, broken windows, knocked a hole in somebody's roof. Now it was windy outside and Leo was flying a kite. Every now and then you could see it, waving past the window. A dragon, with fiery eyes, close to the trees.

The commercial was over, and the show was back on again. Mrs. Grandon took a seat on the sofa. She closed her eyes, leaned her head back, bobbed her foot to the music. Mr. Grandon snapped the paper. His wife opened her eyes and saw that his drink on the table was empty. She stood, picked up his glass, and left the room, trailing perfume. You watched her go: her high heels, her delicate ankles, the swell of her calves below her skirt's hem. Libbie had told you that her mother wanted to have another baby, but couldn't do it, but you weren't sure, exactly, what that meant. Couldn't do what?

Leo's kite was outside the window, and you turned to watch it rise and fall. Libbie reached over and pinched you, hard, on the arm, but you still didn't make a sound. You'd owe a dollar if you did. The next game was even faster, and Libbie won again.

Mrs. Grandon returned with another drink for her husband. She said that dinner was almost ready. You were waiting to be asked to stay. You went into the kitchen to wash your hands. You snooped around, opened the oven—bread—lifted the lid on the pot— some kind of soup. You could see that there were only four places set at the table and wondered what you were going to have to do to get an invitation. You peeked at the salad. Reached in and helped yourself to a piece of carrot.

John came in the back door. He was breathing hard, cold and wet. Rags was right behind him, tracking mud on the floor.

John said hello, but you didn't answer, you only smiled, and he smiled back. Signed: *Hello!* because he'd recognized the game. When you returned to the living room, the radio was off, the television was off, they others were all just sitting there, looking at each other. You signed to Libbie, *What?*, but Libbie didn't respond.

Mr. Grandon turned told you to sit down.

There was a story in the paper. Something about a man in the park. Some guy who had been seen hanging out in the woods. "This is not a joke, girls," Mr. Grandon said, because Libbie was smiling behind her hand.

Mrs. Grandon had gone pale. "Murdered children," she said, her hand at her throat, but her husband told her to knock it off—the drama, the melodrama. Nobody was dead. There wasn't any murder. It was nothing like that. Just a creep, that was all. A pervert. You didn't know what this meant, but at the same time, you did.

John brought the smell of rain into the room with him. Everyone looked at him, his bone white skin, black hair, wet and clinging to his head. "I heard about it, too," he said. "Some guy. A bum of some kind. Whacking off."

Mrs. Grandon was angry now, but it wasn't clear whether she was mad at John or at you and Libbie or at her husband or at Deep Eddie himself.

Before you could figure this out, Mr. Grandon was asking, "Have you seen him?" Libbie looked at you, and you shook your head.

"Is that a no?"

You had no choice then but to break the silence, and Libbie smirked. "Yes," you said. "I mean no. It's a no. We haven't seen anybody like that." Libbie held her hand out. You gave her the dollar, and she put it in her pocket.

Mrs. Grandon said, "You can't go out."

Outside, it was pouring. You were thinking, good, you'd just stay there. For dinner.

But Libbie could talk now that you had; there was nothing to hold her back anymore. She was on her feet. "What do you mean we can't go out?"

"I mean I want you two to stay away from the park."

"Forever?"?

"No, just for now. It's off limits."

You knew, telling Libbie this was just like asking her to do it.

Then the phone was ringing, and it was Josef Krejci, and he was telling you to come home, right now. So, he'd read the paper, too.

Before you were across the driveway, Leo's kite hit the power line, and Wellington Heights went dark.

Another place you and Libbie were forbidden to go on your own was up into the deeper woods of Hollow Hill, so you went there with Matka when she asked you to help her gather the rare and succulent morels that grew in the shaded glens, on the first warm day of spring, in May.

You were embarrassed by your grandmother then—the drab gray skirt and yellowed white apron, the pale dimpled skin of her arms below the short sleeves of her blouse, the lapping rubber tongues of her galoshes in the mud. You were constantly comparing Matka to Libbie's beautiful mother—keeping an agonizingly obvious tally of the one's shortcomings and the other's gifts—but you needn't have been ashamed because Libbie didn't care and she didn't think of her own mother's natural-seeming loveliness as anything more than an annoyance. As far as Libbie was concerned, Mrs. Grandon's looks had made her self-absorbed and vain—she spent too much time in front of the mirror, studying herself, and she walked around her bedroom naked, which Libbie said was disgusting. She claimed she would much rather have had a mother like Matka, whose wholesome fullness, whose modesty and coveredness was much to be preferred.

Matka was as much of a mother as you were ever going to get—and the old woman loved you and said you were a miracle—but still you were ashamed and disgusted by the broad moon of her behind and the cracked plastic bucket that she carried over one arm and the way she had to pull herself along with a heavy wooden stick. Her slowness was so infuriating that you moved past her, to the top of a small rise of land, and stood fidgeting and waiting. The view from there was even worse—it made you even more impatient to have to watch the bob of the old woman's big head, her gray hair dull and dusty looking and glinting with pins.

Maybe you were afraid for her. Or maybe you were afraid for yourself without her.

Matka gripped the hem of her skirt in her fist and lifted it out of the way, exposing the white flesh of her legs above her rolled hose—as pale and yeasty-looking as raw dough—as she struggled to place the stick and heave herself forward, the rest of the way up to the top of the rise, where you stood growling. The bucket banged against her thigh, her galoshes slogged and squelched in the mud and grass, their loose buckles clattering so that even if you couldn't see her, even if you squeezed your eyes shut tight to block out the sight of her altogether, still you would know exactly where she was there in the otherwise hushed thickets of gnarled trees and wild brush that spread out over the gentle roll of land between the river and the road.

When she had caught up, she stopped and put a hand on your shoulder for support. She was breathing hard, and her full cheeks were rosy with exertion; her dark eyes glittered like glass. She pulled a flask out of the pocket of her skirt and took a sip from it, gasping, then tucked it back. You shifted away and slipped out from under her hand. Matka stepped back and leaned heavily on the stick instead.

Libbie was crouched on the ground nearby, her legs folded like hairpins, as she poked at a puddle with a long bent twig. The sunlight fell on her in such a way that the down of fine white hair shimmered on the surface of her bare arms. John had said that bugs and worms and frogs could be spontaneously generated in just such a messy soup of mud and muck, and Libbie seemed to be looking for that, hoping to see it happen. Just as she'd stood outside the bear compound at the park and stared with a kind of eager wonder at the lumbering clumsy stinking beasts after John said that the cubs come into the world as formless blobs of flesh and fur and bones and blood that the mothers hold between their paws and then with their huge hanging tongues lick into sensible shape.

You were leaning back against a tree and idly picking at its bark, when Matka reached out toward you with a grunt and slapped your hand.

"What?"

She slapped your hand again, harder.

"What did I do?"

In the forests of Bohemia, Matka said, when they caught someone harming a tree like that, they nailed his belly to the bark and then they walked him around and around until his skin was torn away and his muscles were shredded and his insides had all come out and undone, unwound from within him to wrap and sheathe and heal the injured trunk. You could, she said, walk through the forest and find remnants of this—bones and bits of cloth and flesh grown into bark, as if the man had in his punishment become the tree, or the tree the man. She sniffed and reared away and spat into the grass while Libbie giggled nervously and you folded your arms around yourself and clenched your offending fingers into fists.

Libbie had found a mushroom and, still squatted on the ground, she held it up for Matka to see. The old woman squinted and shook her heavy head. It was just a common toadstool, she said, a soft white death-cup, not a morel. Disappointed, Libbie tossed the thing away, carelessly, flinching back when it landed in the puddle with a splash. She turned and grinned up at you.

"Look," she whispered, "it's a penis." She sat back and poked at it again, watched it bob and float, whitely, in the murk. And when you didn't answer, Libbie grinned at her again. "Well, doesn't it look like one?"

But the only penis you had ever seen was Deep Eddie's, and this looked nothing like that. You blushed, embarrassed not by what Libbie had said, but at your own ignorance, revealed. Libbie saw this, and it made her laugh.

"It's a penis, and I've planted it here," she said, "so that it can grow up out of the mud big and snaky and wrap around your ankles and pull you in and drag you down all the way to the bottom of the deep eddy and drown you there and eat you!" Laughing, she lunged at you, and you jumped back away as Matka's knife, gleaming, swooped down into the tangled grass and her hand came back holding the golden folded flesh of a morel. She cooked them in cream or baked them with onions or fried them in butter and served them with a tart lemon sauce, but no matter what she did to them, she could never disguise the lingering taste of dirt and decay, the murk and muck of the river bank, alluvial slime, primordial soup, from which some misshapen and grotesque life might decide to impulsively spring.

That summer rolled by, and soon the world was deep into August, floating along on days that were so long and hot and dull, that despite her best intentions Mrs. Grandon couldn't keep you inside. You and Libbie made a plan to go fishing, and you spent the morning creating poles for yourselves out of willow switches and string and safety pins before you took off down Old River Road to what seemed to be the perfect spot, above the roller dam and below the bridge, away from the deep eddy, where the river was wide and still. The afternoon was quiet, lazy, thick with heat. From the cereal mill downtown there wafted the heavy smell of roasted oats and corn. Dragonflies swooped and circled, cicadas screeched in the trees, and a pair of snakes slithered off a rock on the far bank, then skimmed away across the surface of the water as if it were as solid as glass.

"We should cook what we catch," Libbie said, "and eat it." She was lying on her back, dozing, with her pole propped between her knees and her arms folded back behind her head. She had taken to wearing her brother's St. Christopher medal along with the small silver cross that she'd been given for her birthday that year. She'd swiped the medal, she said, but insisted John didn't care. He was too smart to believe in God. Over the summer Libbie's skin had browned and her hair had whitened, changing her in a way that you loved and envied, both. Your own shoulders burned and peeled and burned again, without ever tanning, and your hair always had the same flat colorlessness of coal.

Libbie had been trying to convince you that you ought to be working on a plan for how the two of you would get along on your own if you had to, in case the bomb was dropped and everybody else in the world was annihilated. This was a circumstance that at the time you found appealing. You liked the thought of the two of you and nobody else, having to depend upon each other as you struggled against the elements and the animals to stay alive. You said that if that happened, then you could just go into everybody else's house and eat all their food until it ran out.

Libbie sat up. "But," she argued, "that stuff will be poisoned by fallout."

You smirked at her. "Well, then the fish will be poisoned, too, Libbie, you dope," you said. "We're all going to die," you went on, matter-of-factly. "Might as well get used to it."

You had both already heard your father say that if somebody did drop the bomb there wouldn't be anything left at all—no fish, no people, no trees—and it was foolish for anybody to think otherwise. But that image that he conjured up—of a ghost town world as ruined and empty and lifeless as the shell of an abandoned building—it scared Libbie, even though you pointed out that she wasn't going to be there to experience it anyway, so what's the diff?

"Sometimes I hate you," Libbie said, then stood and tossed her pole aside. It whipped across the grass, string and pin snagged on a low bush, and you called out after her as she walked away: "You're not supposed to be alone!" You came up behind her and grabbed her shoulder, but Libbie tore herself away. She took off on a run, but didn't notice until long after she was home that the cross and the medal were gone.

July 2006

Meena Krejci is in her father's car, and she's driving on the Interstate, headed westward on I-80, across the flat farmland of Iowa into the even flatter farmland of Nebraska. It's late in the afternoon and the traffic on the Interstate is light. Meena doesn't know where she's going because she drives without intent, just following the road, blindly, with both hands on the steering wheel and her seat belt securely fastened, and she's keeping in her lane, she's staying under the speed limit, which she's pretty sure is seventy-five but could be it's only seventy, she can't remember.

About an hour ago she crossed the bridge over the Missouri River, between Council Bluffs and Omaha, and now she's in Nebraska. She's trying hard, doing the best she can, to do anything but think—about what she's done or where she's going or what she'll do next. She keeps an eye on the rear view mirror, expecting to see in it a flash of red lights, and she often holds her breath and listens hard, anticipating the sound of a siren's wail snaking into her senses above the rush of the wind, the hum of the engine, and the radio's low drone. When she passes a trooper on the shoulder of the road, ticketing some other more unfortunate driver, she ducks her head to hide from him, but he isn't looking and he doesn't seem to care. To Meena this turns out to be a relief and a disappointment, both at once.

By the time she finally stops for gas, it is late, past

dinner time. Lightning glitters in the distance, sheet lightning, heat lightning brittle in the blackening sky. She's in a little nowhere town just off the Interstate, a place whose name she won't remember later, after she's moved on. Past a block of boxy white houses with broad front porches and miserly front lawns is the gas station at the corner of the town's center square. Meena pulls over here and fills up, pays at the pump, grateful not to have to go inside and be seen by the cashier, maybe remembered and recognized later after flyers with her picture on them have started to appear on phone poles and lamp posts and in the windows of grocery stores and gas stations like this. *Missing!*

Just a little farther on is a small motel. Outside the car, where Meena stands and stretches, the air smells of summertime: river funk, wet cement, mown grass. The motel is nothing more than a simple long box with curtained windows and numbered doors. A big yellow neon sign hovers, moonlike, overhead.

As nervous as Meena is, the girl at the counter inside doesn't seem to notice, or to care.

"Hey!" she says, looking up brightly as Meena stands gasping at the drastic change in temperature from the humid heat outdoors to this air-conditioned chill. The girl's smile is wide and toothy, and it causes two deep dimples to puncture each milky cheek. "Welcome to the Wizen Inn!"

On the wall behind her is an aerial photograph of the area that has been blown up into mural size—sensuous folds of farmland creased by creeks, slashed on the diagonal by the pale shoals of a dried-up river bed, blemished here and there by the shadowed leafy huddles of spread trees and pocked by the pale buildings of what must be this town. The girl's hair has been bleached a bright white, chopped short and then gelled to spikes above her clear high forehead.

She has pushed a tattered leather bound register book across the counter toward Meena and is offering a pen. "Just go ahead and fill out your name and address, okay?" The dimples twinkle.

Meena nods; she smiles back weakly; she takes the pen and bends to write. She hesitates only for a moment, then: *Elizabeth Grandon. 2340 Otis Road S.E. Linwood Iowa 53402.* Her heart bangs and she can feel the flush of blood that is heating up her face. Do they check on things like this? she wonders. No, how could they? But is the girl going to ask to see a driver's license? And if she does?

Meena hands the pen back, smiles. Well if she does then Meena will just have to turn around and walk away. "Never mind," she'll say. Waving over her shoulder, slipping back outside again into the darkening heat. She'll get back into the car and move on, and try not to worry about the fact that just because of this the girl is going to remember her later when the police finally do come around asking questions.

She'll say, "Yeah, sure, that woman was here all right. In her fifties maybe? Dark hair, graying, about five-foot-six, I guess. Ordinary looking, nothing you would notice. Maybe a little overweight, but not hideous or anything. And she acted a little weird, too, now that I think about it. Scared, like. Paranoid. Guilty?"

But the girl doesn't ask for the license. She merely takes the book back, hardly glances at it. Digs in a drawer for a key, smiles again at Meena. "That'll be thirty-nine dollars," she says. "Plus a dollar seventy-two cents tax."

Meena is digging in her purse. Besides the roll of bills that she took from her father's pocket, she has money of her own in her wallet. A twenty dollar bill and behind that another one and two fives. She pulls both them out and gives them to the girl.

The phone is ringing, and the girl has turned away to answer it. "Wizen Inn!" she chimes, a silvery steel bell. As she hands over the change and the key her fingertips, surprisingly cool and dry, brush Meena's palm. She flashes that young dimpled smile again, waggles fingers, then turns away to huddle over the phone.

Outside in the heat, Meena stands there for a moment and takes a deep breath, of relief. She pulls her suitcase from the trunk, locks the car, eyes the number on the room key, and with a studied casualness now makes her way down the flank of the building to her room—132. She doesn't want to attract any attention to herself, a woman traveling alone, but the place seems to be deserted and no one seems to see her anyway.

The room smells of cigarette smoke and mildew, but at least it's air-conditioned and cool, and she shuts the door, turns the bolt, engages the chain. She sits on the edge of the bed, takes another deep breath, for fortification this time. She finds a cigarette in her purse and lights it. She is thinking she probably should eat something, but she's not really hungry and she sure doesn't want to go out again. The thought of walking into a restaurant, sitting at a table, reading a menu, ordering a meal, eating it, paying for it: the whole thing seems impossible. Instead she scoots back on the bed and falls against the pillows. She pulls the ashtray over close where she can reach it and uses the remote control to turn on the TV.

She didn't know she was this tired, but she's not surprised. It's been a long day.

When Meena awakens later, it's to the sound of a woman's laughter, outside her room. A man's voice, deep, answers back, and then there is silence. The television set flickers wildly before it settles into focus upon a commercial for fast food. A young woman is eating a huge fat hamburger, holding on with both hands but making a mess of it anyway, spilling ketchup on her white shirt. Watching this makes Meena realize how hungry she is. But she can't see how she can go out for food now. In the dark. In the middle of the night. She finds her purse, looks through it, but there isn't anything to eat there, only a roll of mints. So she sits on the bed chewing mints, slowly, one by one, and watching the TV.

After the commercial the evening news comes on and Meena turns up the volume for it, leans forward, feeling slightly foolish even as she does, because what is she looking for? A glimpse of herself maybe? Her own flimsy fifteen minutes of fame? Could be that Josef Krejci's body has been found. And that his daughter's flight out of Linwood has been discovered. If so, then they will be on the lookout for the car, won't they? And might they not find it, parked under that bright yellow sign in the middle of the motel parking lot for everyone to see? Will it be considered stolen, in that case, and is this something that can be added to her crime?

But there's nothing on the news about Meena, so maybe they haven't found him yet, after all. There is, however, an update on that missing man. Ralph Wendell's face fills the screen for a moment—it's bleary-looking and blurred in such a close-up—then that's followed by a shot of the house with the van and the banners, which read better. A short woman is standing in the doorway. She looks ineffectual in that sleeveless summer shift and the cheap strapped sandals on her feet. This will be the wife, of course. To Meena's eyes, she looks forlorn. Lost. Slump-shouldered and much older than expected. She doesn't look like a murderer, that's for sure. And then Meena is wondering: If this woman did kill her husband, then how in the world did she do it? Further: Where's the body? Buried in the garden? Bricked in behind a basement wall? But what about the car?

What follows is a short interview with the detective who has been working on the case since the beginning. He is a bullet-shaped man with piercing blue eyes, a bald head, heavy jowls, thick lips. He has been following every lead, he says, as if that were a promise. But it's clear anyway that he has no idea where the missing man might be. The report ends with the photo of the man again and a sonorous voice-over announcement: "If you have any information as to the whereabouts of this man, please call..."

Meena turns off the TV and allows the darkness to blanket her. This is familiar, and so she doesn't mind it much. She lies back down again, closes her eyes. Figures: Probably that old man wasn't murdered by his wife after all. Figures: Probably he ran away, just like her father said he did. Joe Krejci always was right about so many things, maybe this one too. And in this Meena is able to find a little bit of comfort for herself.

When the morning comes, she doesn't like it that she's still dressed under the covers. This seems slovenly to her. She cracks the curtain to see that the light outside her room is dim with dawn. She has decided what she'll do when they catch up with her, which she expects is likely to be soon. She will give herself up. In fact, she is looking forward to it. She will go without a struggle. Standing in the steam and shower spray, as hot as she can stand it, she is imagining the whole thing: her picture in the newspaper, one hand fanned across her face as a uniformed man escorts her to a police car, waiting. His hand is spread over the top of her head, protectively, as she ducks in. Maybe there will be something on "America's Most Wanted," she thinks, as she works the motel's bottled shampoo into her hair. If she's gone long enough, that is. A woman who murdered her dad. Lizzie Borden. Whack, whack. Even if that isn't how it was.

She also has to wonder what everyone is going to have to say about her: that she is a spinster, a dried up old maid still living at home, taking care of her mean old domineering dad. And then one night, she snapped? Well, he did frustrate her sometimes, she can hardly find any argument with that. He did know how to make her mad.

It would make a good story for "The Whole Truth." She can only guess that they'll all fall back on the same old phrases that everybody uses when something like this happens, nobody has any imagination anymore. They'll say that Meena Krejci sure seemed nice enough. Seemed fond of her father. They got along just fine as far as anyone could tell. And who would have ever guessed that such a thing as this could happen here?

Unless they talk to Mimi Hanrahan, who might have something else to say about a man who gives his daughter his wife's wedding ring for her fiftieth birthday.

"That's sick," Mimi said, when Meena showed up at the restaurant where they'd agreed to meet to celebrate the occasion.

"It's not sick," Meena argued. "It's sweet. It's thoughtful. It's very kind of him."

"You give him too much credit," Mimi said. "That ring is already yours. It was your mother's. It isn't his to give."

Meena didn't agree. She knew better. And who was Mimi Hanrahan to criticize her father?

Mimi Hanrahan, who might have something else to say about a woman who has never left home, a woman who has taken care of the old man for more years than anyone bothers to count anymore, a woman who has given up her own life—a lover, a husband, children of her own—so that she can concentrate all her energies on looking after him.

He needs me, Meena said. I am all he has.

Yes, well. And whose fault is that?

Mimi Hanrahan, who didn't know, who couldn't know, who didn't understand and wouldn't try, either. Meena felt ridiculous trying to explain how it was for her with her father. Trying to describe how safe it felt to be with him—on a summer afternoon when he sat dozing in the shade while she pushed the mower around the back yard grass. She knew exactly who she was at moments such as that. She knew just what was expected of her. She would show him the perfect tomatoes she had grown; he would admire the dinner she cooked for him. He'd praise her sensible nature when she showed him the winter coat she'd found for half-price in the off-season sale at Fairchild's in the mall, and even if he suspected that she was lying and had bought it used from the White Elephant Thrift Shop where she worked five days a week, he would be considerate—and frugal—enough not to let on.

To listen to Mimi Hanrahan judge and criticize their situation, to try to explain and defend herself against it, well that seemed like a betrayal of him, didn't it? Joe Krejci deserved better. He was old. And anyway, he was all that Meena had. And she had long ago made up her mind to be satisfied with that.

Joe Krejci's car is compact and practical. And common—there are black Jettas all over the place, aren't there? So how can anybody seriously expect to be able to single out this one as the one that they've been looking for? When he had the grocery store, Josef Krejci drove a truck that was distinctly his: rust red, with his name spelled out in bold green letters on both doors. He used it for pickup and deliveries, but for a long time now there's been no need for that and five years ago Meena was able to talk him into buying this little car instead. Glad now that she did. And he liked it all right, too. A big man in a small car, he said it gave him a feeling of control, even as he got older and maybe not so confident anymore. He said it felt like he was driving a toy, which brought into Meena's mind this picture of the two of them in it, a couple of cartoon characters, him hunched over the wheel and her beside him with the window rolled down and an elbow hanging out, both of them too big, the car's grille a wide chrome grin, perched on fat crazy-looking rubber tires.

But now that it's just hers, this car feels just right to Meena. It's almost as if she knew that someday it would, although who could have predicted that she'd be driving it here, out on the highway, heading toward the west? She keeps her speed down, partly out of a sense of caution, but more from her own pure enjoyment of these moments and the realization that there is no need for her to hurry because she doesn't even know yet where she's going, so what's the hurry to get there? Right now Meena is just going for the going of it, that's what she's decided. Just for the pure pleasure of the movement, tires rolling, and the thrill that shivers through her, singing out that now she is, finally, moving on.

Add to that the sight and sound and smell of this August morning, which is glorious. Bright and warm, damp and newborn. The phone lines seem to shimmer overhead. Meena has rolled the windows down because she just loves this warm feeling of summertime and freedom blowing by and through and all around her, this early in the morning, when it's still not so hot out yet.

She stops at a drive-through fast food restaurant and sits in the parking lot wolfing down two egg sandwiches and a plastic container of orange juice. The coffee is too hot to drink and so she puts it in the cup holder and then gets back on the Interstate again, still heading west as if maybe she knows what she's doing, with her back to the blinding glare of the rising sun.

Trucks have begun to pull out of the rest stops as their drivers waken and get to work, and it's not too long before Meena realizes that she's been watching the traffic, on the lookout for Ralph Wendell's missing car. Or for his body, on the side of the road. Some khaki fabric, she imagines, a shapeless bundle, maybe a shoe. Hey, it's worth twenty-five thousand dollars, after all, to whoever is lucky enough to find him. Might be worth that, too, if you were to stumble on him now. Because, he's been missing for how long? A couple of weeks anyway. His body will be meat, a meal for some hungry thing.

And with this thought comes a memory of another summer, on an evening when the light stayed late. A Saturday night it must have been because Mrs. Chadima had the day off and Josef had cooked a couple of steaks out on the charcoal grill himself, plus a lettuce and tomato salad and a pair of baked potatoes, buttered, on the side. On Meena's plate lay what looked to her like a huge slab of cold raw flesh and across the table her father was carving into his, chewing, smacking, moaning with pleasure until he saw her staring at him with disgust. Fathers ate their babies, Matka had said.

"What's the matter?" he asked her, seeing that she had not touched her food.

She couldn't speak.

"Eat your steak, Meena. It's good." On the table near his elbow lay a folded section of newspaper that he'd brought with him to look at while he ate.

She shook her head, managed to say, "No."

His fork poised in midair. His eyebrows coming together in a frown, eyes darkening, face flushing with anger, two bright circles of red on either cheek.

"You think everybody gets to eat a steak like this?"

"I don't know."

"Well, they don't. Other people starve. You're one of the lucky ones. Eat." And the fork went up to his mouth, he bit, chewed again, waited for her to do the same.

"I can't."

"Why not?"

She searched for a reason that he might understand. She poked at the meat with her fork and recoiled at the sight of the red juice that spilled out onto the white china of the plate. She set her fork down. Folded her hands in her lap. Lifted her chin to face him—bravely, it seemed to her—and cautiously explain: "It's too bloody."

He pushed away from the table with enough violence to slop the milk over the rim of Meena's glass. He reached across with his big hand as if he might strike her, and she cringed away from him. He stabbed his own fork into the bloody steak, carried it, dripping, outside, and slapped it back down onto the grill. Then he took his place at the table again, across from her, and resumed eating his meal. He turned to the newspaper, chewed, read, ignored his daughter.

She sopped the milk up with her napkin.

"I'm sorry," she said, and thought she meant it. He waved his fork at her, didn't answer, didn't even look up.

Her hope was that he would forget, but no. After he had finished his own dinner he went out and got that steak and brought it back inside. It was blackened on the outside, on the inside it was as gray and dry as a thick piece of cardboard. Meanwhile Meena had eaten all of her potato, she didn't mind that, she liked it. Even the skin, which Mrs. Chadima said had all the vitamins in it. So, she wasn't hungry anymore. She was full and ready to be excused.

She could hear the cries of her friends outside. They had been released from their own dinner tables and were getting up a game of Kick-the-Can out in the Grandon driveway. John Grandon and Leo Spivak, Libbie, the twins Kevin and Keith Mulvaney, Richie Sharpe and Fred Loomis, Lizzie Nathanson and Joanne O'Meara. Meena looked toward the door.

"Eat your steak."

He leaned over her, cut a piece off, handed her the fork.

She took it into her mouth and chewed, doing her best, trying to be good, all hopefulness, but her throat closed and she gagged. Her eyes filled with tears.

"I can't."

"You will."

He cleared the rest of the dishes off the table, turned to the sink and cleaned them up, then left the kitchen, left Meena there to finish by herself. She spit the bite out into her soggy napkin, cut another, put it in her mouth and chewed. Spit it out, took another. She managed to eat the whole steak that way, so that by the time she was finished, her napkin was full of chewed meat. She slipped it under her shirt, tucked it beneath her arm and held it there, waiting for him to come back. When he saw that her plate was empty, he clapped his hands. He grinned. Planted a kiss on top of her head, just at the part. "That's my girl," he said. He smelled of pipe smoke, lemons, scotch.

Upstairs in her room, Meena stuffed the meat-filled napkin in a drawer, then turned and fled, from it and from her father and from her deception of him, which felt like a crime.

That night she slept over at Libbie's. And the next morning Mr. Grandon had an early golf game, and he took the girls with him to the Country Club to swim. So it wasn't until the next night, when Meena came upstairs to bed, that she remembered the napkin and the meat. She opened the drawer and that smell of rotted flesh, cooked and chewed and spat back out, then left to sit in an un-air-conditioned room in the middle of summer… it's the same smell that floated up from her father's corpse when she touched him yesterday.

The Jetta jerks and swerves as Meena pulls it over, hard, and slams to a stop on the shoulder of the highway. And then she has the door open and she's tumbling out. A truck screams past and she buckles, bends, and vomits on the road.

Gasping, Meena leans a hip against the warm front fender of the car. She does not know what to do. She could turn back, go home, and face whatever is waiting for her there. But it seems so far away, worlds behind her, miles at her back. Or, she could continue on ahead, without any expectation except that sooner or later she'll be caught. Or, she might stay put, wait until a trooper comes along, pulls over, asks her what's the trouble.

And then she will be able to tell him everything and he'll put her in his car and he'll carry her back to Linwood, back to Otis Road again. She folds her arms across her chest, shivers, holds herself. *I'm all I have*, she thinks. She tilts her face up at the sun, feels its heat—as if that might burn away the surface and bring some clarity to things—and closes her eyes. When she opens them again, what she sees is the green sign with white letters that's been posted on the roadside several yards ahead: Junction I-76 to Denver, it says. Beyond Denver, Meena knows, are the mountains. And beyond them, the desert. And after that comes the sea. California.

She will climb back into her car, she will shift into gear, she will signal, wait, then pull carefully out into the flow of traffic again, and drive on.

Foreverland

1961

Wellington Heights was a place that was supposed to be safe, that's why people wanted to live there. It was a place where nothing happened. Where any threat of danger was just a story, abstract and exaggerated and remote—whether it was the improbable grotesqueries that Matka concocted and brought to life in her heavily accented Bohemian slur, or the snowy television reports and movie newsreels that Mrs. Grandon watched and couldn't turn away from. Images of foreign countries that she had never seen with her own eyes—to you they were mere splatters of color on a canvas classroom map—and black-and-white snapshots of bearded madmen shaking their fists, angered by the sleepy indifference of the rest of the world and promising to use their supposed hidden arsenals of guns and rockets and bombs and who knows what else to wake everybody up and bring this old world to its glorious end. Living in Wellington Heights, you simply didn't believe it.

But then at the end of that summer, just before Labor Day, a girl went missing from Otis Road, and all of Mrs. Grandon's fears were confirmed. It happened just like that. Like magic. Like a story. Like something that wasn't real. There you have a little girl and then,

Abracadabra and poof! Nothing. One day she was there, and then the next day she was gone, and that was that. She was as gone as if she'd never been. No trace, no trail, no body, no blood, no nothing. Just: gone.

Her name was Julia Bell, and she was no one. She was just a girl like any other; there was nothing special about her, nothing that would have let anybody know that she was special. You and Libbie didn't even like her very much in the first place, and then after she was gone, you liked her even less, maybe because it felt like it was her disappearance that had caused everything to change, as if the world had been darkened by that event, and it would never be the same again. Libbie said, "It's not the world that's changed, it's us," but you disagreed and so did Libbie's mother. Mrs. Grandon didn't see how anyone could ever feel safe in Linwood again after that.

Julia Bell lived in the brick house four doors down from the Grandons, five from you. Mr. Bell, whose first name was Louis, owned the dry-cleaner's on First Avenue, and Mrs. Bell sold magazine subscriptions over the telephone at home. There was a baby sister, too, less than a year old, who slept in a crib in the hallway outside her parents' bedroom or napped in a white wicker basket on the porch.

Julia's straight brown hair was cut in a bowl, and the splatter of freckles on her face and neck and arms gave her a grimy look, as if her skin were always smudged with a fine dusting of dirt. She was a day-dreamer, too, often to be seen dawdling along the sidewalk, lost in her own world, talking or humming or singing softly to herself. You and Libbie didn't go over to her house much, not if you could help it anyway— Mrs. Bell wouldn't allow it, for one thing, because the baby always seemed to be sleeping, and for another, you just didn't like to. It seemed dirty there, or shabby anyway. But maybe it was only old. Maybe they were poor. The few times you did go, Mrs. Bell sat you down at the kitchen table—its speckled Formica surface was warped and buckled at the edges, worn through to the wood in places—and then she served up bowls of wheat germ cereal and milk, or crackers with slices of some cheese so redolent with age that it made Libbie grimace and gag and even you wouldn't touch it. Upstairs, on a table beside the master bed, there was a bowl of foil-wrapped anise drops that Julia encouraged you to steal.

Years later the taste of licorice would have the power to bring back the close dim air of the Bells' crowded bedroom. The red foil wrappers, the chipped crystal bowl, the yellowed lace doily, the hairbrush snagged with hair, the cloying smell of foot powder and perfume, and the sound of Mrs. Bell's voice—on the phone, selling magazines—rising up through the heating ducts, its annoying wheedle as constant and demanding as the high whine of an insect or the squeak of an unoiled hinge.

Josef Krejci thought that Jack Grandon was a fool, and he was not afraid to say so. Mr. Grandon's head was full of names and places and facts that he was quick to cite, as if they were evidence of something, answers to questions that no one else had ever even thought to ask, and he was adamantly convinced that the United States would go to war with the Russians. He believed that it was only a matter of time before one or the other dropped the bomb, and when that happened, he was going to see to it that his family, at least, survived.

Josef Krejci insisted that Mr. Grandon's argument had less to do with survival than real estate, which was his business. He would build a bomb shelter in his back yard and when other people saw what he had, then they would want the same, and so he'd sell them his plans and show them how to build more shelters, just like his, for themselves. It was a racket, Josef said, playing off the deepest fears of the families in Wellington Heights, promising hope in a situation that, if it ever actually came about, would be spectacularly hopeless. At school you heard the sirens wail and ducked down under your desks with your arms folded over your heads—drills that your father claimed were ludicrous. If the bombs were dropped, he said, then that would be the end of it—everyone would be dead. The trick, he argued, was not going to be figuring out how to survive, but finding a way to keep the disaster from ever happening at all.

Mr. Grandon smiled at this—blue eyes sparkling, white teeth shining in his handsome, tanned face—and took old Josef Krejci's reluctant hand and shook it. "Well, then we agree to disagree," he said, "and pray that they can indeed keep it from ever going that far." Meanwhile, the Grandons would continue to prepare.

All that summer long, while you and Libbie were wandering up to the park and back or poking around down at the river, while school was out and the boys were free, Mr. Grandon came home at night and in the long hours before it got dark, he built his fallout shelter. On weekends, sweating in the sun, shirtless, a red bandana tied around his head to keep the sweat out of his eyes, he labored. Digging out the hole in the side of the hill, laying down a cement slab, piling sandbags to reinforce the walls, placing rebar and cinderblock and pouring the concrete to hold it all in place. He paid John and Leo to help him, and you and Libbie, too, although you didn't last as long at it as the boys did. They hauled wheelbarrows of dirt and sand and troweled grout and stirred cement while you and Libbie sat together in the shade eating cherries and spitting out the pits.

Mr. Grandon had ordered a special steel door, painted red with black letters stenciled in—FOREVERLAND—and at the end of the summer it was delivered on the back of a flatbed truck. Ironic or optimistic, however you wanted to read it, that was the shelter's name. After this door had been installed, with a lot of cursing and sweating and groaning from Mr. Grandon and the boys, then the whole thing was done and he let you go inside to have a look. It wasn't anything more than a windowless concrete bunker, as dark and dank as a cave. The door, left ajar, let in a blade of sunlight that cut across the floor and revealed the meager furnishings and supplies that Mr. Grandon had, in his calculations, figured his family would need: cots and blankets, cans of food and bottles of water, books and candles, a kerosene stove and a lantern, a radio and some old board games—checkers and Monopoly and Parcheesi and chess. In one corner, still in its crate, sat a chemical toilet that never would be unpacked, but would be among the other things that Mrs. Grandon dumped on the sidewalk outside the real estate offices years later, when she kicked Mr. Grandon out of the house. And on one wall there hung a plaster crucifix: bowed head, bloodied palms, pale limbs, sinewy with pain.

"How long will we have to live in there?" Mrs. Grandon wanted to know now.

Her husband squinted thoughtfully, then shrugged. Who knew? "Months," he said. "Maybe years." Forever?

"Can Meena come with us?" Libbie asked.

Mrs. Grandon was quick to answer that you were welcome to go in her place, because she was not going to live in a cave with her husband or anybody else. Ever. "I'd go crazy for sure," she said. "I think I'd rather die."

But then when he described for her what that death would be like—hair falling out, skin scabbed over, teeth dropping—she didn't want to know anything more about that either. Those stories were almost as bad as Matka's, you and Libbie agreed.

"What about Rags?" John asked.

But by then his parents were arguing and didn't hear. It looked like the cocker would have to be left behind with Mrs. Grandon, then.

Everybody in the neighborhood wanted to see the shelter, which only confirmed Josef's initial suspicions about why Mr. Grandon had built the thing in the first place. Mrs. Bickel, the old lady who lived next door to the Spivaks, refused to go inside, would only stand cringing in the doorway, peering in with a look of horror and disgust. It didn't take her long to make up her mind: she was in total agreement with Libbie's mother—not even the hard reality of a nuclear attack would ever induce her to spend more than a moment inside that place.

Leo's parents came by for a look, too, but they didn't say a word about it. Only frowned and shrugged, as if the whole idea were beyond them. "What's it for again?" Mrs. Spivak asked, but before Mr. Grandon could answer, Leo's father had pulled her out into the sunshine again, where she stood squinting, blinded by the sudden light and baffled by the prospect of the kind of devastation that would require such a drastic shelter. She spread her hands out on her belly—she was pregnant with Leo's little sister that summer—and wondered, what kind of a world was she bringing this child into? Meanwhile, Mr. Spivak, who was an insurance agent, calculated whether it might be profitable to sell some kind of policy against a thing like that.

The Bells, on the other hand, were very interested in hearing what Libbie's dad had to say, and so it turned out to be Julia's mother who suggested that you three girls sleep over inside the bomb shelter for a night, just to see what that would be like. It seemed like a great idea, a good adventure, you all agreed.

So Mr. Grandon unfolded the cots and unwrapped the blankets and lit the lanterns for you. Mrs. Grandon brought out a thermos of hot chocolate and a bag of cookies and wished you a safe and happy good night, before she slipped away and closed the steel door behind her. You lay in the half-light of the lamplight and pretended that the worst had happened, that the bombs were dropped and all your families were dead. You pretended that beyond the concrete walls there was a barren world, destroyed. But the fright of that soon wore off and it all began to seem tiresome and dull. There wasn't anything to do. How could anybody be expected to live that way for days and weeks and months and years? Libbie suggested a game of cards. Julia had tuned into a top-40 station on the radio, and you were lying on your back on your cot imagining how it would be if what you'd been rehearsing for turned out to be the case after all, and there was nothing left of the world beyond the cinderblock shelter walls, with you and Libbie alone together safe and sound behind them. And Julia Bell, who you figured you'd have to eventually kill and eat as meat.

Then wasn't anything like now—the girls knew nothing about anything, especially not sex. There weren't pictures and movies and magazines that you could look at anytime, any day. The health classes at school would come later. Libbie asked her mother to explain, but Mrs. Grandon was embarrassed and she brushed the questions off. "Oh, you don't want to know about all that," she said. "It's mostly just a mess." And you, how could you ask your father about something like that? He would have thumped you. When you asked Matka she told a story about an old witch who lived alone in the woods and made a baby out of vegetables from her garden.

But there was Leo Spivak, and he was wild and reckless enough to show up at the bomb shelter that night.

Leo Spivak: a scrawny boy in a striped T-shirt, baggy shorts, sagging socks, black high-tops. Crew-cut. Freckles. Standing there in the middle of Otis Road, where everyone could see him as he aimed his shotgun upward. And Mrs. Grandon out on the front porch, her hands on her hips, her face mottled, pale with fear, flushed with anger. Screaming his name, but he ignored her. Mrs. Grandon, shouting, later, as she slammed dishes into the sink: "Who gives a boy like Leo Spivak a gun?" Leo squinting, firing, then whooping in triumph when a bat fell from the sky to land at his feet with a moist thump. It was John who told you the truth: it's no great feat to bring down a bat. Blind, they fly right into the spray, thinking it's a swarm of winged bugs, some providential meal.

A knock at the door, and Libbie was the one who got up off her cot and opened it to find a goblin there in the dark. Rags was barking like crazy and Libbie yelped and Julia started to cry, but you knew it was only Leo Spivak, holding a flashlight under his chin.

"What do you want?" Libbie asked him.

He shouldered past her, into the crowded room.

At first you were afraid, but then you liked that he

was there. Leo was funny. He could do things. He was a boy of many talents and no fear. He could play the accordion, for example. He could do magic tricks. He could juggle oranges. You played a game called The Variety Show. You were the host, and you introduced the acts. First Libbie—and she had talent. She could sing. She could do a back cartwheel. Then Julia, who didn't know what to do. Her dumb face. Can't you do anything? Libbie asked. One thing: she could fit her fist into her mouth. That had you rolling on the floor.

Libbie said that if there was a bomb and her mother didn't want to come hide out in Foreverland, Leo was welcome for sure. He had beer in his backpack. Cans and an opener. And then Julia was complaining—"That tastes awful," and "I'm going to tell."

So you changed the game to Captive. Libbie grabbed Julia and held her and said she'd kill her if she breathed a word of it to anyone. You helped tie her up with her hands behind her back. Her feet were bound at the ankles, too. She was the prisoner. She wanted to go home, but that was impossible. "There are goblins out there, you idiot!" Libbie said. "Go out there, and they'll eat you!" Julia sat on her cot and pouted, unsure which was worse, Libbie Grandon or goblins or an atom bomb.

Then Libbie had the radio on, and it was the Twist, and she was dancing. You were dancing, too, crazy and wild, because Leo was there and Julia was mad. Loud because you all knew no one could hear. Maybe everybody else was disintegrated anyway. For all you knew, they were all dead. Go ahead and scream, Libbie told Julia. Nobody will ever come to save you.

But it was hot. That was something that Mr. Grandon was going to have to work on, the air. Rags farted and it smelled the whole place up. Leo took off his shirt. Though he could have left at any time, of course, he didn't. He was in just his shorts and sneakers. Libbie said, "I wish I could take my shirt off, too," and he said, "You can," and so she did.

And then there was more dancing and the music was playing and Julia was tied up on the cot. Her eyes were closed, and it looked like maybe she was sleeping. Eventually you untied her and tried to get her to dance, too. Libbie was stomping and whirling and making herself delirious. Leo unbuckled his belt. He unzipped his fly and let his shorts drop to the floor around his ankles and then there was Leo Spivak, swaggering in the spotlight of the flashlights, his face in flames, his knees and elbows ragged with scabs—it was a sight that had you all gaping, with Libbie smiling behind her hand and you honking with laughter.

The radio was playing "Purple People Eater" and Julia was whimpering. "What's he doing? Leo, what are you doing?"

"Just shut up and watch," Libbie said.

And so you stood there on that hot cement slab in your bare feet, three schoolgirls in flimsy cotton pajamas huddled together inside the sweltering empty shell of a cinderblock bomb shelter, and you watched while Leo Spivak began to yank at himself.

"That's sick," Julia said. "Leo, stop it."

Libbie didn't take her eyes off him. "Shut up, Julia," she said.

"I'm telling my dad."

"Shut up, Julia," Libbie said again, louder this time.

Leo was playing it for all it was worth. He threw his head back and bent his knees and moaned. "Oh baby, oh baby..." He stuck out his tongue and wagged it at Julia. Her disgust seemed to inspire him. When she backed away, he stepped toward her, still pulling at himself, still moaning. "Oooh Julia, baby, baby, oooh…"

"Stop it, Leo. Libbie, come on. Meena, make him stop."

But Libbie had pulled off her pajama bottoms, too, and she was standing in her white underpants, wiggling next to Leo, ooh-la-la! Her body was straight and smooth—snowy-white above and below the grimy tan lines that marked the outline of her bathing suit, knobbed by the sharp jut of her ribs and joints and bones—and her pink nipples were as flat and round as Leo's. She turned to you, blowing kisses like Marilyn Monroe. "I love you! I love you!" And then, "Come on!" But you couldn't take off your clothes; that was impossible. You just stood there, grinning and gaping at Leo, while Libbie clutched at you, squealing with laughter, shivering with glee.

"Mmmm… Okay baby, come on baby, come on…" Leo had closed his eyes. He swiveled his hips and kissed the air in front of Julia, whose face was hidden in her hands, and he yanked at himself until finally his penis jerked as if it were alive and apart from him and then spit a spurt of gluey milk that hit the concrete floor and filled the air with what smelled like poppy seeds to you.

Libbie whooped and clapped her hands.

Julia scrabbled at the door, clawing at the lever to get it open until you took her by the shoulders and turned her around and shook her.

Leo was pulling up his shorts, grinning, his face on fire.

Julia was curled over herself against the wall near the door, and she was crying, which only infuriated you even more so you kicked at her, and she flinched away.

Libbie bent down to examine the puddle of Leo's

semen. She dipped a finger in, held it up and sniffed it.

Leo lay back on Julia's cot with his hands folded behind his head and closed his eyes.

Libbie leaned over and kissed him.

You were dragging Julia up to her feet. You turned her around and raised the lever on the door, leaned against the steel panel until it swung away. And then you pushed her out of Foreverland and into the night. She faded into shadow as she fled the safety of the shelter and gave herself up instead to the uncertainty of the world.

Julia Bell is alone, shivering in her pajamas, outside in the open air of a late summer night, when the first fall chill has wafted in. The woods crowd toward her on one side, the street is silvery and barren on the other. When a car does pass, she cringes in its lights. She hurries, anxious to be home, only three more houses down, and her steps echo, her hands work at her sides. She's not afraid anymore, now she's only angry. Her face is pinched with outrage and determination—she'll tell her mother, she'll tell her father, she'll tell everybody what you and Libbie and Leo have done.

She passes one streetlight and then another, moving from pool of light to pool of light as if there might be some kind of safety there. Only one more house to go.

Did he jump out of the shadows and grab her, drag her off into the cover of the trees? If so, wouldn't she have screamed, and struggled against him? And if she had screamed, wouldn't someone surely have heard? Or did they mistake her for a peacock?

Did he step out of the trees and stand before her, singing? "Catch a falling star and…"

Did she come upon him sitting on the curb and

stop to wonder whether he needed help? And then he stood up and he had a rock in his fist and he knocked her on the head and lifted her up and held her against his filthy body, with one hand on the back of her head, as if to cradle her, tenderly, in his arms.

It wasn't until the next morning, when you were safe and sound in the Grandons' kitchen eating breakfast like it was any other day, when Mrs. Bell called to tell her daughter to come home, that you knew there was anything wrong. Libbie looked at you. "Julia?" As if she had forgotten all about her. Or had never known her in the first place. "Julia who?"

Mr. and Mrs. Bell talked to news reporters, tearfully begging someone to come forward with any inkling of information about where their daughter might be. Dogs were brought in to help the uniformed men search the woods and the park and the wilderness of Hollow Hill. On that first day, they found an encampment by the river, but it had been abandoned. That Deep Eddie was gone, too, was what made Libbie say that he must have been the one who took Julia Bell, and did something to her. Something unspeakable, but what? That he'd undressed her and made her dance naked for him? That he'd touched her and held her in his filthy arms, kissed her and rolled with her on the ground? That he'd slit her throat and cut her into pieces, stewed her body in a pot, cooked her on a spit above a fire and then gnawed the meat from her bones?

Or maybe she just fell into a hole, some cosmic tear that sucked her in and took her away to another dimension altogether, a Foreverland of another kind. This was what John suggested, later. In his imagination, Julia Bell was trapped in a parallel world behind the thin membrane of matter that defines reality, screaming to be let through again, but forever unheard and forever gone.

Or, you suggested, maybe Deep Eddie really was the King of the Wood. And, maybe Julia went with him willingly, and with her whole heart. Because of who he was and what he promised her if she did. She recognized him and she believed in him and so she followed him into the woods and there in the deepest shadows of the trees he revealed to her his true and secret self— he was not an old raggedy smelly crazy bum after all, but a handsome young man, a knight, a prince, a king. And then, when Julia saw him as he really was, she fell in love and gave herself to him. She put her arms around his neck and let him lift her up and carry her away with him into the river; she lay down beside him in the water, he held her close and she clung to him as together they tumbled over the dam and down into the swirl of the deep eddy itself.

You and Libbie told the police almost everything—skipping only the part about Leo and the music and the dancing and the beer. You agreed that Julia had got scared when you started talking about the bombs and the blasts and the end of the world, that she'd complained and cried and so finally you'd had no choice but to open the door and let her go home, because that was what she said she wanted you to do.

At last Mrs. Grandon stepped forward and told the police to leave you alone. You and Libbie were only children, she said. You'd done nothing wrong, you were the innocent victims of a world gone mad, and everybody had been traumatized enough, without the police harassing you too.

Meanwhile, you two were in lockdown, not allowed to even go outside without a grownup keeping an eye on you. Mrs. Grandon herself came across the driveway every morning to get you before your father left for the store, and all day long she kept you inside, with the air-conditioning turned up and all the windows shut and locked. You played board games and read comic books, baked cookies and made lemonade, staged puppet shows and acted out clues for charades, put records on the hi-fi and belted out show-tunes, from "The Sound of Music" and "My Fair Lady" and "West Side Story." Mrs. Grandon weeping over that one at the end.

This went on for a couple of weeks, and still nobody knew what had happened to Julia Bell, whether she was alive or dead, or who had taken her or why. Summer turned to fall, school started, and after a while there didn't seem to be anything else to do, so they just stopped looking for her. She was given up for dead. Mrs. Bell had had a breakdown and she was in the hospital and her baby, Julia's little sister, was away with relatives somewhere. Mr. Bell still went to work downtown every morning, and he came home alone to his empty house every night. For a while the church ladies brought over their Tupperware casseroles and cakes for him, but then eventually even they gave up, and that was the end of that.

"It wasn't our fault, was it?" you kept asking. And Libbie kept telling you, No. If it was anybody's fault, it was Julia's own. "She was dumb, that's all."

And when you're dumb, you die.

July 2006

If it hadn't been for the old dog, likely Meena would not have stopped where she did for any longer than it took to fill the car with gas and squeegee its windows, and surely she never would have stayed there overnight. Because she was headed for the ocean, wasn't she? At least that's what she had decided by then, and she felt firm in that choice. She was on her way to California; she was only passing through the mountains on her way to starting her life all over again there, reinventing herself as someone new and unknown and other than who she'd been. Hadn't she been set free?

She had begun to allow the thought to cross her mind that she was on her way to finding herself reborn. She had begun to concoct a vision of herself in California, living in an apartment near the sea, turning tan and thin and wearing gauzy pastel-colored clothes. She might be following in the footsteps of a man like Ralph Wendell, for example, who as far as she could tell seemed to have figured out how to run away from his life in Linwood and maybe even successfully start it all over again elsewhere. That he might instead have come to harm was not a possibility that Meena felt like entertaining anymore, never mind whatever other people thought they knew.

And so as far as she was concerned Meena was only crossing over this big range of mountains because she had to do it if she was going to be able to get from here to there. Those craggy peaks were a presence that at that moment seemed to hold no more meaning for her than any shut door or bent fence had ever had, just another obstacle that happened to be where it was, a barrier rising up from the plains to block her view of the ocean and of her new life nearby it—something to be got by, pushed past, climbed over, overcome and then left behind, forgotten.

But then there it was, that dog. It wasn't anything special, really just a geriatric mutt, a nuisance to its owner and good for nothing much, its better days behind it and more trouble than it was worth: unwanted and unloved, arthritic and incontinent, toothless, deaf, and blind.

This incident was nothing that Meena had asked for, then. It was nothing that she'd dreamed of, or in any way hoped to have happen, and it wasn't something that she'd been expecting either. But there are no accidents in this world, according to what Matka knew. This was *osud*, destiny, and all that happens, it happens for a reason, she would insist. It is all connected, and so one thing leads to another just as surely as the daytime will dawn upon the night and the winter will melt into the spring and a young woman will grow into an old one, over time. She will age and fatten and fail and falter toward what is bound by every natural law to be her death. And there is going to be no stopping that, is there?

And so here it is: that dog. He's hobbled out of the sunshine to seek some comfort in the shade, and then he's curled up in that cool place in the dirt behind the Jetta's back tire to take a nap. Meena has filled up at the pump of that little gas station in the middle of nowhere, and she's gone inside to pay for it at the counter. And then it so happens that when she comes back out again there is a battered yellow pickup truck pulled in so close in front of her car that the bumpers kiss.

Which means: before Meena can go forward, first she will have to go back.

Later she will be able to clearly recall the odd amber tint of this singular moment of afternoon light, as it looks to her just now. The color of this light seems somehow familiar, and at first what it brings into Meena's mind is an image of Libbie Grandon modeling a buttercup-colored miniskirt in the Teen Department Fashion Show on-stage at Fairchild's downtown. She restarts the engine on the Jetta, glad to see its gas gauge swing around to full again, and then looks up, annoyed by the matronly wide-hipped presence of that old truck's back fenders looming over its broad chrome bumper here in front of her and in the way. On the left side a bumper sticker reads, *Jesus is Coming: Look Busy*, on the right, *GODISNOWHERE,* and in the middle, *From death he did rise and will come again.*

Meena closes her eyes. She is feeling a little dizzy, a little short of breath, but she figures this must be the effects of the altitude which, she thinks, she'll be down from again soon enough.

She shifts into reverse. She takes a look in her rear view mirror, then turns half around as well, to be sure that the way behind her is clear, which it does seem to be. She takes her foot off the brake, and the car rolls back a bit before rocking to a gentle stop again. She gives it a little gas and feels the tire meet with a soft resistance that in the next moment has been easily overcome.

That wasn't Meena's fault, was it? It was an accident, wasn't it? Something that might have happened to anyone? And Meena knew this and she might have argued about it later, in her own defense, but how could she forget that bump beneath the tires, or that sound: a peacock's scream?

What will soon turn out to be an old yellow dog, at this moment doesn't look like much more than a worthless bundle of rags here in the shadows underneath the body of the car. It struggles for a moment—eyes rolling, tongue lolling, paws scrabbling at the dirt—and then is still. The gravel on the ground is white-gray, bluish even, like bleached bones. An oil stain glistens, rainbow slick, or is it blood? Meena is seeing all of this as if in a roll of film, snapshot by snapshot, one frame at a time: the deep treads of the black tire, the dusty tangle of blond fur, gravel, oil.

And so it's now that all she's been holding inside herself finally breaks through. Maybe it's the ice that froze over her in the car outside the movie theater back in Linwood, after her father's fall. Maybe now that is what comes flowing out of her so fast and hard. Or maybe it's something older, something cold and hard that she's been fostering for years. She's crying, and in a way the pain of this feels very good. The snort and snuffle of it. Sloppy and wet and satisfying. And even if she wanted to, she's sure that she can't stop. Or, even if she had to, she isn't sure she would.

Somewhere in the middle of this Meena has become aware that someone has approached from behind and taken hold of her, and that this person is now drawing her up from her stoop to a standing position and is turning her around to face him so he can get a better look at her, it seems. It's likely that he only means to help her, but Meena lashes out at him with such fury that he doesn't have any choice, short of slapping her face, but to pin her flailing arms against her sides and bring her in close to his own solid self and hold her there before she hurts herself, or him. Then it is only a moment before she stops struggling and he relaxes his grip so that she can shake herself free.

"Christ." In a hopeless attempt at composure, she presses her palms against her clothes to smooth them.

He has flinched at her profanity. "Are you all right?"

His face is soft, even-featured and bland, and his brown eyes are flat and dull. He's a big man, fat, slow. She tries to duck away, but he fills the frame of her vision; she can't seem to see around him.

"Yes," she says. "I'm fine."

She takes a deep breath and swipes at her eyes with the back of her hand. She is hoping that she might still be able to keep this simple. Climb back into the safety of her car, start it up, and drive off, taking care not to run over the dog again. She thinks maybe she can just turn her back on this whole thing and keep on going, as if it hasn't happened. It wasn't her fault, after all. Was it?

Overhead the red and blue lights of the gas station sign flicker weakly in the daylight.

"Hey," he says, squinting at her. "It's going to be okay."

She can see that his fists are clenched at his sides. She's watching his fingers as his knuckles whiten and curl around his thumbs. She's had some experience with this kind of self-containment, and she recognizes it at once. Hard to tell, though, whether his anger is aimed at her, for resisting him, or at himself, for having made the whole thing happen in the first place. He shakes his head, hard, the way a wet dog shudders water off its coat, and then with what seems to be an effort for him, he blows out a sigh and relaxes. Raises his hand and runs his fingers through the fine drizzle of his light hair.

He seems to be embarrassed. Or at least apologetic. Even polite in a way, which is sweet.

"I'm sorry," he's saying. "It's just that you seemed so upset." His smile is crooked. "I hope you don't think..."

Meena bows her head. She thinks nothing.

He has thrust a hand at her. "Well anyway, I'm Will," he says with a smile. "Gidding. Will Gidding."

Meena looks away, wincing at the sky, as Will lifts the limp body of the dog up from the ground and carries it across the gravel, lays it down gently on the flat step, in the shade. Another man has come out of the garage. He's dark, Hispanic. A little boy in overalls, a girl in a plaid skirt. They stand in a huddle around the dead dog. The boy reaches forward and touches its fur, the girl slaps his hand away, and he begins to cry.

Meena turns away. She has her hand on the door handle, feels the fat man behind her again, his hand on her shoulder. "Wait," he says. Then he nods his head in a signal for her to follow, and without thinking she obeys, tagging along after him across the road and into a place that calls itself the Grizzly Grill.

Just inside the door a full-sized stuffed brown bear rears up on its hind legs with its huge front paws raised and its lips curled back from great yellow teeth. Meena reels away from this, caught by Will's hand at her elbow as he urges her onward, into the dimly lit room and over to a padded leather booth along the wall.

Behind the bar a young woman sits hunched on a stool, working a newspaper crossword puzzle. She looks up and smiles broadly at the sight of Will. Her hair is short and dark and straight, parted in the middle and hooked behind her ears. From here and in that light, she's pretty.

"Hey Holly!" Will calls out.

"You're starting early, Will." She moves around the bar and across the coarse boards of the wood floor toward him. A thin steel ring pierces a pucker of flesh above her left eyebrow; the tattoo that bracelets her wrist is of a thorny rose briar. A pink tank top with a pen and ink rendering of the attacking grizzly on its front rides up to show a flash of flat tanned tummy and give a glimpse of another steel ring, this one piercing a fold of skin above her belly button. Baggy boyish brown shorts with big heavy-looking pockets ride low on the hard bones of her hips. Her long legs are thin, tanned and unshaved. Pink rubber flip flops slap at the bottoms of her feet as she walks, and the black polish on her toenails make them look bruised, smashed by hammers.

"This here is my sister, Holly," Will says. He invites her to sit down, and she slips into the booth next to Meena, giving off a mild scent of incense and oranges and alcohol. Holly lights a cigarette. She shakes the match and peers through smoke at Will first, then at Meena. Whatever she sees in their faces, it seems to tell her that something is wrong and Meena watches the bad feeling of the situation come bruising in from the edges of her awareness.

"What?" Holly asks.

Will shakes his head. His hair is blond and thin, silky looking, and Meena is shocked to find herself thinking that it might be nice to touch it. Instead she shifts in the booth and sits on her hands. "Bad news," Will is saying. Holly has taken another drag on her cigarette, and she keeps it in, holds her breath, waits. Her eyes are dark, pinpoints, focused on Will and trying to read him clearly.

"What?" Holly asks him again, exhaling.

And Meena starts to blubber then. "I'm so sorry, it was an accident, I didn't know, I didn't mean, he was…"

Holly's eyes widen.

"Woody," Will says.

Holly taps ash on the floor and grimaces at him. Looking at her more closely now Meena can see that her hair is too evenly dark to be natural, it's dry and ashy-looking on its surface, obviously dyed. And she's so thin, her wrists bony, shoulders sharp, her skin is paste pale. A cluster of pimples festers at the corner of her mouth. Her fingernails are chewed and the skin of her hands look chapped. From dishwater, maybe.

"Stop fucking around, Will, okay?" she says.

"My fault completely," he replies. He clenches his hands tightly together in a fist, glances at Meena, taps his thumbs against his chin before finally launching into it, the whole stupid story about the dog, and hearing it all over again, even in this abbreviated way, Meena feels a sob begin to gather in her throat. She knows that she is more upset than she should be and making it all worse, here is Will reaching across the table to hold her hand between his own. His mild eyes regard her with concern as he explains how sorry he is, that he'd do anything to take it all back, but some things are out of our control, they happen beyond our understanding and we can only accept what is as the will of a higher power than our own. By now tears have begun to glisten in Holly's eyes, too. She squashes her cigarette out in the glass ashtray and is standing up. Meena scrambles out of the booth and pushes past Holly, heading blindly into the depths of the barroom, through a doorway and into a corridor at the end of which there is a bathroom marked with a grizzly in a skirt.

She locks the door and then stands at the sink with

her hands under the icy water running from the tap until she thinks maybe she can feel an inkling of that chill returning to her again, and only now is she able to go back.

Meena has it all rehearsed in her mind now, what she's going to say to them and what she is going to do. First, she will apologize, quickly, without bursting into tears again. Then she'll give Will some money, a twenty maybe, a fifty? She'll apologize again. She'll thank Will first, then Holly, for their forgiveness and understanding. Then she'll go back outside into the sunlight again. She'll cross the street. She'll get into the Jetta. And from there she'll go home. This, at least, is her new plan. Her father is dead. She is alone. And this is what is true.

But when she gets back to the booth she sees that Holly has gone back to work behind the bar again and Will is at the table alone with two glasses of whiskey in front of him.

"You feeling any better?" he asks.

Meena doesn't respond. She's digging in her purse for the money that she means to give him.

"Hey, you know that old dog was sick anyway," Will goes on. "He was just a stray that liked to hang around the pumps. And you probably did him a favor by killing him so quick, the way you did. Saved somebody the trouble of putting a gun to his head, at least."

At first she doesn't answer. What is there to say? And then, "Thank you." She can see, it's obvious, he's only trying to be kind.

He smiles, waves a hand in dismissal. "You going to sit down now, or what?"

She slides into the booth.

"Death isn't the worst thing that can happen to an old dog like that one, you know," Will is saying. "I can think of plenty of other things might be a lot worse."

This observation startles Meena. "Like what?" She doesn't mean for this to sound like a challenge to him, because she really does want to get out of here, before she loses all her resolve. But she also wants to hear his answer and to know what exactly he means.

He shrugs. "Well, illness for example. Cancer. Going crazy. Getting old."

"But I did kill him, didn't I?"

Will shrugs again. "Maybe he was already dead," he offers. "Maybe he was never alive." He picks up one glass of whiskey, slides the other over to Meena, and when she withdraws her hand from her purse to take it her fingers are trembling. "Here's to old Woody then," Will says, his voice deep and somber. He's holding his glass up to the light, peering at her through the dark liquid in it. "May that old dog rest in peace." He drinks and slaps the glass back on the table, upside down.

"So what's your name anyway?" he asks.

"Libbie," Meena answers, without thinking. The name just spills out of her mouth like a gold coin, lands on the tabletop, spins. The tremble in her hand has grown stronger, and now she can feel as well as see it. Carefully, she sets her own glass down before it spills. She looks up and returns Will's thoughtful gaze, feeling courageous now and careful not to blink. "Elizabeth,

she explains. "But everyone's always just called me Libbie." She's still holding her purse clutched close to her body, but maybe he hasn't noticed any of this, because his next question seems merely conversational. They seem to have stopped talking about the dog.

"Where you headed?" he asks.

Meena shakes her head. She honestly doesn't know what to say to this now. He smiles. Seems to understand, maybe people come through there all the time, not on their way to anyplace, just here for the moment, on vacation maybe, time off to get away.

"All right, Libbie," he says. "Then where are you from?"

But she doesn't have an answer for this either. In an effort to avoid the question, she picks up her glass again and takes a sip of the whiskey. She feels it catch in her throat as it burns a path down toward her belly, so that her breath hitches in her chest. Meena doesn't drink much; she isn't used to this. But, she thinks recklessly, what the hell? What is there for her to lose anymore? What is there for her to keep?

"Lost soul," Will is saying. This seems to please him.

Meena agrees: it's true. "I guess I am," she says, and raises the glass and tips her chin and, gasping, throws the whole shot back. Will is grinning. He thinks her name is Libbie. And now he is raising his hand and waggling his fingers, to signal Holly to bring them another round.

The Pilgrim of Prague

1962

As Josef Krejci began to age he was not diminished by time, but rather made larger by it, and at the same time he seemed to grow more restless and shifty in his habits, too. When did he sleep? He was up at dawn and out of the house by six-thirty, turning the lights on in the store by seven, taking deliveries, open for another full day of business by eight. Home for lunch at noon, then again at seven for dinner. You hardly ever saw him.

He was keeping the store open until nine at night by that time, in the first of his many doomed and desperate efforts to compete with the bigger brighter Hawkeye Market two miles away, and he promoted Bo Chadima from bag boy to supervisor to manager so that he'd have someone there that he could count on to help out and fill in the extra hours. Then he hired Bo's wife to come to the house every afternoon to do housework and cook. Her name was Belle, although no one except her husband ever called her that; even to Josef Krejci she was always the more formal Mrs. Chadima, never mind that she was at least thirty years his junior. Mrs. Chadima dusted and vacuumed and scoured and swept and made the huge meals that your father devoured with shameless gusto—good Iowa

Czech food: sausage and apples and noodles, chops and gravy and potatoes, goulash and dumplings and slaw, steak and tomatoes and creamed cucumbers and biscuits and cottage cheese and buttered corn—while you held back and tried (and failed) to starve yourself to beauty.

Bo Chadima was Josef Krejci's opposite—small, thin, nervous and dark, he was a marten with glittery eyes and smooth black hair and a long face that every day he shaved raw. His wife was a cheerful, plump, and milky woman who also baked the breads and rolls and kolaches that were sold from the bakery case under the counter at the front of the grocery store. You and Libbie watched and wondered, trying to imagine what must have been the spectacle of Mr. and Mrs. Chadima having sex: Bo like a blade, burying himself in the soft and fragrant dough of Belle's dimpled, receiving flesh. But they didn't have any children and so, Libbie suggested, maybe they didn't even do it at all.

The rest of the time, when he wasn't eating or working, Josef Krejci walked. He became a pilgrim on the streets of Linwood, a familiar pedestrian figure, a huge ambulatory shadow moving through the snow or across the grass, both hands dug down deep into the pockets of his black wool overcoat or his lightweight cotton duster—depending on the weather, depending on the season—his broad face flushed with exertion below the brim of his dark felt hat.

He just liked to walk, he said. Said the exercise was good for him, said it tired him out, said it helped him digest, claimed it kept him regular and allowed him to fall asleep at night with hardly any effort at all. He was going to live forever that way, he said.

Well all right then, let him wander, if that's what he wanted to do. What harm could there be in that? Let

Linwood be a maze for him to memorize and explore, you thought, if that's what made him happy, if that was what it was going to take for him to find peace.

You didn't come up with the plan to follow him, Libbie did.

It was autumn, late October, a Saturday afternoon, and Mr. Grandon was out working in his yard—he was raking leaves into piles, and he was raking piles down to the street, and then he was setting fires in the gutter. The air was cold and dry and smoke-filled. He leaned on his rake, lit a cigarette, squinted at the flames as if he thought he might find some deeper meaning there. Who knew what he was thinking. The Grandons' yard was long and flat, and cleaning it up was an overwhelming, impossible job that he'd only be able to half-finish before he lost interest, dropped the rake and went into the house to make himself a drink, leaving you and Libbie behind to look after the dying fire. It was legal to burn leaves in the street back then, and on those weekends in the fall the air was filled with the rare smell of smoke—a hint of catastrophe, an inkling of loss.

Libbie's arms were all sinew and bone, poking out of the sleeves of the torn white T-shirt she wore with her old brown corduroy pants, baggy in the butt and worn thin at the knees. She had her hair pulled back into a pony tail, but it was so fine that it kept slipping out from the rubber band and its wisps blew like cobwebs around her head, snagging in her eyes and her mouth.

As for you, you were moving slowly, feeling hot and sweaty and itchy. The dust from the dry leaves was making your eyes run and your nose drip, and so you sneezed and sneezed and Libbie had given up saying, "Bless you, Meena," every time.

You didn't feel like working in the yard anymore. You had never been the outdoor type, not because you were lazy, but you never did seem to get much out of physical activity. Gym class was a torture to you—all that running, jumping, swimming, all that exertion, and for what? To get a ball from one end of a field to the other? You never could see the point. You were the one who was always out of breath. Your feet were too big, your legs were too long, your hands were too small. You were the one who would stumble. You were the one who would drop the catch, bungle the shot, swing too soon, throw too wide, miss by a mile whatever the target was supposed to be.

And so now instead you had found a way to escape. When no one was looking you ducked down and scrambled in behind the trellis by the house to hide. The dirt was exposed there, damp and cold, and you dug your fingers into it. No one noticed, no one missed you, and this was a relief in one way and a disappointment in another.

You could get out of gym class if you told Miss Grissel that you were on your period. You were one of the only girls in the sixth grade class who had that problem already, so soon. The cramps sometimes came so strong that they folded you over yourself, and there were still times, too, when you were careless and forgetful and made mistakes so that dark stains bloomed between your legs or, sometimes, all the way through to the back of your skirt, where everyone could see them. Even Libbie found this disgusting, and honestly, you couldn't argue with her about that.

You squatted in the cool dirt and somehow that felt just right, as if it was exactly where you belonged, and when you put your face up to the trellis to peer past your fingers through the holes you could see Leo

Spivak perched like a big black crow on the lowest branch of the butternut tree in his front yard across the street. He'd been there all morning, watching. He seemed to think that if he didn't move, no one would notice him. He said that he saw everything that way, and you had come to believe him. Ever since Julia Bell's disappearance, Leo had been on the alert.

But she was long gone. Her uncle had been a suspect at first. Now he was dead somehow, and if he did take her and if he did kill her, he wasn't there anymore to tell how or where or why. For a while, too, there had been reports that she was seen—once in Davenport and again in Cedar Rapids, in the company of a clubfoot man wearing a blue seersucker suit, who bought her an ice cream cone at the Dairy Queen downtown. When she asked for extra sprinkles he scolded her and she shouted back at him: "You are not my father!" In the end nothing came of that report though, and after a while there was no one left but Leo who still believed that Julia Bell was alive, somewhere, and that she was going to come back to Wellington Heights and her family again, someday.

It was October, and the butternut tree was almost completely bare of its leaves, which made it that much more difficult for Leo to sit there in its branches without being seen.

Mrs. Grandon liked to say that Leo Spivak was a walking disaster. She laughed when she said it, but it was a self-conscious laugh, and when she shook her head her hair, which she'd grown longer and then curled up into a perfect flip at the ends, bobbed prettily. She was only half-joking when she talked that way about Leo, and the truth was, he made her uncomfortable. Sure, he was just a kid, but there was still something about him that seemed dangerous anyway. Mr.

Grandon claimed that Leo was harmless. Then he qualified that by adding that at least so far the only real damage that Leo had ever done had been to himself.

Every now and then Mrs. Spivak would come out onto the front porch and call to Leo, but he didn't answer her. It was hard to tell whether she was aware of where he was, until Mr. Spivak stood under the butternut tree and ordered him to come down before he fell and broke his neck. But Leo was not about to budge. He was almost sixteen—too old to be sitting around in trees anymore, his father said. Mrs. Grandon worried about what would happen when Leo Spivak got his license and started to drive.

The scarecrow in Mrs. Grandon's garden had his eye on this scene, too. He hung by his wrists from a pair of crossed two-by-fours. He was made of black trousers stuffed with old towels and a white shirt that was yellowed from the weather and the rain and he wore a green tie and a brown wool sport coat with leather patches on the elbows. In fact, he looked a lot like Mr. Grandon, because these were Mr. Grandon's clothes, but also because Mrs. Grandon had designed him that way, with blue painted eyes and yellow yarn hair sewn onto the top of his burlap bag head.

Libbie's mother came out onto the porch. She was drying her hands on a towel. Mr. Grandon had fixed himself a drink. He sat on the stoop, lit another cigarette and squinted again, thoughtfully, into its smoke. Libbie grinned at the both her parents, arched back and flopped down hard into the piled leaves, with her arms outspread and her eyes closed. You were a monster crouched and bleeding in the dirt behind the trellis, as the scarecrow gaped stupidly and Leo Spivak, safe and sound and above it all in his tree, looked on.

It was at that moment that Josef Krejci came out

of his house. He pulled the door closed carefully behind him, turned up the collar of his coat, and tugged at his hat, before heading down the walk to the street. He passed through the smoke that rose up from the piles of burning leaves there, and then, without ever looking up, he disappeared and was gone.

Where did Josef Krejci go? Wandering the neighborhoods without apparent purpose, rambling aimlessly around the labyrinth of Linwood, he walked and walked, from Otis Road north into the country, from Otis Road south into downtown, eastward past the factories and the plants, west beyond the narrow cluttered streets of Oak Hill to the new suburban tracts that had begun to rise up in the fields. Sometimes he headed for the bridge and, under the noses of the saints, he crossed the river and strode straight into Bohemietown, to haunt the old places there. As if maybe he were trying to find some pathway back to that shadowy time long gone, in the olden days before he was married, before you were born, when he was still a young man, when your mother was still alive, when he was courting her and promising to carry her away. Or, was he only lording the present over past, retracing the steps and stages of his own upward movement and telling himself that he was better than all that now, reminding everyone of just how far he'd come, Josef Krejci, from there to here, from that to this?

Mr. Grandon's glass was empty. He stood and started across the porch toward the door. Mrs. Grandon scolded him. Libbie was still lying on her back in the leaves with her hands folded behind her head. She wasn't looking at her parents, she was gazing at the sky—clear blue, bundles of drifting clouds, dark swirls

of smoke from the burning leaves down in the gutter—
and as her mother's voice rose, Libbie closed her eyes.
Mrs. Grandon's voice was shrill, but her husband didn't
answer back, he just worked his jaw. What was she saying? It didn't matter. She was blaming him for something that he'd done. Or scolding him for something
that he didn't do. Or he did it but he did it wrong.

She was so much smaller than him, that was why
her voice had to rise, higher, higher, up to meet him.
She was standing in front of the door with her feet
apart and her knees locked and her back straight, spine
stiffened with resistance—she meant to stop him there,
to block his path. He seemed to tower over her, although he wasn't tall, not nearly as tall as Josef Krejci.
Was he smiling? Did he mock her? He said nothing,
just set his glass down, reached out and put his hands
on her, gently, one on either arm, just below the shoulder, and then he shifted her to the side, easily, away
from him. He simply picked her up and he moved her;
then he got his glass, opened the door and disappeared
inside.

This was how the Grandons's marriage had
evolved. They'd always argued, bickering about one
thing or another, and that was normal, wasn't it? But
lately the tone had changed. Mrs. Grandon's voice rising, piping shrilly, and his face blank, a small smile playing on his lips, as if maybe he was vaguely amused by all
the fuss, but not amused enough to answer back, just
hard and silent now and moving past her, around her,
on by. Ever since last summer, it had been like that between them.

Ever since the week at Lake Vermillion. Ever since
Mrs. Grandon started to talk about a job. At first that
sounded like a threat. Maybe it had been going on

already for a while, probably it had been, privately, but that summer it came out into the open where anyone who wanted to could hear.

Ever since Marilyn Monroe was found dead in her bed with a telephone in her hand.

The Grandons were driving to the lake in Minnesota, where Libbie's grandmother had a cabin and every summer they went to stay, and that year you had been invited to go along, too. It was a long drive then, nine hours in those days of two lane highways before the Interstate was built, and you and Libbie settled in the way back of the station wagon, facing backwards, propped side by side on pillows, watching the road roll off and away, grinning at the man in a car behind you, waving at him and giggling and waving again, until Libbie gave him the finger and he signaled, pulled around, soared away. John was in the back seat with Rags, and Mr. Grandon was behind the wheel.

The voices came to you from the front seat: Mrs. Grandon's pitch rising, Mr. Grandon's voice deeper, his responses measured and slow. Libbie looked at you and raised her eyebrows.

"Is it the money, is that it? You don't have everything you need?"

"No, no, that isn't it at all, and you know it. I only want to get out of the house now and then. Is that so terrible? I just want something to do besides shop and play bridge and talk on the telephone all day."

But what kind of a job did she expect to be able to get? Pretty little Faye Grandon, spoiled little Faye Grandon, who had never worked a day in her life. He was smiling when he said this, warmly, with fondness and amusement. He loved her for her frailty and her dependence upon him. He wasn't angry yet. He reached across the seat to touch her smooth cheek with his thumb, and she batted his hand away.

"But I did too work, once. At Fairchild's in the dress department, that one summer when I was in high school."

He smiled at this, too. Smiled and shook his head. Stepped on the gas, pulled out to swoop around a dawdling truck.

What about holidays, what about summer when the kids were out of school, what about vacations, what about when Mr. Grandon was free and they wanted to take off, spend some time up at the lake, for example, like now? What about that?

And what kind of a job would she be able to get anyway? What skills did she have? Housekeeping? Ironing? Telephone sales? Conjuring up the image of Mrs. Bell, working at the kitchen table at home, selling magazine subscriptions to strangers on the phone.

"No," she screeched at him. "No! That isn't it at all!"

But, he insisted, a woman's place was in the home.

This was the summer of 1962. You were eleven years old, and it was the next summer after Julia Bell had disappeared, the summer you went to Lake Vermillion with the Grandons, the summer you got your period. You and Libbie were sitting at the kitchen table eating breakfast—pancakes and bacon and juice. Libbie was sunburned, her shoulders red, her cheeks pink, her nose peeling, her hair whitened from the sun. You had broken out in a rash of prickly heat on the back of your neck that you couldn't keep from scratching even though Mrs. Grandon had told you more than once to leave it alone, not to touch it, scratching would only make it worse, and she'd given you some lotion to put on it, but you just couldn't help it, your hand crept up to the back of your neck and you scratched when you thought nobody was looking. Scratched and bled.

You were in your bathing suits already: Libbie's two piece with the bumblebees, your old stretchy pink one that was too small because you'd been shooting up so fast. The straps curled in on themselves and bit your shoulders, the legs rode high on your thighs, and you had to keep tugging at the fabric, yanking it down to cover your behind.

You were going to take the rowboat out, paddle the shoreline, explore the inlets and look for caves.

John was wolfing down his breakfast. He ate and ate, helped himself to more, slathered butter on his pancakes, forked up syrup-soaked bacon, but he was still as thin as a stick, his mother liked to say. She stood back and studied him critically; with her arms folded and her head cocked, she eyed the gangle of his legs and arms, his narrow chest, his long neck, his bony feet.

He ignored her. He had been trying to explain something important that he'd learned about numbers. He had been trying to tell them about the square root of two—about the sides of a right triangle laid out on a graph, one inch and one inch and the hypotenuse is equal to the square root of the sum of the squares of the two sides, even the Scarecrow knows that, but if you were to swing that hypotenuse over and lay it down on the graph: Where would it land? If the sum of the squares of two sides is two and if the square root of two is infinitely non-repeating, if it's an imaginary number with no actual place in space, infinitely divisible, infinitely inward?

And hearing this, already Mrs. Grandon was upset. For some reason, the whole discussion had angered her. Why did John have to talk like that? Why did he have to say those things that gave an ordinary person a headache to consider?

"Those ideas of yours make me dizzy," she said.

"But," he explained, "they aren't my ideas." Scattered whiskers splintered his chin. His voice had deepened, his neck had thickened. "It's just the way things are," he said, "that's all. Everybody knows that."

He grinned, gulped his juice, and reached for another helping of the pancakes, but she slapped his hand away and said he'd had enough and so had she. She started clearing away the dishes, scraping them into the trash, slamming them into the sink, and so when Libbie's dad appeared in the doorway, he looked at you and asked, "What's with her?"

You shook your head and Libbie shrugged. "Who knows?"

Already Mrs. Grandon was mad.

She was standing at the counter with her hands in the soapy water, and she was staring out at the trees. Through the heavy leaves, at the end of the winding dirt path, the lake glistened, sunstruck.

Mr. Grandon took a place at the table. He opened his newspaper and read for a moment before he looked up, stirred his coffee, and then said, quietly, "Marilyn Monroe is dead." So quietly that at first Mrs. Grandon didn't hear.

She turned and peered at him over her shoulder, her hands still in the sink. "What did you say?"

"Marilyn Monroe. Says here she killed herself."

And Mrs. Grandon—her dark hair was pulled back from her face with a stretchy yellow band, exposing her high forehead and accentuating the sharp frailty of her bones—she turned around completely and stared at her husband, but he didn't notice this. He had already gone back to reading his newspaper again—he snapped it open and then disappeared behind it.

Libbie was asking, "How?"

Not a gun, no blood, no gore. It was pills. Alcohol. It might have been an accident. Maybe she didn't mean to. They found her body on the floor, or was it in the bed? She was on the telephone.

Mrs. Grandon's hands were still damp and soapy, so the dishwater ran down her forearms from her wrists to her elbows as she lit a cigarette. She seemed to be trembling slightly. She inhaled and started to cough, and her eyes filled with tears. Seeing that you were watching her, she turned away.

Mr. Grandon lowered the paper, eyed her for a moment, then asked, "Faye? Are you all right?"

But she didn't answer, and, coughing again, she raised a hand, nodded her head hard, crushed the cigarette out, pushed away from the counter. The screen door squeaked open, slapped shut behind her. Walking quickly, almost running, she crossed the yard and then disappeared down the path into the woods.

Later she came back and shut herself up in the bedroom, where she stayed all day. Libbie knocked on the door and called to her.

"Mom? You okay?"

The muffled reply: "I'm fine. Go away. Go play. Have fun."

Mr. Grandon went in and then came right back out again. He pulled the door closed after him. Looked at you and smiled. "Don't worry. She's a little upset right now, that's all."

That night she rowed the boat out into the middle of the lake. Mr. Grandon sat on the dock, drinking scotch, watching the water, and waiting for his wife to come back.

"She can't stay out there forever," he said. Then,

"She'll get over it. Pretty soon she'll be fine."

There was no moon. She was a white dot on the black water, hard to make out.

"Why is she out there? What's she doing? What's wrong with her?"

Mr. Grandon shrugged and frowned and shook his head. His look was one of helplessness. "Who knows?"

What seemed like hours later, you and Libbie were lying on your cots on the sleeping porch upstairs, awake. Libbie was sunburned and you were itchy, and you were listening to the Grandons arguing downstairs. Libbie's face was pale, her hair was bright, and her eyes glistened in the dark.

"My mother's crazy," she said.

"She's just a sensitive person, that's all."

"She's nuts."

"Maybe."

"I wish I could be like you, Meena," Libbie said. "I wish my mother was dead, too."

Of course she didn't mean this. She didn't know what she was saying. She was upset, she'd had too much sun, and she was tired, that was all. In the morning she'd be all right. In the morning everything would be fine.

You sat up, slipped off your cot, and climbed in close to Libbie. Then, cradled against each other, belly to butt, you slept.

That's the way it was: Mr. and Mrs. Grandon argued, and you comforted Libbie. Your father walked, and Libbie said never mind.

When Josef Krejci wasn't working, he was walking, and if you saw him, if you happened to be sitting near a window—in school, on the bus, in the back seat of Mrs. Grandon's car—if you looked up, looked out, and recognized your father's dark shape crossing the street, moving down the sidewalk, disappearing around a corner, then you would be squirming with embarrassment, and Libbie would have to tell you, again and again, never mind.

And when you still frowned and fidgeted: "Let's follow him," Libbie said.

You would just see what he was up to; you would find out where he went.

You spent some time with disguises, made a game of it, putting on one thing and then another, throwing each item off until Libbie's bedroom was a mess that you knew her mother would punish her for later, but who cared. You dragged out the trunk of old dresses that Mrs. Grandon had long ago gathered for playing games of dress-up, and Libbie found there a little number that was short and tight, feathery and pale.

You shook your head. No. He would notice her for sure if she dressed up in a bit like that. But Libbie was entranced, studying her reflection in the mirror— her thin shoulders, flat chest, scabby legs. She had slipped her feet into a pair of high heels, dove gray satin with the toes cut out. She cocked a hip, threw back her hair, which made you smile. But how was she going to follow him in those? When she couldn't even walk across the room without falling down?

And yet you were pretty sure you'd seen Mrs. Grandon in that dress. It had been on some Saturday night, wintertime, when dark came early, before dinner, and they were going out to some party at the Club. Mr. Grandon in a black suit, with a bright blue tie that was the same color as his eyes. Mrs. Grandon at the mirror, fastening an earring, her head tilted prettily to one side.

Forgetting for a moment what your purpose was, your gathered up your own hair and twisted it back, away from your face. You sashayed and pursed your lips. Ooh-la-la. But on you it was ridiculous.

In the end, you settled on simplicity and decided to dress like boys. It seemed the best disguise. Most likely he wouldn't even notice you, or even if he did, he wouldn't know he had.

Dark clothes: black pants and sweatshirts with the hoods pulled up and the cords drawn tight, your faces flat white disks. It was perfect: you were nobody or you could have been anybody; you didn't even recognize yourselves.

Then there was nothing left to do but wait for him to leave. You knelt on Libbie's bed, watching from the window. You saw Mrs. Chadima arrive, dropped off by her husband at the bottom of the driveway. The climb up the hill to the house left her breathless; she balanced a bag of groceries in her arms. She let herself in through the side door. You saw John come out of the house, climb on his bike, and ride away. Leo Spivak was in his driveway across the street, washing his father's car. Old Mrs. Bickel was out sweeping her front walk.

And then at last, there he was, your father, Josef Krejci. The front door had opened and he had stepped outside, was standing on the step, with his hands in the pockets of his coat. He looked up into the sky, took a deep breath and then seemed to gather himself in, as his heavy shoes trudged down the steps, down the driveway, to the street.

Libbie was pulling up her hood, drawing the strings tight under her chin. You would let him get a bit ahead, then go after him, she said.

Suddenly you were afraid. "I don't know, Libbie. Maybe we shouldn't be doing this."

Libbie turned, startled. Her face, inside the hood of her sweatshirt, was a thin white mask. "What? Why?"

"If he catches us…"

"He won't catch us. And even if he does, so what?"

You could feel your stomach turning with alarm at the prospect of your father's anger. "He'll be mad," she said.

Libbie shrugged. "He'll get over it."

Still you held back. What you were doing was a mistake, you were sure of it. Libbie stepped up close to you, reached and pulled the hood up over your head. "Come on. It'll be okay. What's the worst that could happen, anyway?"

She took your hand and led you out of the room. You stumbled down the hall and down the stairs, as Libbie called out to her mother, who was playing solitaire at a TV table in the front room: "Bye! Bye!" But Mrs. Grandon didn't look up, only waved a hand, crushed out her cigarette, and slapped down another card.

Libbie cracked the front door open and peeked around it—careful, quiet, sneaky, because what if he stopped and turned, what if just at that moment he looked back over his shoulder and saw her? You could feel the hammer of your heart. But no, he didn't notice anything, he just kept walking away, a big dark shadow getting smaller as it seemed to float down Otis Road toward downtown. One after the other, Libbie first, you slipped out, hurrying to catch up, then keeping a safe distance behind. Hanging back, ducking in and out of doorways, hiding behind hedges, fences, trees, and you began to believe that your father wouldn't be able to see you after all, even if he looked, which he didn't. He was too absorbed in himself, lost in thought as he walked and walked—head down, hands in his pockets, eyes on the ground.

What was the worst that could happen? If he did catch you, what would Josef Krejci do? Send you to your room without supper? Lock you in a closet? Beat you with his belt?

No, worse. He would ignore you. He would pretend you didn't exist. The silent treatment, he called it. He would stop looking at you. He would stop speaking to you.

"Dad?"

You forget to take the trash down to the curb on Monday morning. You leave a pop bottle out on the table in the living room. You break the antenna on the TV set. And he gets quiet.

"Dad, I'm sorry. Dad?"

No answer. He stands up from his chair and walks away, as if he's all alone and nothing bothers him and you aren't even there. He goes into his study and shuts the door.

And then when you're alone together later, eating the dinner that Mrs. Chadima has prepared, he still won't say a single word to you. He'll be reading the paper or focusing on his food, and if he does happen to glance up it will be as if he's seeing right through you, because you don't exist. He knows how to go for days this way, without looking at you and without speaking to you, and he is so good at it that after a while you will begin to believe him. You'll be feeling your own self disappear.

It was early winter, and already there had been some snow, but most of it had melted by then. On a Sunday afternoon in Linwood the stores were closed and the streets were quiet. The sun had come out, and the day had turned warm. Josef Krejci's fingers worked at the buttons of his long wool coat as he walked, and then it was open and flapping after him, like wings. He was wearing a white shirt and dark pants and a thin, silvery tie. His big shoes splattered the sidewalk slush. At the corner of Third Avenue and Nineteenth Street he stopped and stood still, fishing in his pocket for his tobacco pouch and his pipe. He filled the bowl, then lit it, walked on. Smoke billowed around his face, his cheeks were rosy, eyes shining, greedy. He was hatless, and his pink scalp gleamed.

He didn't know that he was being followed. He wasn't aware that behind him hovered a pair of dark shapes, two girls disguised as boys. You'd turned your backs and were standing side by side at the window of the Wendell Ford dealership on Second Avenue. You were looking past the ghosts of your own reflected faces, past the bright colors of the new cars, and when the salesman inside waved at you, it must have seemed to him that you were gaping stupidly back, but what you were really seeing there was the large dark figure of Josef Krejci superimposed on the surface of the glass.

The light changed, and he moved on. You waited, let him go, and then you were moving on too. You skittered across the street at the last second, against the red. It didn't matter—it was Sunday and there wasn't any traffic anyway. The smell of his pipe smoke was so strong and so familiar, you might have followed him by that alone. All the way downtown you hung behind him, slipping from shadow to shadow, along Second Avenue, across Tenth Street and on down to Sixth, over the railroad tracks, behind the factories and the warehouses and then out into the open again, to where the office buildings were, and the stores.

Why would he go there on a Sunday afternoon, when everything was closed? There was nothing to do.

The streets were mostly empty. There were hardly any cars. The lights around the marquee of the World Theater blinked on and off, but no one came or went. First the big show windows of downtown Fairchild's, and after that a shoe store, then the music shop, Haden's furniture, Woolworth's, a jewelry store.

He turned at Second Street, went half a block and then turned again, into the alley where you almost lost him. You stopped and watched as he walked down the middle of the alleyway, past the garbage cans, the locked back doors, loading docks, a delivery truck parked. Pipe smoke wafted after him.

Libbie grabbed your arm and dragged you away—she had a plan. You would circle the block. A woman in a red and green headscarf was coming toward you from the other way. She ducked her head and clutched her purse close to her body, wary of the two wild-looking boys who were bearing down on her. Libbie glared fiercely at her as she passed, and when the woman cringed away, you tried to smile, to let her know that it was okay, really. It was just a game you were playing, that's all.

At the corner you stopped and look left and right, and left again. He should have been there, but he wasn't. He was gone. Nowhere in sight. Libbie held onto your arm, and you stood together looking up and down the street—nothing. She pulled you forward, and you walked carefully, sniffing the air for his pipe smoke.

You were at the front door of the Fielding Hotel. A man in a blue suit brushed past, in a hurry, and the doorman helped him into a waiting car. Libbie's grip on your arm had tightened, and you turned to look past the dizzy spin of the revolving door to see your father, there in the bright lights of the lobby of the old hotel. Above him, a bright cascade of a crystal chandelier.

He was standing by a high-backed green velveteen chair, one hand on its wing. He leaned over for a moment, then stood straight again. A woman, responding, rose to her feet and was turning to face him. She wore a short skirt, fishnet stockings, black high-heeled shoes, a bright orange blouse. Her hair had been pulled up away from her face and piled on top of her head, with dainty tendrils dangling down. She was smiling as she helped Josef Krejci out of his heavy overcoat. He bent and kissed her cheek. She leaned into him, and he held her for a moment—in those heels they were almost the same height.

As they crossed the lobby together he looked up, and when his eyes met yours it was as if he'd reached out and thumped you hard on the forehead with his thumb. But he didn't move. He just held you as you stood there, stunned by his gaze for one long frozen moment, because he wanted to be sure you understood that you'd been seen. And then he frowned, shook his head, and turned away.

The man behind the desk had hooded eyes and a long-jowled face without expression, and he took a key from a hook and handed it to the woman. She carried Josef's coat over her arm as she led him to the elevator. He didn't look at you again. The doors slid open, then shut, and then both of them were gone.

You took the bus home. You and Libbie sat at the back, side by side—two tom-girls in hooded sweatshirts and dark pants and sneakers. A man with a shopping bag balanced on his knees turned and smiled at you. Libbie made a face, and said, "Take a picture, it'll last longer." She nudged you, smirking, then asked, "So, what about that woman? Who do you think she is?"

You didn't answer. You had no idea, and you

weren't sure you wanted to find out.

But Libbie wouldn't stop. What if he's in love with her? What if he brought her home for dinner sometime? What if she stayed overnight? What if he married her?

What if she officially adopted you? She was so young and really sort of pretty, wasn't she?

"She could be more than just a mother," Libbie suggested.

She could also be a friend, a fairy godmother, and you could go places, you could go shopping, she might buy you things—shoes and clothes and records—she would understand and take your side and stand up to Josef when you wanted to cut your hair, wear lipstick, pierce your ears.

"And really," Libbie kept asking, "Meena, why would that be so bad?"

You parted on the sidewalk, at the bottom of the pair of driveways between the two houses. By then it was getting dark, and cold, again. You let yourself into the house through the side door. Mrs. Chadima was in the kitchen, standing at the stove over a steaming pot of something, stirring it with a big spoon. Applesauce. And in the oven, a peppered pork roast. Braised vegetables. Brown gravy. The smell of food was nauseating. Mrs. Chadima's rosy face emerged from the steam as she turned, her smile sweet, the wooden spoon held out in her one hand, the other palm cupped under it: "Meena! Want a taste?"

And later, over dinner, you could not stop staring at him: his hands as he ate, his mouth as he chewed, his big shoes on the floor. You were looking past his clothes, imagining his bare feet, his bare chest, his big belly hanging over his belt. While he pretended you weren't there.

You and your father are in his truck, and he is driving you to school. It's been ten days since you followed him downtown to the Fielding Hotel, and he still isn't speaking to you or looking at you.

He keeps his eyes on the road. He has the radio on, they're giving out the farm reports, and you lean forward to fiddle with the knob and tune in some music, but he slaps your hand away and turns the radio off.

"Why do you want to listen to that crap?"

You hold your breath and feel yourself come back into being again at the sound of his words, addressed to you. His nostrils flare as he breathes. He smells of tobacco, whiskey, shaving lotion, limes. His face is round and fat, his chin has begun to double, he seems to be expanding. When he pulls up to the curb outside the school, he turns to you again. "Have a nice day, Meena," he says. "I'll see you tonight." And then he smiles.

You tumble out of the truck and fall away from him to the sidewalk, your body loose with gratitude and relief.

July 2006

When Meena comes to, it's in total darkness, and she has no idea where she is or how she might have got here. She seems to be afloat, again. Drifting, lost and spinning down into the deep eddy maybe, that's what this feels like, and that's what occurs to her, at first. She flails out to try to save herself, struggles to be free of some entanglement, and finds that she's on a hardwood floor, that she's simply fallen out of bed and is caught up now not in the snarls of Julia Bell's mermaid hair but only the thin web of a crocheted summer blanket. She sits up and puts a hand to her face to feel a tenderness here on her chin. Her lower lip seems to be slightly swollen. Her jaw is sore.

As her eyes adjust to the light now she can see that she's in a bedroom of some kind, small and square, with a single bed, a squat dresser, one door to her left and another to her right, and a window on the far wall.

If she could stand up, if she could pull herself to her feet and stand, then she would wrap herself in this blanket and cross the cold floor to the window and look out and see... what? Trees. All around. Tall trees with narrow straight trunks and high needled branches. Lodge pole pines. And among them, clusters of white-limbed aspens. She seems to be in the middle of a forest. She can see that beyond the spread fan of the swaying firs the sky that rises overhead is spattered with the shine of more stars than she has ever seen before.

Has she been kidnapped? Is she being held prisoner? Has she been raped? Has she been robbed? Oh God, she thinks—the money. Her father's roll of bills inside her purse, it will be gone. Those people in that bar, they got her to drink herself into a stupor, then stole her money and brought her here to this place and left her here to die. Probably they saw her coming. Probably the whole thing was just a setup, even the dead dog.

But here is the purse, on top of the dresser. And in it, the money. What Meena really needs to do, she realizes now, is use the bathroom.

Still wrapped in the blanket, she sits on the toilet with her elbows on her knees and her head cradled in her hands. She's reminded of Mrs. Grandon, who came wobbling through the living room late at night after some wing-ding at the club, carrying her shoes in one hand and her silver sequined handbag in the other. Hissing and spitting at the girls, waving them away as they watched her head for the stairs to disappear up to her room. Mr. Grandon plodded in behind her, all smiles and twirling his key chain. He whistled and snapped his fingers as he stood at the bar and fixed himself another drink. A nightcap, he said.

The next morning, they'd see that the convertible had been parked cockeyed in the driveway, its left front wheel on the lawn, and Mrs. Grandon would not come downstairs again until after lunchtime. She was sick, she said. She had a headache, a cold, or maybe it was the flu. The girls fixed her a piece of plain toast and a bottle of cold Coke with a lime wedge squeezed and poked down into its neck.

What Meena remembers of last night: she was in a bar and she was drinking whiskey with a fat man who said his name was Will. She had run over a dog. Poor old thing. Woody? She shudders, totters, puts out a hand to steady herself. Dizzy, she wonders whether she's still drunk. Stands at the little sink and slurps cold water from the trough of her cupped hands. Splashes her face, gasping. Steps back and takes a look at herself in the cracked mirror on the back of the medicine cabinet to see a stranger there, bleary-eyed and wild-haired and pale.

She finds that her suitcase is on the floor near the bedroom door. She has no idea how it got here. She's not even sure how she got here, although she thinks she does remember something about walking through a mob of standing trees, along a narrow winding path, with an arm of support around her waist on one side, a bony shoulder on the other. The smell of patchouli and pine needles. She touches her face again, tests the soreness, fingers the swelling.

If they kidnapped her, if they beat her up... what for? And then why leave her purse, her money, and her suitcase?

She peers out through the bedroom door to see a small sitting room furnished with a sofa and leather armchair facing a stone fireplace. There is a kitchenette here too, with an old white icebox, a sink, and an enamel stove. She finds ice in the freezer and paper towels on the counter, makes a compress and holds it to her swollen lip. Above the sink there's another window with a view of more trees, standing still and silent sentry around this cabin, as if posted here to guard it.

The clock on the stove reads three-forty-five. Soon it will be dawn.

Memory returns, flickers the past back into being again.

Meena: drinking whiskey with Will Gidding, listening to him tell her of his belief that the world is going to end soon. That only the few shall be saved when it does. That there will be a great tribulation and a battle of Armageddon before the wolf lies down with the lamb. Or something like that. Last days and end-times and apocalypse and revelation.

Holly: telling Meena to pay no attention to her brother. He's crazy, she said, then stood there gazing at him with a look of expectation in her face that seemed to come straight out of the set of her jaw, working. It was time to go home. But he wasn't ready to leave, he said. Not yet.

Will: patting the seat next to him. "Aw come on Holly, just one more." For a man who was expecting for it to be all over at any moment, he seemed pretty content to linger.

Meena: sitting on the broad seat of the yellow truck next to Holly, beside the door, while Will drove. The truck's big tires bouncing in the deeply rutted road that the headlights carved out of the mountain. Climbing the road, so narrow it seemed as if it couldn't be going anywhere, just winding mindlessly upward, and then there was a gate that they passed through and after that the road got worse. Shale and loose gravel, and the truck shimmying over it, like a bag full of loose bones. Meena leaned away from the deep drop-offs on the left, pressed herself against the door toward the high slope of banked rocks and boulders on the right. And then there was another gate and a sign that arched overhead, in a twist of forged iron leaves and raw wood, caught in the flash of headlights—*RAGNAROK.*

Will: getting out of the truck. Telling Meena to sit tight, but she wasn't in any condition to be going anywhere anyway.

Meena: closing her eyes, feeling the world spin.

Holly: lighting a cigarette and handing it to Meena, then lighting another for herself. Holly staring straight out through the windshield, where the twin buds of cinder on the ends of their cigarettes winked back at them.

Meena: trying to coordinate her hand and her mouth.

Meena: falling. The truck door opening and Meena tumbling out. Will trying to catch her, laughing: "Whoa there, Libbie honey. Take it easy now."

Will: holding Meena up and Holly just ahead, pointing out the way.

Meena: singing, "Catch a falling star and put it in your pocket..."

As the wide white beam from Holly's flashlight went swimming through the trees.

Now when Meena cups her hands around her face and peers out the window, she sees there's no sign of her car out there. Only an empty drive and a narrow trail winding away past a woodpile and a stone-circled fire pit before disappearing in the shadows on beyond. When she tries the door, she finds that it isn't locked; it opens easily into the night. From the edge of the shallow plank porch a set of steps leads down to a grassy clearing.

A twig cracks in the woods nearby and Meena starts, loses her balance, nearly falls over, plants a hand on the porch post to steady herself. Just past the clearing there is a shadow moving. A pair of golden discs materialize, gleam, fix on her, then turn away. Meena staggers back into the cabin and leans against the door and locks it.

Her head pounds and she thinks she might be sick, but she wills the nausea away. She's overcome with misery, and shame. She crawls back into the bed and curls in on herself there with the blanket wrapped around her. She closes her eyes and listens to the sound of the forest, which is mostly a deep silence. Some bird twitter and wind flurry, but mostly it's nothing. So quiet that she can hear the zing of her own brain ringing in her ears. She draws herself smaller, becomes a compact self-enfolded bundle, spinning dizzy down toward a deep stupor of sleep.

The Master of Disaster

1963

You were twelve. It was a Saturday, the first warm day of spring, and you were alone at home. Your father was off somewhere, walking. By then that word—walking—had come to be a joke in your vocabulary, a euphemism for something else altogether. Libbie was the one who started this. Said it with a wink. Walking. Walker. Walked. "Ooh baby, walk that walk," Libbie said, screwing up her face, tossing back her hair, one hand on her thrown hip, the other fanned out against the back of her head. Motherwalker. Walking the dog. Walk me. Walk you. You walking son of a bitch. Your father walks with whores.

He would come in later, just at dusk, with his face flushed, cheeks shining pink, and his shirt damp with sweat, and at dinner he would tell you some anecdote about where he'd been, what he'd done, who he'd seen. A man chasing after a rabbit. A woman in a feathered hat carrying something in the crook of her arm—he would swear it was impossible to tell whether the creature was a monkey or a child. Two grown men wrestling with a pig in a puddle of mud. A car engine on fire. A tree full of noisy crows. He never mentioned a doorman. He never described a shining crystal chandelier. He never said a word about a strange young woman in a short black skirt and a bright orange blouse, her hand on his shoulder, his fist in the small of her back. Whether those things that he did talk about were true or not, you couldn't be sure. All you knew was that at the heart of whatever your father said to you, there would always have to be that lie.

But never mind, it didn't matter. You didn't care. This was just the way things were: he was out walking and you were at home all by yourself. Mrs. Chadima wasn't due for hours. Matka was ensconced in her own rooms over the store, where she would be sleeping or watching television or sitting in her chair, soaking her feet and staring out the window, dreaming up more grotesqueries for you to fear.

You had been inside all morning, reading and studying, doing homework, but now you were getting restless and it was hard for you to sit still. The house was too quiet and you'd been nursing a nagging worry that something surprising had happened and maybe the world had gone off someplace else without you. Suppose you'd been left there by yourself, to get by on your own, somehow. Say there'd been a nuclear attack, and you didn't know about it yet, and that not knowing had saved your life in some tricky way, so that it would turn out you were the only one left behind.

You peered out the front window in the dining room just to check on the reality of things, and saw only Leo Spivak backing his father's car out of the driveway, a woman leading a dog on a leash, a boy on a bicycle pedaling past. So it seemed that nothing had changed after all, and maybe that was a relief or maybe it was a disappointment, you couldn't be sure which. You went into the kitchen, opened the refrigerator and then closed it again. You were hungry and not hungry, both at the same time. Some indefinable longing nagged at you.

You were wearing cut-off blue jeans and a short-sleeved sweatshirt, no underpants, no bra, and this seemed to you to be positively daring, so womanly, sexy and comfortable and grubby and accidental, all at once. Your wild hair was held back by a knot of silk ribbon. Your white canvas sneakers were worn and grimy and torn. There was an appealing unintendedness about the way you looked just then, and it felt suddenly beautiful to you. With no one around to notice, no one there to see.

You stepped out the back door and into the yard. It was a nice warm day, balmy and sunny as it hasn't been in months. You imagined that Libbie was watching you. That she was upstairs at her window, looking out but for some reason not saying so. You lingered there on the grass, thinking of Libbie's eyes on you even though you knew they weren't, not really.

In fact, you could be pretty sure that Libbie wasn't even home. Places to go, things to do for a popular girl, with bunches of friends. On a Saturday afternoon like that one, why would a girl like Libbie Grandon be at home? She had gone to watch her brother play baseball, maybe. She was at the movies with her dad. She was at the library, working on a report. She was at her catechism class. She was downtown, shopping for clothes with her mother. She could have been anywhere, and even though you knew this, still you were pretending that Libbie was right there, watching you. You basked in the warmth of that imagined gaze. You tried to see yourself as you were guessing Libbie would have seen you. In the cut-offs and the sweatshirt, your hair, the ribbon, the shoes.

Lately your legs had lengthened and your breasts

had begun to fill out. The angles of your body—shoulders, hips, knees—had started to soften and curve. You had already been wearing a bra for months, but not today.

Mayflowers had begun to poke up through the floor of leaves and debris under the trees up in the woods. And jack-in-the-pulpits, nodding. Bluebells and jonquils. It wouldn't be very long before this all became a riot of green nettles and then the only way to get up the hill unharmed would be along the narrow path. But now it was early still, and still pretty bare.

You took your time climbing the hill. You zig-zagged across it before slipping away from where Libbie could see you, if she were watching, which you knew she wasn't, but...

You faded into the shadows of the trees.

At the top where the property ended there was a wire fence and a wobbly wooden stile that crossed over it at the corner. From there you could see the red roof of Dowland, as it was called, poking up toward the tops of the trees. This was one of the largest and most extravagant properties in Wellington Heights—it was a massive white structure with a red tile roof, gaudy as a wedding cake. There was a ballroom on the third floor and a swimming pool in the back yard.

Mrs. Grandon used to warn you and Libbie away from there. The pool was dangerous, she said. She told you that the youngest of the Dow children had drowned there, but whether that was true, it was impossible to know. Supposedly his body had been found floating. Or was it at the bottom, after a party, all the grownups drunk and no one paying any attention, no one even noticing he was gone, until the next morning, and even then it was hours before they found him, though they said they looked at the pool many times but somehow he'd been hidden, in the shadows or the illusion of blue paint and green water and blinding sun. Until the sky clouded over and it began to rain, and then one last search of the grounds ended when a maid saw the shadow at the bottom of the pool, and she began to scream. Sometimes, Libbie said, you could hear the screams even now. But surely that was just the wind.

This was meant to be a story about the dangers of the world, but what it really was about was the carelessness of the adults who were supposed to be in charge and were expected to know what they were doing. With their money and their gods and their rules and their ghosts and their atom bombs.

You climbed over the fence and crept through the bushes. The path ended at the grass, as the woods opened out onto the long lawn that spread toward the house, around the swimming pool. Drained, empty, it gaped like an open wound. Black stains spread across the bottom from a puddled murk of old leaves and dirty water.

You crossed the lawn and stood at the edge of the pool with the toes of your grimy white sneakers hanging out over the marbled edge. You stared down into the mess at the bottom, entranced. You were squinting into it and studying it hard, looking for a pattern, searching for some sign of a drowned child that wasn't there.

Disappointed, you went home. Later that night it rained.

A few weeks later you went back to look again. You couldn't help it. You just had to. You fought the temptation, without success; somehow you couldn't stay away. Drawn by death and all of that, maybe—thinking of dead babies, dead boys, drowned children, lost children, goblins and ghosts. You were wallowing in the muck and murk of your own misery at that time too, so steeped in your own black unhappiness that it had started to feel like pleasure, in a way. Poor little motherless child, friendless girl, abandoned babe, you were Meena Krejci dawdling in the shadows by yourself.

By then it was the middle of summer already, and there was no pretending about what Libbie might have been busy with, because you knew for sure that she was not up there at her window, silently watching you. Libbie was back up at Lake Vermillion again, with her family. This time you hadn't been invited to go along, and when Libbie told you this you shrugged it off, acted as if it hardly mattered to you, one way or another. Even if it did. Even if it mattered to Libbie.

Instead Libbie had taken Gingi Noone. Gingi Noone of all people. Poor Gingi Noone. Crazy Gingi Noone. That same girl that the other kids used to torment—skinny Gingi Noone with her chopped black hair and sharp white face, who could believe it that Libbie Grandon would have started hanging around with her? They'd got to be friends in catechism class, because Gingi was a Catholic girl, too.

"She's really funny," Libbie said. "She cracks me up." Shrugged, bit her lip, tipped her head to one side and squinted at you. "And she's not all moody all the time like you are," she said, then added, quickly: "I know you can't help it. It's not your fault and it's just the way you are and I'm not saying you should change yourself or anything like that. But..." She paused, shrugged, and finished it: "Gingi Noone and I have fun."

Gingi Noone, poor white goblin girl, who lived on the edge of Nowhere's white trash squalor. The same girl that Libbie used to call Crazy Gingi whenever she saw her riding down the street on her bike, bent over the handlebars, legs furiously pumping, sweater flapping out behind her. Or when she came into the store with her mother.

Gingi Noone laughing too loudly. Shouting across the playground. Running down the street in bright red shorts, the skin of her bare legs so white and exposed that it seemed like she was naked. But she ran on anyway, unashamed and fearless. Shouldn't she have been embarrassed to be herself?

"She doesn't care what anybody thinks," Libbie said. "It's amazing. You should see her in catechism, asking Father Loferski to explain again about Hell." Gingi Noone talked back to a teacher and was sent home. She overturned her lunch tray on the table in the cafeteria, pronounced the food—hamburger gravy and green beans and mashed potatoes—inedible. Once she'd punched a boy in the belly for teasing her. "It's a free country," Gingi Noone would say. "I don't have to answer to anybody but God." "Just try to stop me," she would warn. "See what happens then."

But the fact was, you had explained to Libbie, you couldn't go to the lake with the Grandons that summer anyway. You hadn't been planning on it. You were supposed to be working in the grocery store every day, you said. And looking after your grandmother. "You know how that is," you finished. You rolled your eyes. "My dad..."

Libbie had nodded, pursed her lips, rocked on her heels. "Sure," she said, "I understand."

"Besides," you went on, just to seal it forever, "I didn't really like it up there all that much." There were leeches in the water and mosquitoes in the air. Sunburn. Poison ivy. Chiggers. Too hot in the daytime, and then too cold at night. Not to mention Libbie's parents, yelling at each other all the time. Her mother acting crazy. Her father getting drunk.

Libbie had nodded again. Sure, she knew all right. Better for everybody, then.

Mrs. Grandon had asked you to pick up the mail and the newspapers for her while they were gone. She had given you twenty dollars and a key to the back door. You saw yourself as a shadow moving across the bright background of the Grandons' lives, your stormy hair wild as you wandered through the clean, quiet rooms of their empty house. You didn't snoop around, nothing like that. You were fully respectful of their privacy. Besides, what could there be that you didn't already know about them? You'd been in that house a million times, and had seen all of what there was to see. Such as, Mr. Grandon's dirty paperback books—on the bottom shelf of his nightstand, under a stack of otherwise respectable news magazines. Mrs. Grandon's prescriptions in the bathroom medicine cabinet—valium, codeine, sleeping pills, something called Edrisol, for cramps. Her "face" as she called it—makeup that you and Libbie had experimented with on yourselves plenty of times. John's telescope. His own collection of dirty magazines under the bed, a box of tissues, a bottle of lotion—more of the old Deep Eddie. Libbie's diaries—page after page of nothingness, the boring drivel that Libbie felt compelled to write about herself and her friends. "Went to school. Jeff W. smiled at me. Came home. Not much happened. Rags has ticks."

You'd read all this before, at one time or another. Either when Libbie had shown it to you herself or when you sneaked a peek when she wasn't looking. What's worse than reading someone else's diary? Writing in it, maybe. You flipped through and added words or even, sometimes, whole sentences. That Libbie never said anything to you about it meant that she never noticed—she never went back and read her own pages, probably—but maybe someday, you thought, in some distant future, when she was older and married, with children of her own, maybe then she would want to look back again at herself at this time, to find herself there maybe, or to take the measure of how far she'd come, or how far she was gone—and then she'd see it clearly, your contribution to her life, to her memories, a clarification here, an amplification there. Who is Jeff W. and what happened in the lunch room and how did it feel to have a best friend?

"I love Meena K.," you wrote in the margins. More than once.

Otherwise you didn't bother poking around in their stuff. Instead you just sat there in the living room, with the lights off and the curtains drawn, and you were careful not to disturb a thing. You didn't move, and you didn't make a sound. You listened; you waited... for what? You didn't know. Something. Nothing.

After a while you got up and left. You locked the door behind you, crossed the driveways to your own back yard, set up the sprinkler there, turned the water on, and watched the gentle sway of the spray, filled with sunlight, glistening.

In midsummer the woods were overgrown in wild ragged weeds, impossible tangles of mean nettles, briars, thistles, thorns. Avoiding these, you followed the path up to the fence and the stile at the top. You climbed over and crept to the edge of the yard, where you hovered like a wayward balloon caught up in an electrical wire.

The swimming pool had been cleaned and filled, and it looked nothing now as it had before, because in the middle of that bright blue chlorine rich water there was a canary yellow canvas raft, and on it a youth with gingery hair lay supine, dozing as he sunned himself, one leg bent and one arm folded back behind his head, the other arm outflung, long fingers dabbling the clear clean water, glistening with heat.

So the Dow boy hadn't drowned, after all?

Hidden, you watched him as he floated languidly on his raft. His skin was pink, freckled, his body hairless and slim. There was a movement at the house, a door opened, and a woman in a green dress stepped out, holding one hand up to shield her eyes from the blinding sun, and she called, "Fox! Lunch!"

He opened his eyes and rolled to the side, off the raft and into the water, then glided to the edge of the pool, pulled himself up and shook his head so water spun off his hair in crystal threads that glistened in the sunlight. You covered your eyes, and when you looked again, he was gone.

After that first sighting, you couldn't stop thinking about him. Wondering, who was he? Had you only imagined him? Was he real? Fox. Was that his name? Fox Dow. You longed to go back up the hill to see him again and later that night you did, but Dowland was dark, there was no one home, he wasn't there.

Josef Krejci knew all about the Dows, as you had correctly guessed he would. You brought it up at breakfast the next morning, keeping your eyes on your plate, furiously trying to suppress the heat in your face as you waited for his response, though he didn't seem to notice anyway, his thoughts were somewhere else. He put his fork down and looked out the window—up the hill, toward the trees beyond which the roofs of Dowland rose—dabbed his lips with his napkin, breathed a sniff of contempt. Or was it bitterness? Some struggle in his own mind between his envy of what others had—a world beyond his own reach that could only be accommodated through an effort of denial and disdain—and a sense of unfair disadvantage to his own pursuit of what he had been led to believe was the American Dream, available to anyone who worked hard enough and long enough to make of it whatever they could. But the Dows' dream was a longstanding one, set in motion long before anyone named Krejci came to town. They were one of the oldest families in Linwood— along with the Fairchilds and the Cookes—and they were builders, quarrymen, heirs to a fortune made of limestone. Country Club people, Josef said. They did not shop at Krejci's. Their children were sent away to schools in the east. Old families, with old money. Streets and buildings and mausoleums in the Linwood Cemetery were marked with their names. Oh yes, he knew all about them, all right, everything except anything about this boy whose name was Fox.

That morning you went to the store as usual, and you worked at the cash register there until noon, then walked home in the muggy heat, stopping to pick up the Grandons' mail and take it inside their house, before you allowed yourself to begin to think of going back up there to look at him again. Half believing that you had dreamed him, that he didn't really exist but was a ghost, a drowned boy who had been dead now for many years.

But there he was, sitting at a patio table in the shade of an umbrella, reading a book. You crouched in the brush and watched him. He wore silver-rimmed glasses, and now that it was dry you could see that his hair was longish, longer than any other boy's you knew, shaggy around his ears and on his neck, falling in his eyes so he tossed it back with a snap of his head, a gesture so sudden that it startled you. He was wearing a white, long-sleeved shirt with a button down collar and wrinkled khaki shorts, black high top sneakers without socks. He turned a page, sighed, shifted in his chair. He was so still, and the afternoon was so hot, the air around him shimmered—he might have been a painting and again you found yourself doubting whether he was real.

A plane passed overhead, its engine rattling as it sliced across the perfect blue dome of the airless sky, and he looked up, then turned his intent gaze toward the woods, where you had hidden yourself. You jerked back and, hearing you, he stood. One finger tucked into the book. A hand up to shade his eyes. You were a good fifty feet away, on the far side of the lawn, and you might have slithered back into the shadows and escaped his notice but instead you stood up and stepped forward into the light.

What did he see? A girl with wild dark hair outlined against the trees, pale face stricken with embarrassment and fear as you gaped at him, before you turned and ran, careening through the brush, your blood hammering so loudly in your ears that you hardly heard him call out, "Hey!" and you didn't stop, but tore through the woods, crashed past the fireplace, scrabbled over the stile and skidded wildly down the hill, tromping on mayflowers and crushing bluebells along the way. You sprang into your own yard, blinded by the dazzle of sunlight that languished in the grass.

When you went back the next day, to see him

again, and then the day after that, he was gone.

That fall, as you and Libbie entered seventh grade, Mrs. Grandon finally got her way, and Libbie went to the parochial school while you stayed where you were in the public system and moved up from Johnson Elementary into John Adams Junior High. For you this was a nightmare, and at first you wholly retreated from it. You sank into sleep and went through the days in a half-doze. Where was Libbie?

You kept thinking that it was as if your friend had altogether disappeared from the horizon, a sinking sun. She might have been abducted from the neighborhood, taken away and transformed as surely as Julia Bell had been, and you could almost see it: Libbie's body drifting, floating face down in the water, turning with the current, tumbling over the roller dam, and heading down the river toward the deep eddy, drowned. You could almost see it, but at the same time you knew that what you were almost seeing wasn't anything that was real. It was just an image that kept popping into your head. You knew that Libbie was still Libbie and that she still lived in the house next door, that she went to school every day, and every night she came home again, that she ate meals and worried about her hair and fiddled with her clothes and smirked at her mother and grinned at her father, that she hadn't moved away or gone away or died, and the proof of this was in the fact that you did still see her every now and then.

Mount Mercy School required its students to wear uniforms, so there was Libbie Grandon in a flirty gray skirt that she rolled up at the waist so it wouldn't hang down too far, knee high socks, brown oxford shoes, a green cardigan sweater. When you asked your father if you could go to Mount Mercy too, you saw a flash of anger in his eyes so mean and bright that you knew better than to ever ask him that again. He hated Catholics, that was the long and the short of it. All that pomp, red velvet and holy water, bleeding saints and virgin mothers, incense and Latin, mitered Cardinals, the Pope, even the President of the United States!

"Don't forget who you are, Meena," he said to her, but you had no idea who that was, and he could only tell you who you were not. You were not a Catholic, for one thing. And you were not a Grandon, either. You were different, you were other, maybe you were better, somehow? Too smart to be a Catholic, you were expected to be able to see through all that smoke and mystery. Too good to be a Grandon, you were not allowed to succumb to the whims of the world the way that people like that were, blown here and there by whatever happened to be the passing fad of the day. And at that time there were plenty of those, coming and going so fast. But not for Meena Krejci.

Your father seemed to have nothing but contempt for the Grandons, as well as for some of the other families in Wellington Heights that he judged to be like them, but they never knew the depths of his feelings against them. Because good old Josef Krejci was everybody's friend, wasn't he? The corner grocer, always friendly, always polite. Eager to be useful to them, happy to be of help. Aloof now and then, maybe, moody sometimes, but certainly never rude. He was a thoughtful man, that was it. Complicated, a widower, a Czech prone to laughter, prone to melancholy. In his apron, in his white shirt, in his tie. He was serious and studious, a self-educated man, how could he be otherwise, circumstances being what they were? He knew just what to say. He knew just how to compliment the customers as he rang up their orders. He knew when to wink, how to smile, how to flatter and to flirt. With one hand in his pocket, snapping the thick red rubber band that he'd wrapped around his fattened roll of five and ten and twenty dollar bills.

But you thought you knew better. Because, hadn't you seen for yourself what Mr. Josef Krejci, the grocer, was really all about? Hadn't you followed him, didn't you know where he'd been, weren't you aware of where it was he went, couldn't you guess at what he did? And weren't you his daughter, after all?

So you thought you knew better than anyone that your father was wrong about himself and that he was also, by extension, wrong about you. Truth was: Josef and Meena Krejci were nothing special. You were not, as Matka kept insisting, a miracle, and your father was not a king. Far from it. Josef Krejci was just another fat horny old bald bohunk. A widowed grocer, that was all: he was no one. And if he disappeared tomorrow, who but you, his daughter, would mourn?

And you were the most ordinary girl in the world—there were a million more just like you, too. All over the place. Those days, they were everywhere you looked.

Here's the proof you had of this: no one saw you. You went to school and came back home again, joined the crowds in the halls, went from class to class, unnoticed and unseen. You had become a ghost; bored and lonely, isolated and alone, you were living in a world of your own.

The idea that John Grandon had had about Julia Bell being trapped in some other parallel space: this was just what popped up into your head, and it was just as you were feeling, too, except that unlike Julia, you didn't even have the benefit of really being gone. Instead you were still there, awake and aware of what had happened, what was happening, and you were moving through the world and doing things and saying things, raising your hand in class, turning in your homework, pushing Belle Chadima's food around on your plate with a fork, while at the same time you were somewhere else and watching from a distance this awkward girl who somehow had your own name and your own face, this clumsy creature who went about the business of her life with her shoulders hunched forward and her arms hugging her schoolbooks to her breasts, her head down, her eyes focused on the ground just ahead of her feet. If Libbie had been looking, if she'd been able to see you then, she would have nudged her best friend Gingi Noone, snorted, clucked, shaken her head and rolled her eyes in disgust at the pathetic daily spectacle of you. But Libbie was not around. She had turned her attention elsewhere, and of course that was the problem.

You poked your fingertips with a needle and eyed the spots of blood that spread and dried and then grew dark and blackened on the opened pages of your math book. To you they looked just like the freckles on your arms, the moles on your stomach, the nipples on your breasts. You took hold of your own skin, twisted it and, moaning, yanked it hard between your finger and your thumb so that later you could lie back bare in the bathtub and admire the deep purple blooms that had flowered up high on the insides of your thighs where no one else could see. You had created them and, you thought, maybe they were art.

During the week, days went by and you regularly saw Libbie come and go. In the mornings she rode to school with her father, in the convertible with the top down if the weather was good. If it weren't for the gray skirt and the brown shoes and the knee-his, Libbie might have been a movie star: Marilyn Monroe herself—fair hair covered by a black scarf, sunglasses, pink lipstick, silver bracelets, polished nails. If she happened to look up and if she happened to see you at the window watching, then she would grin and wave—"Goodbye! Goodbye!"—as her father backed the car down the driveway, turned and pulled away. And maybe you would smile and wave back.

In the evenings Libbie came home late, dropped off at the sidewalk by an unfamiliar car, in a carpool with some other girls whose names you didn't know. Libbie had lots of reasons for staying on late after school—cheerleading drills, play rehearsal, choir practice, French club. It was as if she just couldn't bear to be at home.

Some days you might see Mrs. Grandon standing out on her front porch, and she would be watching the street—the victim of a shipwreck she seemed, eyes on a vast empty ocean, searching the bare blank horizon for some flashing beacon of relief. But it was so much simpler than that: Mrs. Grandon was only waiting for her family to come back to her again. She wore a heavy sweater buttoned up and pulled in tight at the throat against the cold. She kept her arms wrapped around herself. On her face the lonesome worry of a frown had begun to etch lines that she would later have to work fiercely to erase.

When you saw her standing alone and waiting like that you felt sorry for her and you went over there and you sat in the kitchen at that table where once Mrs. Grandon had served you meals—eggs and bacon, peanut butter and jelly, fried chicken, coleslaw, French toast, hamburgers, hot dogs, pizza, sloppy Joes—and now you talked to her, recalled out loud the days gone by when John and Libbie were babies, and what that had been like for her.

But they didn't need her anymore now, she said, and asked, "Why should they?" No answer from you on that one. You were stumped. You looked around at the house that Mrs. Grandon had been keeping for her family all those years. Perfect, clean, still. Her checkered curtains at the kitchen window billowed in the breeze. Beyond the window you could just see the garden that was blooming in the back yard—the roses and tomatoes and peppers and mums. But—Mrs. Grandon looked at you then, and, genuinely puzzled, asked: "What for?"

Tears welled in her eyes, before she brusquely brushed them away, shook her head, tugged at her hair. She didn't want to be unhappy, she insisted. She was so pretty—with her careful makeup, perfect teeth, manicured nails. She did her best, she said. Took care of herself. Read books, read the papers, tried to stay in touch. She ironed her husband's underwear, folded his socks. She made glorious meals, worked to keep it different and interesting: escargot, caramelized duck, shrimp cocktail, crab Louie, vichyssoise, an elaborate cream of mushroom soup.

But no matter what, still they scorned her. Turned up their noses. Couldn't be bothered: who could eat that stuff?

Well, you could.

Mrs. Grandon took French lessons, she read novels, she played bridge, she went to Gardening Club, she gave a talk at Ladies' Literary, she volunteered her services to the Junior League, she worked crossword puzzles and acrostics when she could. She was busy all the time, it seemed. And yet...

You had no trouble at all picturing Libbie mocking

this. Rolling her eyes, gesturing the look of gabbing with her fingers and her thumb, open and shut, loose lips, flapped jaw: Blah blah blah. Who cares?

Well, you did.

And so there you sat in that calm quiet clean kitchen while the endless-seeming afternoon finally wound down toward dinnertime, and you listened to Mrs. Grandon talk.

"Watch out for yourself, Meena," she said, more than once. "Don't make the same mistakes that I did."

"I will," you promised. "I mean, I won't."

You were sitting very still so that you might not distract Mrs. Grandon from herself. It might have been that you were so good at this, so quiet, that Libbie's mother forgot you were even there. Invisibility can be an asset, sometimes. You kept your hands folded in your lap, pristine, demure. You politely sipped the milk she poured for you and politely nibbled at the cookies she baked. Maybe for a moment it felt as if it might be possible for you to become Libbie herself, and wouldn't that have been all right? If you couldn't be around your old friend anymore, well then what if you were just to become her for a while instead? Was there any harm in that?

"I almost died once, you know," Mrs. Grandon said. "When I was just a child, an infant, babe in arms." She shook her head. She had both her hands spread out flat on the polished reflective surface of the table—not a speck of dust—and she tilted her head to study them, critically it seemed. She went on: "I fell out a window, toppled down two stories, to the ground. My mother had no idea. She didn't know it. She didn't even miss me. It was my father who found me on my back in the grass when he came home from work that night. What was I doing there? He looked up, saw the open window. I must have climbed out of my crib, he figured. Then crawled across the room, clambered up onto a chair, to the sill, rolled over, and out. All right, I was a toddler then. The window had been left open because it was summer, it was hot, we didn't have air-conditioning in those days. But, I wonder, why was there no screen?"

She took deep breath, sighed. "My mother was napping and she didn't know. It wasn't her fault. She cried and cried. They poked me all over, but they didn't find anything, no scrapes, no bruises, no broken bones." She shrugged, mystified. "I seemed to be okay."

And then she went on, "When my father found me, I wasn't even crying. I was just lying there on my back in the grass, gazing up at the sky. I was happy! Imagine that! Sometimes I think I can see again now what I saw then. I close my eyes and there it is: that perfect vast endless deep unbroken space. Where did I think I was? I was only a baby. So then how was it that I could know? And now, how is it that I can still remember?"

What you were seeing was a pool of cold sunlight. Speckled linoleum. A faucet, dripping. The cold comma of your mother's stolid body and the dark curl of your own self nestled in against it. Your finger, tracing the waxy outline of Agnes Krejci's face. What you were hearing was that buzzing sound, a wasp caught, and the close whisper of your own breath.

Mrs. Grandon had stopped talking. She was studying her hands again, turning the gold band and the diamond on her left ring finger around and around, thoughtfully.

She glanced at the clock above the sink, and sighed. "They'll be home soon," she said. It was getting dark outside. Mrs. Grandon offered you more cookies, more milk, but you declined. "I'd better get going," you said. You leaned in close to kiss her lightly on the cheek. Her skin was like powdered paper, and there was still that faint smell of cloves.

And then it was November, and you were home, not really sick but faking it because you could only take so much and about every two weeks you'd have to give up and stay at home in bed. Just being yourself all the time exhausted you. Shade pulled down, curtains drawn, blankets yanked up over your head. Dreaming, maybe: something vague, dark and wet and warm. Drifting on that imagined boat again, alone in the world, if there still was one. Until a sound brought you back, a banging at the front door, and you came to. You sat up, alarmed. Outside, a siren was wailing. Had there been a nuclear attack then? That was your first thought. It was always your first thought. Fear and longing, both at once. All those images that you and Libbie had dreamed up when you were kids came swimming into your mind: the rubble, the silence, the two of you, alone.

"Meena?"

It was Mrs. Grandon, standing on the front porch. Her hair was all a mess—she hadn't curled or combed it, and it stuck out all over, made her look crazy.

When you opened the door, she stumbled and fell toward you. "Oh thank God, you're here." She'd been crying. Her face was a mess: puffy, no lipstick, eyes outlined in black mascara circles.

Behind her, Otis Road was quiet. No bombs. No rubble. Only old Mrs. Bickel standing in her yard, looking up at the sky as if she thought it might be about to come down all at once all around her. And in the distance, sirens.

If you had been in school, you would have known. Later Libbie told you that they'd announced it over the intercom, just after lunch. The President had been shot, he was dead, school was over, get your things, go home. All those Catholic girls, crying and wailing, grasping at the little gold crosses that they wore around their necks, rolling their eyes heavenward in imitation of the battered saints that glowed in the glass of the cathedral windows and stooped on the pillars of the bridge. Nuns flapping up and down the halls, rattling their rosaries, shooing everyone away.

Friday, November 22, 1963, who could forget it? Even if you wanted to, you couldn't, they wouldn't let you. Everybody has a story, isn't that what they say? If you were alive then, you have to remember. You don't have a choice.

You loved it, that weekend: the crisis, the drama, the unpredictability. It was like a holiday. Stores closed, flags flying at half-mast, the whole public spectacle. It just got better and better. You hung around with the others at the Grandons' house, because they had the best television set, and you watched the news reports, hour after hour, image after image, trying to put the pieces together and follow the story even as it was unfolding before your very eyes. It wasn't that you were wishing for bad things to happen, but that week was the beginning of what would become for you a lifelong habit of gaping at calamity.

Mrs. Grandon was truly in her element, too. John called her "the master of disaster." Making sandwiches, baking cookies, sweeping into the room with a bowl of popcorn, bottles of pop. And crying, she was always crying. With a little laugh, she'd brush away the tears that kept welling up into her eyes. She was so happy.

She loved the crisis, too. "Oh, isn't Jackie beautiful?" she kept asking. In her widow's clothes.

Mr. Grandon stayed as far away from it all as he could. As if he could smell the storm coming, he braced himself against it by simply going on about the business of his life. This man who had been prepared to survive a nuclear attack by taking shelter from it in a concrete bunker that he'd built with his own two hands could not even acknowledge the strange accumulation of thunderclouds that had already begun to build up inexorably around his wife. He went to work in the mornings and came home again in the evenings, as if nothing had happened. As if he thought there might still be people out there shopping for houses.

Josef Krejci also went to work every day as if nothing were happening and nothing had changed. This was one thing he and Mr. Grandon finally could agree on: life goes on, with or without you, whether you like it or not. To your father the spectacle of John Fitzgerald Kennedy's death seemed improper, as it was played over and over again on the television.

"Why dwell on bad news? Why not get on with things, if you can? A grocer can't afford to mourn," he said. And, "Everybody's still got to eat, don't they?"

Yes, they did. The cash register at the store chimed all day long.

Two weeks later, the excitement was all over. Lee Harvey Oswald was dead. JFK was buried. Jack Ruby was in jail. Wellington Heights was quiet again and everyone was back at work or back at school or out shopping, running errands, thinking about the Christmas holidays coming up. Or if they were at home, they were inside. There was no traffic on Otis Road. It was early winter, cold and still, and the afternoon had already begun to sink down toward dusk. In a few more minutes the streetlights would come on.

Faye Grandon dragged a bedroom chair across the carpet, over to the open window. She knelt on the cushion and hoisted herself up to the sill. Ladylike, awkward, in a rose-colored cashmere shift, matching jacket with a fake fur collar, dyed-to-match rose silk pumps. A string of pearls. White cotton gloves. A headband holding her hair back from her face. That slight upward curl, gentle flirty flip at the ends. Jacqueline, the beautiful widow, serene in her horror and noble in her grief. She sat there on the sill with her feet hanging over, legs crossed at the ankles, hands folded in her lap. She wasn't nervous. She was relaxed, in fact, calm, content, happy even. She lit a cigarette, closed her eyes, exhaled smoke. From there she could see the tops of the houses all up and down Otis Road. Chimneys, shake shingles, terra cotta tiles. A glint of the river. A frowning saint.

One of her shoes was loose on her foot. She let it dangle from her toes, let it slip off and fall, leaned forward to see it land. She wobbled, caught her balance, gasped. She stubbed the cigarette out against the sill. She fiddled with her hair. Pursed her lips. Considered the sky. Finally she wrapped her arms around herself and shivered, then leaned, rolling forward, tumbling away from herself toward the momentary indulgence of that one sweet unencumbered fall.

Later, after the ambulance had come and gone, Mr. Grandon stood in his yard with his hands on his hips and his head tilted back as he looked up at the bedroom window and silently measured the distance, trying to puzzle out what had happened, what his wife had meant by what she'd done. Maybe it was an accident, as Libbie suggested. Her father nodded, sucked his teeth, shook his head, mystified. "Had to be," he agreed. "What else?"

Never mind that Mrs. Grandon had paid Leo Spivak ten dollars to take down the storm window for her that morning. When he'd asked her what for, she told him something about how she wanted to clean it up, or paint it, or replace it, he couldn't remember exactly what it was she said. Ten dollars was ten dollars, and that was good enough for Leo.

John shook his head, shivered. His profile was sharp, eyes watery, nose raw. All week he had been coming down with a cold. She'd done it on purpose, according to him. Obviously. She was trying to kill herself. Anybody could see that. He sniffed. Swiped at his face with the back of his hand. What was so pathetic, he went on, was just how poorly she had judged the height and calculated the fall, how greatly she had overestimated what would be the actual force of the impact. He shrugged his shoulders, irritably, and turned away.

A broken collar bone. A concussion. A few bruises. A grass-stained dress that no one would ever wear again. And that was it.

"My wife isn't well," Mr. Grandon explained. She was a danger to herself, as anyone could see. Six weeks at the Cedarcrest Retreat in Rampage, undergoing a rest cure—warm baths, plain food, deep sleep—*that* would help her feel better, *that* would make her good as new.

July 2006

Meena wakes again and outside in the forest it is raining. Not a downpour, not a storm. Just this sweet warm whispery rain coming down like a marvel out of an improbable sunny blue sky. Where are the clouds? The way the bed is placed, against a wall that faces a wide window, and the way that she is lying on it, all she can see is the tops of the trees and the rain like Christmas tinsel falling through them. She gets up and crosses the room to stand at the window, to look out the back into the trees as the rain dwindles, slows, and stops.

The forest is shining damp and fresh, shimmering brand-new, and Meena feels as if she has a newness too, in her way. She seems to be seeing everything so clearly: the very acuity of her vision causes her to squint. The deep black bark of the tall pines. The silvery wind-turned leaves of the aspens. Shafts of yellow sunlight filtering down to the dry needle blanket of the forest floor. And then, as Meena watches, the form of a deer materializes in the forest umbra, then steps out into the light. How long has it been here? Like the hidden figure in a child's picture puzzle, nothing more than an incoherent tangle of contour until you've found a way to eye it just so, and then there it is… a deer.

And now a voice is calling out, from very far away it seems at first. "Libbie!" the call comes, muted. "Libbie?"

The deer freezes in response. It stares, then startles

sideways, turns and bounds off into the shadows of the trees again. There is a tapping at the door, and when Meena responds, there is Holly, smiling.

"You're up," she says.

Meena nods.

"Hungry?"

Meena nods again. She feels like a child, although she is at least twice as old as this girl.

"What time is it?"

"Almost two. You've been asleep all morning."

Holly has pulled her hair back from her forehead with a child's pink plastic headband. The silver ring in her eyebrow glints, and the skin around it is rosy, sore-looking. Infected? She is wearing a thin summer dress under a green wool cardigan sweater, with socks and boots on her feet. The sweater glitters with moisture from the recent rain.

"Listen, Will and I have some lunch made, it's nothing fancy, but if you want to join us?"

Meena starts to beg off, "That's so nice, but I couldn't—"

But Holly interrupts: "Sure you could. Come on. Bring your stuff and I'll give you a lift back down to your car." That settled, she turns away, and Meena doesn't know what else to do but pull her shoes on, grab her purse and her suitcase, and follow. She is starving.

The narrow path takes them through the trees to a wider trail that then wends its way downhill to a dilapidated shack, limp as an old hat. The roof is warped; the front porch sags. The big yellow pickup is parked to the side, and next to it an old school bus kneels on concrete blocks, windshield shattered and going nowhere. The narrow yard is overrun with dandelions. And now here's Will Gidding, stepping away from a smoking barbecue. He's grinning, so glad to see her, it seems. As if he's been expecting her, and hoping she would show up.

"Libbie!" He opens his arms, hugs Meena awkwardly. His body is soft, large, warm, and she feels like a crooked stick caught there in the cushion of his generous embrace. He is wearing rumpled khaki shorts, and a bright flowered shirt hangs over his broad belly, incongruously tropical-looking here in this mountain setting. A black baseball cap covers the thin wisps of his hair. He has been cooking hamburgers for lunch.

He takes her suitcase and sets it on the grass, then guides her to a battered redwood picnic table. "Come on now and sit down. Make yourself at home." He waves a hand to encompass their surroundings. "Welcome to our little compound!"

She sits, keeps her purse in her lap, as if it were a last vestige of her self. "Thank you."

"No sweat," he says. "You want a Coke or a beer or something?"

"Sure… um, Coke."

"Hey, Holly," he calls, heading back to his barbecue again, "be kind enough to serve our guest, wouldja?"

A square red cooler squats in the green shade at the bare base of a nearby pine. Holly obediently digs into the ice, extracts a dripping can, and hands it to Meena with a smile. Will, back at the barbecue again, beams, delighted.

Holly twists the cap off a bottle of beer for herself and takes a seat on the bench across the table from Meena. Behind her, the twisted iron sign—RAGNAROK—is framed between the two tall posts that mark the entrance to the yard.

Meena sips her soda. The fizz stings her sinuses,

the sugar bites her tongue, maybe the caffeine will make her headache go away. What she really wants right now is a cigarette. She's hoping that maybe Holly will light up, and then she can ask to bum one for herself.

Will is happily flipping burgers. He flashes her a smile. "So, how'd the cabin work out?" he asks. "You find everything you need there?"

"Oh, yes, it's nice. Very nice. I love it."

He nods his head. "Good. Good. You staying long?"

She's not sure what he means. But before she can respond, he goes on, "Because of course it's yours for as long as you want it. That's what it's for, you know."

She looks at Holly, who shrugs.

"I'm afraid I don't understand."

Will is pulling buns out of a plastic sack, opening them, spreading them flat upon the grill.

Holly takes a drink of beer, swallows back a burp, leans forward to explain. "This place used to be a lodge, see, about a million years ago. The owners got old and they let it fall apart. Then along comes my brother and he's crazy enough to think he can see some potential in the place. Thinks he's going to bring it back to life again. The old owners were happy to let him take it off their hands."

Will is at once effusive and evasive, behind his wide smile and beyond the nervous-seeming skitter of his eyes. He waves the spatula in a circle that encompasses the shack and the yard, the entryway, the woods all around. "Welcome to my world," he says. "Our refuge, if you will. For when the time comes. For when we need it."

"Need it?"

He nods. "And meanwhile, the cabin you are staying in just happens to be available for rent. Aspenglo, we call it. Pretty, isn't it?"

Holly interrupts. "I already told Libbie I'd give her a lift down to her car."

Will is visibly deflated. "All right, he says. "If that's what she wants."

Before Meena can respond, Holly is nodding and speaking for her. "It's what she wants, Will. You know that."

"Well, all right. I guess that's settled then." He grins at Meena. "You sure weren't in any shape to drive yourself anyplace last night."

Meena blushes, embarrassed. "I was pretty upset, I guess. I don't drink much, normally. Not whiskey anyway. And I didn't have much to eat either. I'm sorry."

He waves the spatula at her, in dismissal. "Not your fault," he says.

"That dog...," Meena starts.

He closes his eyes, shakes his head. "We've been through all that already, haven't we?"

"Can we please not talk about the dog?" Holly asks.

"It was an accident," Will says, setting the record straight, once and for all. "It was an old dog. Old Woody, he was an old dog and he had a good long life. Better and longer than he deserved, probably. Likely wouldn't have made it through another winter up here anyway." He smiles. "Nuff said."

"But still, it was my fault..." Meena isn't sure anymore what, exactly, they are talking about. A dog?

Will has put the buns and the burgers on a platter that he carries over and places on the center of the table. "Hey those Mexicans at the gas station are probably thankful," he says. "One less mouth to feed, right? You did them a favor." He turns away and disappears into his shack.

Holly is absent-mindedly picking at the label on her beer, shaking the shreds of paper from her fingers, letting them flake down onto the grass. The dandelions seem to swarm and nod.

"Well, I still feel like I should do something," Meena says. "At least pay to have it taken care of. Cremated, or whatever." On the platter, the hot hamburgers steam, and Meena's stomach lurches at the smell. She coughs into her fist.

Holly is squinting at her, searching Meena's face carefully. "You know, shit happens. You really shouldn't be so hard on yourself."

Meena nods, and blinks back a sting of tears, overwhelmed by hunger, and misery, and gratitude for what seems to be the easy kindness of this thin girl with her sharp dark hair, her tattooed skin so pale it's almost translucent. Is this what is going on? she wonders. Everything is disintegrating, fading off, becoming less and less distinct until eventually it will all just mist away completely and here she'll be, alone?

Once upon a time, Matka said, people took their unwanted babies out into the forest and they left them there in the open to die. Abandoned and exposed, screaming. Left to freeze in the snow or drown in the rain, to bake in the sun and be eaten by coyotes or bobcats or crows. If an infant cries out in the forest, does anybody hear?

"Will says you're on your way to California."

Meena nods. Is that really where she's headed?

"I've always wanted to go to California," Holly goes on, dreamily, then asks, "So is that where you live?"

Meena doesn't want to lie because that would be ungrateful, wouldn't it? She doesn't want to say yes and agree to something that's so completely untrue, but at the same time she knows it isn't safe for her to say no, either. And maybe she really is going to California. Why not? She solves the problem by not saying anything at all. She nods, distracted by the glint of the eyebrow ring that pierces Holly's face. Why would someone wear such an ugly thing? Why would she do that to herself? Isn't it painful? Or is it beautiful? It looks swollen, inflamed, and Meena feels herself begin to swoon, with nausea and hunger. She braces herself against the table top with both hands. Steady now. Hold on. Get a grip.

"What's it like there?" Holly is asking. "In California, I mean."

Of course the truth is that Meena has never been to California. But: "Well it's like anyplace else, I guess. Except it's warmer. And there are palm trees. And of course the ocean."

"No I mean, what's it like living there? Do you have a house?"

Meena thinks about this for a moment. A house? Or an apartment? A condominium? A bungalow maybe, up in the Hollywood Hills? She can see that Holly is watching her more closely now. Maybe she knows that Meena is lying? Maybe she has known this all along.

"Well it's nothing like this, that's for sure," Meena says, which could mean anything, so she goes on: "I mean, it's so pretty here. And peaceful." Her voice has started to sound more substantial to her now, and that's reassuring. Big and empty.

"You can say that again," Holly replies. "Nowhere, nothing, no one. The wilderness is just up the trail, about three miles. And after that, it just goes on forever."

"The wilderness?"

"Beyond the trails. Get lost there, and you're pretty much lost for good. Lions and tigers and bears, right?

Nobody will find you out there. They won't even bother to look." She snaps her fingers. "Gone! Whoosh."

Meena smiles, nods. She's a normal woman having a normal conversation with another normal person. No big deal. Small talk, that's all this is. "And what about you?" she asks. "Have you lived here long?"

Holly shrugs. "Since winter. We were down in Durango before that. Will wanted us to come up here where we'd be safe."

"Safe?"

Holly grins. "He thinks we're at the End of Days, Libbie, didn't he tell you that last night?" She smirks. "Because if he didn't, then you'd be the first person I know who hasn't had to listen to him go on about it. He loves to go on about it. It's all he thinks about."

Meena nods, remembering. Tribulation. Armageddon. Apocalypse. "He really believes all that?"

Holly smiles. "I suppose you thought it was a come-on or something."

Meena is confused. "A come-on?"

"You thought he was flirting with you, right?"

She can feel the blush rising in her throat, her chest, her ears. "No, I..."

Holly crashes on. "Well, he wasn't. He's dead serious. He says the signs are everywhere. And I guess if you think about it, they are. Flood. Famine. Earthquakes. Plague. If you ask me, I think he's looking forward to it, in his way." She lowers her voice, winks, whispers behind her hand: "It turns him on, if you know what I mean."

Meena doesn't know what to say to this. It is too crazy. Idiot's delight, her father would say. Radical Christian hogwash. But who is Meena Krejci to judge? What does she know, after all? Not much, she thinks. In fact, hardly anything at all. "Well..." That's all she can manage. "Well."

Will comes out of the shack balancing a large tray of plates and napkins and flatware, a bowl of salad, and a bag of potato chips. A bottle of ketchup is tucked under one arm, mustard under the other.

"He has a shelter," Holly says.

Will is proud. "Sure I do."

Holly is mocking, sarcastic. "Loony tunes," she says. "And who'd want to survive something as bad as that anyway?"

Will is unfazed. This is an old argument, long familiar to them both. "That's just fine for you to ask now," he says, still smiling, "when you're sitting here safe and sound, well-fed and cozy, without any real threat to your self or soul."

He bows his head and folds his hands. "Thank you, Lord, for this food. Bless it and bless us poor fools who are about to eat it. Amen."

And Meena murmurs, "Amen."

He's passed a plate to Meena, and she helps herself to a burger. Juicy. Dripping grease. She sniffs at it, then takes a nibble, feels her stomach churn with resistance and puts it down. Dabs at her lips with a napkin, smiles.

Holly is forking salad onto a plate for herself.

"But survival, that's what life is all about, isn't it?" Will goes on. He's eating heartily. He's dribbled mustard on his shirt in the process, but the stain blends nicely with the wild pattern of the fabric and is hardly noticeable.

"Is it?" Meena asks.

"Well sure it is." He grins and chews.

Holly pokes at her salad. "If you ask me I'd say there are plenty of lives around that aren't worth saving."

This embarrasses Meena. She'd like to get away

from here, be on her own, in her car again, traveling, even if she doesn't have any idea where to. But she doesn't want to be rude. These people have been kind to her—they've sheltered her, they've fed her, they've even forgiven what she's done. She owes them something in return, she thinks, even if it's only her interest in them for a while.

"So where is it, this shelter of yours?" she asks Will.

Holly pouts. "Over there. My worst nightmare."

Meena looks, sees nothing. The shack, the pickup, the school bus. Will is grinning.

"Aw now come on, little sister. Some day you're going to be thanking me for this. I promise you, you will." He stands, leans toward Meena. "You want to see it?"

"Jesus, Will, let her eat something first, why dontcha? She's got a long drive ahead of her."

His response is sheepish. He ducks his head. "I'm real sorry, Libbie," he says. He reaches across the table and takes her hand. "Eat, sweetheart, eat!"

She doesn't know whether to be offended by this intimacy or flattered by it. She looks to Holly for help, but she's lighting a cigarette.

Meena has been wondering whether she's been missed yet. Surely Mimi would have been expecting her to be there for work this morning when she opened up the White Elephant Shop at ten, as always. Without Meena there to do it for her, Mimi would have had to fix the coffee herself, and that was apt to make her mad. Maybe she brought donuts to share or maybe not. Likely she's on a diet again—gnawing at celery and carrots, slurping up cottage cheese, and chewing sugarless gum—because she does this often although as far as

Meena can see it never seems to make much difference, in the long run.

Pretty soon she'd start to look at the clock and peer out the front window of the shop, wondering where the heck is Meena? And then by noon she'd have begun to eye the bags and boxes of clothes that got left outside the back door over the weekend and now need to be gone through and sorted, which is usually Meena's job. Who will do that, if Meena doesn't? Not Mimi Hanrahan, that's for sure. Meena is always the one who makes the first cut, deciding what's worth keeping and what's not. She has an eye for this, Mimi has been heard to say, in an admiring way that she means for Meena to take as a compliment. But Meena knows the truth, which is that Mimi just doesn't care for going through those things herself. Because who knows what they'll find?

The White Elephant is a thrift shop in Bohemietown. Mimi buys old clothes on consignment, and she is not set up to take outright donations of other people's junk. "We're not a fucking charity," Mimi says, her voice shrill with her frustration and disgust. But nobody cares about the hairs that Mimi wants to split, and so they leave things anyway. The White Elephant buys and sells used clothes mostly, and sometimes children's toys or other knick-knacks that the women bring in, but always on consignment. Mimi has a sign outside by the back door that says this as clearly as she can think to make it: NOT A DROP OFF PLACE. But no one seems to take that sign seriously, which drives her crazy.

"Can't they read?" she asks, and lights a cigarette, blows smoke and shakes her head. Sure they can read, but they also don't care what Mimi Hanrahan wants or doesn't want. They drop their old things off just to be rid of them, because they can.

The fact of it is, Mimi could very well just have it all hauled away without even looking at it first, if she wanted to, but she can't bring herself to do that either. She just hates to take the chance, because sometimes Meena does find some things that are worth something in those bags and boxes. Mimi doesn't want to think she might be missing out on anything of value. Which leaves it up to Meena to sort through the stuff and see what's there. She wears thick leather work gloves when she does this, just in case of needles or razor blades or what have you.

Maybe because Meena's not there today Mimi will decide she ought to fire her. "Well, fuck her then," she'll say to anybody who's around to hear it. She'll make a big show of writing Meena off her list. Finger drawn across the throat. "Last cut. Finito. Kaput."

But then soon enough she'll realize how much more difficult everything is for her without Meena there to take care of the details and the dirty work.

"It's a charity job anyway," that's what Josef Krejci told his daughter. Sure not something that Meena needs to keep her going. Not by a long shot. Does she do it for the money? "No." And Mimi doesn't really need her either, does she? When Meena tried to insist, he argued, "Well, if she needs you, then why not pay you more?"

But he was wrong. Mimi does too need her. She does. Meena's voice piped higher, shrill with threatened conviction when she tried to explain this to him, but still he would not see.

Just what exactly did she think she was doing working at a job like that, in the White Elephant Shop, in Bohemietown? Knowing as she must have just how such a thing would be a humiliation to him. In these, his later years in life. He'd come so far himself—from a humble birth in one of the poorest white neighborhoods in Linwood, all the way across the river to Wellington Heights, where he made something of himself, where he became a successful businessman and a respected member of the community—and now here was Meena, his daughter, retracing his steps back across the bridge to the other side of the river. On purpose, she did this. If she was trying to get back at him for something, if it was anything he did to anger her, then please, couldn't she just get beyond it?

But it wasn't about him, Meena answered back. It was about her.

His frown was deep, and it was plain to her that he didn't believe it. "Whatever it is that has made you so mad at me, Meena," he said, "you're old enough now to have gotten over it, I think". And then he turned away.

Probably so. How could she argue with him about that? Old enough. Yes.

Meena has done her best to eat some of the food on her plate, and she thinks the result is satisfactory. She's managed to put away half the hamburger and a few bites of some salad. The Coke has settled her stomach and dimmed her headache some.

She has even offered to help clean up, but Will won't have it. He wants to show her his shelter. He's halfway across the yard, and he's calling out to her: "Libbie, come on now. You're going to love this." He's grinning and has one arm extended out toward her. She crosses the skirt of dandelion-spattered grass toward him, but she can't figure out where they're going. She sees no shelter here. And then at the school bus, he stops. Reaches out and yanks the door open. It screams on rusted hinges.

"Here, take a look."

He pulls her closer, stands back, waits while she peers inside. There are no seats, and the interior of the bus is like a big empty room, furnished with a gathering of molded plastic chairs, a pair of cots, metal shelves stocked with bottled water and canned food. Daylight is prismed by the shattered windshield, casting shadow and bringing glimmer both at once.

Will nudges her inside ahead of him, and then heaves himself up after her, pulling the door shut behind them. His bulk crowds the small space, and his smell is warm—salty, sweaty, meaty, smoky. Meena has no choice but to get out of the way, turn and sink into one of the plastic chairs.

"Wow," she says, knowing that her speechlessness will please him.

"Ingenious, isn't it?"

She looks around, nodding, admiring. "Yes. Sure is."

He spreads his arms, to encompass the big picture, and between the buttons of his shirt, his belly button winks.

"See," Will says, "we're completely on our own here. We have everything we need. Our own electric generator by way of an automotive engine—I've added an extra twelve-volt battery there under the hood, and with an inverter we can run an entire household full of appliances off it, if that's what we want to do. I've got the plans to install a solar panel, too. That's next. Then we'll be able to keep the batteries charged, even after all the gas supplies get too expensive or run out. I can boil water from the creek, or use bleach to purify melted snow, if I have to. I've got a stove, I've got wood, and even if I do run out of packaged food, still there's wild game all around here. Deer, elk. Even bear. And, once I get some tires on this thing, then the whole shebang will also be mobile. We'll be able to go wherever we want to. We can show up where we're needed. Anytime."

Meena shifts in her chair. She eyes the cans and bottles on the shelves. "But why? What is it for?"

"I told you. End of days. Bad times coming."

Meena looks at him. "How do you know that?" she asks.

He shrugs. "Signs, Libbie, signs. Israel's return to power, rampant immorality, famines, violence, wars."

"But what if you're wrong?"

His smile is patient now, and smug. "I'm not. Believe me, I'm not. It's all right there in the Bible. They said this would happen, and now it is. Just look around. Earthquakes, fires, hurricanes, floods. Libbie, honey, I'm not making this stuff up." He leans closer. "It's all around us. And it's real."

His eyes are searching hers, and her face feels scorched by the close attention.

Holly is at the door. Sunlight shafts in.

"Sorry, Will," she says. "I hate to spoil your party, but I gotta go. Libbie, you still want that ride?"

Meena stands. "Yes, thank you. And thank you for the food. It's been very nice to meet you both. I... I wish you both the best of luck."

"Our pleasure, Libbie, our pleasure," Will says. He takes her hand between his own and holds it for a moment, as he holds her with his gaze, both serious and entreating. "And when the end comes, now you remember us, all right? If you can find your way back here again, we'll keep you safe. I promise."

She is embarrassed by this, too, but she manages to pull herself away. "Thank you. Thanks. I don't know how to thank you." In the yard she picks up her suitcase, backs awkwardly away, and follows Holly to the yellow pickup.

On the narrow road, the chassis rocks along the shale. On the radio an evangelist rants about sacrifice and salvation. Holly taps the steering wheel with her hand, then reaches forward and shuts the radio off. She turns to Meena, her look serious, the metal in her face glinting. "He's crazy, okay. You don't have to say it, I already know."

"Well, but it's so beautiful here. Even so."

Holly nods. "Sure, if you like trees and a whole lot of nothing going on, that is."

"If that's how you feel, why do you stay?"

She snorts. "Where else am I going to go?"

"Wherever you want to, I guess."

"California?"

"Why not?"

"Well, for one thing, I don't have any way to get there. For another, I'm flat broke. And besides that, if I'm not here, who'll take care of Will?"

"Does he need taking care of?"

She snorts again. "He thinks he knows what he's doing, but he doesn't. You heard him. He's got all these crazy ideas. Somebody's got to keep him real. Might as well be me, I guess. There sure isn't anybody else to do it."

The Jetta has been moved and is parked outside the Grizzly Grill across the street from the gas station. Sunlight twinkles on its chrome.

Holly pulls the truck up alongside it and turns to Meena. "Well it was very nice to meet you Libbie," she says. "You have a nice trip, okay? Say hi to California for me."

Meena has climbed down from the truck and turned to get her suitcase from the back when Holly says, "The license plates on your car are from Iowa."

Meena freezes for a moment, then shrugs. "It's not my car."

Holly frowns, waits to hear more.

"It belongs to my father." Meena clears her throat, and goes on. "He's dead."

This is the first time she's said it out loud.

Tears well up, and now she's crying again, helplessly. Holly scrambles down and takes Meena in her thin arms, holds her. Whispers, "Libbie, it's all right. I'm sorry. Don't cry. Oh Libbie honey, please, please don't cry."

After a while, Meena shakes herself free. "Thank you," she says. And then, "I guess I'd better go."

Not until she's pulled out onto the road will Meena realize she's going the wrong way, away from the main highway instead of back toward it. A glance in the rearview mirror shows Holly standing by the yellow truck, hands on her hips, watching. Shaking her head.

And then it will be the Wal-Mart where she pulls in to turn around that gets Meena thinking about those four or five convicts who escaped from that prison down in Texas a while ago. They were able to get hold of some weapons somehow, and they overcame their guards, changed into uniforms, and rode out in disguise through the front gates, driving a sheriff's van into freedom right under the noses of their jailers. Or anyway, it was something like that. Then there was a car waiting for them in the local Wal-Mart parking lot. It had been left there by a sympathetic relative, and sometime in the middle of the night they broke into the store and helped themselves to clean clothes and toiletries, cigarettes and snack foods, shoes and hats and hair dye. Everything was going along according to plan until the night watchman happened to catch them in the act and they had to kill him, which upped the ante so high that pretty soon they were back in jail again and on death row in Texas.

But during those few weeks before they were caught those boys were on the run and their story got told over and over again, in regular reports on the nightly news. At first it was thought that they'd headed down toward Mexico, and then a while later they were reported sighted in California. Another rumor had it that they were in Oklahoma, or maybe it was Arizona, but when they finally were found it was in a trailer park near Colorado Springs, where they'd been posing as a group of church-going, law-abiding Bible thumpers, friendly young men who were wholly sincere-seeming to the folks who came into contact with them during that time.

The night the men were caught, Meena happened to be watching the news with her father, they were eating supper together on trays set up in front of the TV set and waiting for "Jeopardy" to come on. Joe Krejci liked to play along with that show, and he was pretty good at it, Meena had to admit, considering how old he was. She was waiting for the news to be over so she could go clean up the kitchen and then slip out the back door for a minute to smoke a cigarette, knowing that her father would be so engrossed in the game that he wouldn't get up to see what she was doing, even though she'd sworn to him that she had quit. But then the story came on saying that the fugitives had been apprehended, and so Meena stayed put where she was and watched.

They were saying that one of the men had already killed himself. He blew his own brains out in the bathroom of a motel as soon as he was sure the game was over, but the other two were either more cowardly or more courageous than that, depending on how you wanted to look at it, and they surrendered. They came out with their hands up—one shirtless with his big belly hanging out over his belt and the other one wearing a bandana on his head like a gypsy. They both had neatly trimmed goatees that made them seem stylish, especially with the bleached hair and tattooed shoulders. The one in the bandana wore wire-rimmed glasses that made him seem smart when he was explaining later about the inhumane conditions they'd been forced to live under while they were in jail. It was hard to remember that these two men were both hardened criminals, a danger to themselves and a menace to everybody else. Both men were filmed telling reporters that they'd rather die than go back to prison for the rest of their lives, and if they'd had the chance they would have put their guns to their own heads, too, just as their friend had done. But now they'd be happy to let the state do that dirty work for them, if that's what everybody wanted.

Josef Krejci said that was just bragging and when push came to shove they'd know they didn't mean it, not really. "Nobody wants to die," he said, and Meena didn't disagree. Now it occurs to her that he was probably only talking about himself.

Just those few weeks of freedom that those men had, when nobody knew who they really were, that had made the whole thing seem worth it, they said. Even what happened to the night watchman, though they were sorry about that, it was unavoidable, he'd put himself in the way of harm and they'd had no choice but to shoot him if they wanted to be free. Which they did. In the worst way.

It was all worth it, they insisted, and Meena

thought she understood what they meant then, and she thinks maybe she also has a little bit of understanding of it now even more.

Because here she is at the Wal-Mart herself, stocking up on her own sorts of necessities, including an expensive box of hair color: Golden Honey Blonde.

He'll be buried in the Bohemie Cemetery, Meena thinks, between Matka and my mother, his mother and his wife. There's a space there for Meena, too, a plot that he bought her for her birthday when she turned twenty-one. When Meena mentioned this fact once, at first Mimi thought it was funny but then after she thought about it for a while, she got mad.

"Who gives a cemetery plot to someone on their birthday?" Mimi wanted to know.

Meena appreciated her friend's outrage, but she also knew that her father didn't mean it like that. "A cemetery plot costs a lot of money," Meena explained. "It's like a piece of real estate in a way, an investment."

Mimi studied her nails. "You're full of shit," she said.

"You don't understand," Meena said. "How could you? And anyway, that was a long time ago."

But Mimi just looked at her and shook her head. She lit two cigarettes, one for Meena and one for herself, then shook her head again. They were sitting on stools behind the counter at The White Elephant, taking a break from sorting through a box of winter sweaters, checking them for moth holes before they were folded for display. It had been snowing all morning, and so hardly anyone had come in to buy anything, which made Mimi cranky, but Meena didn't mind it when they had the place to themselves, cozy and warm and all lit up in the middle of the day. She was handling a dove gray cashmere cardigan with white pearl buttons and an embroidered collar and cropped sleeves. It made her think of Christmas and it reminded her of Mrs. Grandon; it looked like something she would have worn.

"You've got that right," Mimi said. "I don't understand a man who could think ahead for his daughter like that. And if you want to know the truth, I hope I never do."

Which made Meena want to explain and make Mimi see the situation, how much she and her father depended upon each other, because between them that was all they had and all that they could do. There just wasn't anybody else. Not Meena's mother. Not Matka. Just Josef and Meena. He looked after her and she looked after him.

"He's a wonderful man," Meena said to Mimi. "He's really brilliant. I admire him. I do."

But Mimi just rolled her eyes. "Okay, Meena, whatever you say." She crushed out her cigarette and heaved herself up to her feet and went back to work on the sweaters again.

Meena wasn't angry. She could see that Mimi just didn't understand. But, how could she? Mimi Hanrahan was just some Rompot trash who'd never even had a father. What would someone like that know about a daughter's true devotion to her dad?

When he had to sell his grocery store, that was a time that just about broke Josef Krejci's heart. But there wasn't any way around it because the bigger Hawkeye store up on Vernon Boulevard had moved in and taken away all his business, and he was losing money every day, whether he stayed open or was closed. The land itself was still worth something though, and so Joe

Krejci made arrangements to sell the lot to a developer who had no interest in groceries but planned to bring in a bulldozer, raze the structure, and put up some apartment units in its place.

At that time, Joe had been keeping up with what little trade he still had from day to day, but he'd let the inventories run way low in order to keep down the cost of operations, only stocking up on those things that he could be certain he could sell. That meant that when it came time to close Krejci's doors for good, there wasn't much left worth salvaging or selling, and so he decided that instead he'd just give it all away. Let the Hawkeye—with their fluorescent lights and their twenty-four hour service, with their bagboys and cashiers and checkout stands, with all their specials and discounts and coupons—let them suffer one night of weakened business then. They deserved it, he said, if anybody did.

Cans of tuna, soup, and Spam, bags of beans and rice, powdered potatoes, onions, carrots, corn, loaves of old bread starting to go stale. It wasn't much, but it was something.

Give it away to who? Meena asked.

"To whoever needs it," he answered, grinning. He opened his arms, a generous man exposing the full breadth of his most expansive self. "To anyone and everyone who comes."

He printed some flyers—"Free Food! Krejci's! 7:00 pm!"—and tacked them up on phone poles. He hired a polka band to set up in the parking lot and play. He strung up lanterns and twinkle lights—to make it festive, he said. Make it seem more like a party, more like a celebration than a loss.

No sense in crying over what was already gone, that was Josef Krejci's philosophy. By which he meant the past, Meena thought. The way things used to be for him, when he was young and his wife was still alive and they still had hope for their future and for their lives in it together. Before Meena came along.

And then, "We're lucky, Meena!" he exclaimed. "We'll never have to work again!"

He put away his white apron for the occasion and spent over fifty dollars on a rented black tuxedo with a crisp white shirt and a peacock blue vest.

"Put on your best dress," he told his daughter, grinning. "We're going out tonight!"

If she was worried at first that they'd be mobbed, by the time it was dark at eight o'clock she was more concerned that no one was going to bother to show up at all. The band was playing and Meena was sitting on the back steps, in the orange chiffon that she'd bought to wear to a dance she went to once when she still did that sort of thing. It was a bit too tight in the waist now for comfort, and much too full in the sleeves to be in fashion anymore, but it was the best she had and the color did flatter her face, she'd been told. Her father was pacing, his polished leather shoes shining in the twinkle lights, and she didn't think she could stand to see him disappointed that night.

But then she didn't have to, because sure enough one by one some people finally did begin to straggle in. First, an old woman pulling a wagon. Then, a young couple pushing a toddler in a stroller. A family with six children and an old dog crouched down low in the bed of a battered pickup truck. And finally, this bum in a big wool overcoat.

Meena saw him coming up the line, feet shuffling in a pair of two-toned leather wing-tip golf shoes that looked at least one size too big for him. His face was half-hidden behind his briary beard and the long matted tangles of his hair, but his eyes were clearly visible, and there was something about them, a look of amusement it seemed. Or recognition, maybe? When she handed him his bag of groceries, he smiled and bowed and thanked her, then turned away, and she kept thinking: "Don't I know that man? Isn't he someone...?"

The band was playing a rousing song—"Oomp-ah-pah, oomp-ah-pah, oomp-ah-pah-pah!"—and from that in Meena's mind there was a melody; it came rising up out of the bog of old memory, unbidden.

"Catch a falling star and put it in your pocket. Save it for a rainy day."

At that moment she looked down to see her father's hand on her arm—his pale skin shining against the bright orange of her sleeve, his face turned and peering down at her, pursed lips, niggling little frown, his voice a heavy rumble that seemed to be coming from somewhere far away, so deep and powerful and reassuring: "Meena? Are you all right?"

And then something happened, there was a shift in things—a baby was crying, a mother had bent to slap out at a child's grasping hand, there was a ruckus in the line, and everybody turned to look.

Deep Eddie.

This was so many years later and of course it wasn't him, it couldn't have been him. Could it? Meena was panting at the possibility of this, feeling her chest lock up and her breath come short, while this mother continued to slap and shout at her child and Joe Krejci had turned to lift another bag of groceries to give away. The polka band was striking up another tune, something slower and more solemn this time. And that baby kept on wailing, a high and rising frantic scream.

But when Meena craned forward, when she stood on tiptoe and tried to look out over what seemed to her then to be a sea of bobbing heads and grateful open faces, the man was gone.

Meena's father was pushing another sack of food into her hands. The teenage girl with the red-faced hitching baby on her hip was reaching out and grinning up at him. Chewing gum. Saying, "Hey, thanks man."

Probably, Meena thinks, Mimi Hanrahan was mad when she didn't show up for work this morning, when she didn't even bother to call to let her know that she was sick or whatever the reason she had for not coming in, and so she tried to call Meena a couple of times this morning, to chew her out, and when there wasn't any answer at lunchtime she got worried, or even more pissed off, so maybe she decided to go over and find out what was wrong. First thing she'd notice would be the mail in the box and the newspapers on the porch. Next thing, no car in the driveway.

She'd be mad, then she'd be worried, then puzzled and finally afraid. She'd try the doors, but they were all locked. She'd peek into the windows and see the empty rooms, clean and still, spotless the way Meena left them. She'd knock and ring the bell, but nobody would answer. She'd go back to work and keep trying to call Meena, and then finally she'd decide to call the police.

Everybody on the block will be watching when the squad car pulls up, Meena thinks. She's seen this on TV a hundred times. The neighbors come out and stand on their porches, or they peek out between the curtains in their windows, or they gather in little groups on the sidewalk at the edge of the yard. Breaking news.

Mimi will show the cops where the key to the back door is kept hidden under a fake rock in the dirt beside the steps, so they won't have to knock the door down. When they go inside, they'll smell him first, and then they'll find him, dead the way Meena left him. In the beginning they are going to wonder what happened to him. Then they'll wonder what happened to Meena. They'll guess that she's been kidnapped, and then the machinery will start to turn and they'll try to find her. Meena thinks: Everyone who knows me must be worried sick.

Outside the Wal-Mart, in the parking lot, Meena sits in her car and fiddles with the radio to try to find some news and maybe learn something about herself that way. But out here in the middle of nowhere, there isn't much reception. And besides, she realizes, her disappearance—if it even gets noticed at all—isn't likely to be a big enough deal to anybody that it would make the national news. Not like some car bomb in the Middle East or a volcano in the Philippines or an execution in Oklahoma.

Finally she gives up and goes back inside to the pay phone, but when she calls home there's no answer. The phone just rings and rings, thin and weak on her end, but slamming into the silence of those dead and empty rooms on the other, she knows. That no one picks up doesn't really mean anything, she reasons. Either they have found him by now, or they haven't yet. Either there is no one there but Meena's dead father, lying in his bed in the heat of that house, rotting down into the mattress, stinking up the place... and who is going to clean it? Meena? But how could anyone be expected to want to come home to something like that?

After a while the sound of the phone ringing in her ear has started to sound like a person who is screaming, somebody small and far away and afraid, and she thinks for a split second that it might be her, but of course it isn't. She hasn't panicked yet. Not yet. She replaces the receiver slowly and carefully, with firm deliberateness, shutting it up like mother putting her hand over a child's mouth to make it stop crying.

Or else he isn't there anymore and they've taken him away. That's just as likely a possibility, isn't it?

She dials Mimi Hanrahan's number next, and Mimi picks up right away, so fast it scares Meena into silence.

Mimi says, "Hello?" three times before she loses patience. Then, "Fuck you!," and she slams down the phone.

Good old Mimi, Meena thinks. She tries again. "Mimi?"

"Meena! Jesus, Meena, where the hell are you?"

Meena's heart is pounding so hard she can hardly hear over the roaring in her ears, and she is thinking: *So, Mimi knows. They have found him, then. And they've been looking for me.* This comes as a relief in a way. Meena doesn't know what to say. Her throat fills, and in spite of herself and in spite of her resolve, she sobs.

"I'm sorry."

But Mimi doesn't hear, because she's still talking. "We had a whole pile of boxes by the back door when I came in this morning, you wouldn't believe it, I think I'm going to have to put a fence up around the place or something. A fucking iron curtain. Everybody's cleaning out their attics at the same time, and it's hot as all fuck, and where the hell are you?"

"My father..."

Mimi waits.

"He..." Meena can't bring herself to say it.

She can hear Mimi light a cigarette. Then exhale, a sigh. "Meena?" Her voice is quiet and soft now. "Are you okay?"

Meena nods.

"Meena?" Mimi knows how it is with Meena and her father, that his needs have to come first, and it makes her impatient sometimes. Meena hears a rattle of ice. Mimi is making herself a drink.

"Have you heard any news about Ralph Wendell?" Meena asks.

"What? Ralph who?"

"Wendell. The car dealer. That guy who disappeared."

"What the fuck does that have to do with anything?"

"Nothing, I guess. I was just wondering, that's all. Do you have to say 'fuck'?"

"Yes. FUCK, Meena. Fuck fuck. FUCK."

She must know that Meena is wincing. "I should have called you this morning," Meena says.

"Shoulda woulda coulda. You need some time off, is that it?"

"He fell down Friday night. Outside the movie theater. He hit his head."

"Oh. Shit. I'm sorry. Did you take him to the hospital?"

"He wouldn't let me."

"Stubborn old bohunk. He's okay then?"

Meena can hear the sound of a car revving, which means that Mimi has gone outside and is sitting in one of the white wicker chairs on her porch. In a big flowered dress, bare legs, rubber sandals on her feet.

"I didn't want to leave him alone," Meena says.

Mimi lives in the same old house in Rompot, where she grew up. Wouldn't think of living anyplace else.

"You should take him to the doctor, Meena."

"But…"

"Just put him in the car and drive him over there. Don't take no for an answer. Boss him around a little. He's an old man. Make him do it."

"I can't."

"You want me to come over and help you?"

"No!"

Mimi's sigh is resigned. She and Meena have had this same conversation so many times already. It's an old argument, Mimi wanting Meena to tell Josef what to do, Meena knowing that she can't.

"Meena, you're a stubborn old bohunk yourself, you know." Mimi grunts as she stands up. Meena can hear the screen squeak open, and the neighborhood noise is hushed, so Mimi must have gone back inside again.

"Don't worry about me," she's saying, as if Meena had somehow indicated that she might. "Go ahead and take tomorrow off too if you have to," she goes on. Good old Mimi.

Hell, take the whole week off, if that's what you need."

"I…"

The clink of ice again. "He's not going to live forever Meena, you know that, right? I don't mean to hurt your feelings, but you just gotta start facing reality."

Meena doesn't know what to say. But it doesn't matter, because Mimi is still going on anyway, she isn't waiting for a response.

"And you need to start looking after yourself some, too." She waits. "Okay?"

"Okay."

"All right then. Call if you want me to come over there and give him some of the old what-for."

For all her faults, Meena thinks, Mimi really does seem to care. And she really does try to be kind, too, in her way. If Meena has one friend in the world, Mimi's it. She's sorry she didn't tell the truth. She thinks she could have, maybe. She thinks it's possible that she still might. Maybe in a while she'll call Mimi back and tell her everything. Mimi will know what to do. Meena only hopes she'll forgive her, when she finds out about the lie. She hopes Mimi will understand. Because if she doesn't, then who in this world will?

Meena is on her way back to her car when she looks up to see Holly Gidding approaching, waving wildly. Calling out, "Libbie! Libbie! You're still here!"

What Remains

1964

Two boys are out walking through the thick woods of Hollow Hill in the middle of the afternoon on a Sunday in early December. The air is sharp with the cold of coming winter; the sky is so bright and white it seems to crackle in the sunshine. As yet, there's been no snow. These boys are brothers, Ralph and James Wendell, ages twelve and eight, friendly, outgoing children from a good family, with a devoted mother and a jovial father. Dad owns the Ford dealership on Second Avenue and Mom's a Fielding, as in the hotel.

Tomorrow is Monday, and with that the freedom of the weekend will be over as school starts up again in the morning, and Christmas vacation is still a couple of weeks away. Ralph dreads going back, he hates the long dull hours in the classroom, the clamor and confusion in the lunch room, the crashing echo of slammed lockers, push and shove in the stairwells, reckless jostle in the hall. This happens to be his first year at Ben Franklin Junior High, and he's not quite used to it yet: the crowds, the noise, the way he's never sure of where he's supposed to be and always afraid of making a mistake, looking foolish, missing a class, going to the wrong room, bringing the wrong books, or being caught out in the hall alone, after the last bell has rung.

He wishes he were bigger, wishes he were older. Or younger, smaller. Anything but this middling thing that he has recently become: man-child, boy-man, neither this nor that, neither here nor there. Two days ago the girl who sits in front of him in Study Hall—whose shapely ass he has been secretly admiring for some time—turned around and flashed a goofy smile, and he didn't know what to do. He thinks her name is Ginny. Jenny? Jean?

James has scrambled up through the brush to the ridge above the railroad tracks. Ralph fishes in his shirt pocket for the cigarette that he swiped that morning from the pack his mother left out on the kitchen table. Lights it, squints through the smoke. A door has closed, he has crossed over, and he will never be just a stupid careless kid again. He understands that the only thing he can do now is go forward and grow up. Say hello to that girl, whatever her name is. Smile back.

James is slapping at the brush with a stick that he's picked up. He's next to what looks like a pile of rocks, hidden in the underbrush. He stoops to look closer, pokes his stick, stands back.

Nearby, an insulated wire. James picks this up, gives it a tug. Above him in the weeds a metal stake shudders in response. He pulls himself up the incline. Puts a hand on the stake, wobbles it back and forth, tries to work it free. And now his eye is caught by a glint of light in the dried grass. The sunshine is bright, he squints against it, then stoops closer to see what he's been seeing all along, without knowing yet exactly what it is: the faint outline of the figure of a girl, a shadow in the shape of a body, ribs and fingers, legs, toes, leathery flesh, and the bare bright dome of a skull.

He screams his brother's name, and Ralph turns to

see him standing in the brush, white hair flashing in the sunshine, face pink around the darker hole of his opened mouth.

Ralph drops the cigarette, steps on it. His heart is pounding, and yet he tells himself, it's nothing. He's sure it is nothing. His little brother is a crybaby, always has been. Probably stubbed his toe or got stung by a bee, something dumb. That's the way it's always been, it's the difference between them—Ralph older, the tough guy gritting his teeth, and James the baby, screaming.

You didn't know them, the Wendell boys. They were just two kids who lived on the far side of Hollow Hill, in the big house that had once belonged to Senator Elwood, and they were younger than you, and they went to another school.

But that doesn't mean you don't know how it happened. It was in all the papers, and on the television news, too. Ralph and James Wendell had gone out walking in the woods of Hollow Hill on that Sunday in December. They had followed the path toward Dowland, and James found a steel stake, and next to the stake, a skeleton. He called out to his brother and Ralph thought at first it had to be an animal, a dog, maybe, too big for a cat.

But what about what about the rope, what about her hands? The paper only said that Ralph used a stick to poke at the skull, and as it rolled away down the slope, that was when he saw her face, and that was when he knew that the body they had found was human.

The police didn't contact the Bells until after dinnertime, not until they were sure that what the Wendell boys had found out there in Hollow Hill was what they thought it was—Julia Bell's remains. There would be a news report on the TV that night at ten. It wasn't much of a report, just a snippet with no names mentioned and no speculations offered, only a wide shot of the woods, taped off, with a group of people, mostly men, standing around on the road with their collars turned up and their hands in their pockets. And there were the Wendell boys, too, posed beside a squad car, blinking in the lights.

The newspaper said that what was left of her wasn't much more than a skeleton, with all of the flesh from the torso area of the body gone. The hands had been tied at the wrists, and the feet at the ankles. Curtain cord, it looked like. Or window blind. Clothesline, maybe. And the glint that had caught James Wendell's eye that sunny Sunday morning in December? It was the St. Christopher medal that Libbie had lost, the one that John Grandon had always worn around his neck.

Two weeks later, when school was out for Christmas break, you and Libbie went up to Hollow Hill together to take a look at the place where Julia's body had been found. It was Libbie's idea to do this, and you were surprised—and pleased—when she crossed the driveways, just like old times, to knock on the door and invite you to come along. Libbie just wanted to see it, she said, and why not? She was thinking you might look for evidence, maybe you would notice something that everybody else had missed, maybe you would recognize a trace of Deep Eddie there that the police had overlooked. Because, in your way, she said, you had known him.

Your boots crunched across the thin snow. Frozen fingers. Collars turned up. Chins tipped, faces lifted, eyes raised toward a sky that was hanging low and leaden overhead. Clouds snagged by bare treetops that groped blindly toward the dim nickel of late afternoon sun.

So Julia Bell was not at the bottom of the deep eddy after all. So she had not been carried down into its murk, as you had imagined, and she had not found another kind of life there in the watery embrace of a River King.

And she was not, as John had insisted, trapped beyond the skin of an alternate universe either. Not lost and found in a new family, on some other street, in a different town. Not wandering around in a haze of dimwit forgetfulness, faint memories of some other lifetime nagging at the vivid hems of her dreams. No, she was still right there with you, and she had been there all along, for three years, the flesh withering over her bones and her bones sinking down into the dirt, nestled in the grasses that grew up through and around and over her. May apples in spring, flying Dutchmen, bluebells, forget-me-nots. Rampant weeds, thistles, nettles, thorns in summer. A sea of dropped leaves in the fall. And now, snow.

You didn't have any trouble finding the spot. The path that led to it was clear, trampled flat by the feet of all the cops and reporters who had come out there to investigate, take pictures, sift through the leaves and dirt for clues, or simply gape. A bit of yellow police tape had got caught in a tangle of dry undergrowth, flapping there like some misplaced remnant of a late summer bloom. The steel stake had been removed. Evidence.

"We didn't kill her?" Libbie's hand on your arm, her fingers scrabbling, clawing, clinging to her sleeve. "Did we?" She'd explained about the medal. And John had been questioned, too. The little silver cross was never found.

"Of course not," you told her. "No."

Libbie's thin face a splinter of worry and doubt made more pale by the cold reflection of drab snow and low sky and yours a doubtful moon, aglow with bland resistance: No.

You were just kids. You'd done nothing wrong.

"But Meena, are you sure?"

You shrugged her off: "What are you talking about?"

Libbie circled the site, tromping over it, stomping purposefully upon the ample detectives' footprints with her inconsequential boots: "Well we always did hate Julia." Stopping to peer at you again: "Didn't we?"

And hadn't you taunted her? Didn't you laugh at her? Didn't you scold Julia and kick her and push her out the door, into the night?

So maybe you were guilty, after all. Had you gone after her? That's what Libbie was asking. Had you come upon her hiding in the shadows of the yard beyond the shelter door, shivering, cowering, afraid of breaking every scolded rule and walking home alone? You on one side and Libbie on the other—the two of you squatting beside her, trapping her there on the lawn. Libbie holds her down, you have the rock, and you raise it up high, bring it down hard against the surface of Julia's skull. She is as fragile and flimsy as a blown egg. In silence and surprise, she falls forward, softly crumples to the ground.

But no, that wasn't what happened, it wasn't like that at all. The St. Christopher was proof positive that it was Deep Eddie who had killed Julia Bell. He'd found John's medal in the brush, where Libbie had lost it. He'd picked it up, he'd put it in his pocket, he'd kept it with him, he'd saved it like a souvenir. Then when the time was right, he gave it to Julia, or maybe he used it to tempt her, or maybe he meant it to be a signature of some kind, to let you know that it was him and you were next. Besides, you argued, you and Libbie had been inside the fallout shelter that night. You'd been listening to the radio and dancing in your underpants with Leo and laughing about how stupid Julia was. The newspaper said that there had been no evidence of any violence. No breaks, no fractures, no broken bones, no bullet holes.

This you did know: her hands had been tied, behind her back. Her feet had been tied, too, and trussed. Hands first, she must have been standing. Force her to her knees, then further to her belly, bring her ankles up to meet her wrists, wrap, tie, knot.

She snivels.

"Baby."

She moans.

"Shut up!"

Cries.

"Boo-hoo."

She begs and pleads and snuffles in the dirt, but that only makes it worse.

The searchers hadn't found her body in the woods because when they went to look for it, it wasn't there. Because while they were searching for her, she was still alive. All those days, she'd been kept hidden, gagged and tied. How long, before he killed her? Or did she die of suffocation, a mistake? He comes back to check on her, to look at her, again and again. And then, after the furor has died down, after the searches have ended and no one is trying to find her anymore, then he can let her go.

Julia Bell, she was just a kid after all. Ten years old, and small, even for her age. Deep Eddie picks her up, easily. He swings her back and forth a few times, and then he lets her fly. She dips low, rises high, spins on in a wide and graceful arc before she falls and crashes, rolls and settles against the ground, for good.

You could see that Libbie was crying. It wasn't just the cold wind stinging her eyes. She sank to her knees in the thin snow and clenched her bare hands together. She was praying, murmuring some Latin gobbledygook, some Catholic mumbo-jumbo that she'd picked up in her classes at Mount Mercy—her lips moving, her eyes squeezed shut, tears gleaming, spilling over, tracing stinging lines down along her cheeks to her chin. You wanted to comfort her. You knelt near. You wrapped an arm around Libbie's shoulders, as any friend would do, and you pulled Libbie close. You would protect her. You would save her from her own self-destructive self. You were Libbie's friend. You loved her.

You told her: "It's not your fault."

You said: "We didn't kill anybody."

You whispered: "I love you."

And then you kissed her.

Later, you would deny it. Maybe that was what Gingi Noone said, and maybe that was what Libbie went and told everybody afterward, but you would insist: that was not what happened.

You did not kiss Libbie Grandon. And you didn't murder Julia Bell.

Did you?

July 2006

At nine thousand feet the air is thin and clear and from this new perspective of such height, it seems to Meena as if the darkness that has obscured her vision of the world until now is burning clean away, and everything looks brighter. That fog, that smoke, the haze, the veil, the caul—it is lifting, and now what she can see seems almost too brilliantly, blindingly, painfully clear. The sharp sunlight, a swirl of dust motes, the fine pores and creases in her skin, the icy white glint of the diamond clenched in the gold teeth of her mother's wedding ring on her right hand. Even as she understands that this heightened perception might not be real, she squints against it. Her father would mock her, if she told him; she understands this, too. He would not hesitate to let her know, in no uncertain terms, exactly what he thinks of what she thinks she is experiencing. Delirium, he might call it. Hysteria. Sleep deprivation.

Her heart pounding, her pulse fluttering in her throat.

His voice convincingly deep and decisive as he paces, slapping the newspaper against his leg for emphasis.

Dehydration. A lack of oxygen to the brain.

Leaving the room long enough to give the impression that he's finished, then popping back in again to add:

Hypoglycemia. Altitude sickness. Psychotic break.

Or maybe it's an aneurysm, a slow leakage of blood in her head.

Well all right, she thinks. *Maybe so. Could be. Fair enough.* But, she smiles, just let him go ahead and explain to her how wrong she is this time, if he can do it. In his own current mute and immobile situation, that is.

Not that it would make any difference to her at this moment anyway, what he thinks or doesn't think. What he says or not. Because the fact is: all of her senses have been sharpened. Everything is real. She is Meena Krejci. She is the grocer's daughter. She has run away from home. It's taken her more than thirty years to do it, but now she's done it, and now she is gone. She has been gone for three days. And her father, Josef, he is dead.

She thinks she might have an even greater understanding now of what Mrs. Grandon thought she was up to when she let herself fall out her bedroom window that day all those years ago, after President Kennedy was shot. This state Meena feels herself to be in right now might be something like what Mrs. Grandon was after then. Just the clear clean experience of it, that's all. The razor's edge of a disaster. Now.

Not suicide though. Definitely not suicide. That wasn't it at all. That was the mistake that everybody made. That was the crucial misinterpretation of what Mrs. Grandon's gesture was for on that bright winter afternoon in 1963. Not self-destruction. Nothing like that. Exactly the opposite, in fact. Re-creation. Faye Grandon would fall out of her second story bedroom window, she would drift into the blue, and be reborn.

Meena recalls the bitterness of John Grandon's scorn for his mother's judgment—not that she would choose to end her own life, if she could, but that she was too stupid to do it with any measure of success.

Why not a gun? Or a handful of pills, a bottle of vodka, a plastic bag over her head? If she was serious about wanting to jump to her death, why not off the rooftop of the twelve story Roosevelt Hotel, or from the shoulders of a saint down on Bohemie Bridge, why not into the deep eddy, which would be sure to suck her down and hold her there forever?

She wasn't serious, that's why. According to John, it was a failure of intent. It was all just drama, melodrama, it was craziness that was too overwrought and too feminine to be taken seriously. It was something to be laughed at, embarrassed about, ashamed of, even scorned.

But Meena knows that John Grandon had it all wrong. Death was never the point. Life, that was the point. Galloping heart, adrenaline thrum. And now that Meena can see it all so clearly, now that she knows what it really was that Mrs. Grandon was after—that same free fall, a letting go to gravity—well, she wonders, why then can't she have something like it for herself, too? An air-clearing, mind-cleaning, breath-taking sort of tumble through thin air. With the wind of it strong enough to blow away everything else that used to hurt so much but doesn't have to matter anymore. Isn't that what Mrs. Grandon wanted? Meena thinks it is. And now she's finding it to be something that she is after, too.

At Holly's urging she has bought herself a few days in the Aspenglo cabin here at Will Gidding's Paradox Compound, and until next Sunday the place will be hers, all four rooms—bedroom, living room, kitchen, and bath. What more does Meena need? She has paid in cash, with bills snapped off the roll that she took from her father's pocket, and she can't tell whether or not Will Gidding was made suspicious by this or not. She hopes not.

He told her that these woods are full of wildlife. Critters, he called them. Deer and elk and fox. Coyotes, but not wolves. Bobcats and black bears. This last had sounded dangerous, but he was quick to reassure her— "Those kind like to keep to themselves," he said. "They're smart and they don't want to have anything to do with you, not if they can help it, especially if you let them know you don't want to have anything to do with them."

She is thinking: maybe there's some way she can stay here, if not in quaint little Aspenglo itself, at least in this area, in these mountains and this forest, where everything seems clear. Maybe she can come up with some way to work it so she won't have to go back to Linwood after all. Or on to California, either. Is it crazy for her to be considering such a thing? she wonders. What kind of miracle would it take for Meena Krejci to have a life of her own from now on? After all this time. Why can't she just stay gone, leave her father where he is— where he belongs? In his bed, in his room, in his stone house on Otis Road. Just leave the house as it is, too— let it be a museum, a tomb, an archive of the past, perfectly preserved—just up and leave that whole mess of the first half of her life behind, forget all about everything and begin herself over again right here?

She is fifty-five years old.

Is that the first half of her life?

What if it's more? Much more.

Her heart tumbles at the thought, pounding with an urgency that launches Meena to her feet, across the room, and out the door into the woods.

In Linwood, Mimi Hanrahan has fixed herself another drink and carried it outside to the wicker chaise on the front porch of her house in Rompot. She peers at two children chasing fireflies in the yard across the street and thinks of her friend Meena Krejci. So many times she tried to get her to go out, have some fun, live a little, without success. Meena always had too many reasons why not and after a while Mimi threw up her hands and quit. Fuck it. Some things are not meant to change.

And then that turned out to be just exactly what she loves best about Meena now: her reliability. The reassuring sameness of her self. Meena is always Meena, nothing more and nothing less, steady as a stone. The job at The White Elephant started out as a simple act of charity, because Mimi felt sorry for her, but lately she isn't sure what she'd do without Meena there to help her out and fill in. To keep her company. To be her friend.

And anyway, who is Mimi Hanrahan to talk, still living right here herself, in this same old rundown poor white neighborhood of Rompot where she grew up and now, decades later, nothing much has changed? Where kids still chase after fireflies in the twilight, men swagger off to the bars with their friends, and overweight middle-aged women like herself sit out on the porches drinking themselves into a forgetful stupor of contentment.

She shifts her weight in the chaise and the wicker creaks. The kids stop and look up. They peer through the shadows at her. One raises a hand, gives her the finger. The other giggles, then both squeal and skid away. Little fuckers. Mimi should get up and go after them, but she doesn't have the energy for it anymore. Way too fat and old and slow.

She sips her drink, rattles ice, fans her face with the back of her hand. Fuckem, she thinks. Then, "Fuck you!" she shouts. From somewhere down the block a car radio thumps a deep bass beat. "Fuck you!" Mimi shouts again. The neighborhood is still. Fireflies signal fitfully in the grass. Mimi heaves herself up again, pads back into the house for another splash of gin.

And isn't it just like Meena to fixate on a guy like Ralph Wendell? she thinks. Shakes her head. But what's the big mystery? Obviously the guy is dead. Most likely he killed himself. Most likely he's fish food, at the bottom of the lake. Or he's lying in a cornfield somewhere, with his brains blown out. Who knows why. Who cares?

Somebody must because there are flyers all over the place and people out looking for him on horseback and in helicopter and a reward has been offered for any information regarding his whereabouts. The paper said they're going to use sonar to search the lake tomorrow. The wife was quoted in the newspaper just this morning, telling about a dream she'd had where her husband was found alive in the woods, thin and unshaven, with a broken leg and a busted collarbone, curled up in a bed of leaves next to a kindly deer, who gazed up with liquid black doe eyes, smiled, and whispered, "Welcome."

Weird.

But didn't Meena see that story? Mimi wonders now. Seems like she must not have or else why would she have asked whether there had been any more news? Must have been so busy taking care of her old man that she didn't have a chance to look at the paper.

Mimi picks up the phone and calls Meena back, but there's no answer. Maybe they went out for a Dairy Queen.

Poor Meena. Her father was in his nineties already. And didn't Mimi try to be a friend, didn't she keep telling her and telling her, trying her best to get Meena to wake up and face facts: "He's going to die, you know he's so old!" But Meena didn't want to hear it: "Not yet, he's not. He's fine. Look at him! He's twenty years younger than he really is!"

Whatever.

But what Meena will do, once he does go, Mimi can't imagine.

She waits a half hour, then tries the number again, and still there is no answer. Must've already gone to bed, she thinks. Tomorrow she'll stop by the house to see just how bad Joe Krejci is and whether Meena needs her.

Keep positive thoughts, Ralph Wendell's wife had said at the end of the article about the dream and the deer. That's what to do. Keep positive thoughts, and stay hopeful for the best.

All shall be well and all manner of thing shall be well...

Old Ralph Wendell will turn up again soon enough, Mimi's sure of it. And when he does, then the mystery will be over and he'll be forgotten and nobody but the wife and maybe the kids will bother to think twice about him again.

Meena veers away from the path that leads down toward Will Gidding's compound and trudges upward instead, following a narrow dirt trail toward the silver aspens that stand shimmering in the sunlight at the top of the rocky hill. The climb is hard, she's out of shape, not used to this, and by the time she gets to the top she's short of breath and panting, but she presses on as the path flattens out again and winds around to the left, into the cathedral shade of the lodge pole pines.

The world seems full of possibility, suddenly, in her dazzled state of mind. Fanciful alternatives; lucid dreaming. What if she stayed here? What if she got a job at the Wal-Mart? Stocking shelves, handing out shopping carts, helping customers, it doesn't matter what exactly, almost anything would do. What if she rented a house or a room someplace and made up another identity for herself, what if she kept telling people that her name is Libbie Grandon and she made a birth certificate and then got a Social Security number and a bank account and a credit card? Hasn't she seen such stories in the movies, plenty of times, and on television and in her magazines? Don't people do this, don't they start themselves all over again for all kinds of reasons, some innocent and some not? Isn't that what America's supposed to be all about, the land of opportunity? Reinvention, starting over, new life, new self, new world?

Too bad Meena never had a chance to make up a real plan, though, the way that man Ralph Wendell must have done. He had to have spent years and years at it, she thinks, coming up with forged ID cards and the phony bank accounts that he squirreled his money into a little bit at a time so his wife wouldn't notice it was missing, until he had enough piled up to last a while. Long enough to get him going, anyway.

Meena has always admired that quality in a person, the ability to think ahead. Because she's never been much good at it herself. Maybe after a while she and Mr. Gidding will get to know each other better, maybe they'll get to like each other, they might get married and then she'll be Libbie Gidding and her identity will be secure. Maybe she will never go home, why should she? Maybe she'll just stay right here. Maybe this is exactly where she belongs. Maybe it's her fate. The dog stopping her, the cabin keeping her, and now the forest, drawing her in.

Because, honestly, how can she go back now? Isn't

it too late? And what would it be like if she did? Pulling into the driveway as if nothing's happened, acting as if nothing's changed. Letting herself in through the back door, into the kitchen. The house quiet. Dark. Stuffy and hot. But also clean. Spotless. And undisturbed.

Mail piled up on the floor inside the front door. Newspapers scattered outside on the porch. Haven't the neighbors noticed that something's wrong? Maybe not. Or if they have, maybe they'd rather not get involved. Maybe they prefer to believe that the Krejcis are on vacation, out of town for a few days, that's all. As if anything like that has ever happened before.

And Josef doesn't have any friends anymore, no one to check up on him, no one to come calling: all of them are dead. Did he ever have friends? Seems like it's always been just the two of them—Meena and Josef—all along.

He will still be there, upstairs in his bed, just the way she left him, but she won't go in to look, she'll just go straight to the telephone, call the police, turn herself in. Or maybe she should make the call now, before she goes back, so that when she gets home someone will have found him, someone will have taken him away, and then it will be as if it never happened.

They would know she didn't kill him, wouldn't they? Of course she didn't. Someone must have seen him fall. There would have been witnesses, people who will come forward and tell the truth about what happened. This isn't what it looks like, they will say. It's not what it seems. Maybe that bullet-headed detective that she saw on the television will be waiting for her, wanting to ask her a few questions about her father's death. And her involvement in it.

As Meena trudges along the trail, her canvas sneakers—smooth-soled and not made for hiking—skid on the soft dirt, but she doesn't slow, she presses on, enjoying the rhythm and the movement, heart beating, blood pumping, alive and alert. On either side of her the tall narrow trunks of the pines shoulder each other, so close together they form a solid seeming wall that rises toward a widespread canopy of needled branches that creak and sway with breeze.

And, she thinks, her anger rising with the effort of ascent as the trail angles upward at a steeper slant: isn't it just like him to leave her like this? Holding the bag. It isn't fair. After she's given him everything she has, everything she is, her whole life, in fact. These inconsiderate men, thoughtless of the women, their wives and daughters, left behind to clean up after them when they're gone. That coward Ed Madrick, sick with cancer at seventy years old—locked himself in the bathroom and put a gun to his head, leaving an unspeakable mess for his wife to come home to after an otherwise unremarkable day spent playing bridge with her friends. Ronnie Fleming, recently widowed, closing up the garage and starting up the car, so he could be found dead by his granddaughter, who'd dropped by for a surprise visit, hoping to maybe cheer him up a little with her company. Barnes McGregor, whose emphysema, after a lifetime of smoking, was so bad that even though he was hooked up to oxygen all the time, still he had to sleep sitting up—alone in an extra bedroom downstairs—until he fell out of bed one night and broke his neck. Lying there in his own mess for his wife to find when she came down to wake him up the next morning. Peter Stepanek, drove his car into a brick wall. Ozzie Pickering fell down the basement stairs. Mark Bloomberg lost both his legs to diabetes. George Hendricks: colon cancer. Mike Ingalls: heart attack. Ernie Chapman: stroke. What a mess.

It's all very well for Mimi Hanrahan to keep warning her, fine for her to say that Josef Krejci is going to die someday, too. Just like everybody else. Mimi taking Meena by the shoulders to get her attention, pulling her close to look her in the eye. "Meena, you understand that, don't you? He *will* die." How many times had she heard that? Why hadn't she listened? But if she had, what would she have done?

And all very well, too, for Josef Krejci to decide to retire, to give away what was left of his groceries and then turn the building over to a developer who would tear it down to the ground as if it had never existed, what did he care? He was already an old man by that time, past a reasonable retirement age, plus he had a couple of office spaces and small houses over in Bohemietown that he'd bought for a song a long time ago, and he could still count on an income from the rents that he collected on them.

But what about Meena? What was she supposed to do once the grocery store was gone? She'd graduated from high school with honors in her classes and then not gone on to college because she had agreed to stay there in Linwood and work for him.

"You don't need a job, Meena," he said. "What do you need a job for? A girl like you."

But Meena always worked anyway. She always had a job, she would have gone crazy otherwise. What else was she supposed to do all day? She was in the credit department at Fairchild's downtown for six years. Cooped up all day in a windowless office on the top floor where no one ever went, riding the escalator downstairs at lunch time to eat alone in the tearoom on two, ducking into the ladies' lounge on three for a smoke twice a day, home in time to fix supper for her father every night. And she worked in circulation at the newspaper for a while, too, filing, until they switched over to computers and didn't need her anymore. All for a few dollars an hour—she never did earn enough money that she could afford to move out of her father's house, rent an apartment, and support herself on her own. Not that she would have done that anyway. But she did make enough to keep her dignity at least, she believed.

Over one summer she was a housekeeper for a family down the street. The Brainards: Jay and Dana, he was an attorney and she worked in public relations. They were busy people and they needed someone to come in and keep the place clean and cook sometimes and also take care of the kids. Out of the blue Meena went ahead and applied for the job and right away they hired her, no problem. She was exactly what they were looking for—an adult woman with good references and no family of her own.

She wasn't abandoning her father, although maybe he believed she was. She told him, "I'm not leaving you." And it was true. Meena wasn't going anywhere, but she knew he worried that she would.

"It's just the two of us," he'd say. "You know we're all we've got." And she would tell him, "Don't worry, Dad. I'll always be here for you." And she meant it. And she was.

The Brainards had two children, a girl and a boy. Lily was eight and Sam was five.

Meena was there six days a week looking after them that summer, sometimes for twelve hours at a stretch, but she didn't mind that. It wasn't like sitting at a desk or working behind a counter, it was more like being a part of someone's normal everyday life. She took them to the park, and to the pool. They drove downtown to the library or walked around the zoo. She packed a picnic lunch and they ate outside on the grass under a tree. They watched cartoons and she told them stories and they drew pictures and they played with clay. Meena took them to the doctor and the dentist and they went with her to the grocery store, and more often than not people who didn't know better thought she was their mother. It was a natural assumption, and Meena didn't try to correct it. Why should she? What did it hurt if she wanted to pretend?

That was a happy time for her, the time that she was able to spend with those children. In that house.

She told the kids about Leo Spivak. She held him up as an example whenever she wanted to make a point about not doing something that was dangerous.

"Don't play with matches," Meena said to Sam, who frowned back at her. "I knew a boy once, his name was Leo Spivak." And then she'd say that Leo set his bed on fire and burned off all his hair. While Sam's eyes widened and Lily groaned. Or, "Don't go in the street." Leo Spivak had been run over by a car, crushing his foot so flat that the doctors had to cut it off. "Stay away from firecrackers." Leo Spivak put some in a jar once, and the explosion blew his hand to pieces. Leo Spivak blinded by a BB gun. Leo Spivak bit by a rabid squirrel. Leo Spivak falling off a roof and breaking his back, paralyzing him from the neck down so he was confined to a wheelchair for the rest of his life. On and on it went, Leo Spivak this and Leo Spivak that—by the time Meena was finished with him, he was a legend of calamity in the Brainard household, blind and deaf and scarred and maimed, hairless and limbless, just lucky to still be alive.

Some years after that she was downtown and she came out of Fairchild's to see Leo Spivak standing on the corner, waiting for the light. There he was, the real thing, in the flesh, wearing a wool coat over a suit and tie. He was respectable looking—and still in one piece. A little bit overweight, even. And although she knew, as she had always known, that everything she'd told those Brainard kids had been made up just to scare them, still it seemed to Meena to be a miracle that Leo Spivak was alive. And whole. She didn't dare say hello. Instead, she spun away from him and didn't look back until she was at the end of the block, to see that he was gone.

Intact. Unharmed. She never saw him again, but she believed that he must still be out there somewhere, a rough boy transformed by time into an ordinary man living an ordinary life, free from blame and unbothered by his memories or the small consequences of a childhood long past and mostly forgotten.

First it will be the view that stops Meena in her tracks. The path has widened, the trees have thinned, and she's on the lantern jaw of a bluff that juts out over the highway winding into a crease between the mountains. The river is a thin slip of silver breaking through the green.

And then, at her feet, fresh kill: the headless carcass of a fawn—softly speckled pelt, curved hip, sharp backward angle of the knee, hooves paired, daintily, demur as a young girl's feet in glossy black ballet slippers, folded modestly to the side, knees clenched.

Frails

1968-1969

Mrs. Grandon always had been drawn to drama, everyone knew this about her already and so maybe they
should have known that when the time came she would
make sure her marriage ended with a bang and not a
whimper, with the quick relief of one last big blowout
of a fight, a knockdown drag-out disaster that began
with accusations and counter-accusations, escalated to
doors slammed, fists clenched, teeth bared, and then
peaked in a bloodbath of flashing lights from a patrol
car parked in their driveway askew. The cop calls for
backup, unsnaps the holster that holds his gun, picks
his way through a debris-strewn aftermath, warily
climbs the steps up to Mrs. Grandon's locked front
door.

Those who were watching from their own yards or
porches or windows, depending on how discreet they
were trying to be about it, should have guessed that
something like that was bound to happen. Most of you
had been well aware of what was going on with the
Grandons for some time already. You ought to have
been expecting the worst, and not been surprised or
scandalized when that was what you got.

All except for poor little Rags, who didn't seem to

know whose side he was on or whether it was only a game after all, and so he limped hopefully back and forth across the yard, from the house to the car and back again, in a confused obsessive loop. While Mr. Grandon sat there at the wheel of his blue convertible, turned the radio on and up loud, pounded his fist against the horn, made such a racket that he had to know everybody heard and everyone was watching, but what did he care?

Mrs. Grandon was standing in the doorway on the front porch, a backlit silhouette, throwing things. It didn't matter what—anything she could get her hands on, that would do.

In your father's considered opinion, this was a waste of everybody's time, his own included. The cops would come, there would be paperwork, and for what? Everyone was losing sleep, as well as peace of mind. That woman was only making a mess she'd have to clean up later. A pity, he said. Unfortunate for every-one, all around. Waste of time, not to mention money, not to mention well-being.

And sure enough, there she was out there in her bathrobe the next morning. Just as dawn was breaking Mrs. Grandon was stooped in the grass, searching the bushes by the house for the bits and pieces of all her broken stuff. And later she would be resolutely sweep-ing the sidewalk, determined to pick up every single shard, dustpan in one hand, straw broom in the other. Her hair tied up under a pretty red bandana, big cotton gardening gloves on her hands. Shattered glass glittered on the pavement—bits of crystal, fine porcelain, paint-ed china. Books tumbled out into the yard, their pages flayed against the ground and curling into the damp grass. After a while your father couldn't stand it any-more and he went out to help—dragging the garbage can across the grass and setting it down on the walkway near her, taking hold of the dustpan, bending over it, backing away from the broom as she swept toward him.

As for Mr. Grandon, he almost got away clean. With one last long sorrowful bellow from the car's horn, he gave up, shifted into gear and retreated, backed out to the street, swept around and was gone. He only cared about his car, Libbie said later, arching a skeptical eyebrow in her judgment of him. He had only been considering the consequences of something banging into a fender, she insisted. Or crashing into the windshield. Or tearing through the precious fabric of that white canvas top.

It was Mrs. Spivak who called the police. She explained later, patting a palm against her breathless chest, that she thought the neighborhood was under attack, that the Negroes were rioting in the streets and had brought their terror over here to Otis Road. That they might be about to set the world on fire and burn the whole town down.

Meanwhile, Mr. Grandon had been stopped and pulled over down the street, at the corner where Vernon Boulevard crosses over the Old River Road and begins to turn in toward the tracks. A flashlight shining in his face, blinding him as he did his best to explain. His voice soft, controlled, conciliatory. No, he was not drunk. He was stone cold sober and only trying to get away, running for his life in fact. Had they been to his house yet, for God's sake? Had they seen it, what she'd done? Jesus. They could test him, if they wanted to, if they didn't believe him. Go ahead.

But he never touched her. If anything, she was the one who had pummeled him. This, with a smile. Indulgent. Her small fists. A wink and a shrug. No damage done.

Mr. Grandon was convincing. He was a salesman, after all. Who could argue with a man like that? As decent as he was. He was sincere; he seemed to be honest. Maybe he had said something to his wife that he shouldn't have, and maybe in reaction she had got a little upset. But that was all there was to it. No big deal, really. And he had circumstances on his side, besides. She had been hospitalized, after all. She'd been in and out of the Cedarcrest Retreat for years now, that was a documented fact. It was the medication, if you want to know the truth. Difficult to balance and get exactly right. But he had already put a call in to her doctor, and so she was going to be good as gold again soon. You could be sure of that.

He was sorry for the disturbance, sorry for the inconvenience, sorry for the mess. But, he insisted, it was over now, and done with. No need for any worry. He had everything under control. She'd be okay, he'd see to it himself. He'd lie low for a few days. Give her a little time to cool down. Winking at them. They must know what he meant; didn't they see stuff like this going on all the time?

Your father claimed that he had seen it coming, too, the Grandons' estrangement. He was quick to judge the situation, ready to come to a conclusion and eager to say that he, for one, couldn't blame a man for walking out on an ugly mess like that one next door: what it looked to him that the Grandon family who were his neighbors had become.

His evidence? Mrs. Grandon came into the store one afternoon and she rolled a shopping cart up and down the aisles, took her time, picking up this and then that, examining it, putting it in the cart. Then when she was finished with her shopping, she rolled up to the register. Started setting her items on the counter: crab-meat, sardines, capers, hearts of palm, smoked oysters and fancy mustard. Josef was all smiles. "Will there be anything else?" he asked.

She eyed him, frowned, seemed to consider, then shook her head. "No, I don't believe so," she said. Running a hand through the close curls of her hair. Chewing on her lip. "I believe that will be all." Considered further, then adding, "Thank you very much."

"Having a party?"

She shook her head, lifted her chin, touched her throat with her fingertips. All but batted her eyes. "Oh no," she says. "Just stocking up."

He rang in the items, told her the cost.

She listened carefully, concentrating to be sure she'd got it right. Then she beamed back at him. "Just put it on our account, would you please?"

His face was shiny, cheeks rosy—with embarrassment, amusement, concern? His skin seemed to be stretched tight as a drum over the big bones of his face, and you could tell just by looking at him what he was thinking. He was imagining what kind of a world poor Mr. Grandon had to wake up to every day there in his own home across the two driveways next door. With his son away at school and his daughter seething with contempt at home and that distracted woman beside him in his bed, that wife with her crabmeat and her capers and her credit account.

"A house full of women," he said to you, at dinner, as if that said it all. He shook his head, sucked on his teeth, dabbed at his lips with the corner of his napkin. The gold band on his finger gleaming, as you looked up to see the blurred reflection of your own face in the glass pane of the window across the room, and Mrs. Chadima pushed in and out through the swinging door carrying one plate of food after another to him at the dining room table, offering water, coffee, more wine? Matka was there too, but she kept her own counsel, she was only watching, only chewing and chewing, and breathing heavily and nodding, "*Ano, ano.*" Yes.

"Frails," Josef called you. Even your mother, frozen in time within the confines of the silver frame that he kept on a shelf in the living room. Women. He shook his head. He was, it seemed, resigned.

And yet, what you knew was that your father had it all wrong. Because, as you tried to tell Libbie over and over again, it wasn't Mr. Grandon who had left his family. It was Mrs. Grandon who had kicked him out.

She spent the next few days after their big fight packing up what she could of her husband's stuff. It was over, as far as she was concerned, and now she wanted him gone. She set her jaw; she blinked back tears. Her face was thin as a splinter, pale as a petal, and she had taken to wearing a darker, more dramatic lipstick: blood red. She was beautiful. Short bangs feathered her forehead, her hair fell straight to her shoulders from a tender middle part, fine lines fanned from the corners of her eyes, they cupped the sides of her mouth and puckered the edges of her lips as she drew in smoke from her cigarette, then nervously tapped off its ash. A black velvet turtleneck, the graceful stem of her throat, the sharp angle of her squared shoulders and the softer curve of her breasts.

What she wanted, she said, was for you to help her out, and you believed you owed her that much, it was the least you could do, wasn't it? After all that Mrs. Grandon had done for you? She could get you out of school, if necessary, and she'd be happy to put a call in to the attendance office, if need be. She would tell them that you were otherwise engaged that day. Or she could write a note, if you thought that would be better.

You could take the truck, couldn't you? Might you be able to arrange such a thing? And if so, would you mind? Her Thunderbird was too small; with it they'd have to make more than one trip, which would completely spoil the drama of what she meant to do.

You told your father that Mrs. Grandon was paying you to help with some spring cleaning; you probably wouldn't need the truck for more than an hour, you said, or at the most two.

Mrs. Grandon already had all of her husband's things packed up in suitcases and boxes, ready to go, but it took some time to get it loaded into the truck bed. You had to drag it down the back steps, pile it up onto a dolly from the garage, roll it across one driveway over to the other.

Early spring, a drizzly gray day.

"You sure this is what you want to do, Mrs. Grandon?"

Her face, set like concrete. "Yes, Meena, I'm sure." A hectic blush in her cheeks.

Mrs. Grandon didn't know how to work a stick shift, so you did the driving. And then even after you'd been so careful—a perfectly maintained twenty-five miles an hour, signals at every turn, full stops at the four-way intersections—Mrs. Grandon wanted you to pull over right out front of the real estate offices, in a no parking zone. She said not to worry, that if you did get a ticket, she'd take care of it. She patted your knee, smiled, unfolded a plastic rain bonnet and tied it under her chin. No problem.

Together you unloaded the stuff—the suitcases, the boxes, a sack of bathroom things, books, papers, car wax, records, photographs, tools, and that chemical toilet from the bomb shelter. You dragged it all out piece by piece and dumped it there on the sidewalk at the front door, under the snapshots of houses tacked up to a bulletin board in the front show window, beneath the black and white sign—"Grandon Homes"—spelled out in boldface letters overhead. A woman in a green raincoat stopped to watch you work; the look on her face was both puzzled and amused. She stood under the awning with her arms folded over her chest, while you struggled with a heavy box. You stopped what you were doing, stood, and glared, set the box down, waved your arms, until, embarrassed or frightened maybe, the woman turned and walked quickly away.

Someone was shouting, "Hey!" And Mrs. Grandon grabbed at your arm, yanked you toward the street. "Come on! Come on!" She was squealing with excitement, tripping over herself, clambering up into the truck, as Mr. Grandon skidded out the front door of the building, calling out again, "Hey!" and then falling over the piles of his own things. "What the hell?"

Mrs. Grandon laughed, throwing her head back with hilarity at the sight of her husband. His look of surprise. Bewilderment. Affront. And you behind the wheel, pulling away. You had your eye out for the cops, but what you saw in the rear view mirror was Mr. Grandon, surrounded by the piles of his own possessions, both feet planted squarely on the shining damp pavement of the sidewalk, his hands on his head, his mouth a hole that formed a crater in his face as he hollered after you, wailing with outrage.

"I have every right to this, you know," Mrs. Grandon said, as you drove off. She pulled the rain bonnet off, shook her hair free. "Every right," she said again. She lit a cigarette, sat back, satisfied. She leaned forward, turned up the radio. It was like she was a girl again, just like Libbie and you.

Mr. Grandon took a room down at the Fielding Hotel, on the ninth floor, overlooking the river. What else could he do? And it wasn't so bad, really. He was high up, and he had a view: of downtown Linwood, the cereal plant, the packing plant, the unlit vast expanse of cornfields rolling on beyond the edges of the city lights. He had a television set and a big bed, a mirror and a sofa and a chair. He had clean towels and small bars of soap, bottles of shampoo and room service whenever he wanted it, night or day, hot meals made to order and then kept warm for him under domed silver lids. He could go out, too, if that was what he preferred. There was the coffee shop in the lobby. Or, more to his taste maybe, the Pickwick Club in the basement downstairs. Out front there was the doorman to greet him, to say, cheerfully, "Good morning, sir," or "Good night." An elevator operator asking, "Which floor?" A concierge prepared to answer any question, meet any need. The uniformed man behind the reception desk was all smiles as he gave Mr. Grandon his messages, handed over his mail. Everyone seemed genuinely glad to see him, after all. This was nothing at all like home, and so maybe that was a relief? "Good morning, Mr. Grandon." "Hi there, Jack." "Nice day, isn't it?" "Good to see you again, sir." And so on. Because, everybody loved Jack Grandon, didn't they? How could they help it? How could you not?

The way you saw it though, Mrs. Grandon had made a big mistake, she'd committed a serious tactical error. Because by kicking her husband out, hadn't she also set him free? There he was, living by himself at the same hotel that Josef Krejci had been known to frequent, where he might find a woman in the lobby who would be happy to join him for a cocktail in the bar or dinner in the restaurant. Someone who might even be happy to follow him up to his room. Mr. Grandon could do just about anything he wanted now, and what was there to stop him? You asked Mrs. Grandon, didn't this bother her at all? No, was her answer. Because now she was free, too, she explained.

"Free to do what?"

"Whatever I want. Anything at all."

She slammed the truck door. Turned, squared her shoulders, marched back up the driveway to her house.

You were working school-day afternoons and weekend nights at the grocery store, where it was your job to keep track of the orders and the billings. Your father had put you on the payroll. You clocked in and out like everybody else, and he paid you by the hour. You used the money that you made this way to buy records and books in the bargain basement of Sanford's Everyday downtown. At Krejci's you sat at the desk under the stairs, just the way your mother once had done, and your fingers flew over the adding machine as you tallied the accounts. Your father told you that you were very good at this, and you wallowed in his praise.

And so it was that on the last Saturday in February you got up early to ride to work with him in the frozen dawn. The weathermen had been saying that Linwood was in for a storm that afternoon, so the store was unusually busy all morning, with people coming in to stock up on what they thought they might need in case they got snowed in for a day or even more.

Maybe you noticed the silence upstairs when you came in, or maybe you didn't. It wasn't until later, when you were at your desk there under the stairs, with all those numbers swirling in your head, and you looked up from your work to see the snowflakes that had begun to fall, big and fat and thick beyond the cold sheen of the front window glass. Early afternoon, but already outside it was dark as dusk and the streetlights had popped on one by one.

Your father was standing in the open doorway looking out and letting the cold air blow in, and maybe you both had the same thought at the same time, but he was the first to move. He looked up and you looked up and together you were listening but there was nothing to hear. No creaking floorboards, no television blare.

You watched him start up the steep stairs to the apartment overhead, an old man moving slowly, as if he were being dragged up there against his will. And then you were on your feet, too, away from your desk and coming around to follow him as he climbed. When he got to the top he stopped and so you stopped too, right behind, so close that you could smell him: pipe smoke, limes, sweat, the ointment he rubbed into his shoulder muscles, the oil he used on his hair.

A panic had begun to flutter in your chest, but you were trying not to think about it. Your breath was coming short, and you were gasping. Maybe you knew what was about to happen, but you were hoping not to know. You knew it and you didn't want to know it, so you closed your eyes and tried to disappear.

He knocked first, a courtesy that was so beside the point it brought you back and made you want to laugh out loud. And then he turned the knob and pushed at the door, expecting it to open, but it resisted him. He hesitated—maybe he was already beginning to guess at what he was going to find and was bracing himself against an expectation of the worst. He tried again, but still the door didn't budge. It was locked maybe? He turned to you, a pinched look on his face, and then with a groan he threw himself at the door, expecting to shoulder it open with the brute force of his body and his weight. His ears were pink with anger and frustration, and he was calling out to her by then, in emergency and hope: "Matka! Matka!"

He stopped a moment to listen, and then called out to her again, in the same way. "Matka! Matka!"

You heard the bell tinkle on the front door downstairs as a customer came in. You peered over the banister to see a woman in a fur coat standing near the counter below you. She looked up, her attention drawn to the racket that your father was making up there, and whatever she saw in your face at that moment must have frightened her, as she put a hand to her throat and stepped back.

It was only old Mrs. Krauss, from up on Vernon Hill. She shopped at Krejci's weekly and at that time she owed you a little over three hundred dollars on her account from December. You didn't even pause to say hello. You just tumbled down the stairs and elbowed your way past, barreling through the store and outside into the snow and around the back and up again to Matka's outer door. You used the key from under the mat to let yourself in. The apartment was dark, and cold, but you could see the shape of your grandmother there in the shadows on the other side of the room. She was sitting on the floor, propped up with her back against the door, and that was why your father hadn't been able to open it. Her knotted hands were folded in her lap in such a way that she almost seemed to have been posed there, with her swollen ankles encased in their dark stockings and her misshapen feet sticking out from under the hem of the black skirt that was spread out around her on the hardwood floor like a spill of inky water. Her eyes were open and her head was tilted slightly to one side, as if in puzzle over some question that she hadn't yet found an answer for.

Josef had come around after you and was pushing his way into the apartment, calling out to his mother, kneeling over her and wailing words that you didn't understand, Czech that sounded so crazy you had to turn away.

You went downstairs to turn off the lights and close the store. Outside the snow was falling, thick and cold. It was going to be a bad night, and everybody knew it. The storm that you'd been waiting for had turned into the blizzard they were predicting. Already the streets were piling up with snow and there was little traffic, just a deep cold stillness, with snowfall muffling down all around.

Inside the store it was warmer, and Mrs. Krauss was still there. She had finished her shopping and was standing patiently at the counter, waiting for you to ring her up as if this might be any other day and business as usual. In her basket there was a bag of sugar, a jug of milk, a box of butter, and a half-carton of eggs. You turned the sign on the door around and explained as kindly as you could that the store was closed. But this was not something that Mrs. Krauss wanted to hear. She'd come all that way, she argued, and in such weather.

"Couldn't you just allow me buy these few things?" she asked, smiling.

You shook your head. "We're closed, Mrs. Krauss. I'm sorry, but my grandmother..."

The old woman frowned and raised a gloved hand. She pursed her lips, which were thin and bright red with fresh lipstick. Her old skin was leathery-looking and powdered, her cheeks were pink with rouge.

"Please, dear?" she begged. Her eyes twinkled with expectation, or maybe it was fear.

"Just take it then," you said.

Mrs. Krauss started to thank you, and began digging in her purse for her billfold.

"I'm locking up," you told her. "Get out of here," you said. "Please. Just go." You put the things in a bag and pushed it at her. You'd come around the counter then and you were nudging her toward the door, prepared to shove her out into the snow, when you looked up and saw your father standing there, watching.

"What are you doing, Meena?"

"I was just…"

His face was white, and fallen-seeming, slack and slipping from his bones. His eyes were dull. He shook his head, then turned to Mrs. Krauss and seemed to brighten at the sight of her. "Here dear, let me help you with that," he said, and took the bag of groceries from her arms. He reached and pulled her collar up around her neck for her, straightened the hat on her head, then took her by the arm and guided her toward the door.

"This weather," you heard him saying, his voice deep, soothing. "Terrible. You shouldn't be out in it. You should have called us, let us bring your things to you. Watch your step now. It might be slick."

He helped her into her car and then stood in the snow to wave her back out of the space where she'd parked, guiding her forward toward the street and sending her off with an encouraging thumbs up, calling after her, "Be careful now. Good night!"

That was Josef Krejci. The customer always came first and the customer was always right. He'd told you this over and over again: Without the customer a grocery store is nothing. Service, that's what people expect. Generosity. Kindness. Attention. Understanding. Love.

And that's what you have to give them, if you want to get ahead. No matter what.

He left you there to finish closing up and went upstairs to Matka's rooms again. You emptied the cash drawer. Checked the coolers. Swept the floor and turned off the lights.

Maybe you heard the siren as the ambulance approached or maybe you didn't. There were voices first, and then the clamber of men's feet up the stairs and across the floor, shaking the ceiling overhead so it sounded as if there must have been a dozen firemen and paramedics up there, but later you would learn that there were only three.

Instead of locking up from inside the store and going up the stairs to the apartment, you put on your coat and scarf and hat and went out the back, locking the door behind you. You stood at the edge of the parking lot, away from the light and the ambulance and the folks in the houses nearby who had come outside to see what happened and you watched as the men struggled to bring the stretcher with Matka's big body laid out on it down those narrow stairs.

By the time it was all over, the snow was so thick that it had piled up on your shoulders and your head, and maybe it would have buried you after a while if your father hadn't found you and brought you inside again where it was warm and light, but by then the apartment was empty, and your grandmother was gone.

Matka was buried in the Bohemie Cemetery behind St. Wenceslas church, in a plot beside her husband, near where Agnes Krejci lay. That there were so many people at the service should not have come as a surprise to you, because you ought to have known how many friends your father had, how popular he was: Josef

Krejci, the neighborhood grocer who had a smile for everyone, the most eligible widower, who'd been given the burden of having to raise his only daughter all alone. Some of them you knew from the store, some you recognized but couldn't name, and others you were sure you'd never met.

Libbie was not there, but her mother was. Mrs. Grandon kissed you on the cheek, then turned to Josef and shook his hand. She was wearing a high-collared black dress with full sleeves and a narrow waist that flattered her figure and a pillbox hat with a spotty veil meant to hide her eyes and conceal her grief, such as it was.

It was so cold and snowy still that few people came outside to the graveyard after the service was over. The snow was still fresh-seeming and white, piled all around and weighing down the branches of the trees, which creaked against the weight. There was a canopy over the open grave, and plastic grass laid down across the snow, edging the hole and its deep black Iowa dirt. The wind whistled in your ears. So cold! And colder still, the thought of Matka in her thin black dress, a large shadow huddled down there all alone. It had to be even worse than death itself, you thought—that coldness, that blackness, that emptiness, that dark.

Compared to a warming summer sun. Compared to a cozy yellow fire. Compared to the buttery quiet light of an empty kitchen in the middle of a humid August afternoon with a wasp trapped and buzzing angrily against the screen.

There was your mother's own grave nearby. The stone—simple, square, her name and the dates of her life carved in plain frank letters—"Dearest Departed Too Soon Gone"—was covered with a cap of snow that Josef swiped away with his gloved hand. You looked up at his face, pinkened by the cold and damp, to see that he was crying. You pretended not to notice. You were embarrassed, and you believed he'd be ashamed.

When you got home you went straight upstairs and thawed yourself out in a hot bath, put on pajamas and a sweater and climbed into your bed, even though it was only the middle of the day. You could hear music downstairs—your father in his study, listening to opera. Mrs. Chadima would be in the kitchen, sorting through the food that the neighbors had dropped off, putting a dinner together for you to eat later.

You fell asleep and dreamed of a golem, some shared figment of your grandmother's imagination, a concoction of vegetables and fruit that emerged from the basement of the grocery store to move through the streets of Linwood. He was looking for you, it seemed. His body was half rotten and the soles of his feet squelched on the pavement as he moved, solid with intent. You saw him coming, and you tried to turn and run away, but something was holding you in place and you couldn't move. Until he came so close that you could smell him. Ferment. Putrefaction. Desiccation. Rot. He reached for you, shriveled pickle fingers waggling, and you woke up in a sweat, both terrified and enthralled, to find your father there, standing by the bed, watching you.

"Remember who you are, Meena," he said.

You sat up, pulled your damp hair away from your face. He was so large, looming over you—his broad face bobbed above his wide shoulders; he held his big hands folded together into one huge fist, which he shook at you. "Remember," he said again.

"Who am I?" you asked him.

"You are my daughter," he replied. "And now you

are all that I have."

It was sometime in the week after Matka's funeral that you found Libbie waiting for you when you got home from the store. She seemed to have materialized from out of nothing, from the shadows she was there. You knew that she had dropped out of Mount Mercy. Well, to be exact, she didn't drop out. To be exact, she got kicked out.

When you asked her about it—"What happened? Why?"—she just rolled her eyes. Coughed into her fist and blew on her hands. They were chapped, and the nails were chewed, bitten to the bone like a fox paw caught in a trap.

She shrugged and sniffed. "They caught us smoking on the grounds," she said. You knew that "us" meant her and Gingi Noone.

Her face, a bright white saucer, glistened; it shone mask-like in the growing dark as you stood outside in the double driveways that ran between the two yards. The hard tweak of winter was gnawing, so you had to keep moving if you wanted to stay warm.

"Fucking nuns," Libbie went on. She moled her hands down into the deep pockets of her pea coat and hunched her shoulders up to her ears. That coat of hers was a hideous old moth-eaten thing, several sizes too big for her, that she'd picked up for a couple of bucks at a thrift shop downtown. "Frigid pussies," she said, shuddering. "Frozen cunts."

You bared your teeth, grimaced, gasped at the cold air and at these words, which frankly shocked you. You wanted to think that Libbie didn't mean what she was saying, not really. You wanted to believe that Libbie was only trying to be tough, like Gingi Noone. But you also knew that Libbie was nothing like Gingi Noone.

Libbie was almost eighteen then too, but she looked much younger. She was so small, thin and shivery inside her big coat. Her lips were chapped and her cheeks were bright with two twin nickels of winter's pinch. She was kicking at a stone in the driveway, and with each kick she flinched. To you just then it looked as if Libbie were feeling the blows in her own body, as if she might really only be driving her own foot into herself.

What she was saying was only half—if even that— of the real truth. Because it wasn't just the smoking. It was also the lying. It was also the swearing. It was the blasphemy and the anger, and it was the temper tantrums that she was known to throw when she wasn't given her way. The disobedience and the insubordination. It was skipping classes. And it was sneaking out of her mother's house after dark to meet her friends and hang out at the new hamburger stand on First Avenue, talking to the boys, flirting and smoking and sometimes going off with one of them in his car.

So they kicked her out. And now, no more uniforms. No more catechism and no more morning chapel and no more midday prayer.

What would Libbie do? She seemed so small and thin and pale, she might have been fading away before yours eyes.

Your own situation at school wasn't much better. Not that you were ever in any kind of trouble. That wasn't it. Not that you'd been singled out in any way. That wasn't it either.

No, you were a hopeless case, scorned by the popular girls and worse off even than the most unpopular ones. They were at least made fun of, and even felt sorry for by some, but no one even saw you, you were altogether ignored. When you moved through the stream of students in the hall the way before you would part, mindlessly, no one even seemed to be aware that you were there. You went from room to room that way, from hall to hall, from class to class. Maybe the teachers took a kind of notice, but their awareness of you was oblique, sunlight bounced off the magnifying glass of the work you did, and it caused you to blush and stammer with embarrassment at the heat of their attention, even when what was being offered was praise.

Mr. Grandon was the only one who treated you as if you might be someone who was normal. He was all smiles and jokes and friendliness. "How's it going, kiddo?" he asked, his blue eyes brilliant, white teeth gleaming, blond hair glossy. Then he nodded happily when you stammered back that it was going just fine.

Captured forever in the school yearbook at the end of that year, your face would look as plain and vague as if someone might have rubbed it out with her thumb.

Libbie led the way, and you followed her around the back of the house to the Foreverland bomb shelter, where she shouldered the heavy steel door open, and when you hesitated Libbie took you by the hand and dragged you inside, where it was even colder and dark as death besides. She lit a match and held it to a camping lantern hooked to a chain that hung from the ceiling overhead. You could see now that Libbie had made a small private place for herself here. It was an encampment, with hanging fabrics that hid all the junk that had been pushed into piles against the cinderblock walls. In the center of the room, where the cots used to be, she'd unfolded a pair of lawn chairs next to a cracked plastic parson's table with a blue crocheted placemat on it. She'd plugged a space heater and a small television set into a thick black extension cord that ran out under the red steel door and across the grass to the garage.

"What do you think, Meena?" she asked. "Pretty homey, huh?" Her smile gleamed just like her dad's.

She flopped down onto a chair and gestured for you to take the other. She offered a cigarette, and when you declined, lit one for herself. The pea coat swam around her.

You were surrounded by boxes of old clothes, old shoes, suitcases and picture frames, broken appliances, rakes and brooms, lawnmowers, furniture, lamps. A lifetime's accumulation of extra and unnecessary stuff. Libbie, looking around and recalling the cots and the blankets and the cans of soup and vegetables, scoffed now at the idea that there might have been a place of safety here, in a world that would have otherwise, and for other reasons, been destroyed.

Because her mother was crazy, she said. Rolled the cone of ash at the end of her cigarette, raised an eyebrow, smirked: "Certifiable." And her father was even worse, he was a fool, flirting with anything in a skirt, even Gingi Noone.

She shook her head, then smirked. "Even you, Meena, for Christ's sake."

The dog was deaf and blind and arthritic; the cat was dead and so was old Mrs. Bickel, for that matter. Matka, too. John was away at school in California, off into his own life there. He didn't even come home for holidays anymore. Even poor old Leo Spivak had been drafted and shipped off to Vietnam, where he was flying helicopters, where he'd probably get blown to bits.

Libbie was feeling sorry for herself now, and who could blame her? The stuffed animals and dolls and childhood toys that once cluttered her bedroom had been packed into boxes that she'd dragged downstairs, out the back door and across the grass to this place, the bomb shelter, where they were piled up with everything else unidentifiable and forgotten that had accumulated there.

Her entire life seemed to be falling to pieces, and if something didn't happen soon, well, she did not believe that she could take it anymore.

She lit a second cigarette off the embers of the first.

"I was really sorry to hear about your grandmother," she said, blowing smoke. Then paused, thoughtfully. "Remember those crazy stories she used to tell us?" Grinning, shaking her head, tapping her ashes on the floor.

You nodded. "Yes, sure."

Later you would listen to Libbie swear that Matka's ghost still haunted the rooms of the apartment over the store. And couldn't you just about see the old woman sitting right there the same as she always had, in her chair by the window, watching the street, waiting for something to happen—but what? Soaking her feet in Epsom salts dissolved in a bowl of warm water, knitting, sewing, working away at something, one thing or another, with her knobbed fingers and her bolted joints, while she talked and talked, telling you a story of some kind: the Golem, the bears, the goblins, the pilgrim, the forest, the river, the mushrooms, the mud. Her hairpins glinting in the sunlight, her teeth sharp and white in the broad moon of her face, and a sheer bright buoyant glimmer of tears afloat there in the corners of her eyes.

"Once upon a time…"

Now Libbie was asking, "Remember how we used to pretend to be each other? How we lied about our names? How we were a pair of princesses, mistakenly switched at birth? I was you and you were me?"

Yes, you remembered that, too.

"Well now…," Libbie went on, thoughtfully,

"…now I wish I really could be you."

The lawn chair creaked beneath her as she shifted and brought her arms around to hug herself. You peered through the dim light, through the gray whorl of cigarette smoke to study your friend's beautiful pale face.

"Me?"

Libbie sat up, excited now, and intent. "Yes. You."

And you knew then that of course Libbie had no idea at all who you were. Something she'd invented maybe, but surely not yourself.

Libbie was talking so fast now that it was hard for you to keep up, difficult to follow the train of her thought. She was talking about a boyfriend, how much she loved him. And you were lucky, weren't you, not to be loving anybody? Wasn't it all so much simpler that way?

"You can't imagine what it's like, to want someone this much. To feel that you are only half a person, you are nobody, without him. Without him, you might as well be dead."

Libbie sighed, then sat up, stomped out her cigarette and lit yet another.

"I wake up in the morning and the first thing I can think of is his face," she said. The phone would ring… and there it was, his voice, a deep thrill to hear. She was up until all hours of the night, in her room, talking to him. Sometimes she fell asleep that way, listening to him murmuring to her.

She made a face. "Sickening, isn't it?"

When you were young, you used to laugh about love. You used to think it was something sappy and ridiculous, slightly disgusting, something googlely-eyed and crazy, having to do with sweat and saliva and Deep Eddie yanking at his Thing. "Pee You," Libbie would say, if she caught her parents kissing. "Cooties!" she'd exclaim.

"Who is he?" you asked. "What's his name?"

Libbie shook her head. "You don't know him. He's older. And he's not from around here."

Oh, but he was beautiful, she went on. If you could call a man beautiful. And amazingly smart. He knew about everything. Absolutely everything.

"Where did you meet him? When?"

"Last summer. Here. He just showed up one night."

Libbie had been sitting outside on the front steps, smoking and listening to the crickets and complaining about the heat and the mosquitoes. She'd flicked her cigarette off, watched it bounce and spark against the sidewalk, and at that same moment the street lamp snapped on to reveal the shape of a boy outlined against the darker tangle of the boxwood hedge that rimmed the side yard.

How long had he been standing there?

He said something that made Libbie laugh, and right away she liked him. She liked the way his eyes were green and his hair was red, and he had a crooked thin half-smile that made him seem as if he knew something she didn't know, and that he thought it was funny. He took her hand and held it up to the light, comparing hers childish and pale to his freckled and raw-boned.

But he was not really a boy—he was a young man, four years older than Libbie, the same age as her brother. He worked at the used bookstore down on 4th Street, near the railroad tracks, and maybe he was also dealing dope.

He had a car, too—a yellow Mercury, with a black convertible top that he put down so they could cool off a little, let the wind blow through their hair. Mess things up some. They cruised up and down First Avenue and then he took her up to Twinkle Hill and they parked there under the trees with the whole of Linwood spread out below them like this great big glittery gift, theirs for the taking if they wanted it. If they knew how to take it.

They listened to the radio. Sly and the Family Stone. Simon and Garfunkel. In a white room with no curtains... C'mon baby, light my fire... Don't you need somebody to love? They smoked cigarettes. They smoked a joint. He talked and she listened—revolution, the man, the pigs, anarchy, peace. Policemen in Chicago. Soldiers in Vietnam. Tear gas and billy clubs, napalm and body bags. When he finally stopped to kiss her, well, that was all it took.

Libbie Grandon was in love.

She went on: some day she was going to marry him, but for now they only wanted to live together, if only they had a place of their own.

And so: "What will your father do with Matka's apartment?" Libbie was asking you now. "I mean, do you think maybe he'd be interested in renting it out? To me?"

Faye Grandon was outside in her yard planting pansies along the edges of her front walk in the first warm days of spring. She squatted in the dirt, wiped her forehead with the back of her hand. She stood, arched her back, raised a hand to her face, cupped one palm across her forehead to shade her eyes from the sun. She was wearing yellow shorts and blue rubber flip flops. She'd painted her toenails the color of tomatoes.

Across the driveway, on the other side of the hedge Josef Krejci—the grocer, a big old Bohemie in a flowered shirt, brown shorts, thick belt, socks and leather sandals—stood near the hedge. He was puffing on his pipe and looking thoughtfully up through his own smoke into the sky.

On her knees now in the rose garden, Faye Grandon was sitting back on her heels. Her ankles were slim. She sighed. She held a pair of shears in her hand; they glinted in the sun. She wiped a wrist across her forehead again, pushed her hair back from her face, sniffed, smelled smoke.

And at the same time Josef Krejci was sniffing too. Maybe he was smelling the roses. Or was it the scent of her perfume?

She turned to look, and her blue eyes meet his green. This was an awkward moment, and at first neither of them seemed to know what to say. She smiled; he nodded. He tapped his pipe against his palm; she dug her trowel into the dirt. He lingered, rocking on his heels.

You stood at the upstairs window, keeping an eye on the two of them. Faye Grandon laughed; you listened. Josef Krejci smiled; you saw.

And then later, at dinner that night, you told him, "I think I know somebody who will rent Matka's apartment. If you're interested."

He paused to consider this. Took a bite of meat, chewed. "Who?"

"Libbie Grandon."

This puzzled him. "Libbie? Why would she want to do that?"

"She's got a boyfriend."

He snorted. This he understood. "How much?"

"I don't know. What would you want for it?"

He was thinking. Thinking and chewing. "What's it cost us?"

You were the one who kept the books and paid the bills. "Not much," you said. "About thirty dollars a month for the utilities, except in winter, then it's more. Probably something like, oh, maybe two hundred a year in taxes on it, as part of the store. That works out to a little more than five hundred a year. A little less than fifty dollars a month, maybe. Not counting the phone."

"How much will she pay?"

"Probably double that, at least. The boyfriend's got some money, I think. They both have jobs."

In the end, you settled on one hundred dollars a month, for one bedroom, a living room, a kitchen and a bath, all utilities paid, except for the phone.

And so that spring Libbie moved out of her mother's house and into Matka's empty rooms. Where your grandmother's bed used to be now there was a mattress on the floor. India print fabric throws were draped across the windows. A beaded curtain hung in the doorway. A lamp with a frosted glass shade sat on a table made from a telephone wire spool turned flat on its side and painted Day-Glo green. A battered loveseat slip-cased in blue chintz was placed against the wall, beside a bookcase made of cinderblocks and old barn planks. On the wall: a Jefferson Airplane poster, with fat white letters that billowed out around Grace Slick's cool-eyed, hair-framed face, a print of Picasso's "Guernica," an American flag, hung upside down and backwards. On the floor: tied rag rugs, ashtrays, beer cans and wine bottles. In the air: a hanging haze of sunlight and dust, incense and smoke.

And at the door: Fox Dow knocking, standing back, waiting for Libbie Grandon to open up and let him in.

July 2006

Meena has been following the trail back down to the cabin, not paying much attention to it, only keeping her eyes on her feet skidding in the dirt and noticing the ache in her knees that jolts her with every step. It's dusk, and she's dizzy with exertion and vertigo and the hectic joy of her new freedom, here in this strange and beautiful, and vast, place.

Just moments ago, when she was standing at what felt to her to be the top of the world, gaping at the countryside spread below her—far away and small and toy-like and unreal—it seemed simple enough to just turn around and retrace her steps, come back here the same way she went, but when she emerges from the shadows of the forest she realizes she's made some mistake, although in her confusion she can't understand what it is, exactly. The place is familiar, but at the same time it's different—it's what it is and something else, too, both at once. More and less. The same and not the same. For one thing, the woodpile is much smaller. There is a bentwood rocker on the back porch and a hammock strung between a pair of trees and a stone-rimmed fire pit in the yard. And the cabin itself is askew somehow—lopsided in its very structure, it sags on its foundation, and the tarpaper roof is peeling back in places, weeds flock the porch steps, the log walls are weathered, soft and gray. But the door has been painted purple, and there are wind chimes hanging from the eaves.

So—time has passed, she thinks, while she's been away. That must be it. There's been an enchantment; months have gone by, maybe even years. Her life here must have become settled, in the meantime. All those other problems and questions and worries, somehow resolved.

As if to confirm this, and to welcome her back from her long and miserable absence, the cabin glows with warm light now as twilight spreads through the forest, and the shadows smudge toward night. There is even a thin swirl of white smoke rising from the chimney, quaint as a picture book. A breeze tinkles charmingly through the chimes.

Meena approaches this scene cautiously, slowly, quietly, sneaking up on herself in what seems to her to be a dream, taking great care not to come crashing back in again too quickly, because she doesn't want to shake herself awake, not if she can help it. Could it be this easy then? Might she be able to Rip Van Winkle herself forward into a simplified future, push past this complicated present into another time, a stand-alone future in which the past has been forgotten or resolved or, at least, outlived?

She creeps up onto the porch and peers in through the window to see a room that is warm and bright and welcoming, aglow with lamp and fire light. She expects to see her older wiser self sitting there by the fire, too—and, she wonders, what will she have become, in the meantime? Matka?

But it is not herself that Meena sees, it's a changeling replica, smaller, thinner, paler, younger... it's Holly Gidding.

Meena blinks. Wrong path. Wrong cabin. A simple mistake, and she struggles to hold herself together and not be devastated by it.

Tonight Holly's dark hair is wet-looking and pulled back and slicked down like a helmet, flat against her skull. A single glittery butterfly clip lifts and holds her bangs back, clearing her brow above her sharp features. Her skin, though still pale, looks clear, even pretty in this light, and she has removed the metal from her face. The bud of her mouth is pursed in concentration as she squints down at some needlework in her lap. This whole picture forms an old-fashioned tableau: except for the clip in her hair, Holly might be a settler, a trapper's daughter, a pioneer wife.

She's so young, though, and self-absorbed. Meena finds herself transfixed by this vision of this girl, innocent of her attention. Holly tugs at a caught thread, frowns, brings it up to her mouth, and bites it off with sharp white teeth. Meena knows that she should turn away now—she's seen enough and has no good reason for being here—she knows she ought to drift back into the forest again, regain the trail, and find there the right way back to her own cabin, where she, at least for now, belongs—but she hesitates. She doesn't want to go. She doesn't want to be alone. She leans closer instead, and as she brings her hands up to frame her face against the window glass her shoulder bumps the bentwood chair and sets it rocking with a clatter against the rugged floorboards of the porch. Holly hears, looks up, and, caught spying, Meena swoons with shame. Her heart hammers in her throat, but Holly is smiling and bounding toward the door, calling, "Libbie!"

She's wearing overalls, a silky pink T-shirt, a baby blue cardigan sweater with white plastic rabbit-shaped buttons. She really is smiling, and she really does seem glad to see Meena.

"I'm sorry, I'm, I...," Meena stammers, but Holly

has reached out and is pulling her inside, and isn't this just what she wanted?

"Come in, sit down, no one ever visits me, this is so nice."

Meena allows herself to be led to a chair—green velvet, with an old lace antimacassar on the back—and she sinks into it, suddenly limp with exhaustion, resignation, relief.

Holly's eyes glitter in the firelight. She pushes up the sleeves of her sweater, revealing the rose briar tattoo on her wrist. "I wasn't expecting you."

"I'll just catch my breath, if that's okay. I don't want to be a bother."

"It's no bother, really."

The fire is warm, comforting. "I was out walking. I guess I took a wrong turn. I thought I was home."

"Do you miss it?"

"What?"

"Home."

"I guess so, maybe."

"If I lived in California, I would never leave it. I'd never go anyplace else."

"And what would you do if you lived there?"

Holly shrugs. Her smile is self-conscious, shy. "Maybe I could be an actress," she says. Her face reddens. "Isn't that what everybody wants? What if I got famous? What if I was a star?"

"Well, if you're ever going to get away from here," Meena hears herself saying, "you should do it now, while you're still young enough to take chances." She might be Mimi Hanrahan, squawking at some hopeless-looking kid who's come into the White Elephant to shop.

"Is that what you did?" Holly asks.

"Yes, it is. But I was lucky. I had a boyfriend. We

ran off to California together."

"What was his name?"

"Fox. "

Holly smiles at this. "And was he a fox?"

Meena grins. "Was he ever."

She's ashamed of these lies that she keeps telling. But she can't seem to stop them. She feels dizzied by the make-believe and the possibilities that it seems to be offering. Or maybe it's the altitude.

Holly is leaning closer. "Take me with you?"

Startled by the suggestion, Meena frowns. "Oh no, she says, no, no, I couldn't do that."

Holly shrugs. "Why not?"

Why not. "It's just not a good idea, that's all."

"Sure it is."

"But what about your brother?"

Now Holly is frowning. She peers at Meena. "You know, Libbie, everything isn't always what it seems."

"I'm afraid I don't…"

"Look, he lied to you, all right? It was a trick."

Meena still doesn't understand. "Who lied?"

"My brother. The great Will Gidding, full-time survival expert and part-time Armageddon freak."

Meena shakes her head. "I don't think I know what you're talking about."

"The whole thing with the dog. He set it up." Holly sits back, folds her hands in her lap. She seems to be enjoying Meena's confusion. "It wasn't dead."

Meena stares. "It wasn't?"

"No, it wasn't even real."

"But… How could it not have been real? There was blood, wasn't there?" Hadn't she seen blood?

"He just put it there so you'd run over it."

"But why?"

"To save you, why else?"

"Save me from what?"

"Damnation." Holly is smiling now. "But don't feel bad. You're not the only one who's fallen for it. It's this thing he does, on purpose, to catch lost souls. It's bait, he says, that's all. Like fishing. He's a fisher of men, he says. And women."

"That's crazy."

Holly nods. "No shit it's crazy. I thought I already told you that—my brother is a lunatic." Her own grin is goofy. She waves a hand at Meena and goes on, "Mostly people just give him money, to take care of the dead dog, and that's okay, too. But you're the first one who ever cried like that. I think you scared him."

Meena shakes her head. "Why are you telling me this?"

"So you can see what I'm up against and take me with you. When you go." She leans forward again, reaches out, lifts Meena's hand and enfolds it in her own. "I'll be good," she says. "I promise, I won't be any bother. And I can help you out, too. I'm really useful that way. Like, if you get a flat tire, or something, I know what to do. You'll be glad to have me around, I swear you will." She's squeezing Meena's hand now. "Please? I have to go, I have to get out of here. This is my life. It's my whole life, and I can't just sit here and watch it waste away…"

Meena pulls her hand back. "He's done this before?"

Holly nods. "Plenty of times."

"But I saw the dog move…"

"Did you? Are you sure?"

Meena tries to remember. She doesn't know what to think. She struggles to stand up, but her head is spinning, and so instead she slumps back down into the chair.

"Hey, I'm sorry." Holly's voice seems distant and dim.

Meena closes her eyes.

"I didn't mean to scare you." And then, "Hey Libbie, are you okay?"

Meena hears the squeak of alarm in this, but she keeps her eyes closed, and her head is filled with a swarming darkness in which she thinks she can imagine her father's death. She's feeling the blackness that came folding down over him as he lay in his bed, the bed he'd slept in alone for almost fifty years, almost her whole life. His senses closing down, slowly, one by one. First, taste and smell. Then touch, he's floating, can't feel the bed beneath him, can't feel the warm air around him, his skin has opened up, the flesh that separates him from the world has begun to disintegrate, it frays and thins and shreds, worn away to such nothingness that his inner self is exposed, vibrant as bare wire. Then his hearing goes—dimming, muffled, muted—and a deafening inward silence fills him. His eyes pop open, and he stares and stares, watches the ceiling open up and retreat. The objects in the room dim and disappear, they become one with the blackness, the world closes in and his eyes widen, straining to see, straining to stay.

Josef Krejci is an old man—he lies alone in his empty bed, in his dark room, in the middle of a hot August night. He doesn't feel the heat, he doesn't see the darkness, he doesn't hear the screams of the cicadas in the trees. His breath catches in his throat, it rattles in his chest: he gasps, he stares, and then the silence that surrounds him is his own.

"Libbie?"

Meena's eyes snap open.

Holly has come close and is bending near, her face a crumple of concern. "Please, let me help you," she says. "What can I do?"

The needlework that Holly has set aside seems to be a sampler of some kind—the letters of the alphabet entwined in deep green leafy vines and gaudy flowers. Such domesticity in a young woman, Meena thinks. A girl, really. Here in this cabin, on the verge of the rest of her life. Lucky that way. Nearby is a box of sewing supplies: threads, buttons, measuring tape, needles, pins. A small pair of steel scissors.

Meena takes a deep breath. She turns to Holly, smiling weakly. "Just glass of water, dear. Would you mind?" she asks.

And Holly is quick to respond; she's eager to be of help. As soon as her back is turned, it doesn't take Meena more than a moment to snatch the scissors from the sewing box and hide them in the crook of her folded arms as she struggles to her feet.

Cupboard door opening and closing. Ice clattering into a plastic glass. Water running from the tap.

The wind chimes shiver on the porch—and by the time Holly returns to the firelit room, her visitor will be gone.

And now the Aspenglo cabin is warm with lamp and fire light, too. And here is Meena Krejci crouched before a fire of her own—which it took her some time to light, struggling with matches, newspaper, shreds of bark and needles tucked beneath an arrangement of split logs that she carried in from the woodpile out back. The twilight in the forest around her has darkened, and night has arrived.

Her father has been dead for four nights. She has been away from home, alone, for three. Only once before in her life has she been gone from Linwood for this long—when she went with him to Chicago for a weekend—and never alone, never without him, never on her own. They drove in on a Friday afternoon and home again on Sunday morning and stayed those two nights at the Drake Hotel, in separate but adjoining rooms. They saw a baseball game, they ate dinner in a skyscraper, high above the street, they walked along the lake shore, and shopped in the department stores on Michigan Avenue—it was his birthday.

Now she kneels before the fire she's built, pleased to see that it has caught and grown to fill the room with warmth and a flickering orange and yellow light. The darkness outside the cabin feels deep, the forest seems thick with shadowy life. Meena imagines the animals that prowl its paths, recalling her old childhood dreams of wild beasts lurking in the bushes around her father's house on Otis Road. Someone had opened up the cages in the zoo at the park and the animals were free and were approaching, traveling swiftly through the woods, their paws silent on the narrow paths, now and then a growl, resounding, a growing murmur of movement as the monkeys went swinging silently from limb to limb in the canopy of trees overhead. The beasts lay in wait for her, breathing deeply, slowly. Eyes aglow in the dark, teeth agleam in the moonlight, the animals were infinitely patient, they could wait for her forever. She might have stepped into the darkness and let them have her. She might have chosen to give herself to them.

Some nights her father would retreat to his study after dinner and once the kitchen was clean she would slip in after him—maybe he knew she was there and tolerated her, or maybe he wasn't aware. As a child she had crouched in the shadow behind his chair, near the ornate wall vent billowing warm air from the old heater in the basement, blowing in her hair. Outside, snow, or rain? She couldn't see, because it was night and the windows were wet and black, reflecting back the inside of the room, so she could look up and see him there in the glass, reading a big book, history maybe it was, or philosophy, what was it? The newspaper? And there was music playing, piano and violin and flute. When she was older she found a reason to come in—bringing him coffee, pouring brandy, looking for a book. Maybe she lingered and he didn't look up, maybe he ignored her, maybe he didn't complain when she eased herself down on a chair near the book case and pretended to read, sharing his company, breathing him in—pipe smoke, lemons, alcohol, wet wool—growing sleepy in the warm room until the print on the page blurred, the book slipped from her hand and landed on the floor with a smack that startled her awake, disoriented and craving a cigarette. Or maybe he gave her a look of dismissal and so she stood in the hallway for a while, outside the open door, instead. Before retreating to the living room to watch television alone.

She and her father had stood together outside the bear compound in Ellis Park one afternoon, sniffing at the stench of the animals' close confinement, and he said not to bother feeling sorry for them because they liked it. Said if you opened up the cage to let them out, they wouldn't know what to do. They wouldn't run off, escape into the woods, rampage through the gardens, terrorize the neighborhood, no, they would just stand there and stare at you, uncomprehending. "They don't want freedom," he said. "They don't want to be let loose." They would stay put because captivity is safety, awash with the familiar reek of home.

And later Meena, in her nightgown, will be leaning over the sink in the tiny Aspenglo kitchen, working Holly's sewing scissors through her hair. Steel blades chewing, the hair coming away in her fist, dropped into the basin, curling like a dead animal, to be ground up in the fierce teeth of the disposal, and washed away. Then she'll look up to see a stranger's face reflected in the fire brightened pane of window glass above the sink— longer, paler, thinner than her own. Bladelike. Eyes wide, dark, shocked. Cheekbones sharp. Jaw long. The mouth a fierce gash, aslant with resolve.

A changeling child, Meena Krejci will have shed her outer shell of self. And thus exposed, she will have been reborn as someone else, a new person, pure being loose in the world—this solitary woman who has been calling herself Libbie.

Accounting

1969

Mrs. Grandon had stopped paying her bill at the store months ago, but Josef Krejci didn't know this because you were in charge of the books and he had entrusted their upkeep to you. Mrs. Grandon owed over four thousand dollars, a sum of such breathtaking extravagance at that time that you knew your father was not going to be able to take it lightly. First he would be angry with you, for letting the situation get so far out of hand, and then he would be angry with Mrs. Grandon, for what he would judge to be her recklessness and irresponsibility, and finally he would be angry with Mr. Grandon, for neglecting the financial obligations of his wife.

Everybody knew, your father had a policy: no more charges allowed on accounts totaling over three hundred dollars in debt. Who could ask him to carry any more than that? He was not a banker, after all, he was only a grocer, and he had a right to expect his customers to pay. He had every right. And it was your job to make certain that they did.

When Mrs. Grandon came in to pick up a few things that she thought she needed, you knew what she owed, so you should have stopped her. Her name was supposed to be on The List. That was what it was called, The List. There were other families who were on The List too of course, families like the Noones, who were turned away at the register—in a humiliating contest of their small want against Josef Krejci's stone will—if they couldn't pay cash. Gingi's mother thin and pale in a pair of men's pants, baggy, and a blue work shirt, stained, and a wool sweater coat, buttons missing. Mrs. Noone was known to drink whiskey; maybe she smoked pot. She went to bars and sometimes was asked to get up and sing with the band, her voice was deep and smoky, and she slept with Negroes.

Letters were sent, dignified, distant, and polite at first, then fixed and firm, and finally when all else had failed, vaguely threatening. "Dear Mrs. Noone, kindly remit." Or else. Although everybody knew that a person such as Mrs. Noone was likely to ignore the letters—or to laugh them off, or to try to work her way around them if she could, falling back on her family, that whole squalid clan of Noones, uncivilized and inbred, monsters that they were—most people responded to these tactics. They liked Josef Krejci, for one thing; they respected him. And why not? He was a good example: he worked hard and he didn't ask of anybody any more than what he asked of himself. He offered people simple payment plans. With a little interest added in, for his trouble. That was only fair.

Still, because of who she was and all that she had done for you, it didn't seem right that Mrs. Grandon's name should be there on The List, right next to somebody like Mrs. Noone. You watched Faye Grandon do her shopping, you saw her stand in line at the register, you saw Josef's fingers on the register keys, you saw the exchange of pleasantries between the two of them—his grin, her smile—and you saw him hand Faye a pen, you saw her sign the slip and hand it back to him, you watched Faye bundle her bags into her arms, you watched Josef watching Faye, and you tucked the Grandon account aside, in a drawer.

It wasn't that you lied, it was only that you didn't tell him. You couldn't, you didn't want to, you wouldn't. You were hoping you might be able to spare both yourself and Mrs. Grandon, even though you knew it had to be only a matter of time before your father found out the truth, and then there would be hell to pay. As you saw it, you had no choice but to go and have a talk with her yourself. Before the situation got very much more out of hand. You would explain the problem and then see if you couldn't take care of it between the two of you, without Josef Krejci having to know anything about it, without him ever having to be involved.

Mrs. Grandon was at home when you went by, and she was alone, sitting all by herself at the kitchen table and playing solitaire. She looked up, startled when you knocked at the back door, and then she invited you in with a wave of her hand, a gesture that seemed so natural and normal, so familiar, that for a minute you were thinking this was just like old times, when you would be here together waiting for Libbie and John and Mr. Grandon to come home from play and school and work. Except it wasn't anything like that now, because nobody was coming home—they didn't any of them even live there anymore. Libbie had Matka's apartment with Fox, and John was off at college in California, and Mr. Grandon was camped downtown in a room of his own at the Fielding Hotel.

The house was clean and quiet as usual, perfectly presentable, hushed and hopeful as a museum, the rooms untouched and unused and on display for anyone who might care to come and look and see. The oven was cold, but the sink was scrubbed. The floor was polished. The appliances gleamed.

Mrs. Grandon lit a match, lit a cigarette, squinted at you. "How are you?" she asked. She nodded at an empty chair, and you sat down in it.

"Fine. Good. I'm okay." Shrug. "The same."

She cocked her head and studied you for a moment, her own face open, eyes wide, expression frank. She was kind, as always. Worried for your welfare, it seemed, careful of your feelings, thoughtful for your well-being. Just as she had been when you and Libbie were younger and maybe you argued and Libbie went upstairs to her room to pout and Mrs. Grandon would be there, looking at you, poor Meena Krejci, motherless girl on her own. She'd take you into the kitchen, give you something sweet. Send you home with a soft kiss and a gentle pat.

"Come back tomorrow, Meena. Little Miss Princess will be over her snit by then."

But: "What's wrong, Meena?" she was asking now. "I can tell just by looking at you, your face all fisted up. Something's wrong." She sat back, blew smoke, pleased with herself and what she believed to be her sensitive perceptions. "Isn't it?"

You weren't sure what to say, didn't know where to start.

"Not sick are you?"

You shook your head. "No. No. Nothing like that."

Mrs. Grandon smiled. Tilted her chin. "Boy trouble?

You winced. "No, not that either."

Mrs. Grandon crushed her cigarette out in the

ashtray, sighed, leaned on her elbows and studied the cards that she'd laid out on the table. Drew one from the pile in her hand and placed it—an ace. From this she looked up and fixed her eyes on you—ice blue, stone cold, lashes heavy with black mascara. She'd cut her bangs short so that they feathered her forehead, against skin as softly creased as the chamois that her husband used to polish the curvy fenders of his convertible. She was wearing a dress with big blocks of bright color, meant to imitate a painting by Mondrian.

"Tell me about Fox Dow," she said.

That took you aback. And anyway, you didn't know much. Just that after their first encounter he called Libbie on the phone and asked her to meet him.

"Where?"

The woods. On Hollow Hill.

You knew this because you had been watching from your window and you'd seen Libbie climbing through the overgrowth, up the hill behind the houses. The path was a treachery of nettles and weeds then, but that didn't stop her, she didn't seem to mind. In her shorts and her tank top. Her hair pulled back into a pony tail. Sneakers on her feet—black boys' high-tops that you knew she'd swiped from Sanford's, just put them on and walked out of the store.

"Jesus, Libbie," you had scolded when Libbie told you about it, bragging, proud. "What if you'd got caught?"

A careless shrug. Her white hair shining in the street lamp, so bright even the moths were drawn to it.

"I didn't," she'd replied. "But I didn't."

And now, exposed to the wiser scrutiny of Mrs. Grandon's judgment, you could feel the heat rising in your face. "What do you want to know?"

"Everything."

"Well, I sure don't know everything."

"All right." Mrs. Grandon nodded.

"Just... his name is Dow." What else was there to say? "He's rich."

She nodded again. "What's he like then?"

"He seems okay. I think maybe he loves her."

"Love." Mrs. Grandon spat the word. Lips shining, tangerine orange. "Well that's not going be enough. Love." She lit another cigarette. "Not near enough by half."

But this was nothing new; it was just the same old story that you had already heard so many times you had it down by heart. How Jack and Faye Grandon had been sweethearts all their lives. They were the real thing, everybody said, admiring. Jack and Faye Grandon. Just look at them. Love birds. Can't get enough of each other, isn't it sweet?

"And," she said, sighing, tapping ash, "for a while, it was so."

"What happened?"

She smirked. Took a sip of her cold coffee. "What happened?" she echoed back.

What happened is what always happens: flames grow cold, energy runs downhill. She got tired; he got tired. And then in the end it was all just too much trouble anymore, wasn't it?

"And now?"

He had betrayed everything. He had made a mockery of her life, and of their children's lives, and of himself. Dating a bar girl down at the Pickwick, for Christ's sake.

"But she does love him," you said, meaning Libbie, meaning Fox.

And in reply Mrs. Grandon snorted, coughed, squashed out her cigarette and fixed you with that hard blue frozen look of her contempt.

"Love. What can Libbie possibly know about love?"

She got up from the table, poured herself another cup. It seemed to amuse her: Libbie and her youth. That innocence, that ignorance, that hope that Faye Grandon seemed to be in her own way working so hard to try to recapture for herself, even as she scorned it in her daughter. Standing there in her short dress. With her cheap jewelry gleaming, with her hair growing longer in the back and her eyes made up, while all the while her face was aging, and time was running out.

This house next door, this house that you had envied once and wanted for your own, this house that had been so full of light and sound and life, it had now become an empty shell with Mrs. Grandon rattling around alone inside it, like a seed in a dried up pod. How could she stand to stay there by herself?

And maybe it was then that you had your big idea, or maybe it was earlier. When did it first occur to you that Faye Grandon's loneliness might be the question and at the same time the answer, to everything? Because, what if you knew of a way to fix it? What you had in mind seemed like the most obvious answer in the world: that Mrs. Grandon should cross the double driveways and move into your house next door, with you.

What if one night, after dark, out of the blue, the doorbell rang, and there she was, standing on the front porch?

Josef wouldn't hesitate, how could he? Faye was too beautiful for him to resist. He would reach out into the night and take her by the elbow and bring her inside with him, where it was safe. He'd lead her through the dining room and into the kitchen; he'd sit her at the table and pour her a glass of sherry. She would talk, and he would listen. She'd been frightened by a noise outside the house, but it was probably just a raccoon. She was sorry for the mess she'd made of her marriage, but maybe it wasn't really all her fault. She was lonely, and wasn't he a little bit lonely, too?

You dreamed: you were huddled in the shadows of the staircase of your father's house, and you were holding your breath, in hope and in wonder. What you were listening to was only the most ordinary sound—the murmur of two adult voices, talking. Hers high and plaintive, his deep and reassuring. And that was all it would take—just such a simple, most commonplace phenomenon, a conversation between two lonely people, a man and a woman, in a warm kitchen in the middle of the night—that's all it would take to vanquish the familiar emptiness of your world, to fill it up with being other than your own. When you finally did dare to breathe again, when you picked yourself up and crept back through the shadows to your bed, then you would lie there in the dark and know, for once, that you were not alone.

And later, when you got up in the morning, Mrs. Grandon would still be there. She'd be standing at the stove in your own kitchen, making breakfast for you and your father, frying bacon, scrambling eggs, buttering toast. Josef Krejci would sit at the table with his coffee and his newspaper, and when you came in he and Faye Grandon would both look up and smile. As if there hadn't been a miracle. As if this was maybe how it had always been.

"Good morning, Meena!" So cheerful!

Where did Mrs. Grandon sleep? You wouldn't ask; you would be afraid to look. You'd have to talk about something else, for now.

"How was your night, dear?" Faye would ask you. And then, "That's such a pretty blouse you're wearing," she'd say. "A great color on you. Brings out the green in your eyes." Her face would be pale but beautiful, clean, without makeup, except for lipstick—Creamsicle Orange that went with the dress she wore. She'd lean forward to touch your hair, while you sniffed at her powdered flowery scent, with its familiar hint of clove.

After breakfast Josef would fold his paper, look at his watch, and say, It's time for us to go to work. You would follow him out the back door to the truck, and you'd leave Faye Grandon there to clean up after you, the way that mothers do. Plates piled up next to the sink, juice glasses on the table, a napkin on the floor. She'd be standing at the door, waving as Josef backed the truck away. And from then on that was how it would be: the two of you, Meena and Josef Krejci, same as any other day, except that then Mrs. Grandon would be there, too.

You would not say anything about it to your father. He would drive, and you wouldn't talk. You'd hold yourself as still and steady as you could, and all day as you sat at your desk under the stairs, recording numbers and calculating accounts, reading invoices and sending out bills, you would hardly even dare to breathe. You'd jump at every sound, startle whenever the front bell chimed or a can fell off a shelf, when the phone rang or a customer laughed or the register drawer got slammed shut. You'd have to keep quiet. You'd have to be careful, because any abrupt movement or sudden noise might tear the delicate skin of your bubble and shatter the contents of this fragile new world that you had dreamed up for yourself.

"So, how's your father, Meena?" Faye Grandon was asking.

"Oh, he's all right, I guess. A little lonely maybe."

"I'm sorry to hear that. But I guess I'm not surprised."

"Maybe you could go out with him sometime. You're lonely too, aren't you Mrs. Grandon?"

"Go out with your father? Me?" Her small laugh was like a cough. Just a little hiccup.

You leaned toward her, all business now. "You know you owe him money, don't you?"

Mrs. Grandon's eyes widened.

"Four thousand one hundred thirty-one dollars and sixty-seven cents, to be exact."

"What do you want from me?"

"I think he might forgive the debt if, you know, if the two of you were... friends?"

Mrs. Grandon lurched to her feet, toppling the chair behind her, splattering her playing cards on the floor. She steadied herself, raised a hand, pointed a finger at the door. "Get out."

She always had been dramatic.

But you held your ground. "I know I should have stopped you sooner," you said. "We never should have let it get so high."

Mrs. Grandon wasn't listening. She had come around the table and she'd taken you by the arm, hauled you up out of the chair. "Get out!"

Her fingers bruised, but still you pleaded: "Or maybe you could pay it off a little bit at a time? Just enough to make it so I wouldn't have to mention it to him. Could you manage that?"

Mrs. Grandon was hissing as she guided you across the room and toward the back door. "Talk to my husband," she said. "Go get your goddamned money from him."

She ushered you out, so brusquely, so roughly, so rudely. No smile, no kiss, no pat, she just shut the door, and locked it. You could hear the bolt slam into place. You stood there on the back porch for a while. Saw Mrs. Grandon's face at the glass, peering out. Saw her wave her hand, shooing you away.

You found Mr. Grandon at his office. You had to hang around outside for a while first and pretend to be absorbed in the bulletin board with its photos of houses for sale before he noticed you. You strolled from one end of it to the other, reading about floor plans, architectural styles, prices and financing terms, while you worked at mustering the courage to go inside and confront him. You almost gave it up. You couldn't do this. You thought, "How can I do this?"

You'd just have to let your father take care of the situation. Bear his anger and his silence for however long he decided to hold it. This was not your problem, after all. Maybe he would fire you. Send you off to college somewhere. And so maybe that would be all right, too.

But then you heard your name, and you looked up and there he was, Jack Grandon, coming toward you, grinning big, all bright teeth and glowing cheeks. Reaching out to take your hand in his. He was so handsome. His blond hair and his blue eyes.

"Meena! How are you?"

Hands on your shoulders, he held you away to get a better look, then pulled you close and hugged you. A drowning man hanging on to a life belt. If he could have, he might have picked you up. Or dragged you down with him.

But Mr. Grandon was not a big man; he was

nothing like Josef Krejci. He was only a few inches taller than you, and small-boned, thin, boyish. He seemed so young, too, maybe because of how he was dressed, fashionably, in a turtleneck sweater and black pants, zippered leather boots, a wide black belt with a big silver buckle. His hair was modishly shaggy. He could have been somebody's boyfriend. He was wearing English Leather cologne.

Now that you'd come that far, you didn't bother to beat around the bush—you pulled the bill out of your purse and handed it to him. He looked at it, sucked on his teeth, frowned and looked at you.

Whatever it was he saw, it caused him to shift gears. He was all smiles again, affable and talkative. Of course he'd pay his wife's grocery bill. No problem. But first, would you mind keeping him company for a little while? You were a reminder of the old days, he said, a glimpse back at the way things used to be. He looked at you, and from that sight he was able to remember everything. He missed the neighborhood. He missed his family. He was a little lonely, he was reluctant to admit.

How about if you came back to the hotel with him? Right now. To keep him company. He'd buy you dinner downstairs at the Pickwick, would you like that? Would that make all the bother of the rest of it worth your while? For now?

You slid into the leather booth across from Mr. Grandon. You ran a hand over the deep polished wood of the table, and squinted up at the brass light fixtures overhead. You wondered, what would you do if your father were to come in and find you here like this? What would you say and what would he think, what would he do, in return?

Across from you, Libbie's father grinned. He

ordered drinks—a scotch and water for himself, a Shirley Temple for you. The waitress—a Playboy Bunny imitation in seamed fishnet stockings, low-cut black leotard, bow tie, spiked heels—bent over and pecked him on the cheek. He grinned, blushed and introduced you as his daughter. The waitress winked at you.

"Lucky girl," she said.

Mr. Grandon sat back, watched the waitress walk away, then turned to you and shrugged.

"Well," he reasoned, "we can't have everybody thinking you're my girlfriend, can we?"

Jack Grandon and Meena Krejci sitting together in a booth at the back of the Pickwick Club, downstairs in the basement of the Fielding Hotel. You listened while he talked about his wife and his daughter and his son. He wanted you to understand, he wanted everybody to know, he had not abandoned his family. The current situation was not his doing, it was not his choice, he had not left his wife and his children to come downtown and live there at the hotel all by himself. No.

His wife had kicked him out. That was the truth. She took all of his things and she drove them downtown and she dumped them on the sidewalk, told him not to come back. She kicked him out of his own house.

He said this again and again, insisting, disbelieving maybe. But you had seen it for yourself, hadn't you? He seemed to want you to confirm it, how his wife had been.

"Impossible."

Nevertheless, it didn't matter. Ultimately. Because, there had been no convincing Libbie. No matter what the facts were, still she was going to blame him. For everything. He was her father, after all.

He sighed when he said her name: "Libbie." Shook

his head, ground his teeth. "Libbie."

He said: they were both trying to kill him, his wife and his daughter. They wanted him out of the way, out of the house. Dead of a heart attack now, in the prime of his life. And that would make them happy, wouldn't it? As if maybe he deserved it?

Well but no, it was not going to be that easy. No sir. Oh no, Jack Grandon was not going to just disappear, he was not going to give up. They were his family. Even though they treated him like this.

The waitress brought the drinks and handed over the menus. You wondered if she knew Josef Krejci. Did he eat there? With someone else across the table from him, some girl he'd found upstairs in the lobby?

"You hungry, Meena?" Mr. Grandon was asking. He closed his menu with a snap and lit a cigarette, drew on it deeply, tapped ashes nervously. "I'm not," he said. "Late lunch. You go ahead and order some dinner for yourself. Whatever you want. My treat. A steak? Lobster? Don't look at the price."

You had a bowl of onion soup. Mr. Grandon nibbled on nuts. He shook the ice in his glass, waved at the waitress to bring him another scotch.

"You know this guy she's with, Meena? You know him? What's he like, is he a good person? A troublemaker? Smart? Stupid? What?"

"Fox Dow. I'm afraid I don't really know him, Mr. Grandon."

"Dow. Well I guess he can't be too stupid if he's managed to shack up with my daughter. She's something else, that kid. Pretty. Smart. But angry. Boy is she angry. Slamming doors and calling everybody names. You know what she said? 'I wish you were dead.' Said that to me. Said that to her mother, too. It was all I could do not to take a hand to her when she said that.

All I could do. You want some dessert? Ice cream? Chocolate mousse? They have a terrific chocolate mousse here."

He waved to the waitress again, called her over, ordered you a chocolate mousse, and you all but licked the dish clean.

Upstairs, in his room, he made a big deal of writing a check for the full amount that was owed, plus an extra fifty thrown in for your trouble. A tip, sort of. Interest, if that felt better to you. He signed it with a flourish, ripped it from the book, and all the while he was telling you about how he was glad to do it, more than glad, it was nothing, really. Really. It was, he said, "the least I can do."

You stood at the window and looked out over the river at the lights of the cereal plant, the packing plant, the railroad tracks downtown. Mr. Grandon handed you the check, took your hand again, leaned close, and said, "Thank you." Even as he paid his estranged wife's grocery bill, he was thanking you. For your loyalty, he explained. For your steadfast friendship. For all you'd done for him—and for his daughter and for his family and for his wife.

You wondered: Did he know who was driving the truck with all his stuff in the back that day?

"She's not herself," he said, meaning Mrs. Grandon. "Hasn't been herself for years." He shook his head and sucked his teeth and frowned.

But if Mrs. Grandon was not herself, then who was she?

He was still holding your hand. He got so lonely sometimes, he said. He drew you closer to him, wrapped his arms around you, held you for a moment, and you allowed him to do this, you did not protest.

You felt sorry for him, maybe. Or maybe you liked it, the warmth of his embrace. He was sorry for what he'd done, he said. He didn't want to be there. He wanted to go home. He trembled. Was he crying? He moved his head, and you felt the burr of his cheek against your skin, the warmth of his breath in your hair. He had slipped his fingers under your sweater and his hand slid up over your belly to cup your breast. His mouth covered yours, he was kissing you, and then you were tipping your chin and you were kissing him back.

You wondered: What would Faye Grandon think, if she knew her husband was holding Meena Krejci and kissing her this way? And what would Josef Krejci do?

You dreamed: You and your father came home in the evening after work, after closing up the store, and Libbie's mother was still there, she'd been waiting for you. She'd been there all day, picking up, polishing, and playing solitaire, and she'd made dinner for you, too, one of Josef's favorites—pork chops and gravy, green beans and potatoes, buttered bread and cucumber salad and pie. You sat down together, just the three of you, a real family gathered at the kitchen table, telling each other about what you'd done that day, talking about the weather, the news, the war, the astronauts, the moon.

July 2006

Meena wakes to find herself curled on a blanket on the floor in front of the Aspenglo hearth, but the fire is out, only embers glowing, and the cabin is cold around her. It is the middle of the night. She shivers and sits up to peer sleepily into the shadows of the room. She holds her breath and stiffens, works to keep herself still, to listen for a sound of someone else here in the cabin with her. Someone who is waiting. Breathing. Watching her.

This is a new feeling, this sensation that maybe she is not alone, after all. As a child she lay in her bed at night and she listened, just as she is listening now, tried to imagine there was someone else there, someone who was standing in the hallway just beyond the door, or crouched inside the shadows of the closet, or pressed against the window pane and longing to be let in. Listening, watching, waiting. Just out of reach.

Maybe it was her father or maybe it was a dream. Maybe it was the ghost of her mother or maybe it was Julia Bell. Or maybe it was no one other than her own still self.

Now she is staring into the shadows, and she is holding her breath, and she is waiting, listening for some sigh of movement, straining to hear the whisper of another's presence, feeling for a pulse that might be other than her own.

"Holly?"

No answer.

And then that silence, falling over her like a shroud. Her worst fear, realized—that here she is, after all: alone.

She stands, her joints stiff and aching from her hike of the day before, knees, hips, shoulders—she is getting old. She is old. And yet... She puts her hand on her head, feels the scruff of her new hairdo. She stands there for a while, in her nightgown with the blanket wrapped around her shoulders, posed and staring at the last glowing embers of the fire. Indecisive and unsure. Should she get some more wood and build the flames back up again, fill the room with light and heat? Or creep over to the bed, slip in under the warm down comforter, tumble back into a more forgiving oblivion of sleep?

In the window glass her ghost is reflected back, a dim outline shapeless and indistinct. And beyond that, the trees, the forest surging forth.

Meena will choose to rebuild the fire. She will leave the cabin and go outside to the log pile. There is the path up toward the wilderness, shining through the trees. The pine needles are soft against the soles of her bare feet. The moon seems to be friendly and her newly cropped hair makes her feel lightheaded. Small. As if she might have become a girl again, after all.

She stands at the woodpile, considering it. The neatly split logs have been stacked in the space between the two trees that stand as bookends on either side. Meena lifts one from the top and cradles it against her chest. The blanket slips off one shoulder and she yanks it back up, tucks it in around her, but as she reaches for another log there is a sound. Something in the woods is watching her. A deer? A fox? She peers toward the trees, thinking to see the twin disks of eyes again, but nothing. She waits until the sound begins to seem like a memory, or something that she has imagined for herself.

Another log, and then another. She has turned back toward the cabin when she hears it again, the sound. Gentle thud of shifted weight, brief snicker of teeth. Flurry of ruffled fur, pant of animal breath, whisper of paw, click of claw. She carefully sets the logs down on the ground and turns her body fully toward the path. The blanket slips from her shoulders and puddles at her feet. She should be cold, but she is no longer shivering, she is no longer feeling the chill that's in the air. The white fabric of her nightgown shimmers in the moonlight.

Overhead the sky is black but at the same time bright, aglow with the gleam of more stars than Meena has ever seen before. There are the constellations that John Grandon once pointed out to her—scorpions and crabs and belts and bears—and what she was unable to decipher in them then now seems completely clear—shapes and beings made manifest in a measured placement of stars.

They are the dead saints leaning close, their faces welcoming and kind.

They are her dead mother, reaching out with open arms.

They are her dead father, howling in his loneliness.

And there is Matka, too, and she is rising, a full-blown powdery moon.

"You are a miracle," Matka said, holding her granddaughter in her lap, nestled against the generous spill of her bosom so that the coarse dark wool of her dress chafed the little girl's cheek.

"Your mother is a princess, she is an angel, she is a star. And your father? He's a king!"

"Remember who you are," her father said.

And now, Meena Krejci, alone in the forest, cries out to herself, she calls out her own name, and it echoes back to her through the thin air, clearly:

"Meena?"

"Meena!"

Come With Us

1969

It was June, and you were still the grocer's daughter. You were eighteen years old, a recent high school graduate, a working girl. If asked, you would have said that you were happy enough, you guessed, overall. As happy as you'd ever been, at least. You had your whole life ahead of you, and you were taking it very seriously. You had been given certain responsibilities. You had a regular paycheck, you had a checking account and a savings account, and you stood to inherit your father's business for yourself one day. Some of the older customers who still came into the store to shop would note that Meena Krejci—in her brown skirt and her blue blouse and her sensible shoes—had grown up to become the very picture of her mother Agnes Krejci there at the desk beneath the stairs. And maybe your father had noticed this, too.

It was your job to keep track of the accounts for him—you wrote bills, addressed envelopes, tallied payments, and prepared the deposits that your father would be taking to the bank. He didn't let you handle any of the cash yet, that was still his department.

But it was only a part time job, and at noon your day was over. Then you'd put away the files, turn off the lamp, lock up the drawers, and leave your desk to walk home. You'd stop at the mailbox on Vernon Avenue to drop a stack of letters in, then turn the corner at Otis Road and climb the low hill toward the house. You'd fix yourself something for lunch, you'd take meat out of the freezer for dinner, you'd vacuum the carpet in the living room, start the laundry in the basement, change the sheets on the beds upstairs.

At your desk, you chewed on your pencil, shifted in your chair. Looked upward as a sound of footsteps crossed overhead, the ceiling creaking under the weight of someone walking, or was it someone dancing? At that time of the morning? Had they been up all night? Faint sound of music, dim pounding bass. Your watch said eight-thirty. You looked up to catch your father's eye, see his frown. So he'd heard them up there, too.

Libbie and Fox, Fox and Libbie. Inseparable, they were always together, they were in love! They both worked downtown now, at the used bookstore near the tracks, selling incense and candles and books and records to the hippies and the high school kids, and maybe he was selling a little pot on the side besides, or maybe not. He had money of his own anyway, family money, he was a Dow after all and the Dows were rich. He drove a yellow Mercury convertible, with the top down and the radio turned up loud and Libbie beside him in a long gauzy skirt and halter top, peasant blouse, leather sandals, round-rimmed red plastic sunglasses, a floppy purple felt hat with a paper daisy in its brim. Trippy!

She often came into the store to buy groceries— milk and cigarettes and cereal—and usually she smiled at you, but she almost never stopped to talk. You two had gone your separate ways, it seemed. And Libbie was in a hurry. Besides, what was there to say? Fox lingered outside, sitting on the back steps, smoking. When he saw you he smiled, too, and flashed you a peace sign, but you ducked your head away, embarrassed, your face in flames. He called out your name, but you wouldn't turn, you'd pretend not to have heard. Why couldn't you stop and talk to him? Why not smile and flirt, why not come up with something clever to say, something that would let him know that you were more than just that plain timid girl who sat under the stairs with her numbers and her books, that girl who just happened to also be Josef Krejci's daughter. Much more.

Furious with yourself—with your shyness and awkwardness and ugliness and stupidity—you pinched your own inner thigh, hard. "Stop it! Stop it!"

Maybe they thought you disapproved of them, that you supported the war in Vietnam and agreed with Spiro Agnew and Richard Nixon, that you ignored Libbie and Fox because you were prudish and straight and believed yourself to be morally and mentally superior to them, but that wasn't it at all. No, it was that just then you had problems of your own.

For one thing, you had signed up to take a few night classes at Linwood Community College in the fall—not a full load, nothing like that, because you weren't going for a degree and you weren't trying to find a career, you were just thinking that a continuing education might be something that would keep you busy, and hadn't you always been good at school, if at not much else? Good grades, good reports, honors in some classes, and high scores on tests. If you'd had the money for it, you would have gone away to a university somewhere. But as it was, you'd registered for a survey of American literature, a general philosophy seminar, and introductory Czech—why not, maybe that would please him, although he didn't speak the language anymore himself.

But you had yet to tell your father about these plans that you'd been making, because you were sure he would object. If you were bored, he could think of something else for you to do to make yourself useful. Plenty else. He'd give you more hours at the store, more responsibility, was that what you wanted? Or, more work at home. You would have liked to find some way to stand up to him about it, you'd have liked to have your own way for once—it was your life, wasn't it?—but talking to him about yourself, about anything, was too hard.

Maybe that wasn't Josef Krejci's fault. He wanted only what was best for you, you knew that. But his opinions were strong, and the way he thought, the way he reasoned when he argued, he always made it seem that you were wrong. Ridiculously so.

And, maybe he was right. Maybe such classes were a waste of time, and money, for a person such as yourself. You should have been studying accounting instead. And even if you did agree to do that, what for? You already had a job. He could teach you anything you might need to know. The grocery store was a business that some day would be yours to run on your own. Or to sell, if that was what you decided you'd rather do with it, when the time came.

Josef Krejci, in 1969, was already an old man, after all. And he couldn't live forever. Could he?

If all this was not enough to drive you to distraction, there was more. Because for another thing—that check that Mr. Grandon wrote to pay off his wife's account? It had come back. Insufficient funds.

You thought first of phoning him. Not from the store, where your father might walk by and overhear and wonder—what were you doing? Who were you talking to? About what? You'd have to wait until you got home. But then what were you supposed to say? "Mr. Grandon, I guess there's been some kind of a mistake." Though you were pretty sure it wasn't a mistake. He knew what he was doing, and it wasn't fair, that he'd done this to you.

Your anger boiled up. How dare he? When he'd told you how grateful he was for your friendship and your kindness. When you'd trusted him. You'd known him just about all your life, and to you Mr. Grandon had been, if not like a father exactly, at least like some kindly uncle. And he'd said it himself, you were like a second daughter to him. When you'd trusted him enough to let him touch you, and to kiss him, because that was what he'd needed just then, wasn't it? And when you stopped it there, because he was drunk and lonely and weak and didn't know what he was doing and would only have been sorry later. Wouldn't have been able to forgive himself, if anything else had happened. Which it hadn't, thanks to you. You could have made it otherwise. Easily.

You wanted to scream, storm around, break things, slam doors, make a scene, but you didn't dare do that, because what would your father say, if he knew? You had the feeling he was watching you already. Eyeing you from his place at the register, sensing something was wrong, but what? You held yourself together—biting down on your anger and resentment and humiliation, chewing on it, feeling it burning at the back of your throat first, then in the pit of your stomach, later it would roil ferociously through your gut and leave you moaning—and you went off at lunch, as usual, carrying your bundle of letters and bills, as always, making sure that there was nothing odd-seeming about your behavior, nothing your father might pick up on, nothing he would notice, nothing that would cause him to stop you, ask you, "What's wrong?"

You smiled at him, waved goodbye, slipped out and walked the three blocks to the mail box before you turned, not east toward Otis Road, but west toward downtown. You walked all the way down to the real estate office, sweating in the midday, midsummer heat, rehearsing what you would to say to him: "I guess there's been some mistake. I'm sure you never meant for this to happen. You must have so many things to look after, and probably this is the least of your worries. I'm sure you have bigger fish to fry!" You were not your father's daughter for nothing. "But you've put me in an awkward position, see, and I'd appreciate it if we could take care of this right now?" You meant to walk over to the bank with him, right then and there. Have him pay you in cash. If not all of it, at least some.

But the real estate office was closed. Door locked, lights off. In fact, it looked like it had been closed for some time. Yellowing newspapers had piled up on the pavement outside, and the For Sale sign in the window seemed to be offering up the business itself rather than the properties pictured in the photos and the flyers on the bulletin boards inside.

You couldn't believe it. You took hold of the door handle and shook it, rattling the glass, uselessly. You stepped back to the middle of the sidewalk, looked up and down the street as if you thought you might find him there, even though you knew it was impossible. It was too late; you had missed him. Mr. Grandon was gone.

Meanwhile the Iowa sky had clouded over, and now it opened up, releasing a lazy downpour of hot summer rain.

The lobby of the Fielding Hotel was rich and warm and bright, and outside the sidewalks were slick with rain, greased with neon light. The doorman in his stiff brimmed hat and braided jacket opened the door, stepped aside, smiled at the serious young woman who whirled past him. You were there to visit your father— that's what the doorman believed as he watched you stride past the front desk toward the elevators—and that would be Mr. Grandon, a nice man, big tipper. Sold houses, didn't he? And had been having some marital difficulties, that's why he was living at the hotel. It was the times—so much freedom, so much chaos in the world, everybody was getting into some kind of trouble, it seemed.

A red-haired woman in a yellow dress stepped off the elevator, brushed past, left a smell of flowers in her wake, and the elevator operator offered you his toothy smile, said something about the weather—too much rain? Not enough? On the ninth floor, the elevator stopped and the brass doors opened out onto a long narrow hallway. Your shoes skimmed the geometrically patterned carpet; your double glanced back at you from within the mirrored wall—stony face set beneath a troubled storm of hair. Flowers in a glass vase nodded in the breeze of your passing as you ticked off the numbers on the doors. 908, 910, 912—Mr. Grandon was in 916.

You knocked, stood back. Nervously shifted your weight from one foot to the other, hand on a hip, head cocked, as you listened for the sound of his approach. Hoping to see a shadow cross the peephole and the door swing open, hoping to see him there before you, grinning from ear to ear.

You tried to tell yourself: he had his reasons. He'd be able to explain, you would understand, together you'd find a way to work things out. You'd think of something. And if you had to kiss him again, you would.

You waited.

You knocked again.

But, of course he wasn't there.

What an idiot you were. What had you been thinking? Why would a man like Jack Grandon be in his room now, in the middle of the day? Of course he was out somewhere, conferring with a client or sitting at an open house, or whatever it is he did all day at his job.

If you left him a note at the front desk, then they'd give it to him that evening when he came in, he'd know that you were looking for him, he'd go up to his room, and he'd call you back.

But the front desk clerk was shaking his head. "Mr. Grandon? I'm sorry, but he checked out a few days ago."

"What?"

"He's not here, Miss. He's gone."

"Gone? Gone where?"

A shrug. "Now that I do not know."

"But when will he be back?"

Seeing the look of desperation on your face and hearing the squeak of panic in your voice, the clerk stopped. He cocked his head suspiciously. "Say now, aren't you his daughter?"

You were backing away.

"Would you like to leave a message?"

Ducking your head, turning on your heel.

He called after you, "What's your name again, Miss?"

But you didn't stop to answer. You whirled through the lobby, toward the tall glass doors, away from the Grandons and back to yourself, out of the light and into the falling rain.

Seen from afar, as you moved along those streets of Linwood on that wet summer afternoon, you were no more than a shadow of a girl, huddled in upon yourself, small and inconsequential, hardly noticed, easily overlooked. You might have been a pilgrim like your father, wandering aimlessly from one neighborhood to another without direction or intent, but beneath the dark surface of that apparent calm you seethed, and it was the power of your flaming hatred for the Grandons that drove you on. You were cursing them, damning them, wishing death and disaster on them all—Mr. and Mrs., Libbie and John. And didn't they deserve it? Not only because they'd let you down, yet again. Not just because they had rejected you, yet again. They had failed you and at the same time they had failed themselves, hadn't they? But worse, they had been ungrateful, careless and thoughtless and neglectful of the many gifts that had been given them in their lives.

Josef Krejci was right about them; he had been right about them all along. Shallow, stupid people. Why in the world did you ever think you wanted to be like that? Or, one of them. How dare they be so unhappy, and such a mess? Your neighbors who had always had everything. Everything! All the comforts of an intact family and a crowded home—noisy, lively, bright and welcoming and warm—all of it handed to them, as if they deserved it. As if it were nothing more than their just due. And yet without thinking, without looking back, without even understanding what it was they had or what there was to lose—they'd just tossed it all away. As if it were junk. Piece by piece by piece.

And to think that you, poor pathetic lonely

motherless Meena Krejci, had ever envied them. Had ever wished that what was theirs might someday also be your own. This was what was hurting you the most just then. This was the deep pain that fueled the rage that was driving you on, away from downtown and back toward Otis Road. Fourth Street, Fifth Street, Sixth Street.

You had decided: before you went home, you would stop at the grocery store and tell your father everything. The bill, the kiss, the touch, the check. He'd take care of things for you. He'd find Mr. Grandon and demand to be paid the money that he owed. Maybe he'd even go to the police. It was likely that he was going to be angry with you, too, at first, and maybe his anger would linger for a while, but he'd get over it, finally. In time, he would forgive you. How could he not? You were his daughter, after all, and hadn't he said it already, that you were all he had?

Maybe he'd even kick Libbie out of the apartment, while he was at it. If you asked him to, you were sure he would.

You didn't have a chance of going to community college now, you knew that too, much less to a real university. But maybe that had been a bad idea anyway. As absurd as thinking that Josef Krejci and Faye Grandon might find something in common with each other—their loneliness—and decide to do something about it between them. Maybe it was all just as well, now the situation was clear.

By the time you got back to the store, the rain had stopped and the streets were steaming. Josef Krejci was at the register, cheerfully ringing up a big order for a woman with three children—one on her hip, one clinging to her skirt, and the other seated in the cart—and he looked up when you came in, surprised to see you back.

"I need to talk to you."

He shrugged you off. "Not now, Meena. I'm busy."

You could see that there was a line of customers, and that he would be busy for a while, which was just the way he liked it anyway. You would have liked to tell them all to go away. You needed him for yourself just then so you could tell him everything, before your anger dissipated and you lost what resolve you had, but you knew better than to even suggest such a thing. The customers came first, of course, the customers always came first, that was how his world worked.

You went to your desk under the stairs, took your place there as if you had something to do, but you didn't unlock the drawers, didn't take out your adding machine, didn't turn on the lamp. You sat quietly, with your hands in your lap, and you waited. You felt your temper cool, your breathing deepen, your heartbeat slow. When he was free he'd come to you and ask you what was the matter, why were you there, why weren't you home, what was wrong, were you all right? And then in the face of his concern you'd be able to tell him everything, and maybe he'd be angry, all right, sure he'd be upset, but he'd also know what to do, he'd be on your side, he was always on your side. He was your father, you were his daughter, you each were all you had. There was nothing that either of you could do that would ever be able to change that fact. He would not abandon you. And you would not abandon him.

You pulled out a pen and paper, and you wrote him a note.

Dear ~~Dad Josef Sir~~ Dad,

I have made a terrible mistake and I am sorry. As you can see by the attached statement, the Grandons owe us more than four thousand dollars in unpaid bills. It's all my fault. I've tried to collect ~~and~~ but have been unsuccessful. I'd hoped to spare you the trouble of this ~~but they~~ . Can we talk about it later this evening, when you come home?

~~Love~~ ~~With love~~ With sincere apology,

Your daughter, Meena

Outside the back door of the store, Fox Dow was lounging on the stairs. His coppery hair, his ginger grin. Your first thought was that you would duck back before he saw you, pretend you'd just remembered something you'd left behind, turn quickly and go back inside again, cross the store and leave through the front door to avoid him altogether. But why? What were you afraid of? What was there to keep you from returning his greeting, why not smile back, why not stop and talk to him? Why not?

He saw you hesitate and pounced. "Meena!" He seemed so glad to see you. Or maybe it was your obvious embarrassment that delighted him. "What's happenin', Meena?"

You shook your head. "Not much. Nothing." You didn't know how to talk like that: groovy and far out and right on and like, wow. "I guess I'm okay, Fox. How are you?"

This made him smile. He nodded. "Sure. I guess I'm okay, too." He ran a hand through his hair, blew out a long puff of breath, shook his head. Now that the rain had stopped and the sky was clear again, the world steamed, the air was thick, the sun blinding. You squinted at him. A swarm of gnats hovered near the bushes that edged the parking lot and crept against the stairs. Fox waved a hand to scatter them. He was wearing a blue plaid cotton cowboy shirt with pearled snap buttons, open at the front, and faded jeans, torn at the knees. A rope belt, bare feet. His body was pale, freckled, frosted with coppery coils of chest and belly hair. His hair was long and tangled. He looked like a bum, Josef Krejci said.

"Where's Libbie?"

He shrugged. "She split about an hour ago. She should be back pretty soon."

You nodded. Well… You had begun to turn away just as Fox was stepping toward you. He was tall and thin, and his hair fell in his face as he leaned closer. His smell was smoky, musky, sour. He reached out, skimmed a fingertip across your cheek, tapped your chin and tipped your face toward him, just as Mr. Grandon had done.

"Hey, you want to come upstairs for a minute?"

"What for?"

"Because it's too fucking hot out here!"

He had backed away, turned and bounded halfway up the stairs before he stopped and looked over his shoulder, down at you. "Come on!"

The screen door creaked open, slapped shut.

The world steamed. Cicadas hummed. Gnats swirled. Your hand slid along the rickety wooden banister as you followed Fox upstairs.

"My grandmother lived up here you know. And when I was a little kid I spent every day here, with her."

You were sitting on the old flowered loveseat, rolling a cold bottle of beer between your palms. Fox perched, birdlike, on a straight-back caned chair that you recognized from Mrs. Grandon's dining room. You were struck by how unlikely this seemed, that you should be there, in that place, then, alone, with Fox Dow. Unlikely, but there you were. He had lit a cigarette, smoke swirled around his head. He offered one to you, but you shook your head, No thanks. He was laughing at something, but you weren't sure what, unless it was you. He had turned on the stereo and there was music playing, music that sounded strange to you, some foreign instrument that vibrated up a scale alongside a shiver of tambourine, behind a wail of voices chanting nonsense syllables. And although you could see Fox clearly, and smell and hear, somehow that moment was less substantial to you than what you could remember of yourself there before, with Matka: the summer heat caught in the stillness of these attic rooms, the low growl of a delivery truck pulling up to the door downstairs, a clatter of conversation from the store, your father's deep voice, his hearty laugh. Matka, dozing in her chair, a blade of sunlight glinting in her hairpins. The sheen of her black dress, the mottle of her swollen feet, the comforting rhythmic surf of her breathing, her delicate snore.

"And then what happened?" Fox was asking. His posture in the chair was effeminate, one leg crossed over the other, elbow cupped in palm, cigarette dangling from curled fingertips.

"And then I met Libbie. We were friends. Her family sort of... well, I guess they took me in."

"That was kind of them."

"I guess it was."

You eyed his freckled fingers. Through the holes in his jeans, you could see that his knees were freckled, too.

You would have liked to tell him about how you saw him, in the pool, all those years ago. You'd have liked to let him know you'd hidden in the woods and watched him then, but you couldn't bring yourself to say it. He already thought you were a freak, as appealing as some strange animal in a zoo. Worth gawking at as a creature from another planet. An alien being left behind by a U.F.O. Abandoned changeling child. What would he say if he knew you'd spied on him?

His look was puzzled, curious: head tilted to one side, his golden eyes searching yours, a questioning crease furrowing his brow, a frown of bewilderment on his lips. You couldn't hold his gaze; your own eyes slid away.

And then the screen door banged open, and there was Libbie whirling in, smelling of incense and patchouli. Her fine blond hair braided in the back. Beads and tank top, soft cotton skirt, heavy leather sandals, her small shoulders nut brown, her smile like a lightning flash.

"Meena!"

Dazzled, you were stammering an excuse for being there, as if that were something that needed an excuse. "I... I was... I was just trying to find your dad."

Libbie had tumbled into Fox's lap and thrown her arms over his shoulders. She kissed his cheek, nuzzled his throat, catlike. "Mmmm..."

You blundered on: "Where is he, do you know?"

"Why do you want him?"

You told her: "Money."

Libbie snorted. "Good luck then." She had taken Fox's cigarette and was smoking it herself.

"It's really your mother's bill," you said. "Over four thousand dollars."

Fox whistled.

"And when my father finds out..." You would have liked to explain the situation; you'd have liked to make Libbie understand what you'd been risking by protecting her family the way that you had. You'd have liked some sympathy, some gratitude, something.

But: "Fuck your father," Libbie said.

You stood.

"No, really. Listen…" Libbie was on her feet too. She'd bounded out of Fox's lap and landed next to you. "Hey wait, I'm sorry." She put an arm around your shoulder, squeezed you close. "Friends forever, right?"

Fox was grinning at this. He sat with his feet planted on the floor, his elbows on his knees. His long red hair framed his face like flames.

"Sure, I guess so. Right."

"Oh, Fox," Libbie went on. "You should have seen us. Best friends. Meena and me."

Shadow and light.

"We were like sisters. We were! Weren't we, Meena?"

You nodded.

"We were always together. Always. We played in the woods. We went to the park." She was counting these things out on her fingers. "We were in all the same classes at school. We had games and dolls," she told Fox. "And not a care in the world, right?" She sighed. "Those were the days, weren't they? Weren't they the days?"

Before you could answer, Libbie had stumbled on: "Remember poor Julia? And Leo!" Libbie was grinning. A giggle bubbled up.

Fox was mystified. "What?"

Leo Spivak, scabbed and scarred, naked in the spotlight of your flashlights. You kicking poor Julia and pushing her out the door. Libbie in just her underpants, wagging her hips and blowing kisses: "Ooh la la."

And now here was Libbie, with her flowing clothes

and her brown summer skin, her white lipstick and heavily shadowed eyes, her wispy blond hair, as fine and filmy as cobwebs, and she was grinning at you, she was standing next to you and squeezing your hand, flashing a glance at Fox, who squinted through a fog of cigarette smoke and shrugged. Indifference or assent.

"Sure," he said, go ahead. "Tell her."

Libbie shivering with the thrill of it. "Okay." Then calming herself down. "Okay. Want to know a secret?"

You felt like a plain white wall, expressionless and unmoved. Did you want to know? Not sure. Know what? "I guess."

"You can't tell anybody."

"All right."

"Not anyone. Not my mother, not my father... Not your father... Especially not him."

"All right."

"Promise?"

"Sure. I can't find your father anyway. That's why I'm here, remember?"

But, was that why you were there? You were trying to guess at what it could be that Libbie was trying to tell you... She was pregnant... They were getting married...

"We're running away."

"What?" As dumb as that.

"We're going to run away."

"Who?" And dumber still.

"Me and Fox, who else?"

"But, why... and where? When?"

"In a few days." California. Because they could. And, why not?

So, that was it. Libbie Grandon and Fox Dow were leaving Linwood. They'd walk out on the rent they owed Josef Krejci, but who cared about that? Capitalist pig. They'd drive Fox's Mercury all the way across the country—through the prairies over the mountains across the desert to Los Angeles, California, where John was waiting for them. It had been his idea, as a matter of fact. Hollywood! Malibu! He was in his last year at Caltech; he had an apartment in Pasadena, and maybe they'd crash with him for a while or maybe they'd head north to San Francisco, where it was really happening. Big Sur. Carmel. Maybe they'd join a commune that John had heard about up there. Another kind of Foreverland.

Fox's amber eyes, regarding you. "Come with us?"

Libbie's small hand, squeezing yours. "Oh Fox, that's a great idea. Yes, Meena, come with us. Why don't you?"

You pulled your hand away. "No, oh no. I couldn't." Thinking of... your father, downstairs, in the store. Thinking of... your life there, in Linwood, on Otis Road. How could you leave that and what would you do for money, what about all your things, and what about your father? Fox and Libbie weren't serious, were they? What would Josef Krejci do without you? How would he get on? And besides, your place was here, wasn't it? You had a job. You had a... career. In groceries.

"No," you said. "Oh no. I couldn't... No, I'd better not."

Libbie sat down. Folded her arms over her chest. Frowned with disapproval. "So you're going to stay here for the rest of your life, Meena? Is that it?"

"No. I don't know. Yes. Maybe. So what?"

"And die a virgin?"

Fox was grinning. "Looks like we'll have to kidnap her, Libbie. If she won't go willingly."

Libbie giggled at this. "Yes! We'll steal you from

him. We'll come into your house in the middle of the night, and we'll spirit you away. We'll leave an old moldy scarecrow in your place, and then when he sees that, won't he be the sorry one."

Fox raised his fist. "Foreverland forever!"

Right on.

But of course they didn't mean it. After you left, they forgot all about you. And for years you would think about that moment, you would wonder, what if you had gone with them? What then? But you couldn't get yourself to imagine the difference that might have made in your life. To see clearly what might have happened, what you might have become.

No, your father's shadow was too great, it loomed too large and dark upon the possibilities of your imagination. Of course he would have stopped you. Or, even if you did manage to get away, he would have come after you. He would have tracked you down, he would have found you, and he would have brought you back home. Where you belonged.

This was summer, 1969. It was a time of madness and confusion: riots and revolution, massacre and murder, assassination and war. Everything was changing. Everybody had gone crazy. Nobody was safe, and nothing was sacred anymore.

When you rounded the corner onto Otis Road and turned toward your father's house halfway up the hill, you would see the sign in the Grandons' front yard next door: FOR SALE.

Then Mr. Grandon's blue convertible would come down the hill from the direction of the park. It would pull into the driveway and stop, and as you watched he would get out and climb the steps up to the kitchen door, where he would smooth back his hair, square his shoulders, and cough into his fist. Then he would knock, step back, and wait.

The door opened. Mrs. Grandon was framed in light. She shook her head. He leaned toward her, took her hand, brought her close and held her. After a while he let her go, and she turned away, allowing him just enough space to sidle inside.

July 2006

Now Meena has left the main trail, and she is lost. She's climbed up away from the cabin and into the wilderness. Pale sylph, she is following the moonlight, chasing after the stars, and even if she wanted to she would not know how to find her way back again.

She is not alone. There is something else here with her, and she's aware that it's been tracking her for a while. Its presence is huge and warm. She can hear it, lumbering heavily, too cumbersome and clumsy to be a fox or a deer. Now and then she sees it, a patient shadow, hanging back. A monstrous presence, stalking her. A bear.

She stops, and it stops, too.

Holds her breath. Listens. She shivers. Looks around. Peers into the trees to see. Calls out.

"Hello?"

There's no answer. Only the chuffing of its breath and the soft shifting of its weight as it stirs.

Again: "Hello?" The sound of her own voice shakes her.

And now: an approach, cautious. Heavy footsteps, twigs breaking, a being moving closer... And then the huge black shadow swaggers forth.

Panting with fear and expectation, Meena steps toward it.

The bear holds its ground. Black eyes gleaming, it watches. And then it lifts its forefeet, heaves itself back, rises up, and stands. Half again her height, it looms. Head wagging. Teeth gleaming. Soiled snout, matted filthy fur. It sways and murmurs, belches out a deep low growl.

Meena steps closer still.

A paw swipes out at her, testing. She shows a palm. Then swipes back. It rears away, regains its balance, snorts and heaves itself forth in full charge.

She brings her hands up to her face and tumbles backward. It gnashes at her folded arms, cradles her head, lacerates her scalp with curled claws. There is a loud crack and she feels her left arm snap out of its shoulder socket and hang. Her eyes are closed, blinded by blood. Now it is lifting her off the ground and throwing her down onto her stomach. She moans. Hunkered over her, it works in silence. Her bones shatter and grind inside her flesh. She pulls her head in, humps over herself. Teeth sink into the small of her back. Slide up her spine, gnaw at her shoulder, her neck, her head.

Its weight on top of her. Crushing her. With a scream, she thrashes free and rolls away, gasping for gurgled breath, coughing on blood. Its breath in her face, foul and hot. She flails, it takes her forearm in its teeth, stands, pulls her up and tosses her away. She flies, falls, lands with a groan, the wind knocked out of her.

And then it's over her again.

It picks her up, tucks her close and, hobbling three-legged, it carries her a few yards before it drops her. It stands over her, shaking its big head, spraying slobber, blood, phlegm, flesh. She clings to the ground, holding her face and stomach down. It cuffs her, bends and sinks its teeth into one soft buttock. Chews. Sits back, waits. Prods her lifeless body with a paw. Waits. Prods again.

And then, just as it's giving up, just as its turning away to leave her there, Meena is rolling over, she's opening her arms, and so, with a groan of pleasure, it's thrown itself upon her once again.

As she surrenders herself, as it splits and tears her open, Meena is whispering: "Yes."

All her self containment, all her self-restraint, the years of saying no and no and denying herself, punishing herself—for what happened, for what she didn't know and what she didn't do, for who she was and who she wasn't—now they are over, now she is saying yes.

She is screaming: "Yes."

Howling: "Yes."

Yes.

Nowhere

1969

There was a time in your life when you thought it was possible that Mrs. Grandon might marry your father and become your mother. There was a time in your life when you thought that with Libbie out of the way and Mr. Grandon gone such a thing could actually happen to you. You would be a family and you would live happily ever after: your father, your stepmother, and you.

But no. Instead, by the end of that October, they were all gone. Libbie and Fox had run off to California and left your father in the lurch, as promised. Mr. and Mrs. Grandon had sold their house and paid off all their bills, including what they owed your father. They'd come back to each other and, choosing discord over loneliness, they'd found a way to make a new start for themselves elsewhere. For a few years there were Christmas cards: postmarked Chicago first, then Minneapolis, and finally Davenport, before they stopped altogether, and you never did hear any more word from the Grandons again.

When Libbie got a Ouija board for her twelfth birthday, she thought you ought to use it to try and conjure the spirit of your dead mother. You locked yourselves up in Libbie's room, turned off the lights, lit a candle for effect. You sat on the floor, facing each other, cross-legged Indian style, with the board placed just so between you. Libbie was serious, but you had your doubts. Libbie closed her eyes and bowed her head, and at first you did the same. Then you peeked, eyed Libbie's white hair shining, her fingertips poised on the planchette, nails chewed ragged.

Nothing happened; the planchette was still. The room was quiet. Your breathing the only sound. A sputter of the candle, guttering. Libbie's eyes popped open and she saw that you were watching her. She cried your name, drawing out the e's, stretching it into six syllables of frustration, in the high cicadic whine of her high soprano: Me-e-e-na-ah-ahhh. She said, "You have to close your eyes."

Chastised less by Libbie's intent than by the sound itself, you squeezed your eyes tight and murmured: "Sorry, sorry, sorry, okay, okay. " Libbie's sigh, a billow of a breeze. And still she had to reach across to punish you with a pinch. Scolding: "Concentrate!"

You flinched away, dropped your fingertips down onto the planchette again and held your breath and waited, waited, waited, until: it began to move. All on its own, it seemed. Stopped in the high right corner. "YES." And you were trying to remember, what was the question again?

"Are you here with us?" Libbie asked.

And "YES," the board replied.

"Are you Agnes Krejci?"

Again the planchette moved and circled around and came back: "YES."

You could hear a basketball pounding on the driveway outside. John, his sneakers squeaking against the cement. Rags at his heels, barking. A car honking on the street, a siren wailing in the distance, a squirrel chittering in a tree.

Libbie whispering, "Where are you now?"

Spider legs, high-stepping up the nape of your neck, a whisper up your spine as Libbie read out the message: I-A-M-N-O-W-H-E-R-E.

Then, at that moment, thunder at the door so loud that you and Libbie both screamed.

But it was only Mrs. Grandon, knocking, calling out, "Libbie! Telephone!"

Libbie, running downstairs to the phone, Gingi Noone calling. You were left behind, upstairs, alone with the Ouija board. Whispering, "Are you still here?" Your fingers on the planchette. "Mother?"

But nothing happened. She wasn't there.

Never had been.

By the end of that October, they were all gone. And by the end of that October your father had not spoken to you for more than two months. It was a matter of stubborn principle, in his view. He had your confession—that you had let Mrs. Grandon take advantage of you, that you had allowed Mr. Grandon to kiss and fondle you, that you had not told him of Libbie and Fox's plans—and he had your respectful apology and he even had his money, too, except for the unpaid rent, but the fact of it was that you had purposefully deceived him. This was a breech that Josef Krejci simply could not, in good conscience, overlook or overcome. His silence was for your own good. It would teach you a lesson. Because if you couldn't be counted on to behave yourself with propriety, if you could not tell right from wrong, if you could not be trusted...

And so in those weeks that you lived in the empty spotlight of his willful abandonment, you felt yourself begin, again, to disappear.

The Grandons' house had been sold to a young

family from St. Louis, who had not yet moved in. Its rooms were empty; its windows were dark. The street was quiet, and the neighborhood seemed deserted, as if the world had been abandoned, but for you.

And your father. The front door opened, and there was Josef Krejci, heading out on one of his walks. Coat collar turned up. Hands in his pockets. The inchoate shade of his body, framed as it was in the light of the streetlamp. A large man dressed in a dark wool coat, his body squared by the padded shoulders, the wide double-breasted front as flat and formless as a soldier's armored shield.

From your window, you watched him walk away. The early evening light drifted gray as chalk dust against a schoolroom's blackboard slate. He rounded the corner and was gone. The bare branches of the butternut tree in the Spivaks' yard across the street rose up into the twilight sky, and in the midst of their tangle could be seen the even darker and senseless-seeming knot of a squirrel's nest way up high.

You would be downstairs in the living room when he came back, bringing the smell of early winter inside with him. Stamping his feet, cheeks rosy with the cold, breath steaming. He would pull off his gloves, shrug out of his coat, and hang it up in the hall closet. He would look up, see you, turn away. Go into his study and close the door. A moment later, there would be music. The smell of pipe smoke. Clink of bottle against glass.

Soon you would get up and go into the kitchen and fix dinner. You would sit down together at the kitchen table to eat it. Josef would read the newspaper as he ate. You might ask him where he'd been. What he'd done. Who he'd seen. But he wouldn't say. He would clear his throat. He would not utter a word. Maybe you'd turn on the television later. Or maybe he would build a fire and you'd sit together in silence, watching the flames. Maybe you'd go to bed early and tomorrow would be another working day and the next day after that and then the next one after that. While your secret screams, muffled by the unfathomable distance that he'd put between you, went unheeded and unheard.

You had to break a window at the back to get into the Grandons' house, and you cut yourself on the glass. You had a flashlight, even though you knew your way around and didn't really need it. Its white light skimmed the walls, made shadows lunge forward, then cringe back.

You went into every room, and you looked in every closet, but there was nothing, no one there. Only your own footsteps echoing. Your own breath, your own shadow, your own pulse.

You opened some windows upstairs.

You sat in the middle of the floor in what had been Mrs. Grandon's bedroom. You took off your clothes. You were bleeding.

Somehow your father knew. Somehow he was there.

You lounge in your father's chair in the living room of the small stone house on Otis Road, and you wait for him to come home. You sit quietly, with a book open on your lap, but you aren't reading, you're keeping an eye on the summer twilight beyond the window glass, and from here you will have a full view of the front door when it opens, framing the inchoate shade of Joseph Krejci's body when he returns from his evening walk.

Julia Bell's hands had been tied at the wrists, that's what Leo said. And her feet, at the ankles. Curtain cord, it looked like. Window shade. Clothesline. Tossed into the woods, she rises, spins upward in a wide and graceful arc before she falls and crashes, lands moaning, rolls and then settles against the hard ground into which her flesh will, with stunning slowness, soften and spread, liquefy and sink and, finally, blend.

Your mind circles around and around, but always it comes back to this: the bones, the skull, the ropes, the guy wire, the steel pin. The leathery flesh of a dead girl, stringy as old meat and cobwebbed with rot. Bones bleached clean. The pearly gleam of her smooth, socketed skull.

But where is Julia now?

"Your mother is an angel," Matka says, and her hand reaches out toward the little girl and her bent knobbed fingers clumsily brush from her glittering eyes a web of windblown hair. "Your mother is a star."

You lounge in the chair, with the book opened in your lap. You aren't reading, you are waiting. The book is balanced upright on your knees, and hidden in the crease of its spine is Libbie Grandon's silver cross, plucked from the woodland floor.

Soon your father will be home. Soon the front door will be opening and you'll be looking up to see him there, his expression full of expectation. Dinner. Some small conversation. Maybe you'll wonder, only for a moment, where he's been. What he's done. Who he's seen. Only for a moment, and then you'll let it go. You won't ask him. He won't tell you. It doesn't matter. Maybe you'll watch television. Maybe you'll sit together reading for a while. Maybe you'll go to bed early, because after all, tomorrow is another day.

July 2006

Down at Aspenglo a shadow moves. Thin and quick, it skitters across the yard like a blown leaf, drifts up the steps to the porch, and slips through a crack in the door into the cabin's main room, where the fire has died and the air is cold and still.

The shadow is Holly Gidding, and even in the dark of the middle of the night she knows her way around because she's been in here many times before, and also this cabin is an exact replica of her own. Sure of herself and of her intent, she creeps barefoot across the cold floor, steering carefully around table, sofa, and chair before stopping to peer into the bedroom to see the tousled bed and suppose that somewhere underneath the mounded comforter a lady named Libbie Grandon is sound asleep, knocked senseless by an afternoon of hiking in the invigorating mountain air.

It didn't have to be this way, Holly thinks. The lady could have been more understanding. She could have agreed to let Holly come along, but she didn't. Too bad.

The lady's suitcase is open on the floor amid a spill of clothes, and her purse is on the dresser, within such easy reach that Holly can snap it up without taking another step. She cradles it close to her body as she glides back toward the window where a haze of yellow moonlight floats in to help her see what she has. Now Holly's arm is elbow-deep inside the purse and she is digging through its contents: car keys, glasses, Kleenex, billfold, and a blunt roll of bills wrapped in a thick rubber band.

Outside in the forest, a scream: bobcat shriek, owl screech, rabbit squeal, coyote howl, or maybe it's the coloratura ululations of the mating elk. Holly freezes at the sound, holds her breath, waits for the shape beneath the covers in the bedroom to stir, but that woman in there sleeps on, undisturbed.

As silence settles back over the scene again, Holly makes her getaway. She glides off, out the door, over the porch, down the steps, and across the thin yard to the Jetta, parked in its sea of dandelions and summer weeds. Gritting her teeth, she opens the door, cautiously. Warns herself: Careful now, be quiet! Sets the purse gently down on the seat. Reaches in and slips the keys into the ignition. Cheers herself on: Almost there now, almost... Pulls the gearshift into neutral, and bracing her body against the door frame, pushes the car back, rolls it down the slope of the driveway to the shale strewn road.

Congratulates herself: *Okay, yes, good!* One last look at Aspenglo, still as a painting in its wash of enchanted mountain moonlight, before she makes up her mind— *Now!*—and turns away, hops in, slams the door, grips the key and starts the engine. The Jetta's tires spew stones as the car wheels around and Holly, expecting to see the cabin door fly open and the woman running after her, guns it and tears off. No headlights yet, and she teeters dangerously toward the dropoff edge before regaining the road and slowing to a safer crawl. Brake lights glowing, the black Jetta winds downward to the highway, where it stops. A semi-trailer truck roars by, leaving silence in its wake. Holly leans forward, flicks the headlights on, and turns toward the Interstate, where she'll climb the westbound ramp, merge with the sparse midnight traffic, and be gone, to the triumphant clamor of her own whoops and cheers.

Later Holly will stop for gas and breakfast, and after she's ordered what feels to her to be an extravagant meal of eggs and bacon and toast and juice, then she'll sit back and take the time to more closely examine the contents of the purse she's stolen. The cash. The checkbook from the Farmer's Bank in Linwood. The Iowa driver's license, with Meena's photo on it, the Social Security card and the credit cards with her name.

In Linwood Mimi Hanrahan will be waking up with a bad feeling gnawing at her gut. On the table by the bed sits a glass with the dregs of her gin from the night before, a fly floating indelicately on top. She should stop drinking, she thinks. Next to the glass, an ashtray, overflowing with lipstick tainted butts. She should stop smoking, too. She finds a butt of decent length and uses a match to light it. Takes a drag, then crushes it out among the others. Peers at the clock. Almost ten-thirty. Shit.

She pulls her legs around and sits up. Runs a hand through her hair, stands and crosses to the bathroom. Uses the toilet, splashes water on her face, brushes her teeth. Outside, a child shrieks with laughter and Mimi winces. A headache hovers, and the bad feeling in her gut turns. She'd like to crawl back into bed, stay there for the rest of the day, but she can't do that.

No rest for the wicked, she tells herself, sneering at the reflection of a middle-aged stranger's face in her mirror—softened, bloated, blotched by nests of spider veins, crowned by a yellowing tangle of thinning bleached hair: When did this happen?

She can't go back to bed. She'll take a shower, get dressed, maybe stop for donuts on the way down to the shop, where Meena Krejci will be waiting with a pot of coffee and a pile of sorted clothes. Except, she remembers now that in an inebriated fit of generosity she gave Meena the day off, the week off, all the time she needs, to take care of her fat decrepit old fuck of a father, who is probably dying, and maybe he's even already kicked it, and hell if it's not about time.

Which means: Meena wasn't there to open up the shop again this morning. Which means: it's still closed. Half a day of business down the drain. Shit. Not that folks have been breaking the doors down, exactly, but still a sale's a sale and a buck's a buck, after all. Maybe she should offer a part time job to one of those high school kids who are always coming by to rummage through the old clothes, calling them "vintage" now instead of simple "second hand." Pay them cheap and give them discounts on the stuff to make up for it.

She goes into the kitchen, finds a fresh pack of cigarettes there on the table where she left them last night, makes a pot of coffee. She turns on the television set to keep her company while she waits for it to brew. Opens the back door and stands in the sunlight, peering across the street to see a couple of kids in the yard there running through a swaying sprinkler, naked and squealing like a pair of pink pigs.

On the TV a woman is breathlessly announcing Channel 2 Breaking News, but Mimi isn't listening to it, until she hears the name, Ralph Wendell. Whose car has been towed from the lake, where it was found this morning, about forty feet from shore.

Mimi has already dialed Meena's number. She listens to it ring four times, and then the machine picks up. Meena's voice is soft and shy and proper-sounding: "Hello, you've reached the Krejci residence. We can't come to the phone right now..."

Mimi hangs up. Maybe Meena took her father to

the hospital then. That would be a relief for everyone, she thinks. But in that case, wouldn't Meena have called? Sure she would. Unless she's mad about what Mimi said about her dad, that he's a stubborn old bohunk, that he's going to die and she'd just better get used to it. Mimi feels her face fill with the heat of her shame. How could she continue to be so cruel? And wouldn't it be just like Meena to say nothing more about it, to keep her feelings to herself and pretend that everything was just fine, even when it wasn't?

The bad feeling in her stomach turns again.

On the television, the blue Galaxy, sheathed in mud, and a shuffling group of onlookers, gaping beyond a line of yellow tape. This is followed by a long shot of the Wendell house, with its closed door and banner and poster and the smattering of flyers on the trees. Someone is saying the words now: "Probable suicide."

After she's showered and dressed, Mimi tries phoning Meena again, but there still isn't any answer. On her way downtown to the White Elephant, she takes the long way around, out of Rompot and through the park, so that she can cruise past Meena's house on Otis Road, and on Vernon Boulevard she encounters a small traffic jam as the news vans and police cars and lookie-loos swarm the street outside the Wendell house.

Josef Krejci's black Jetta is not in the driveway at 2338 Otis Road. Mimi pulls in and stops. She sees the Sunday paper still out there on the front porch, and when she peers through the glass she'll see that there is mail piled up on the floor inside the foyer.

She rings the bell, a formality really, because it's obvious that there is no one home here. Listens to it echo through the empty rooms. Waits and rings again. She trudges up the driveway and bangs at the back door, peeks into the kitchen, but it's spotless and empty.

She uses her cell phone to call the hospitals. First St. Anne's and then Mother of Mercy, but neither has taken in a patient by the name of Josef Krejci, and: "Yes ma'am, I'm sure."

Now Mimi will find the back door key that Meena keeps hidden inside the fake plastic rock in the dirt beside the steps—*In case of an emergency...*—and now Mimi will let herself into the house where Josef Krejci lies dead.

August 2006

It ends on a Friday at the end of the August, when Josef Krejci's body is laid to rest between his parents and his wife in the Bohemie Cemetery behind St. Wenceslas Church, across the river from Wellington Heights. Many mourners show up for this: some to pay their respects, others out of a morbid curiosity. This is the man who lay dead in his house for four days. This is the one whose daughter has disappeared.

Four rectangular brass markers have been set flat upon the grass in a row near the fish pond, and his is the most succinct.

First, Josef Vaclav Krejci: 1907-2001.

Then his wife, Agnes Anna Krejci: 1912-1954. Dearest Departed Too Soon Gone.

Then his father, Tomas Milos Krejci: 1882-1910. Noble Father.

And finally his mother, Meena Ludmilla Krejci: 1890-1968 Beloved Matka Sorely Missed.

But there, beyond them all and closest to the pond, the daughter's plot is empty.

There are plenty of people who witnessed the old grocer's fatal fall outside the movie theater that night. They saw him hit his head on the pavement, and they saw that he was bleeding. They assumed that his companion would take him to the emergency room for treatment and then didn't think about it again. His injuries were consistent with what the medical examiner concluded was the ultimate cause of his sudden death: respiratory failure due to severe head trauma. For a man of his advanced age, this should come as no surprise. Something of a mercy, maybe.

But where is the daughter? She's not been seen again. A missing persons report was filed by her employer, and some people have suggested that the most likely answer is that Ms. Krejci, overcome by her fear and grief at the death of her father, has done away with herself. But if that's the case, then where is Josef Krejci's car? Others have suggested that she has been the victim of foul play. Still others like to think that she has simply run away. That she has assumed a new identity and bank account and credit cards and made her escape. Mimi Hanrahan, for one, has been heard to say that she fully expects to hear from Meena Krejci again some day. There will be a phone call, or a letter, or a post card. With palm trees on the front. *Dear Mimi. Having a marvelous time. What took me so long? Wish you were here. Love, M.*

Out of the blue, one day the call will come. One day she will come back.

At Ragnarok in the Colorado forest, Will Gidding prays.

"Our Father who art in heaven, hallowed be Thy name…"

He prays for his lost sister, asks the Lord to send her back to him again, before it's too late.

"Thy kingdom come, Thy will be done…"

He knows she ran away to California, and he regrets that he ever had anything to do with bringing that other woman up here to stay, even for a few days.

"Forgive us our trespasses, as we forgive those who trespass against us…"

He guesses she's the one who lured Holly away.

"And lead us not into temptation, but deliver us from evil…"

They were in such a big hurry to go that they left all their stuff behind. He hasn't called the police; what would be the point? Holly is an adult. She can do whatever she wants, including go to hell. Ungrateful bitch.

"For Thine is the kingdom, and the power, and the glory…"

Will Gidding sits outside on his porch, and he keeps one eye on the sky, the other on the road. He is waiting for what he knows is coming; he is certain that sooner or later it will be here. Sometimes he feels himself getting impatient for it, even though he knows that he is not quite ready yet. The school bus is almost finished. Most of his supplies are here. He still has to install a solar panel. He still needs to put on the tires. He sniffs the air. He's looking for a sign. He's waiting for the end of the world.

"…forever and ever. Amen."

July 2007

In Los Angeles, California, there is a young woman who lives in a rented bungalow near the ocean. She waits tables in a diner on Venice Boulevard, and she goes to acting classes at night. Maybe someday she'll be discovered—she's pretty enough, and she does know something about the art of self-invention, it seems. On Saturdays she goes to the beach and lies in the sun all day, and on Sundays she shops for fresh flowers and vegetables at the Farmer's Market in Santa Monica. When questioned about her family, or where she's from, she becomes evasive, and the new friends that she's made here assume this to be because her past is somehow painful to her, so they kindly leave it alone. She tells them simply that she hasn't been this happy in a long, long time, and they have to agree, it's true, she does look stronger and healthier than she did when they first met her, months ago. She's eating well, her skin has cleared up, she's even put on some weight.

Recently she traded in her old black Jetta for a red convertible Bug. She has an authentic-looking birth certificate and a new California driver's license and a new Social Security card and a debit card and a credit card and over five thousand dollars in the bank.

Your name is Meena Krejci, and you have your whole life ahead of you now. You got away. You made it. You're on your own, and you are free.

It ends...

...in silence—in silence and illusion.

It ends somewhere deep in the forest, where these mauled and mangled remains have been dragged off and hidden away, half buried in a pawed over bed of pine needles, torn bark, and dried leaves.

Soon the animals will have picked the bones clean and they'll leave them where they lie, unknown and unnamed. Winter will come, and they'll be blanketed by snow—the shattered vase that was her skull, the open basket of her ribcage, abandoned pelvic cradle, spindle of spread legs. In the enduring sanctuary of the wilderness they will sink and settle, and this is how...

...it will end.

ALSO BY SUSAN TAYLOR CHEHAK

It's Not About the Dog: Stories

"The turns these stories take, structurally and emotionally, prove that Chehak is not only a daring literary artisan, but a connoisseur of human frailty. An acerbic, stirring collection from a master of the craft." —Kirkus Reviews

The Great Disappointment, A Confession

"[Chehak's] ambitiously imaginative novel questions the very nature of reality... [a] diverting exploration of metaphysical concepts. Winsome and smartly playful." —Kirkus Reviews

Rampage

"Chehak's darkly evocative Midwestern gothic is a stunning exploration of love, lust, greed, envy, innocence, murder, and obsession. Unforgettable characters, a grim and riveting plot, and darkly lyrical prose add up to great reading." —*Booklist*

Smithereens

"Vivid [and] intense SMITHEREENS has brooding, ominous atmosphere, sexual awakening, loss of innocence, murder. It could be described as a gothic coming-of-age novel, but it's far too good to lend itself to any label. Susan Taylor Chehak is a meticulous writer, an evocative stylist whose mastery is evident on every page." —*The Boston Globe*

Dancing on Glass

"A deeply chilling, disturbing, beautifully written novel. Shocking, stunningly written Faulkner himself would have admired and respected [DANCING ON GLASS]. Its events should linger in the reader's mind long after it has been read." —*Los Angeles Daily News*

Harmony

"One of those novels that returns to haunt you long after it's been replaced on the shelf." —*The Cleveland Plain Dealer*

The Story of Annie D.

"Absolutely stunning. Reads with the force and generational sweep of some ancient rural myth. Like the author, Annie D. is such a mesmerizing storyteller that you can almost feel the fire at your back." —*The New York Times Book Review*

ABOUT SUSAN TAYLOR CHEHAK

Susan Taylor Chehak is a graduate of the University of Iowa Writers' Workshop and the author of several novels, including *Smithereens*, *The Story of Annie D.*, and *Harmony*. Her most recent publications include a collection of stories, *It's Not About the Dog*, and a work of nonfiction, *What Happened to Paula: The Anatomy of a True Crime*. Susan has taught fiction writing in the low residency MFA program at Antioch University, Los Angeles, the UCLA Extension Writers' Program, the University of Southern California, and the Summer Writing Festival at the University of Iowa. She grew up in Cedar Rapids, Iowa, spent many years in Los Angeles, lives occasionally in Toronto, and at present calls Colorado her home.

Website: www.susantaylorchehak.com
Twitter: http://twitter.com/stchehak
Facebook: www.facebook.com/stchehak
Blog: www.tumblr.com/blog/susantaylorchehak

Find more good books at
Foreverland Press
www.foreverlandpress.com